The ROAD to GODERICH

The ROAD to GODERICH

Linda McQuaig

Copyright © Linda McQuaig, 2025

All rights reserved. No part of this publication may be reproduced, stored in a retrieval system, or transmitted in any form or by any means, electronic, mechanical, photocopying, recording, or otherwise (except for brief passages for purpose of review) without the prior permission of Dundurn Press. Permission to photocopy should be requested from Access Copyright.

All characters in this work are fictitious or are used fictitiously. Any resemblance to real persons, living or dead, is purely coincidental.

Publisher: Meghan Macdonald | Acquiring editor: Kwame Scott Fraser & Megan Beadle | Editor: Shannon Whibbs | Cover designer: Karen Alexiou
Cover image: from *Julie Le Brun (1780–1819) Looking in a Mirror* by Elisabeth Louise Vigée Le Brun, MET 2019.141.23, bequest of Mrs. Charles Wrightsman, 2019 (public domain); flourish: Cloudniners/istock.com
Interior map: Anna McQuaig

Library and Archives Canada Cataloguing in Publication

Title: The road to Goderich / Linda McQuaig.
Names: McQuaig, Linda, 1951- author
Identifiers: Canadiana (print) 20240461320 | Canadiana (ebook) 20240461339 | ISBN 9781459754898 (softcover) | ISBN 9781459754904 (PDF) | ISBN 9781459754911 (EPUB)
Subjects: LCGFT: Historical fiction. | LCGFT: Novels.
Classification: LCC PS8625.Q84 R63 2025 | DDC C813/.6—dc23

We acknowledge the support of the Canada Council for the Arts and the Ontario Arts Council for our publishing program. We also acknowledge the financial support of the Government of Ontario, through the Ontario Book Publishing Tax Credit and Ontario Creates, and the Government of Canada.

Care has been taken to trace the ownership of copyright material used in this book. The author and the publisher welcome any information enabling them to rectify any references or credits in subsequent editions.

The publisher is not responsible for websites or their content unless they are owned by the publisher.

Printed and bound in Canada.

Dundurn Press
1382 Queen Street East
Toronto, Ontario, Canada M4L 1C9
dundurn.com, @dundurnpress

To Amy, forever my pride and joy
And to Neil, for the happiness he's brought

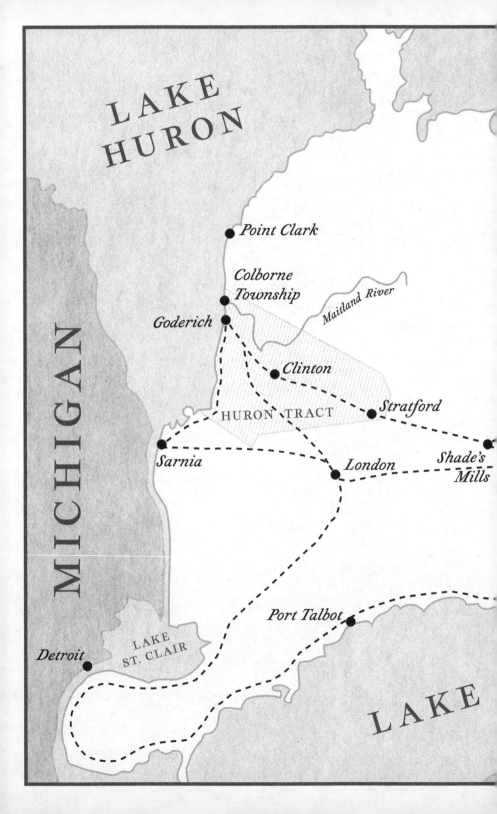

N
nw
ne
W
E
sw
se
S
LAKE SIMCOE
UPPER CANADA
Port Hope
Whitby
LAKE ONTARIO
Toronto
Guelph
Burlington
Hamilton
Niagara-on-the-Lake
Fort Erie
Buffalo
ERIE
NEW YORK

Prologue

Upper Canada, 1862

When I finally saw Momma again, standing with outstretched arms just behind the small wooden gate, I could feel joy pumping wildly through my little body. I still have dreams about that morning. I can close my eyes and see us hugging, then walking hand in hand down to the sandy bay where I played with the ducks.

There is something about the motion of the train that allows my mind to wander, lulled by the endless forest on the other side of the glass. The images come flooding back. Soon I'll be confronted directly with the dark memories, too. At least Luke will be there; his breezy ways always lift my spirits.

I often wonder how differently our lives might have been, if only I hadn't made that stupid remark. I was just five at the time, and Momma always insisted it hadn't been my fault. Still, it was my remark that began unravelling all the deception. In her mind, I must have been forever linked to the devastating events that followed.

After Momma died of pneumonia, I mostly raised Luke myself. He was seven and I was twelve, but I'd promised Momma I would take care of him. We stayed on in Goderich, living with a

Presbyterian family brave enough to take us in, despite the stigma. Luke was a skinny little kid back then, but he had a lot of courage and spunk. When other boys accused him of being the son of a traitor, he boldly declared that his father was a hero. That was grounds for a fight and Luke often came home bloodied.

The train slows down and there are clearings and farmhouses, then a few two-storey buildings, a warehouse, some stores. As we pull into Hamilton station, people wave and cheer. The womenfolk are wearing their finest bonnets and the men their best Sunday jackets.

I spot Luke easily in the crowd. He is even taller and stronger after two years on the farm, his face and arms brown from the sun. It would break Momma's heart to see him now, so much like his father. No wonder Luke was always her favourite.

Chapter One

Fenwick, Ayrshire County, Scotland, 1832

Mr. Abernathy often lauded the courage of the clans in the Battle of Culloden Moor. So Callandra's answer — that the clans were outnumbered and should have retreated — was not what he wanted to hear.

"If you would pay more attention to history and less to your appearance, you wouldn't make such foolish mistakes," he bellowed. "Take off that beret. French affectations have no place in Scottish education."

With the full attention of her classmates, Callandra removed the beret. Hair that had been held in check cascaded from captivity. Mr. Abernathy ordered her to write twenty times on the blackboard: I WILL NOT WEAR A BERET TO CLASS.

As he resumed teaching, she went to the board and performed her penance, a sense of injustice building inside her. When she reached the last line, she wrote: I WILL WEAR WHAT I LIKE TO CLASS!

A couple of students noticed and suppressed giggles. She quickly erased the final sentence and was writing in the correct one just as Mr. Abernathy turned to check. She took her seat, savouring her moment of defiance.

Walking home that afternoon, with three of her younger siblings, she enjoyed the feeling of loose hair in the pleasant May weather. The ash trees along the lane had freshly sprouted leaves, and the air was crisp with spring. Callandra and her siblings were nearly home when Alex McLeod caught up with them. Alex was sixteen, just a few months older than Callandra. He lived down the road, and their families had always known each other.

"I like what you wrote on the board," he said.

She smiled and kept walking.

Her eight-year-old brother Duncan asked Alex for a piggyback ride. He obliged and soon all three children were laughing and climbing onto his back.

"You going to the Stewarton Fair on Saturday?" Alex asked Callandra, when the children had run off in pursuit of a rabbit.

"I don't know. Depends if we get the seeding done."

"Well, if you need a ride, we'll have space in the wagon," he said, sounding casual about his brash suggestion.

Callandra's siblings returned and began a competition over who could walk the straightest line, leaving Callandra's gentle "thank you" lost in the clatter of voices.

"I've never seen so many perfectly straight lines," said Alex, responding to requests that he select a winner. "I think the only way to resolve this is to do it again — backward."

The backward-walking began, with all the contestants soon declaring victory and returning to Alex's back. He let them climb up and then charged ahead, as if into battle.

Callandra caught up to them at the top of a hillock. From there, they could see her family's modest farm tucked behind a cluster of trees, nestled among gently rolling hills and fields of rich, dark earth. Their wagon was in the lane, and today two others were parked behind it.

Alex was out of breath.

"That's enough," said Callandra, curtailing further demands from her siblings.

"One more contest!" said Alex, an eye on Callandra. "Whoever builds the best castle in the sandpile ... gets to go to the Stewarton Fair!"

"Oh! What if my parents say no? Look at the trouble you've got me in!"

They stopped by the majestic oak tree in front of her house, as her siblings headed toward the sandpile near the barn.

"See you tomorrow." A few paces away, he turned and said: "Oh, I almost forgot ... You left this in the classroom."

He pulled her beret from his pocket and tossed it gently in the air, aiming it to land on her head; it did, with the help of her hand.

He walked closer and gently altered its angle. Her heart raced. He kept adjusting the beret, shifting it slightly from one side to another, as if each position pleased him more than the one before. He moved a strand of hair this way and that, then tucked another behind her ear, leaving his hands gently cupping the back of her head.

"You should wear the beret to class again — if only to torment old Abernathy."

"Really?"

"Yeah, I'm sure he was put off because you looked so pretty. He doesn't want to notice things like that."

Callandra looked down shyly.

"I should get going," he said. "But first I better check how those sandcastles are doing ... or maybe I'll leave the judging till tomorrow."

"Aye," said Callandra, smiling.

"If Abernathy could see you now, he'd never get his mind back to Culloden Moor."

She didn't move but felt a blush heating up her cheeks.

"I can't wait to see those sandcastles tomorrow," he said, releasing her with a look of longing. He started to walk away.

She stood by the tree, stunned by what had just happened, watching him walk down the road until he disappeared around the bend.

It felt like the happiest day of her life. But when she walked into the farmhouse, she discovered that the extra wagons were in the driveway because her father had died.

Ross Buchanan had been such a strong presence in Callandra's life that it was hard to imagine him gone. He'd loved all of his children, but had particularly doted on her. The eldest of seven, Callandra had absorbed his freethinking ideas and ways of looking at the world. It had been his disapproval of war that had prompted her to counter Mr. Abernathy's patriotic view that courage alone is enough to win battles.

She felt a sudden, stinging sadness in realizing she would never get to tell her father how she'd challenged Mr. Abernathy and then flouted his orders in front of the class. He would have been proud.

Sadie Buchanan wept openly in the days leading up to her husband's funeral. She had always been stable and steady, focused on the needs of everyone but herself, so Callandra was devastated to see her mother so blank-faced and dispirited.

The little country church was packed for the funeral. Ross Buchanan had managed his small farm without apparent strain, growing potatoes and raising chickens and pigs. So, family and friends were still in shock from his sudden death, apparently from heart failure. Callandra sat on the wooden bench between her mother and her fourteen-year-old sister, Beitiris. So many times she'd sat on this same bench, but with her father there, too. She realized now how comforting his presence had been, how secure it had made her little world. He never took Christian dogma too seriously, but he spoke highly about the church for the way it brought the community together each Sunday. And so Callandra had come to appreciate it for that, too. But now, without his gentle smile and kind eyes, the church felt like a very cold place.

Trying to avoid crying, Callandra kept her eyes forward, away from her grieving family. But this left her staring straight at her father's coffin, intensifying her sadness. When the minister appeared at the pulpit, she was relieved to have somewhere else to fix her gaze.

There was much to study in this peculiar-looking man. She'd heard that he'd come from Glasgow, due to the illness of Reverend Patterson, who had been the local pastor since her father was a child. This preacher had none of Reverend Patterson's warmth. He was short, and had pallid skin; deeply set, narrow eyes; and strange, protruding lips. His eulogy was almost completely impersonal, referring to her father only as "this good man" after once using his name. He even had to check his notes before mentioning that Fenwick was the town where they were gathered together on this sad day. It was such a sharp contrast to the eulogy that would have been delivered by Reverend Patterson, and its remoteness drove home Callandra's feelings of pain and loss. It was made worse by the Glasgow minister's stutter. "F-F-F-F-Fenwick," he had said.

After the service, Callandra and her mother led the small crowd from the church to the burial site, the warmth of the sun softening the bleakness of the event. Still, the comforting words about her father going to a better place were rudely contradicted by the facts — the coffin in the cold ground, her mother a tearful shroud of black, her brothers and sisters all cleanly attired to say goodbye. There was no escape from the cavalcade of saddening sights.

She allowed herself to search the crowd and spotted Mr. and Mrs. McLeod with their two oldest children, Alex and Bernadette.

———— * ————

Everyone came back to the house afterward. It was warm enough to sit outside, and no one was crying now. Sandwiches and cakes were served with punch; the men drank whisky.

Callandra helped with the younger children, conscious of Alex standing a short distance away. She went to her brother Duncan, who had spilled his plate of food, bringing her closer to Alex. She cringed as she heard Duncan ask Alex if they were all still going to the Stewarton Fair.

Before she could scold him, she sensed someone approaching from behind.

"Excuse me, miss."

Callandra looked around; it was the minister. He was shorter than he'd looked in the church, not much taller than her.

"I'm Reverend Scott," he said. "You're the eldest child, I believe."

"Aye, sir," she responded.

"I hope I've been a comfort to your family in this t-t-t-t-t-terrible time."

"Yes."

"The death of a loved one takes an enormous toll," he continued. "Fortunately, we have the Lord and the scriptures to help us through it."

Callandra had no response.

"You seem very t-t-t-t-t-troubled," said the minister, taking her hand.

"Oh no. I'm fine," she said, pulling it back. "I mean, I'm doing fine."

He reached again for her hand, this time securing it. "Let's take a little walk."

A request from a minister was difficult to decline. They walked a short distance from the gathering, with her hand held firmly in his.

"I'm not used to these simple country churches," he said. "My own church is in Glasgow, and is much more elaborate."

She stopped to pick up a child's bonnet in the grass, enabling her to break free of the minister's grasp without appearing rude.

"I think you'd find my church very grand," he said. "Perhaps you'll visit it someday."

Callandra nodded faintly, ambiguously. "I think I should go and help my mother, Reverend Scott."

"Yes, she'll be needing you, and I must be off anyway," he said.

Then, worrying she might have seemed rude, she added, "Thank you for coming, sir."

"It was my pleasure," he responded with a small bow.

As he disappeared, Callandra spotted Alex alone near the oak tree where they'd dallied the other day. Before she could move in his direction, she was summoned to help her aunt in the kitchen. One chore led to another and, by the time she'd finished, it was late afternoon and the warmth was going out of the day, leaving a golden haze in the air. The gathering had thinned. She spotted the McLeod family getting into their wagon, with Alex facing toward the road, not even looking back at the farmhouse. As he disappeared from view, she was struck by how different his departure felt this time.

The next day, Reverend Scott returned. The sight of his fine carriage was distinctly out of place now. Callandra watched from the barn, as he walked to the house and was welcomed at the door by her mother, who hastily removed her apron.

It occurred to Callandra that he must have stayed overnight nearby, perhaps at the inn in Kilmarnock. A follow-up visit the day after the funeral was perhaps part of his duties.

After a while, he emerged from the house and turned toward the barn, where Callandra was feeding the pigs. She watched him through the slats.

"Callandra," he called, stopping at the entrance. "Callandra."

She stood motionless, but he kept calling her name and started to advance into the barn.

"Yes, sir," she said, emerging from the pen in a stained smock, her hair covered by a bonnet.

"Your mother told me I would find you here."

She stood silent, confused by his presence. With his lips pursed and his head tilted upward, he looked even more self-important and silly than yesterday. She had a strong wish for him to leave.

"I have some news I trust you will be happy to hear," he continued. "I've just spoken with your mother. I've indicated an intention to seek your hand in m-m-m-marriage."

"But sir," she finally mustered. "It is so soon after my father's death, I cannot ..."

"Of course, my dear," he interrupted her. "I intend to help you through your grief. Don't forget I am a man of the c-c-c-c-cloth."

"No, I would never forget that," she said, cringing at the memory of his hand on hers. "I can't even think of marriage ..."

He motioned dismissively, reaching to take her hands.

She pulled them back. "Sir, my hands are dirty. Please, you embarrass me."

"I intend to change your life for the better, dear girl. You'll be a minister's wife, and you'll have no occasion to be cleaning barns." He grabbed one of her hands and kissed it, saying he would return the following week, then walked to the waiting carriage without looking back.

Callandra felt sure her mother would not force her to marry against her will, but she urgently wanted this confirmed. As soon as his carriage pulled out of sight, she rushed into the house and found her mother sitting alone in the rocking chair in the kitchen.

"Oh, Mother, I don't want to marry that man! You won't make me marry him, will you? I'm not ready for marriage."

Sadie looked up with sad, forlorn eyes. She was clearly surprised by her daughter's vehemence, and quickly replied, "Of course not, dear."

Callandra felt an enormous sense of relief. But she also quickly became aware, in a way she hadn't fully appreciated before, just how much her father's death was going to change all of their lives. The family now faced a dire situation. There was no longer an able-bodied man to run the farm; her mother's small, irregular income as a midwife wasn't much. Without sufficient funds, they'd have to leave the farm.

They could live with Sadie's sister's family in Paisley. But their modest home couldn't accommodate eight extra people, and they were the prosperous side of the family.

Sadie considered moving to a humble flat in Kilmarnock, where she could earn a meagre living as a servant while taking in laundry and sewing.

"I could help with the laundry and sewing," offered Callandra.

"Aye ... aye ..." said her mother.

"I couldn't possibly abandon the family," Callandra added.

"Well, it wouldn't exactly be like that," said her mother, sighing heavily as she shifted in the chair. "You see, the minister proposed to take you to live with him in a grand house in Glasgow, with the family staying here on the farm."

"What do you mean?"

"He said that he would take care of the mortgage, and we could stay here."

It took a few seconds for this new landscape to come fully into view. So her family didn't need her — at least not scrubbing laundry in a hovel in Kilmarnock. Rather, they needed her to go to Glasgow, reside in a fine house, and live a life of leisure. She felt cornered, realizing the moral high ground had been yanked out from under her.

"But you don't think you'd be happy with that life?" asked her mother blankly.

"I'd hate every minute of it!" cried Callandra, imagining his jutting lips touching hers.

The forcefulness of her response shook Sadie from her torpor. "Then you shan't do it. That's decided," she said, showing her old vitality.

Callandra ran over and hugged her, murmuring, "Thank you, thank you, Mother."

Sadie kept her word. In the following days, as she moved from grieving to preparing for the changes ahead, she never let on to anyone that there was another option. Callandra's siblings bemoaned the prospect of leaving the farm, but no one blamed Callandra.

The depth of the family crisis became clearer still three days after the funeral when Mr. McTavish, their neighbour, drove Sadie and her three eldest daughters to Kilmarnock to help them find a place to live. Almost everything was beyond their means. The only option turned out to be a tiny two-room flat in a decrepit house in the centre of town. Dingy and musty, it contained nothing more than a woodstove and washbasin — a washbasin that would undoubtedly be used every waking hour of the day, doing other people's laundry. There was one small window, which looked out back on to a row of latrines.

As they drove away, through the town's busy main street, Callandra noticed the impressive facade of the King's Arms Hotel, where she assumed the minister had stayed.

On the ride home, her mother sat up front beside Mr. McTavish, so Callandra couldn't see her face, but she saw the vivid pain on her sisters' faces. For them, moving off the farm meant the end of school and the beginning of a life devoted to washing and cleaning. It was difficult to imagine a happy existence in that dismal flat. The rolling hills and neat hedgerows they passed seemed part of a paradise now beyond reach.

Callandra felt consumed by grief and despair. As the carriage trundled on, she was bothered by the thought that she had the power to save her family from further desolation, from descending into lives of misery. She couldn't bring her father back; his death would forever sadden them all. But she could protect those she loved from bleakness and hopelessness. She was overwhelmed, one minute feeling distraught about her family's fate and her role in perpetuating it, the next indignantly rejecting any responsibility.

Her mind wandered onto the memory of Alex adjusting her beret; it was like a fresh discovery of a distant past. The cart drove past a particularly lovely clump of hawthorn trees, with their creamy white blossoms, and she let the memory of Alex dance in her brain.

She would never feel for the minister the excitement she felt for Alex. Yet when she'd seen Alex the day of the funeral, he hadn't even spoken to her.

Was she putting her family — and herself — into a wretched state, all so she could cling to the dream of something that may have existed only in her own mind? She even considered the possibility that Alex had betrayed her, teasing her with feelings that to him were just part of a warm spring afternoon. When harsh realities like death entered, he was no longer there.

The next day, after a tormented night of little sleep, she approached her mother.

"I've changed my mind," Callandra said. "It will take some adjustment, but I think I'll be fine marrying Reverend Scott. It will be better for all of us. At least, this way I'll have a happy place to come home to."

"Oh, that you always would!" said Sadie. Callandra knew that the image of a happy homecoming was just what was needed to assuage her mother's fears.

"But are you sure that's what you wish, dear?" Sadie asked.

So that would be the extent of her mother's probing about a marriage her daughter clearly didn't want? What had happened to the spirited Sadie Buchanan, who had once been such a loyal advocate for her daughter?

"It is," said Callandra, forcing resolution into her voice.

At dinner that night, her mother told the family that Callandra was to marry Reverend Norbert Scott and live in Glasgow, and that the minister would help the family stay on the farm. There was considerable shock and curiosity that Callandra would be marrying the pastor who presided at their father's funeral less than a week ago. But overall there was relief and delight that they would not have to move to Kilmarnock. In the commotion over the developments and the crush of attention, Callandra felt, if not sure of her decision, at least gratified by the thought that she had done her duty to protect the people she loved.

The next day, as she fixed her mind on preparing for her new life, a letter was slipped under the door with her name on it.

> Dear Callandra:
>
> I hope you will be back at school soon. Walking home isn't the same without you.
>
> Please tell Duncan we shall all go to the Stewarton Fair next year, for sure. And promise me you'll wear the beret.
>
> Alex

Chapter Two

"I've found a girl to marry," Norbert declared to his mother.

Mrs. Scott braced herself. Much of her life had been spent protecting her son from rejection and suffering. Without ever saying so, she had assumed he would live out his days at home, unmarried. So this news was shocking and became more so when he revealed that he had already made a proposal and it had been accepted.

"I believe it will give me confidence to have a wife," he said, as he and his mother sat alone in the parlour of the family's stately Glasgow home.

"I understand," she said, her deep-set eyes staring at the pattern on her teacup. A linen cap held her greying hair in place, displaying a sharp-featured face that, even in youth, had not been described as pretty.

And in some ways, she did. Certainly she understood that Norbert was deeply lacking in confidence. Growing up the eldest son of Thomas Scott had meant comfort and privilege. But these advantages were undermined by a profound sense of inadequacy — a sense inculcated in him since childhood by his father.

From an early age, it had been clear that Norbert lacked the quickness, vigour, and self-assurance of his father, a successful textile manufacturer. Then there was the stutter. When it became evident, by age three, that no amount of drilling or instruction could correct the stutter, Mr. Scott insisted that his son no longer be referred to as Thomas Jr., but rather be called by his middle name — Norbert, a family name on Mrs. Scott's side. Mr. Scott was convinced that a son with a stutter would never amount to anything in the business world.

Mrs. Scott countered that a stutter was not nearly the disability her husband implied.

On one occasion, she had gone further and added that her husband perhaps overstated his own accomplishments; he had built his business when the demand for fine fabrics happened to be expanding rapidly; moreover, he'd been able to draw on her fortune to make the necessary investments. Ever since that conversation many years earlier, there had been strained relations between husband and wife, particularly in relation to Norbert. Mr. Scott's harsh attitude toward the boy made Mrs. Scott all the more protective, and that made Norbert seem even more pathetic to his father.

With the business world ruled out, Mrs. Scott had groomed Norbert for the clergy. He'd obtained the necessary university degree, but the guest sermons he gave upon graduation to small Presbyterian congregations outside Glasgow were not well received, despite generous contributions from Mrs. Scott to local parish funds. Eventually, Norbert had ended up assistant pastor at the grand Glasgow church where his mother's family had long been preeminent. His title suggested a certain status, but that was misleading. Nobody was under the impression that Norbert was being trained to take over as pastor some day. In fact, Norbert's responsibilities were light; filling in for ailing ministers at inconsequential county churches was one of his few duties.

But even if Mrs. Scott had managed to arrange the semblance of a career for Norbert, she had more difficulty protecting him from the pain of watching his father dote on his ten-year-old brother. The boy had been born long after Norbert and his sister Isobel, both now in their twenties. Mr. Scott had insisted that the boy be called Thomas Jr. — a name that was no longer in use — and openly groomed him to take over the family business. The younger son spoke without a stutter, and his brash, outgoing ways bore a striking likeness to those of his father. Tommy basked in the attention, and seemed to derive pleasure from the way his father's adoration created a distinct discomfort in his older brother.

"I do believe this is the appropriate kind of girl," Norbert continued, looking into the fire. Above the marble mantel was a heavy, gold-rimmed mirror, in which was reflected the room's darkly panelled walls, finely woven upholstery and richly coloured tapestries. "She is modest and meek."

Modesty and meekness were certainly desirable qualities for Norbert's bride, in Mrs. Scott's view. Even better qualities would be loyalty and devotion, although she never really expected anyone — except herself — to feel such attachment to Norbert.

"Very well," she said, drawing the matter to a close after less than an hour of discussion, including the financial details.

Mrs. Scott retired to her private bedroom, inclined to believe that, although she hadn't anticipated or wished for this development, perhaps it was for the best. Over the years, she had avoided pushing Norbert toward the parade of debutantes — not because she wanted to keep him celibate — but because she worried that he might be rudely rebuffed by young ladies with options. She savoured the possibility that he had found a suitable young lady without options.

Her acceptance of the new situation grew in the three weeks leading up to Callandra's arrival, as Mrs. Scott saw a more confident manner in her soon-to-be-married son. Young Tommy was no longer the sole centre of attention. Isobel bustled about the house with an air of excitement that her older brother was to marry. The fact that Norbert's betrothed had a humble background seemed unimportant since the marriage had the blessing of Mrs. Scott, whose sense of propriety was never questioned.

So, when Miss Callandra Buchanan alighted from the carriage after her long ride from Fenwick, Mrs. Scott was predisposed to accept her. But what she saw, as the girl was presented in the hallway, was not to her liking. It wasn't that she was offended by Callandra's simple look — a slender country waif in a calico dress. Rather, it was something in her face: something a little too animated, a little too alert, a little too comely. Callandra did not look like the modest, meek girl Mrs. Scott felt she'd been promised.

"Hello," said Mrs. Scott. "I trust your journey has been satisfactory."

The words sounded cold, but they communicated more warmth than Mrs. Scott actually felt.

In the days that followed, Mrs. Scott came to wonder if she'd been mistaken in her assessment of Callandra. Rather than being animated, the girl seemed quite subdued. At the small, quiet wedding reception in the parlour, Callandra seemed dispirited, even docile. The wedding was attended only by close Scott family relatives. Since Callandra's family was in mourning, they had not been invited to the reception — an obstacle waived in Callandra's case. Whatever alertness Mrs. Scott felt she had detected in the girl's face upon arrival was no longer evident. Callandra was so lifeless and gloomy that she hardly seemed like the bride at all. Her ill-fitting, high-necked, off-white organza dress — borrowed from Isobel's cache of discarded garments — appeared as out of place and lacklustre as Callandra herself at her own wedding.

"Am I pulling too hard, ma'am?" asked Lottie, the young maid who handled the hairbrush with authority.

"Oh no, not at all."

After a week in Glasgow, Callandra still hadn't adjusted to being called "ma'am," especially by someone her age.

"Just call me Callandra — really," she said.

"Yes, ma'am," said Lottie, with no hint of disobedience.

They returned to brushing in silence. In the large mirror in front of her, Callandra's eyes wandered onto Lottie's face and was struck by its beauty — full, heart-shaped lips, skin like porcelain, and a dimpled chin. Braided and covered by a kerchief, her hair was long and blond.

With the brushing done, Lottie arranged Callandra's hair, pulling it back off her face but leaving it flowing down her back. Although neatly styled, it looked different than the way Mrs. Scott and Isobel wore their hair, pinned back sharply and structured into a bun.

"I have an idea," said Lottie, going to the large bureau where she had installed Callandra's meagre wardrobe. Opening a lower drawer, she pulled out the beret. "What if you wore this with it? It would look nice with your frock, ma'am."

This was just the sort of reminder of her past that Callandra had been struggling to avoid. But Lottie seemed so energized by her plan that Callandra didn't have the will to crush her sweet helpfulness. She sat still as Lottie deftly arranged her hair under the beret.

Heading down to tea, Callandra was struck again, as on her arrival, by the grandness and opulence of the house. The central staircase was massive, with oak banisters, elaborately carved railings and a thick, wine-coloured carpet. Heavy candelabra adorned the walls in between portraits of dour-looking older men, scowling from inside gilded frames. A large marble statue of an angel stood at the bottom of the stairs, like a sentinel watching over the spacious main-floor foyer. Light filtered in from above through stained-glass windows, decorated with Biblical scenes and framed by weighty brocade drapes that kept the stately hallway dark and grim.

As she approached the double doors to the parlour, she was aware — for the first time since her arrival — of feeling lighthearted. Someone had been nice to her; kindness had been displayed in this vast, cold house.

The gathering included only Norbert, his mother and sister, but Callandra's appearance in the doorway drew little attention. Indeed, scant attention had been paid to her since her arrival in Glasgow the previous week, including at her own wedding. She was directed back to the same chair where she'd been seated each day, slightly removed from where the others sat near the hearth.

"Dr. Anders suspects gout. I spoke with him this morning," said Norbert, continuing yesterday's discussion of the ailments of a Mrs. Lumley. Callandra noticed how little Norbert stuttered in the intimacy of this group.

Mrs. Scott rang a bell and Lottie, along with an older female servant, appeared with the tea service. Callandra watched Lottie as she quietly went about her work, while Norbert outlined the case for gout over a spleen-related disorder.

"We must pay her a visit," said Mrs. Scott, stirring her tea. She was dressed in a grey taffeta dress and matching cap. Her hair was pulled back, revealing the sharpness of her features and the lines on her face. She was devoid of any jewellery or scarf that might have brightened her appearance or softened the effects of aging. It was hard to imagine there had ever been any youthful gaiety in that face, or that she had borne a child — let alone engaged in the activity that would have led to such a result — as recently as a decade ago.

Norbert and Isobel nodded in agreement to the idea of visiting Mrs. Lumley.

A lull in the conversation prompted Callandra to say, "Today is my birthday. I'm sixteen."

She had resolved that morning not to focus on her birthday, fearing an unleashing of memories of past birthdays happily spent with her family. But her pleasant exchange with Lottie had left her feeling whimsical and a little reckless.

"Oh, happy birthday, ma'am," Lottie said warmly.

"Our best wishes to you," said Mrs. Scott, her curtness quashing Lottie's exuberance. "Would you like a ginger cake?"

Callandra accepted a piece from the cake tray offered by the older serving woman, thereby apparently completing the matter of celebrating her sixteenth birthday. Mrs. Scott noted that the cake tray should be refilled, as relatives would soon be arriving.

But Callandra's announcement — her first intervention at a family event — had drawn Norbert's attention.

"My dear, I understand your wardrobe is limited for now, but I find the beret unsuitable," he said. "I shouldn't think you'd want to present yourself to my cousins that way."

The implication that she was an embarrassment to Norbert hit Callandra hard. With Mrs. Scott's gaze echoing Norbert's disapproval, Callandra reached up to remove the beret. But it was fastened on with clips and she fumbled to get it free. Lottie rushed over to help. Callandra could feel her chin quiver and tears gather in her eyes.

"Don't worry, your new clothes will be ready soon," consoled Isobel.

By now, Lottie had gotten the clips free and removed the beret.

"You can discard that, Lottie," said Mrs. Scott.

Callandra trembled. All her attempts to blot out thinking about her family, about her dead father, about Alex, about the bliss of once wearing that beret, suddenly gave way. Tears rolled down her cheeks, dropping onto her slice of ginger cake.

"It was all my fault, ma'am," said Lottie to Mrs. Scott. "I selected the —"

"That will be enough," said Mrs. Scott, abruptly cutting off Lottie's interjection. Then, turning to Callandra: "Perhaps you might want to go upstairs and rest. We'll give your regrets to the guests."

As Callandra rose to leave, Mr. Scott suddenly appeared in the doorway.

"Good heavens, what have we here?" he exclaimed.

"Callandra's not feeling well," replied Mrs. Scott.

"Well, well, what's the matter?" said Mr. Scott, who had none of his wife's distaste for emotional displays, especially at times like this, when he'd been drinking at his club.

"She's simply not well," Mrs. Scott continued. "Florence and Nathaniel and the children are expected any minute. If you're going to join us, Mr. Scott, you may wish to change." Even from across the room, the smell of cigars, snuff, and liquor could be detected.

"What's upset you, my dear?" Mr. Scott asked Callandra. With a full head of silver hair, chiselled features and a florid face, he looked like he'd been handsome in his youth.

"I'm all right," said Callandra.

"Nonsense! What's going on?" stormed the head of the family.

"Nothing … I guess … I guess I'm just a little homesick," said Callandra.

There was a long pause, shattered by Mr. Scott's bellowing laughter.

"Homesick! Homesick! Unbelievable!" he scoffed, crossing the room to pour himself a brandy.

"Two days after all your girlish dreams are realized in marriage and you're homesick!" he roared.

As the focus shifted to guests arriving in the hallway, Callandra caught a sideways glance of her husband and noticed his lips were trembling.

---　*　---

She woke to a darkened room, and feelings of despair.

There was a soft knock on the door and then Lottie appeared, carrying a candle and a small tray of food.

"I thought you might want to have dinner up here," she said, almost in a whisper, as she placed the tray in front of Callandra.

"Oh, Lottie, this is so kind of you."

"I best get back downstairs," said Lottie, then added shyly, "I understand what you said about homesickness, ma'am. I feel it, too. If it wasn't for my brother being here in Glasgow, sometimes I think I'd die of loneliness in this house."

Callandra wanted to learn more about Lottie's loneliness, but sensed the girl had already risked punishment by bringing the food. It was shepherd's pie — a meal likely taken from the servants' kitchen, possibly Lottie's own dinner.

Callandra felt deeply moved by this gesture of kindness. She thanked Lottie, not wanting to detain her further. But Lottie put a finger to her lips to suggest silence, then pulled Callandra's beret from a pocket beneath her apron.

"I'm hiding this," she whispered, putting it in a bottom drawer.

"Oh," sighed Callandra, stunned by Lottie's thoughtfulness; the servant girl was openly defying an order given by Mrs. Scott. All this, on Callandra's behalf. She felt overwhelmed by Lottie's sweetness and benevolence.

"Good night," Lottie whispered as she paused at the bedroom door, "And happy birthday — *Callandra.*"

For Norbert, the evening was unbearable. The simpering smiles of his cousins, the stiff formality of Aunt Florence, the quiet dullness of Uncle Nathaniel, all blended into a colourless background for Norbert's raging hurt.

His marriage hadn't solved a problem, but rather made it worse. He had never been comfortable approaching young ladies, with their proud and flighty ways. He suspected he would have been happy with a quiet life, living at home and spending evenings in the parlour with his mother, sister, and the occasional guest. But he knew his father viewed such behaviour as evidence of his inadequacy. The dilemma of finding a presentable young lady who posed no risk should she reject him — since no one in Glasgow would ever know — appeared solvable in the person of Callandra.

Like most of the parishioners in the Fenwick congregation that day, she was unsophisticated, but she spoke without the strong local accent and seemed bright and attractive despite her simple ways. The fact that her father had just died was awkward, but it allowed Norbert to present himself to her mother as she adjusted to the family's new financial difficulties, taking advantage of a sense of vulnerability that might wane over time.

In presenting his offer to Callandra's mother, he had been cordial, but had handled the matter with detachment, not unlike he would have dealt with the purchase of a horse which he admired but regarded as one of a number of possible choices.

Norbert realized that the whole point of the marriage had been to gain the respect of his father, to demonstrate his ability to function as a man in the world. But now Callandra's tears and homesickness had exposed the lie behind the project.

The more Norbert thought about it, the more he saw her behaviour as a violation of the trust that should exist between man and wife. Did she really have to parade her misery in front of his family? How dare she reveal the depth of her unhappiness, which couldn't help but reflect negatively on her new husband! Were his feelings of no consequence to her whatsoever?

Thomas Scott held court over dinner, expounding on politics and business with his usual flair. Norbert sank low in his chair, managing to avoid his father's notice until, over dessert, Aunt Florence turned to Norbert and asked about Mrs. Lumley's condition.

"It seems she may have g-g-g-g-g-gout."

Mrs. Scott quickly intervened with details favouring a gout diagnosis, having retained them perfectly from her son's recounting earlier.

With the conversation now about the health of someone of no interest to him, Mr. Scott announced he had to leave for a "business meeting."

Norbert excused himself from joining the others in the parlour after dinner. He arrived in the bedroom to find Callandra asleep in their large, canopied bed in the darkened chamber. This only fuelled his resentment; while he had been suffering through one of the most humiliating evenings of his life, she had drifted off to sleep! Her motionless body now presented itself to him as a picture of tranquility, mocking his anguish.

---- * ----

Callandra awoke with a start, to find his hand groping under her nightdress. The touch was so sudden, so out of keeping with anything that had happened between them, including on their wedding night, that she let out a small scream.

"It's your husband," he said, putting his hand over her mouth.

She stopped screaming; he was entitled to do this.

She could see he was naked, and that his soft, fleshy body was clammy with sweat. He lifted her nightdress up over her face, and his other hand moved quickly all over her, grabbing roughly at her legs and breasts. She tried to pull the nightdress down, but he held it firmly over her face as he climbed on top of her. She sensed it was better not to resist, and lay still as he completed their marriage commitment.

Chapter Three

In the weeks and months that followed, Callandra became even more homesick — particularly for her mother, whose failure to protect her from this dreadful marriage somehow filled Callandra with even more longing for the deeply caring mother she'd once known. And, of course, she missed her father, with his smile and his quiet strength. He would never have let his favourite daughter marry a man she didn't love. The memory of the farm, with her parents and siblings gathered around the hearth, made Callandra detest all the more the heartless grandeur of the Scott mansion. Callandra realized that Norbert's plan was that they would eventually move out on their own — a prospect that was just as chilling.

The only solace that made her life in Glasgow bearable was Lottie, whose loveliness was matched by her thoughtfulness. When Lottie came upon Callandra crying in bed, as she frequently did, she would sit quietly next to her, gently stroking her arm or holding her hand, humming or softly singing Gaelic lullabies to her. Lottie's touch was so warm and comforting that Callandra would almost forget her sadness. Sometimes Lottie would leave fresh flowers on Callandra's pillow, along with a little candy.

Most of Callandra's time was now spent with Lottie in the long daily routines of hair-brushing and dressing. These routines were not only a chance for her to avoid the family, but they had the approval of Mrs. Scott, who saw them as a sign of Callandra adjusting to her role as Norbert's wife. A seamstress came and took her measurements and produced fine dresses of richly textured French cotton, wool, silk, brocade, and linen. With their puffy gigot sleeves, corseted waists, and flaring skirts over corded petticoats, the dresses were more elaborate than anything she'd ever worn. And, although uncomfortable to wear, she accepted them as part of the wardrobe and grooming rituals that allowed her to spend time alone with Lottie.

The bond between Callandra and Lottie was cemented by their shared sense of loneliness, and the realization that they had both suffered the loss of a father. Indeed, Lottie had lost both parents, ending up in an orphanage along with her older brother, Sam, her one living relative. She had only faint memories of her parents and found it painful to talk about her childhood. Callandra didn't probe.

However, Lottie spoke with great enthusiasm and admiration about her brother. They had always been close; he had sustained her through the sadness of her childhood, and she looked to him for guidance and reassurance. She described him as very smart — the only child at the orphanage who could read, having mostly taught himself. He had run away from the orphanage at the age of twelve and found employment cleaning and oiling the power looms in Mr. Scott's factory, where he proved himself a reliable worker with a knack for carpentry. Mr. Scott came to consider him a valued employee and later agreed to hire his sister to work as a live-in maid in the Scott household, allowing her to leave the orphanage, too.

One day, Lottie told Callandra that she'd heard her brother was coming that afternoon to repair the woodshed. Callandra was intrigued to see this brother she'd heard so much about, and she stood with Lottie watching out her dressing room window.

When he appeared, a tall figure walking across the lawn, Lottie let out a yelp of delight as she waved in vain, trying to get his attention.

"Let's take a walk outside," said Callandra.

Lottie's eyes widened. Callandra grabbed two shawls from her drawer, wrapping one around Lottie. Then, taking her friend by the hand, she headed for the backstairs.

Rushing down the narrow staircase, they almost collided with an older servant, Mrs. Metcalfe, who lost her balance and dropped a basket of freshly laundered towels. At first Mrs. Metcalfe only noticed Lottie, who apologized as she rushed to help.

"What in the good Lord's name are you doing, girl, charging down the stairs like a mad bull?" Then, noticing Callandra, Mrs. Metcalfe changed her tone. "Excuse me, ma'am."

"No, it's my fault. So sorry," said Callandra, pulling Lottie past the woman.

The doorway at the bottom opened into a bustling kitchen, which Callandra had never seen before. It was full of female servants, who looked up surprised at the sight of her.

"This way," murmured Lottie, motioning toward the scullery, which led to the back door.

Suddenly they were outside, moving swiftly across the lawn, hand in hand. Inside the shed, Sam was crouched over, measuring something, when he turned and saw his sister.

"Lottie!" he exclaimed, as she rushed into his embrace. "They told me there'd be no chance of seeing you today."

"It's all because of Callandra," said Lottie, turning to introduce her new friend.

"Hello, ma'am, very pleased to meet you. I'm Samuel Hunter. You're most kind to let my sister visit with me."

His words were clearly meant to be agreeable, but they irked Callandra. He was addressing her with formality, as Reverend Scott's wife. Had Lottie not told him about her? Why didn't he treat her as his sister's trusted confidante? All of a sudden, Callandra felt acutely conscious of her elevated rank, exemplified by the fineness of her dress, while Lottie wore a servant's dress and apron. The gap in their status in the household — which Callandra always tried to ignore — loomed unmistakeably huge.

Lottie immediately put her arm around Callandra and drew her over to Sam.

"You can just call her Callandra. I do," said Lottie, confidently. "She's my friend."

Sam seemed hesitant, unsure whether his sister was reading the situation correctly.

"Aye, please call me Callandra," she said.

Lottie told her brother how much better things had been, and how much time she and Callandra got to spend together away from the rest of the household.

"But I could be in trouble if Mrs. Metcalfe reports me," said Lottie, and then related what had happened on the backstairs. "She might say nothing because Callandra was there."

"Oh, don't count on that," Callandra interjected. "I'll be in trouble, too, if Mrs. Scott hears about it."

"Do you think it would go all the way up to the old hag herself?" asked Lottie.

"Whooa, hold on," said Sam, cutting off his sister's reckless language.

Callandra felt excluded. "I think I'm going to take a walk in the garden," she said, pulling her shawl back up over her shoulders. "I'll come back in a while, Lottie."

"I hope I haven't offended you, ma'am," said Sam. He had a pleasing face, but she felt annoyed that he kept using the address she so disliked.

"No, not at all," she replied.

"I'm coming with you, then," said Lottie.

"No, no," insisted Callandra. "This is a chance for you to visit with Sam."

Walking away, Callandra felt sad, disappointed that such an important encounter — meeting Lottie's beloved brother — had gone so strangely sour.

The next morning, Callandra was summoned to see Mrs. Scott in the sun parlour.

The room was bright and plant-filled, and unlike the other principal rooms in the house, there was no dark wood panelling on its walls. With its large, southern-facing windows, it was the prettiest room in the house — almost cheery. However, Callandra avoided it because, when it was at its finest with the morning sun streaming in, it was spoiled by the presence of her mother-in-law. As Callandra entered now, Mrs. Scott was sitting by one the windows, wearing a high-necked, charcoal-grey dress that even the sunlight didn't liven up.

"You sent for me, ma'am?" said Callandra, her heart pounding.

"Yes. Do sit down." Mrs. Scott's hair was pulled back beneath a white linen cap that drew attention to her stern demeanour. "I understand there was some disorderly behaviour yesterday on the servants' stairs."

"Yes, ma'am," said Callandra. "It was my fault. I meant no harm. I was just having fun."

"If you choose to have fun, do so with Norbert or Isobel. Not with a servant."

Callandra meekly nodded. Then seizing her chance, she continued: "Mrs. Scott, I know I've been a disappointment. Perhaps you want to send me back home."

Mrs. Scott was silent for a moment. "No," she said. "That won't be necessary ... I'm making a few changes. From now on, Mrs. Metcalfe will take charge of your grooming."

"What about Lottie?"

"She wasn't doing a good job. She's been reassigned to the scullery."

"Oh, Mrs. Scott," pleaded Callandra. "It was my idea to go down the backstairs —"

"That's enough," Mrs. Scott said, cutting her off curtly. "It's simple. Follow Norbert's direction in all things. And stay away from Mr. Scott."

"Yes, ma'am."

"Now you may go."

Walking back to her bedroom, Callandra felt devastated by the prospect of losing all access to Lottie, which was clearly what Mrs. Scott intended. Suddenly dizzy, Callandra sensed the stairs were moving beneath her feet. She clung to the banister, trying to regain her balance.

She awoke a while later in bed, with a doctor standing over her, and Mr. and Mrs. Scott, Isobel, and Norbert gathered in the adjacent sitting room. The doctor, who introduced himself as Dr. Anders, explained to Callandra that a maid had found her slumped over at the top of the stairs.

"But you're going to be fine," he said. Then turning toward Norbert and the family, he declared with a smile, "Congratulations, Reverend. I do believe you're going to be a father."

The months of Callandra's pregnancy were the most serene in Norbert's life; he seemed an important person, busy both with church and family responsibilities. The Scott household buzzed with preparations for the birth. Isobel devoted herself to supervising the embroidery work necessary for the decoration of the nursery.

Now that a product of their union had been created, Norbert no longer had to worry about Callandra seeking permission from his mother to escape the marriage and return home. As a goodwill gesture, Norbert intervened with his mother to allow Callandra the return of her favourite maid.

It was early June when Norbert's child was born, after two days of wrenching labour for Callandra, during which, day and night, Lottie never left her side. Isobel watched much of the drama as well, with curiosity, while Norbert waited in the parlour with his mother. Yet even after he was summoned and his daughter — wrapped in meticulously embroidered sheets — was presented to him, he felt a sense of detachment, a strange foreboding that it would take more than this to impress his father.

Chapter Four

With the birth of her child, Callandra's life changed for the better. She now had someone who was truly hers, and she felt overwhelmed by feelings of love and attachment. Her focus changed to nurturing her daughter, and protecting her from the coldness of Norbert and his mother, who both seemed largely indifferent to the girl, as if she wasn't really part of their family. Surprisingly, no one objected when Callandra said she wanted to call the child Emma — even though the name had no significance to the Scott family.

Callandra's relationship with Norbert also became less openly contentious. Emma's birth had at least provided some proof of his normalcy, his maturity, and even his manliness. As a result, Norbert's father was less inclined to belittle him, and that seemed to make Norbert less antagonistic in his dealings with Callandra. In bed, he rarely approached her with the hostility that he'd often shown in the early months of their marriage. Indeed, after two years of married life, he largely ignored her, in bed and out of it. When he did speak to her, it was usually to criticize her for something she'd said or done or for failing to be sufficiently deferential to him. He certainly never showed any affection or basic consideration, and he clearly preferred the company of his mother and sister and the dreary guests who regularly visited.

Overall, however, as the mother of Norbert's progeny, Callandra fit less awkwardly into the Scott household, although she was sure that Mrs. Scott still regarded her with disapproval. Isobel was less judgmental, and even invited Callandra to join her in attending the Ladies Reading and Improvement Club. Callandra readily accepted; it was an opportunity to leave the house, and the concept of books triggered a pleasant, poignant memory of school, childhood, and her father.

The club did not disappoint. It consisted mostly of young women, all well coiffed and fashionably dressed, who met once a month at a member's home. Some of the ladies were married, others not, but all were of sufficient means that they had ample time and little to do. Each month they read a book — usually a romantic novel — and then discussed the plot and characters. Callandra took to it immediately, finding it a pleasing alternative to the languor of the Scott household.

Her interest was particularly aroused by the selection one month of a very different little book. It had been suggested by a member who had just returned from a stay in London where she'd belonged to another ladies' reading club. The book, *A Vindication of the Rights of Woman* by Mary Wollstonecraft, had been popular with the London club. And, opening it in her dressing room one afternoon, Callandra quickly understood why.

Mrs. Wollstonecraft insisted women didn't have to be inferior in status to men! It wasn't nature, but lack of education and social custom that relegated women to their subordinate role, transforming them into passive, vain, coquettish creatures obsessed with pleasing men, rather than being strong, thinking beings in their own right.

There was so much to absorb in all this that Callandra found herself pondering little else for the next few days. It seemed that an important truth had been revealed to her — one that helped explain the sadness in her own life. Her father's death had plunged her family into desperate financial straits, leading to her being effectively sold off in marriage. The financial security that marriage offered was supposed to bring happiness to a woman, but for Callandra it had brought despair. It wasn't just the callousness of Norbert and his family; it was the empty nature of her life. The very richness and idleness of it — considered so desirable by most — made her world feel like an ornate prison.

"The most respectable women are the most oppressed," Mrs. Wollstonecraft wrote. "How many women … waste life away, the prey of discontent, who might have practiced as physicians, regulated a farm, managed a shop, and stood erect, supported by their own industry." Callandra felt downright inspired by Mrs. Wollstonecraft's description of the possibility of expanding women's minds beyond the confining world of gossip and vanity to "comprehend the moral duties of life, and in what human virtue and dignity consist," and her urging women of leisure to give up their privileges of rank in exchange for "the privileges of humanity."

This little book — and its courageous, clear-headed author — filled Callandra with palpable excitement. Even in her quiet sitting room, in this big house where she was of little consequence, she felt she understood the world as never before.

She assumed the book was having a similar effect on others. But Isobel said she hadn't made it past the first chapter. At the meeting, most of the ladies seemed uninterested.

"There is much talk in London about the 'Woman Question,'" said Priscilla Hopkins, the young woman who had introduced the book. "Sadly, it has generated little support from men."

The suggestion that the book dealt with a subject that provoked resistance in men made the group even more reluctant to discuss it.

"The author certainly didn't make much of her own life," snarled Mrs. Wade, an older woman who had said little at previous meetings, but was animated on the subject of Mary Wollstonecraft. "Her life was a disgrace, you know. She had an affair with a married man, and a child out of wedlock."

"Still, there is much in the book that is so ... well, interesting," said Callandra, nervously.

"I think her behaviour shows the folly of her ideas about men and women," said Mrs. Wade. "When I learned of her transgressions, I decided not to read the book. I can't imagine why this club would want to discuss the thoughts of such a woman. It might suggest we condone disreputable behaviour."

"I don't know about her behaviour —" began Callandra.

"Well, I do," Mrs. Wade interrupted. "It's been revealed in a book — a book authored by her lover, of all people!"

There were clucks of disapproval around the room, clarifying that further defence of Mrs. Wollstonecraft would be tantamount to advocating marital infidelity.

Callandra struggled to regain her composure, feeling rebuked and humiliated, angry at Mrs. Wade for her domineering ways and more intrigued than ever about the inner thoughts of the brilliant and rebellious Mary Wollstonecraft.

———— * ————

After that, the book club returned to novels, and *A Vindication of the Rights of Woman* was not referred to again. But its ideas remained alive in Callandra. She read the book multiple times, finding strength and beauty in its words. She read them out loud to

Lottie, with the sound of them spoken providing a reminder that they existed beyond her own mind.

> Gentleness, docility, and a spaniel-like affection are, on this ground, consistently recommended as the cardinal virtues of the sex; and, disregarding the economy of nature, one writer has declared that it is masculine for a woman to be melancholy. She was created to be the toy of man, his rattle, and it must jingle in his ears, whenever, dismissing reason, he chooses to be amused.

Lottie listened attentively. Although Sam had taught her how to read, she didn't read well and preferred listening to Callandra. Lottie agreed that women were treated unfairly, but the ideas in the book seemed to resonate less with her.

"Sometimes you remind me of Sam," said Lottie one morning, after a reading session.

"Your brother?" asked Callandra. "Is he interested in the emancipation of women?"

"Well, uh, no. At least I don't think so. But he's very passionate about equality."

Lottie said that Sam also resembled Callandra in that he, too, was always reading and talking about what was wrong with the world. Instead of books, he discussed pamphlets he got at political meetings or publications he read in coffee houses downtown. Pressed by Callandra, Lottie recalled the name of one — *The Poor Man's Journal.*

The thought that Sam was passionate about equality — even if he hadn't applied that passion to the plight of women — was intriguing, and left Callandra wondering if perhaps there was some merit in him after all.

Callandra was conscious of her driver watching with curiosity when she had him stop by a street vendor. After two years in Glasgow, she still felt uncomfortable in the bustling city streets, and she had not gotten used to having a driver to transport her around, on the rare occasion when she left the house. Although her status was clearly higher than his, it sometimes didn't feel like that, and she worried that he might be regarding her with suspicion.

She quickly purchased a copy of *The Poor Man's Guardian*, the actual title of the newspaper, and slipped it into her purse.

The publication seemed extraordinary when she opened it in the privacy of her dressing room. It was full of articles about things she knew nothing about — the Great Reform Act, the Factory Act, the Corn Laws, the Manchester Strike. The pages reverberated with talk of injustice, exciting in her the same feelings that Wollstonecraft's book had. The only disappointment was that it had nothing on the plight of women. Indeed, women only appeared in cartoons, as nags trying to coral their menfolk home from the tavern.

Callandra soon returned to the street vendor, but this time, feeling more confident, she had the driver wait as she stood scanning the racks, looking for what else was on offer. The vendor directed her to journals and almanacs concerned with domestic themes. Then he picked up a copy of *Tait's Edinburgh Magazine*.

"Some of the ladies read this one," he said.

She was struck by how much *Tait's Edinburgh Magazine* resembled *The Poor Man's Guardian*. The issue was devoted to something called Poor Law reform. To her surprise, she noticed that one of the articles was written by a woman — Harriet Martineau, whose name appeared on the magazine's cover. Callandra indicated she would take a copy, energized at the thought there was a woman writing in these journals.

"And these, too," Callandra said, picking up *The Loyal Reformers' Gazette* and *The Weaver's Magazine and Literary Companion*, because they were positioned near *The Poor Man's Guardian*.

At tea that afternoon, the conversation seemed even duller than usual. She made her exit as soon as she could, disappearing up to her dressing room.

She sat down with the magazines, turning first to the article by Harriet Martineau in *Tait's*. It was about a new law that forced poor people into grim workhouses, with mothers separated from their children. Martineau attacked the law and sharply criticized leading political figures who endorsed it. Callandra was thrilled by Martineau's boldness. Here was a woman publicly challenging some of society's most powerful men, on behalf of a powerless group!

It was getting dark outside by the time she finished reading. She slipped the magazines into the bottom drawer of her dressing table where Norbert would never find them. She felt a pang of pleasure knowing how disapproving he would be — particularly if he knew how happy she felt just knowing there were women like Mary Wollstonecraft and Harriet Martineau out there trying to change the world.

For the first time since Callandra had lived with the Scott family, the drawing room was full of people. A couple dozen gentlemen and ladies, dressed in glittering evening wear, sat in small clusters around the ornately decorated room, with its rosewood panelling and massive fireplace. Heavy portraits featuring beady-eyed gentlemen were bracketed by elaborate wall sconces, with dangling crystals. The mood of the party was more dignified than jovial, but the sound of so many voices in the house was striking.

The guests were businessmen and their wives, and Callandra found herself paying attention in a way she rarely did at the duller afternoon tea events. She listened intently as the conversation veered on to politics, indeed on to the very issues she knew from her reading: Poor Law reform, the Factory Act, unionization.

"So, we should be on the hook for their indolence?" said one of the men, with a lean frame and gaunt face. "Our taxes are high enough without having to pay for opulent housing for those who won't work."

"Well, you've got that wrong, Humphrey," replied a man with ruddy complexion. "There's nothing opulent about this housing, I can assure you. The conditions are quite atrocious — as they should be!"

"It's a roof over their head and something to eat every day," shot back the gaunt-faced man. "Why in heaven's name would they work with all that provided?"

"Well, otherwise they'll be getting handouts, and then taking off to do as they please," replied the other. "This way, they're penned up and made to suffer plenty."

"Suffering isn't enough. They should be working."

Callandra listened in amazement. What had the poor ever done, other than work hard serving these men, whose lives seemed unduly charmed!

"If they're not prepared to work, let them go hungry. They'll soon figure it out," said the gaunt-faced man, pleased by his succinctness.

"Well, the issue remains whether you want reform — or revolution," said an older, previously silent gentleman with a beak-like nose.

"What are you suggesting, Gilbert? That we just give in, so they don't bludgeon us in the streets? Isn't that what we have a constabulary for?" insisted Thomas Scott.

Over dinner, the conversation switched to more mundane topics, but Callandra found herself still thinking about the outrageous things the men had said. After the main course, she was distracted when Lottie appeared from the kitchen to help clear the plates. Her hair was fully tucked under a tight cap, making her less noticeably pretty than when she wore her usual kerchief, which allowed her lovely blond hair to show. Callandra was contemplating whether Lottie was deliberately trying to avoid male attention, when she happened to notice Mr. Scott discreetly touch Lottie's thigh, placing his hand on her skirt. Callandra was stunned, horrified by her father-in-law's action and frustrated by her inability to do something to help her dear friend.

The sheer dullness of the conversation prompted a return to an animated political discussion. Once more, the failings of the poor were decried amid general agreement that hunger was a useful prod.

"Ah, gentlemen," said the gaunt-faced man. Callandra watched as Lottie cleared crumbs from the table. "We can continue this over cigars. Let's not forget there are ladies present — even some young ones, who might prefer a more agreeable topic."

To Callandra's surprise, the man was staring directly at her, apparently inviting her to select a topic of interest to young women or to simply blush modestly.

"Please don't discontinue your discussion on my account," she said, finding her voice. "In fact, I consider that topic of great interest and importance."

"Oh really," the man replied, apparently amused by the notion Callandra might have any understanding of the topic.

"Yes," she continued, feeling her confidence rising as the diners all looked in her direction, with Lottie's face discernible behind them.

"And what would be of great 'interest and importance' to you? Pray tell, what does a young lady know about these things?" he continued playfully.

"Well," she said, with a burning desire not to let him humiliate her. "In my life, I've experienced both genteel and humble living."

The smirk faded from man's gaunt face. Norbert looked at Callandra disapprovingly, as did Mrs. Scott.

"And I can tell you," Callandra continued, "from my observation of both worlds first-hand, that when it comes to diligence and industry ... I'm most impressed by what I've seen in the humble ranks."

There was silence around the table, making the muffled noise of servers flawlessly delivering dessert plates all the more audible.

It wasn't clear for a few moments what the repercussions of Callandra's statement would be. She hadn't said anything overtly rude. But she'd failed to show deference to a roomful of powerful older men.

"Ha!" said Mr. Scott, smiling and breaking the awkward silence from his seat at the head of the table. His meaning was unclear, but he seemed to be signalling that he found Callandra's words acceptable, despite — or perhaps because of — the displeasure evident on the faces of Norbert and Mrs. Scott.

And so, to Callandra's surprise, there were no negative consequences. When dessert was over and the guests were filing out to their separate sitting rooms, Callandra and Lottie briefly found themselves in a quiet corner of the dining room.

"That was brave of you! My brother would have been impressed!" whispered Lottie.

―――― ❖ ――――

In her dressing room the next morning, Callandra reflected on her father-in-law's lecherous conduct, as well as on her own intervention at the dinner party. She was anxious to review the dramatic events with Lottie and was trying to figure out how to broach the subject of Mr. Scott's behaviour, when Lottie arrived for hair-brushing.

"What a hateful group of men last night," Callandra said, plunging in quickly.

"Aye," said Lottie, without elaboration.

"They have such disdain for the poor," Callandra continued. "And they think so well of themselves."

"Aye, it was good you said what you did," responded Lottie, as she pulled the brush through a particularly thick knot of hair.

"And Mr. Scott — he's as bad as the rest of them," ventured Callandra, trying to prompt Lottie to open up about what had happened. But Lottie just kept brushing.

"Well, he gave me my employment here … so that's good," she said eventually.

Callandra sensed Lottie didn't want to say more. While Lottie was always loving and sweet, Callandra had learned she could be very private and tight-lipped when she wanted to be.

"I was thinking — you said your brother goes to political meetings," Callandra continued in a different vein. "Do you think we could go with him to a meeting some time?"

"Oh, I don't know. I've never been to one."

"I'd really like to go," said Callandra, realizing how much the idea appealed to her, especially now that she had gotten a taste of articulating her views out loud.

"I'll ask him then," she said with a smile.

But a few days later, after Lottie had seen Sam, she reported to Callandra that he'd said no to the request.

"Why?"

"He just didn't think it was a good idea," said Lottie vaguely.

"Did you tell him about how I confronted those men at the dinner party?" asked Callandra, wondering if Lottie had failed to describe how she had stood up for the poor.

"Aye, I told him about that."

"And — didn't he think that was good?"

"Aye, he did," said Lottie with a smile.

"Well, then? I don't understand. Why can't we come to a political meeting?"

Lottie hesitated, then responded: "I think he worries you might tell your husband."

"Tell my husband? Oh, heavens! I'd never do that!"

"I know. I've told him he can trust you — as I do. But he's different. He doesn't trust people — except maybe me."

Callandra felt Sam was being most unfair. She read the same publications he did, and cared about injustice, just as he did. Yet he considered her untrustworthy. She felt hurt and offended but, most of all, excluded.

Chapter Five

1837

It was a fine spring afternoon, and the family gathering was being held outdoors in the Scotts' back garden. Tommy, now almost fifteen years old, was holding forth confidently in front of aunts, uncles, and cousins, bringing a proud look to his father's face and making his older brother acutely uncomfortable.

It had been five years since his marriage to Callandra, and Norbert was increasingly conscious of feeling he should be living independently as a grown man with his wife and child, and not in his parents' home. Isobel, now twenty-seven, had finally married and moved in with her husband. As always, Mr. Scott spent most evenings at his club, but when he was at home, he retreated into his den with Tommy after dinner to play chess or educate the boy about politics and the ways of the business world. Norbert, now thirty, remained distant from Callandra and Emma, who spent most of their time with Lottie. When he wasn't attending to church business, Norbert was visiting relatives with his mother or just spending time with her alone in the parlour.

As Tommy continued to dominate the garden party, Norbert readily agreed to his mother's suggestion that he supervise the children's game of quoits, which was taking place at the far end of the lawn. But Tommy soon wandered over and joined the game. As Tommy took extra turns for himself, the children grew frustrated and demanded that Norbert intervene to discipline his brother.

At first, Norbert ignored the demands, but the objections of the children grew louder, drawing the attention of the adults a short distance away. Mrs. Scott would normally intervene to rein in the behaviour of her younger son, but she was caught up in a conversation and had not noticed the problem.

"Tommy," said Norbert eventually. "You have to wait your t-t-t-t-t-turn."

By now, the adults were watching. Tommy placed his hand on his hip and, looking Norbert square in the face, laughed as he loudly declared: "No, I d-d-d-d-d-don't."

Norbert was relieved that he had a meeting on church business to attend.

As the carriage wound up Argyle Street, he nursed his wound. He had been embarrassed the previous month when the Presbyterian congregation in Barrhead had rejected his application to be their minister, but this episode with Tommy in the garden stung more. Barrhead was an inconsequential town where he had no family, and his father would probably never find out that he'd applied for the position. But this humiliation by his younger brother occurred in front of all his relatives, with his father watching.

His carriage pulled up in front of the large brick home half an hour before the meeting of the Glasgow Colonial Society was to begin, the consequence of having fled the family gathering early. Norbert assured the butler he'd be fine waiting by himself, but his host soon appeared alongside the meeting's special guest, Reverend

James Kirkpatrick, who held forth zealously about the spiritual needs of Presbyterians in Upper Canada.

"In the more remote townships, there are often no places of worship, nor even songbooks or Bibles," he declared.

Norbert nodded. "Hmm."

"They see only the occasional Baptist or Methodist preacher passing through — and these men are quite lacking in knowledge and piety," insisted Reverend Kirkpatrick. "In some places I visited, the desire for a Presbyterian minister was so great I was almost besieged by the people."

Other guests began to arrive, enabling Norbert to relocate across the room, where he could still hear the pastor tell each new listener how he'd been "besieged."

Norbert was pleased to fade further into the background during the meeting, but his peace was disturbed when Reverend Kirkpatrick started talking about the need for a financial commitment from the Church's Head Office. This prompted an earnest young man, who introduced himself to the gathering as Reverend Jonathan Blair, to stand up and denounce that suggestion, insisting that Presbyterians in the colonies should continue to rely solely on the generosity of groups like the Glasgow Colonial Society rather than succumb to the "spiritual tyranny" of Head Office.

At this fierce language, heads turned toward Norbert, who was known to be associated with Head Office and therefore presumably representative of the tyranny just mentioned. Norbert attributed this annoying bit of attention to the young minister's overzealousness. Fortunately, the tense moment passed without Norbert having to say anything.

Flushed from the attention, Norbert was left wondering how many of these people had heard about his rejection by the Barrhead congregation. Images began crowding into his head: the glum expressions of the Barrhead parishioners, Tommy's taunting face in the garden, his father's bemused look as Norbert walked away mortified, his mother's hand raised to her mouth, Reverend Kirkpatrick besieged by people desperate for his wisdom.

It wasn't clear to Norbert when the idea first came to him, but as the meeting wore on, it started to take shape as a possibility — a possibility both terrifying and strangely exhilarating: what if he were to offer himself up for spiritual duty in the colonies?

Callandra put on her nightgown, doing the buttons up to the top.

Her sexual encounters with Norbert were mostly brief and impersonal on the rare occasion that they happened. But after the humiliation he had suffered in the backyard that afternoon, she feared a return to his hostility and sexual aggression.

Lying in bed, she awaited his return with apprehension.

When he entered, holding a lamp, she saw right away that he was agitated.

"I've decided something important," he said, approaching the bed.

His expression was odd, more disturbed than angry.

"We shall go to Canada," he said. "It's the right thing, I'm certain."

Callandra realized this was his way of responding to his father laughing at him. She had always disliked Mr. Scott's cruelty toward his eldest son, and was almost tempted to offer consoling words, but she knew Norbert would just rebuke her. And she dared not express opposition to his plan to move to Canada, even though she was appalled at the idea that she and Emma would have to go with him. But she suspected that any protest on her part would only strengthen his resolve to follow through with his crazy plan. So she said nothing.

He went into his dressing room, then reappeared in his nightclothes and climbed into bed on his side. For a long time, Callandra lay silent, wondering if he would move toward her, but he didn't. She fell into a light sleep, waking several times, still half alert to a potential attack. But each time, all was silent and still.

She awoke again hours later, this time to hear him, well over on his side of the bed, sobbing quietly into his pillow, with a pain that filled the room.

---- * ----

Any hopes that Norbert wasn't serious about moving to Canada were quickly dispelled the next morning at breakfast. He announced the plan as if it had long been in the works, not a response to his mortification the day before.

Callandra felt overwhelmingly sad at the prospect, realizing it would likely mean never seeing her mother or siblings or the farm again. And what kind of life would that be for Emma, growing up in such a cold, faraway place?

But, above all, she feared being separated from Lottie.

She had already been preparing herself for Lottie moving out to live with her brother. Now twenty-six, Sam was earning enough as a carpenter at Mr. Scott's company for him to move from a rooming house to a small flat where he and Lottie could live together. Lottie wanted to retain her job in the Scott household — a plan Callandra supported, even though she knew it would never be the same with Lottie living elsewhere.

But Norbert's insistence on moving to Canada threatened to separate Callandra from Lottie completely — unless Lottie came to Canada, too. But it was impossible to imagine Lottie willingly leaving her brother.

Norbert's keenness for the Canadian venture seemed to grow with each passing day, as he basked in the attention surrounding his departure.

"I've received a letter just this afternoon," he said, as he sat down to tea with Callandra, his mother, and Isobel, who was visiting. "My ministry is to be in Goderich, in Upper Canada."

This gave the plan a cruel specificity. The mention of Goderich — as if it were a well-known city — revealed to Callandra how irrational and swept away by the whole scheme he had become.

"And there's to be a new church built there, in honour of my arrival," he continued.

"Oh, I'm sure it will be a grand church, brother!" said Isobel.

"I believe so," said Norbert. "Although, of course, they aren't as advanced there."

"Well, we could take Sam along with us. He could build you a grand church," suggested Callandra.

After five years in the Scott household, it was still rare for Callandra to say much at tea. To have spoken out so boldly like this, and on so weighty a matter, was extraordinary.

"And who is Sam?" asked Isobel.

"Lottie's brother. He works for your father as a carpenter. He could build a very nice church, I'm sure," said Callandra.

"I think that would *not* be a good idea," said Mrs. Scott firmly.

This was the first time Mrs. Scott had expressed a negative opinion related to the Canada venture, giving the remark special significance and dashing Callandra's faint hope of salvaging some prospect of happiness for herself.

———— ✻ ————

They were to sail on the vessel *Christina* on July 2. With the departure less than three weeks away, Norbert and his mother set out for Edinburgh so he could bid farewell to relatives.

It was a luxury knowing they would be gone for five days. Callandra's first night alone, she rummaged in his closets until she found the bottle of whisky he tucked away. She took a sip, her first taste of liquor, and choked and coughed from the harshness. Even so, she liked the stinging sensation. She poured a small amount into a glass by the washbasin and took it to bed with her.

Its impact was almost immediate. She sat up in bed, glass in hand, intrigued by how such a harsh smell and taste could be so strangely pleasant. Her despair over Canada mellowed into a whimsical reverie.

She had finished her whisky and was drifting peacefully off to sleep, still in the no man's land of strangely contorted yet familiar images, when Lottie appeared at her bedside.

"I haven't brushed your hair," she half whispered.

"Thank you, but it's fine," said Callandra. Moments later, she added: "I've done something wrong."

"What?" asked Lottie softly, putting down her candle.

"I've asked Norbert to bring you with us to Canada," said Callandra, watching Lottie's reaction.

"Oh."

"Don't worry," Callandra quickly followed up. "I would never press you to come if you didn't want to."

"I can't stand the idea of us not being together," said Lottie, "But ... my brother ... I'd never see him again ..."

"Of course," said Callandra, sympathetically. *But you'll never see me again if you don't come.* Lottie seemed ready to take her leave.

"Stay with me, Lottie. I don't mean come to Canada. I just mean here, now."

Callandra went to Norbert's dressing room, refilling her glass of whisky. "Try some of this. It makes things better."

Lottie took a tiny sip and responded as Callandra had, but soon adjusted to its sharpness and seemed to enjoy it. Callandra got back into bed and Lottie sat on the bed beside her, both occasionally sipping from the glass.

After a while, Callandra blurted out: "Oh, Lottie, I should never have married Norbert. He's so mean to me …"

Lottie listened, her eyes heavy with sympathy.

"I haven't told you the whole story …"

"I understand," she said.

"It's not that I don't trust you. I trust you with my life," said Callandra.

Lottie gently put her finger to her lips, signalling that Callandra needn't say more.

"I can't stand having a secret from you!" said Callandra. "You're too important to me."

"There's nothing wrong with having a secret."

"Do you have one?"

"Maybe … no, not really … no," said Lottie.

Callandra took another sip, pondering Lottie's evasive response. She concluded that Lottie probably did have a secret, and began trying to figure out what it was. Could it be that Mr. Scott had lewdly touched Lottie at that dinner party a few years earlier — and perhaps that he did so regularly?

"Let's trade secrets," Callandra said, excited at the prospect of learning Lottie's secret in exchange for one she wanted to impart anyway.

But it became apparent that Lottie was less interested in divulging hers. The more Callandra goaded, the more resistant her friend became. Callandra moved on to lighter topics, eased by the alcohol.

After a while, with Lottie preparing to leave for the night, Callandra blurted out: "I'm going to tell you my secret anyway. Norbert is rough with me in bed … even violent."

Lottie didn't push for details, but she stroked Callandra's arm gently and said, "That's terrible."

Callandra awoke later in the night. She had gone to sleep with Lottie singing to her, leaving her feeling loved and comforted. But now Lottie was gone, and the harsh reality that had been softened by the alcohol freshly jolted her. In only two weeks, she would be aboard a ship bound for Canada. The conversation with Lottie came back now, too. It suddenly hit Callandra that perhaps Lottie's secret wasn't about Mr. Scott's improper conduct, but rather Norbert's. That would explain why Lottie hadn't seemed particularly surprised by Callandra's revelation; maybe she already knew about Norbert's violent ways — because she had experienced them herself. Could it be that they shared the same secret?

Callandra lay awake imagining Norbert's desire for Lottie, the fierceness of his angry lust. She shuddered, realizing how much she hated him. She also realized that her strongest reaction to the thought that she might in some grotesque way be sharing her husband with her dearest friend was to do everything she could to protect her friend.

———— ✼ ————

Mrs. Scott had resolved not to interfere with Norbert's plan to move to Canada, hoping he would change his mind on his own. But with the departure fast approaching, he showed no hesitation or doubt. As the carriage moved steadily through the drizzling rain, she realized this trip to Edinburgh was a final chance to bring him to his senses.

They stopped for tea in Airdrie. Already, less than a day out of Glasgow, she sensed him relaxing, leaving her feeling less guilty for having failed to intervene to prevent Tommy's cruel taunt at the garden party. The strain that had existed between Norbert and herself over the incident seemed to have finally subsided.

Over tea, mother and son drifted in and out of conversation, mostly about the relatives they were about to visit. Much of their time together over the years had been spent in this sort of subdued engagement. Norbert never stuttered when they were alone like this, and Mrs. Scott knew that was because he understood it wouldn't matter if he did.

She surveyed her son's face as he talked. It wasn't actually ugly, but the eyes were a little too deeply set and there was something odd about the mouth. The lips seemed in an almost perpetual pout. She watched as Norbert chewed on his tea biscuit, conscious of the waiter observing her son with curiosity, prompting her to feel both embarrassed and annoyed lest Norbert should become aware of the man's prying eyes.

It would be all the more difficult, of course, to protect him from such affronts once he was on the other side of the Atlantic. She didn't trust Callandra to do so; the girl was primarily concerned about herself, lacking any wifely sense of loyalty or duty. She would obviously pay Norbert little heed once they were beyond the reach of the Scott household. Mrs. Scott was convinced that Callandra had only ever been interested in Norbert for his money, and she now regretted she hadn't tried to block the marriage.

After all, she had learned that lesson the hard way herself many years earlier, when youthful naïveté had prevented her from seeing that her betrothed was principally entranced by her fortune. The discovery, after their marriage, that he was also a philanderer had strained things further between them, even before Norbert was born.

As they drove on toward Edinburgh, the rain picked up, sharply pelting the roof of the carriage and helping Mrs. Scott refocus her thoughts on more practical matters. If she couldn't protect Norbert from emotional pain, she could at least take steps to ensure his physical safety, given the dangers he would soon face travelling and living in such a cold, uncivilized place.

"You know, son, I've been thinking," she began, interrupting the silence between them. "I believe I've misjudged something."

Norbert looked over at her, his thin dark eyes revealing surprise at such an admission.

"Perhaps Callandra was right," she continued, realizing that such an out-of-character statement would highlight the importance of what she was about to say. "You should have a fine church built for you in Goderich. And Lottie's brother may be just the man to supervise its construction."

"Hmm," said Norbert, apparently pleased by evidence his mother respected his ability to choose a wife and navigate his own course. "I'll give it some thought."

———❖———

With Norbert and Mrs. Scott away, Callandra decided that she would visit her family in Fenwick.

She had kept in touch with her mother only by letter since moving to Glasgow, suspecting it would be too painful to leave home again if she went back. But now that she was about to cross the Atlantic and probably never return, she realized how much she wanted to see them all one last time. She decided to take Lottie and Emma with her, sensing that would make the parting easier.

As she gave orders for a carriage to be readied for the trip, she realized that the staff in the Scott household seemed as unsure of her authority as she was herself.

"I'm going to visit my family before leaving for Canada," she explained to Miss McNeil, the housekeeper.

"Mrs. Scott didn't mention this," she said, looking at her with a mixture of suspicion and condescension.

"Well, that's because I didn't think of it until now."

"Mrs. Scott and your husband will be back by the weekend. Perhaps it would be best if you waited until then."

Although Miss McNeil had framed this as a suggestion, her tone indicated she expected it to be the end of the matter.

"I have no instructions from Mrs. Scott," the housekeeper repeated icily. "You'll simply have to wait."

"No, I don't want to wait. I want to go now," said Callandra, pleased by the firmness in her voice.

"I see," said Miss McNeil through tightened lips.

Callandra headed back to her room, and quickly put on one of her old frocks for the trip. The little excursion was taking on the feel of an escape.

She decided not to call for a butler, instead bringing their small bags down to the front door herself. There was no sign of a carriage, so she told Lottie and Emma to wait in the parlour while she headed out to the stable, leaving by the front door to avoid running into Miss McNeil in the back of the house. Clyde, the large, good-natured stable hand, was clearly surprised by her sudden appearance and request for a coach to drive her to Fenwick for two days. But he assured her a carriage and driver would appear shortly at the front door.

Walking back to the front door, she noticed a carriage parked near the large portico. When she got a closer look, she was relieved to see that it wasn't Norbert and his mother home early. It turned out to be a young cleric who had come looking for Norbert. She found him in the parlour with Lottie and Emma, but was able to deftly dispatch him, suggesting he return on the weekend. With a pleasant smile, he departed, leaving a card identifying himself as Reverend Jonathan Blair.

On the long drive to Fenwick, Callandra felt buoyed and pleased with herself for insisting on this expedition, wondering why she hadn't done it before. There was a strange sense of freedom as the horses pulled the fugitive caravan toward her childhood home. It was late afternoon by the time they reached the richly green terrain that she readily recognized from her girlhood, and the memories became more vivid and poignant. Emma's face was pressed against the window, as her mother pointed out important sights until finally, rounding the last bend she remembered so well, the little farmhouse came into view.

Although there had been no advance notice of their visit, Sadie Buchanan quickly appeared in the doorway. She was fleshier and older-looking around the eyes than Callandra's memory of her. But she was clearly thrilled to see her long-gone daughter, and seemed more like the tender, caring mother she had once been. Did she perhaps have regrets about being so quick to accept her daughter marrying an unlikeable young man in order to save the family farm? She greeted Emma for the first time with a loving embrace, leaving Callandra pondering how differently her mother and Mrs. Scott responded to their granddaughter.

Being back at the farm, surrounded by sisters and brothers — changed and yet the same — felt so natural to Callandra that the idea of leaving it forever seemed profoundly wrong. The simple furnishings she remembered so well — even the earthy smell of the country air — was delightful compared to the stuffy grandeur of the Glasgow house or the cold isolation of Canada. As the evening wore on, Callandra found herself pondering the possibility of not returning to Glasgow.

Fortunately, Norbert had paid off the mortgage on the farm, so she could move back home without causing any reversal of fortune for her family. She wondered if Norbert might even be relieved; he could head over to the New World without the wife he so clearly disliked. He could explain that his wife and child planned to join him there later. And then, hopefully, later would never come.

"There," said Sadie, holding up a shawl which she'd just finished knitting for Jessie. "You can wear it to the dance tomorrow."

Jessie blushed. She had been just a child when Callandra left. Almost sixteen now, she had turned into a very pretty girl.

"There may be a proposal tomorrow," Sadie said to Callandra.

Jessie admired the shawl, obviously excited about tomorrow night. Callandra recognized that look, remembered that feeling. The sweet radiance on her sister's face brought back a flood of memories that filled Callandra with envy.

"We have our fingers crossed," her mother said privately later to Callandra, wanting to finish filling in her eldest daughter about Jessie's marriage prospects. "He's such a fine young man, and he adores Jessie. He'd make a very good husband."

"That's wonderful," said Callandra.

"You may remember him, dear," her mother continued. "I think you knew his sister Bernadette. Do you remember Alex — the McLeod boy — from down the road?"

Chapter Six

Reverend Blair felt immensely satisfied that he'd embarrassed Norbert Scott at the meeting of the Glasgow Colonial Society. It wasn't that he bore any personal animosity toward Norbert, whom he did not know. It was just that Norbert represented the Church establishment, which Blair considered acutely in need of reform.

The meeting ended early and Blair, feeling charged up after all the stimulation, decided to call on Nadine Erskine. He had known her before moving to Upper Canada three years earlier and, upon hearing she was still unmarried, had begun unofficially courting her during his current stay in Glasgow. It had occurred to him that it would be advantageous to have a wife when he returned to Upper Canada.

Nadine seemed an obvious choice; he admired her family, which was strongly associated with dissenting positions in the Church. Her great-grandfather, Ebenezer Erskine, had led the first secession movement, with its clear dedication to spiritual independence for congregations. Marrying Nadine was like attaching himself to a legend.

Nadine agreed with Blair's strong views on Church matters — hardly surprising given her pedigree. And on a personal level, she seemed agreeable. Although not quite handsome, she had clear skin and bright eyes, as well as a strong, sturdy build which would be an asset in the backwoods.

There was a bounce in his step as he walked up to her front door. He was disappointed, however, to learn that her parents were out; it would have been interesting to hear her father's reaction to what had happened at the meeting.

He was waiting in the family's small parlour when Nadine eventually entered, wearing a structured, puce-coloured dress that made a crinkly sound when she moved.

"I'm sorry to keep you waiting," she said. "I had no idea you might drop by tonight, but I'm so glad you did."

"I told you I was going to a meeting of the Glasgow Colonial Society?"

"Oh, yes. I hope it went well," she said. "Would you have some dinner? You must be famished."

"Oh, no thank you. There were refreshments at the meeting," he said.

"It must have been just a light supper. Was it enough?"

"Yes," said Blair. "It turned out to be more interesting than I expected."

"The supper?"

"No. What?" Blair looked at her in confusion. "Not the supper! The meeting!"

"Oh really?" she said. "Why? What happened?"

With the question put so directly, Blair had trouble thinking of an answer. There had been no momentous development. What had seemed so interesting was his intervention about spiritual tyranny. But he felt self-conscious making a fuss about his own statement; he wanted it to emerge gradually as part of a conversation about the meeting.

"Well, nothing of great note," he said. "But there was something of a split in the group."

"Are some people opposed to missionary work in the colonies?"

"Well, no, not opposed," he said, struggling with her overly simple questions. "But some would like to see the financing come from Head Office."

"Ah," said Nadine, recognizing an issue for which her family was well known. "That would mean compromising spiritual independence."

"Precisely," said Blair. "You can't tear down the Church establishment when you're counting on it for your subsistence."

"Aye, you're right," she replied, and looked off into the distance, as if digesting the hugeness of his thought. He felt rather pleased with the way he'd expressed it. But before he could continue, she turned to him and excitedly exclaimed: "My cousin Shona has become engaged, just this afternoon!"

"Oh," he said flatly, frustrated that this bit of news interrupted a conversation leading toward his dramatic intervention at the meeting. "That's very nice."

"They'll be married just before Christmas. I'm so thrilled for her!"

A servant brought tea and biscuits and they discussed Shona, her skill with the cello, and the long courtship that had just come to fruition.

"You know who was at the meeting?" said Blair, still preoccupied with his thoughts, "The minister rejected by Barrhead."

"You mean Norbert Scott?"

"Yes, I think that's his name. Do you know him?"

Nadine rolled her eyes. "He's a real ninny."

At this, Blair's attention picked up, exclaiming, "How could anyone feel justified preaching when the call hadn't come from the congregation!"

"And how could any congregation want *him*?" scoffed Nadine.

"Why? What's the matter with him?"

"He's unpleasant, and he stutters," she said.

"Oh."

"You know he married beneath himself?" she added.

"No, I didn't know that," said Blair, immediately regretting that his reply suggested he agreed with the concept that one could "marry beneath" oneself. The gossipy drift of the conversation, and his interest in it embarrassed him.

"Yes, he married a poor country girl," said Nadine. "They almost never go out."

"Really?" said Blair, now intrigued. But she switched back to her cousin's wedding plans, which seemed quite advanced considering the engagement had only just happened.

Bidding Nadine good night as he left, Blair felt relieved to be spared further details of the upcoming nuptials, and energized by what he had learned about one Norbert Scott.

While Reverend Blair's attitude toward Norbert Scott had softened considerably in the conversation with Nadine, it became downright sympathetic the following day when he heard about Norbert's decision to take up a ministry in the colonies. Blair was favourably disposed toward any minister willing to give up his homeland to answer the needs of far-flung parishioners. But he was particularly impressed when he learned that Norbert was also giving up a life of wealth and comfort.

Blair wondered if he'd been too quick to judge him on the Barrhead affair. Perhaps Norbert had simply wanted to serve in a disadvantaged area — which Barrhead was — and had not understood that there might be local resistance to his appointment. In any event, Norbert's response had not been to seek redress in the civil courts, like some rejected ministers, but rather to turn the other cheek and offer himself up for service in even more humble circumstances abroad.

Most fascinating to Blair was that Norbert had married a poor country girl. This suggested a willingness to defy social convention, to put at risk advancement in the Church — for the sake of marrying a simple girl whom he evidently loved.

Blair found himself curious to learn more about Norbert, and in his next visit with Nadine casually raised the subject. She offered up details of the grandness of the Scotts' house, which she'd seen from the outside, and a recollection of having once encountered Norbert at a church social event and finding him awkward. She remembered him stuttering. She also volunteered that she'd heard that his stutter was a factor with the Barrhead congregation. "That would drive anyone crazy," she said, then, changing her tone, added: "Head Office clearly thought they could get away with dumping him there, because it's a poor area."

Blair had taken to walking to and from Nadine's house, and found himself enjoying the walks and opportunity for peaceful contemplation almost as much, if not more, than the visits. If he were to achieve resolution on the marriage question, it would surely come in the course of these meditations.

But as he set out for Nadine's one morning, he realized he was pleased primarily by the thought that all his uncertainty would soon be over and he'd return to Canada, with or without her. Oddly, the thought of her aboard ship did not appeal to him. The advantages of marriage seemed more long-term than immediate. He paced on, trying to force a decision, but felt uncertainty creeping back.

While walking down Union Street, Blair was struck by the idea that he should pay a visit to Norbert Scott. Checking his watch, he realized he could still make it to Nadine's before noon if he briefly dropped in on Norbert. He hired a hackney to take him there.

Blair found the house easily from Nadine's description. Even by the standards of the street, it was large and imposing, with a grand portico and thick ivy covering the stone facade. Requesting the driver wait, Blair knocked softly on the heavy front door and was surprised how quickly it was opened by a blond-haired young woman wearing a simple, lilac-coloured frock.

The sight of this lovely creature — rather than a formally attired butler — was perplexing.

Blair wondered if she could be Norbert's wife.

"I'm looking for Reverend Scott," he said.

"He's away in Edinburgh."

"And would you be his wife?" asked Blair.

"Oh no," said Lottie, "She's in the stable." Lottie explained they were about to take a trip and Reverend Scott's wife was making arrangements. "She'll be back shortly. Please come in."

"That's very kind of you, but I don't want to intrude," he said. "I just wanted to leave my card. I'm Reverend Blair. I'm stationed in Upper Canada, and I thought I might be able to answer questions for Reverend Scott and his family about their new life."

"Oh, do come in. This is Emma," Lottie said, as the girl peered out from behind her.

Blair hesitated. It seemed wrong to impose when they were about to leave, but this young woman in the lilac dress — whoever she was — was inviting him in with such authority. She was clearly a friend of Norbert's wife, and knew the family well.

After they sat down in the parlour, she quickly revealed she was a servant.

"It will be a big adjustment, I'm sure, for Callandra and Emma," she said, taking Emma's hand as the little girl sat on a footstool at her feet. "It would be so helpful for them to have a friend there in Canada."

"I would welcome their friendship," he said.

"That could make such a difference," continued Lottie, her face animated. "They will be so alone there."

"As a family, they will of course have each other," said Blair, reminding himself of the unresolved matter with Nadine.

"Well, yes," said Lottie, adding, "What is it like there? Is it bleak and remote, or is there something wonderful about the place?"

"Both," said Blair, thinking she had summed up well his entire experience of Canada.

"And are you happy there?" she asked.

"Uh, well," he stammered. "I don't know. I mean, I'm there to offer spiritual guidance, which I feel to some extent I've been able to do, although not nearly enough, of course."

"Well, that must make you happy then ... helping all those people."

"Well, yes, you could say that," he replied, uneasy about the suggestion he was helping others in order to make himself happy, rather than out of concern for their needs. He was puzzling over how to clarify this, without sounding as if he were boasting about his self-sacrifices, when a slender, brown-haired young woman entered the room.

This, clearly, was Norbert's country wife. She was wearing a simple dress, and she moved about quickly, without the poise and composure of a well-bred lady. But she had nicely braided hair, dark brown eyes and was rather fetching. There was also something in her expression that hinted at sadness.

During his short visit, Blair was struck by how pleasant the experience was, how much he liked both these young women. He was now more intrigued than ever by Norbert Scott, who clearly had spotted a warmth and spontaneity in Callandra and not been dissuaded by her humble roots. The fact that Lottie was comfortable entertaining visitors in the parlour suggested an informality and indifference to social custom on Norbert's part which deeply impressed Blair. The one unfortunate thing was that Lottie was apparently not going with them to Canada. Was this perhaps part of Norbert's desire for a simpler way of life, leaving servants behind?

Returning to the waiting hackney, Blair gave the driver Nadine's address and they moved quickly — too quickly — toward her house. Blair realized he didn't want to be there quite yet. But then, with so little time left before his departure for Canada, it was wrong to further delay the marriage offer, if there was to be one. He was conscious of biting his lip, a habit he associated with his dithering on the Nadine question.

As it started to rain, the driver picked up speed, which helped clarify things for Blair. There was something about the delight he'd felt minutes earlier during his encounter with Callandra and Lottie, and the knot he felt in his stomach as the carriage hurtled toward Nadine's house, that made the obvious finally clear: Nadine was wrong. Almost the instant he announced this to himself, he felt a strange elation. Not only did the knot in his stomach disappear, but a thought took hold of his mind and body: he wanted Lottie.

Blair tapped for the driver to stop the carriage and happily jumped down into the driving rain. As he strode along the sidewalk, he felt certain that he wanted to marry the entrancing young woman he'd just met.

He arrived at Nadine's house, thoroughly drenched, but with an energy that he'd been lacking of late, particularly, he realized, when he visited this house. His course was now clear: to emphasize his imminent return to Canada and clarify that he had no intention of marrying right away. This would be tricky. Although he had said nothing to suggest a courtship, he suspected his visits had been viewed this way, particularly by Nadine. And she would have a case. He must be prepared for criticism; in fact, he deserved it.

The female servant who answered the door made a fuss about his wet garments and went to fetch a towel. Hopefully, this would distract from his lateness. On her return, the servant advised him that Nadine's father wanted to have a word with him in his study.

This was not at all what Blair wanted to hear. He liked and respected Nadine's father, with whom he had often discussed spiritual matters. Clearly, however, Reverend Erskine was now summoning him to insist he clarify his intentions toward Nadine. He winced as he approached the study, frustrated that he hadn't experienced his revelation a few days earlier and thus been able to avert what was sure to be an awkward encounter.

Reverend Erskine, a stout man with thick sideburns and a wide, honest face, greeted Blair with his usual warmth, which only made Blair feel worse about the situation and his responsibility for creating it. The older man immediately offered him a set of dry clothes. But Blair, standing in front of the fire, insisted he was fine; it would take more than dry clothes to soothe his torment.

The smallness of the room seemed to highlight the largeness of Reverend Erskine. Blair was struck, as he'd been before, by the bodily resemblance between Nadine and other members of her family. Not that Nadine was stout, but both she and her brothers had their father's large bone structure. While that would indeed be helpful in the backwoods, Blair saw now how much he disliked it — in a woman.

As he thought about it, Blair realized she strongly resembled her father — but without his big heart and mind. Nadine had been raised a dissenter within the Church, but, beyond her familiarity with the language of reform, she was sadly conventional. When she'd said Norbert had "married beneath himself," she wasn't mocking social rigidities, she was reflecting them in the most cowardly and repugnant way.

As he prepared himself for Reverend Erskine's lecture, Blair reminded himself to praise Nadine for her many fine qualities but to tell her father that he had never actually considered marriage. He realized this was a lie, so quickly adjusted it to the vaguer position that marriage just wasn't something he was ready for yet. But he also didn't want to leave the impression he was suggesting she wait for him.

"Well, let me get to the point, Jonathan," said Reverend Erskine. The big man's straightforward manner left Blair doubly miserable about his lack of candour. "Of course, Mrs. Erskine and I have noticed your attention to Nadine."

"She's a splendid girl, sir," said Blair, trying to steady the vibration that had crept into his voice. He feared his words sounded as insincere as they were.

"Aye," said the older man. Then, looking more serious, he continued. "Now, I don't know what your intentions are, whether you're planning to ask her to marry you …"

There was a pause in which Blair could have said something, but he remained silent, affecting a look of almost surprise, and then felt instantly ashamed of his fraudulence. He knew he had to muster the courage to be more forthright, to admit everything short of his infatuation — not a word he would have ever used before — for another girl he'd just met.

"Uh," said Blair weakly, struggling to begin his miserable task.

"Well," Reverend Erskine continued. "The truth is that my wife would be heartsick to see her only daughter move so far away. It is with great reluctance — because you know our fondness for you — that I ask you not to think of marriage, unless you plan to reconsider your commitment to remaining in the colonies."

Blair took a second to digest the news.

"Sir, uh, I couldn't abandon my commitment to my parishioners," said Blair, shuddering at his own shamelessness in invoking the spiritual needs of others to get himself out of an awkward bind. He held himself back from embellishing further with expressions of sadness that he wouldn't be able to spend his life with Nadine.

"I quite understand," said her father, apparently satisfied that Blair's idealistic commitments simply won out over his personal self-interest, even if the decision was rather rapidly delivered. Then the big man leaned forward, confiding, "It may not seem so, right at this moment, but I'm sure you'll find someone else to join you on your journey through life, perhaps sooner than you think."

Blair's final act of duplicity was trying to sound unconvinced as he replied: "I suppose."

In fact, there was one more bit of duplicity — his willingness to use his apparent disappointment to excuse himself from sitting through lunch with the Erskine family. Surely a young man could be forgiven for wanting to lick his wounds privately after such a crushing turn of events. Rejecting more offers of dry clothing, Blair insisted on heading out into pouring rain with only an umbrella. He jumped over puddles on the street, overwhelmed to realize he was not only completely off the hook with Nadine, but now unencumbered — a man who could, in all conscience, make an impetuous proposal to Lottie and, hopefully, in just two and a half weeks, take her with him to Canada.

Chapter Seven

The prospect of her sister becoming engaged to Alex McLeod was deeply upsetting. But it brought a sharp clarity to the situation, ruling out the possibility of Callandra staying on in Fenwick, and prompting her to depart the next morning even earlier than planned.

Upon their return to Glasgow, Miss McNeil said little, only noting that a Reverend Blair had called earlier in the day.

"He called yesterday as well," noted Callandra. "He wants to speak to Norbert about Canada."

"Well, this morning he said he wants to speak to either you or your husband. And he asked me to convey the urgency of his request."

Although tired after the long trek, Callandra was intrigued by the prospect that something had gone wrong; perhaps, the Church no longer had a posting abroad for Norbert.

She ordered that a message be sent right away to Reverend Blair, informing him that she would receive him later that afternoon.

——— ✽ ———

It was after five when Reverend Blair arrived and was ushered into the parlour, where Callandra sat alone.

"I've come on a matter that is of some urgency. I apologize for not waiting for your husband's return, but I feel that I can waste no time."

Callandra surveyed him, increasingly curious and hopeful about his purpose.

He looked shy and uncomfortable but proceeded, "I've come to ask for Miss Lottie's hand in marriage."

"Oh."

"I would intend to bring her with me to Upper Canada, of course. I'm sailing on the *Christina* on the second as well."

Callandra's heart was suddenly racing. Of course, this would mean Lottie coming to Canada! She looked him over with fresh interest, concluding that Lottie might well consider him a reasonable suitor.

He was of medium height and build with a head of thick, brown hair and a rather bland, but not unpleasant face. He seemed to have a slightly nervous manner about him, but perhaps that was due to the matter being discussed. Callandra found herself comparing him favourably to Norbert. Whereas Norbert was pompous and pretentious, Reverend Blair conveyed a quiet seriousness that seemed both warm and reserved at the same time.

"And where in Canada do you reside? Are you in Goderich as well?"

"Well, not exactly in Goderich. I'm based in Toronto. You may have heard of it? It used to be called York. But I travel to the outlying regions from time to time."

For the first time, Callandra felt an intense curiosity about the geography of Canada. She wanted to know how far the two towns lay apart, how good the connecting roads were, and, crucially, did Reverend Blair intend to bring his wife on his travels and allow her to visit for extended periods? But she caught herself, realizing this was an inappropriate response to news of his marriage proposal.

"Well, Reverend Blair, this is most interesting," she said carefully.

"I would promise to take excellent care of her. She would be a clergyman's wife, with all the accompanying privileges."

"I think she would make you a very good wife, Reverend," said Callandra.

"Do I have your permission then to make my proposal to Miss Lottie?"

"Ah, yes, yes, indeed," she said. "Shall I call for her?"

"Oh, please do!"

Callandra rang for a servant. When the butler appeared, she asked that Lottie be sent for.

"I'll leave you now," she said to Blair, slipping out to the terrace.

Reverend Blair did seem like a fine man, decent and kind. He wouldn't be considered handsome or dashing, but he was certainly presentable, his attentive manner was pleasing, and there was a gentleness about his eyes. She realized she felt comfortable with her decision that Lottie should marry Reverend Blair.

———— ✱ ————

Callandra was seated in her dressing room when Lottie came in just before supper to do her hair. She had resolved to let Lottie raise the subject.

"Well? Have you nothing to tell me?" asked Callandra, unable to stick to her plan. Lottie could be so infuriatingly discreet at times.

A nervous smile came over Lottie's face, as she picked up Callandra's brush.

"No, come and sit down here with me," Callandra implored.

"Reverend Blair has asked me to marry him," Lottie began, sitting next to Callandra. "I guess you know that."

"Yes. And does that please you?"

Lottie looked away from Callandra's intense gaze, fidgeting with the edge of a cushion. "I'm a little overwhelmed," she said finally. "I barely know him."

"Of course," Callandra said.

"I mean, he seems like a very nice man … it's just so sudden."

"What did you tell him?"

"I said I would think about it."

With that frustratingly vague answer, the conversation came to an end. Callandra felt irritated by the thought that her encouragement of this marriage was not unlike what her mother had done to her; indeed, she was being more assertive than her mother had been. But then Reverend Blair had none of Norbert's meanness, making the comparison unfair.

Along with Emma, they had supper in Callandra's dressing room. While Lottie's willingness to consider the marriage proposal didn't guarantee the hoped-for result, it helped dull Callandra's pain of knowing that, even as she quietly ate her evening meal, Jessie was almost certainly in the arms of the man they both loved.

——— * ———

The next morning, Reverend Blair sent a message to Callandra, asking if he might visit Lottie again. Callandra made the messenger wait in the hall while she wrote in reply that he could come that afternoon, having rejected her first inclination to suggest that he come immediately. She then went into Norbert's study and found a map of Canada. She quickly located York, but was unable to find Goderich.

Reverend Blair's visit was longer this time. Callandra watched from her dressing room window as the couple strolled in the garden together, the rain holding off to make the setting pleasant and hopefully romantic. She caught a glimpse of Lottie smiling.

When he left that afternoon, Callandra waited in her dressing room, but Lottie didn't appear for nearly an hour. And when she did show up, she was evasive. Worse, she had declined the cleric's offer to visit again the following day, because her brother was scheduled to take her for a walk. That infernal brother! Couldn't he wait, just this once!

"I'm sure Sam wouldn't mind if you cancelled your walk. I could send a messenger."

"Oh no," Lottie replied.

Callandra said nothing further and tried to conceal her frustration the next day when, from a front window, she saw Lottie disappear down the street with her brother. By late afternoon, Norbert and his mother had arrived home, shattering the tranquility of the house.

At dinner that evening, Callandra waited until after Mrs. Scott and Norbert had recounted details of their trip, then mentioned Reverend Blair and his proposal to Lottie. Everyone was surprised by the news, although little was said. Mr. Scott let out a sigh that sounded like part whistle, while Mrs. Scott looked even more dismissive than usual. Norbert, on the other hand, looked rather pleased, apparently regarding Reverend Blair's proposal as affirmation of his own decision to marry a simple country girl.

The next morning, a note was delivered to Callandra in her bedchamber, requesting she come to the servants' entrance at the back of the kitchen. It was signed "Samuel Hunter."

She dressed quickly and went down the main stairs and out the doors to the back lawn. Sam was sitting on a bench just outside the entrance to the kitchen, and he rose as he saw her approach. He seemed more carefully groomed than usual, but still looked like someone who should be outdoors rather than indoors.

"I'm sorry to trouble you, ma'am," he said. Encounters between Sam and Callandra had been infrequent over the years, but when they did meet, he had usually avoided calling her "ma'am," knowing she disliked it. He had seemed unable to bring himself to call her "Callandra," so instead used no form of address. His return to formality now irked her.

"But I thought I should tell you first," he continued. "Lottie doesn't wish to accept Reverend Blair's proposal."

Callandra felt like she had just received a heavy blow.

"I'm sorry to have to tell you this. I know how much you want her to be with you in Canada," he said, sympathetically.

"I don't understand," Callandra stammered. "Why are *you* telling me this? Why isn't this coming from Lottie herself?"

"The reason I'm telling you," he replied, ignoring her hostile tone, "is because she just can't bear to tell you herself. She doesn't want to disappoint you. I think she would have liked to say yes, if only to make you happy."

Callandra didn't know how to respond. She resented his implication that her support for the marriage proposal was prompted by self-interest; it was surely also in Lottie's best interest. Indeed, Lottie had appeared to enjoy Blair's company and seemed to be moving toward accepting his offer. Then she'd spent the previous afternoon with Sam and now, abruptly, her hesitation had turned into refusal.

But Callandra realized she had to be careful what she said, as Sam's sway over Lottie was immense. When she was slow to reply, he took her silence to indicate that the matter was resolved. Moving on, he pulled an envelope from his shirt pocket and handed it to her. "I wonder if you could give this to your husband, so he could pass it on to Reverend Blair."

"Well, just a minute," she said, reluctantly taking hold of the letter. "I'd like to speak to Lottie first."

Callandra saw the first flash of annoyance move across Sam's face.

"I don't think that's a good idea," he said.

"What do you mean?"

"I think it would be unfair. It would put too much pressure on her."

"Too much pressure? I don't put pressure on Lottie … I wonder if it isn't *you* who's been pressuring her," said Callandra.

"What?" said Sam, as he pulled away from her slightly. He really was a powerful-looking man. "I only want what's best for my sister."

"And that's all I want for her, too."

"Then why don't you let her make up her own mind?"

"That's exactly what I want her to do. But I'm not convinced she's had a chance to," said Callandra. "All I want to do is talk to her. That's all."

"I don't want you to try to change her mind, to confuse her. We spoke about this at length yesterday. I know how she feels."

Their exchange had become heated, and several maids were now watching from the pantry. Callandra realized how odd the scene must look.

"You know Lottie will do anything to please you," she said, dropping her voice without removing the jagged edge from her tone.

"I wish you would leave this matter to our family," he said. "Since the death of our father, Lottie has come under my care."

Callandra hesitated, aware that she had already jeopardized her future relations with Lottie by having an open rupture with her cherished brother.

But then she suddenly realized there would be no future relations of any substance with Lottie. Callandra had been so distracted quarrelling with Sam that she hadn't absorbed the fact that her last hope of getting Lottie to come to Canada had just been dashed. Now, as well as being angry, she felt the urge to cry.

"May I ask," she began, trying to avoid tears, "Why doesn't Lottie want to marry Reverend Blair?"

Sam's expression softened. "She just doesn't love him."

"He could give her a better life," she said.

There was truth to this: Lottie would have a kind husband, an escape from servitude, and close proximity to her dearest friend. But Callandra realized it might sound like she was advocating that Lottie marry for money.

Sam put his hands in his pockets and looked away from her, as if to disengage and avoid exploiting the vulnerable position she had put herself in with talk of a "better life."

"I know Lottie," he said simply and softly. "She would never be happy married to a man she didn't love."

"Well, of course, no woman would be happy married to a man she doesn't love," Callandra shot back defensively. What right did he have to lecture her about marriage without love? She had lived it, had felt the pain daily.

"I don't know what others feel," he said calmly. "But I do know Lottie. I know she would feel … defiled."

Callandra looked at him in disbelief. His impertinence, his insult was now clear. He was suggesting that women like herself may be capable of marrying without love — of prostituting themselves — but his sister wasn't; she was made of finer stuff.

Thrusting the letter back into his hands, she slapped him hard across the face.

"My husband is in his study. You can deliver this yourself," she said and walked away, feeling enraged, resentful, and ashamed that she had just referred to Norbert as her husband.

---- ❖ ----

By tea time, Callandra had sufficiently composed herself to join the family in the parlour. Her outward composure masked a despair she hadn't previously experienced. She was accustomed to thinking of her unhappiness in terms of noble suffering, a sacrifice she had made for her mother and siblings (who now showed so little gratitude!). But Sam had implied something different, that her decision to marry Norbert revealed a deep unworthiness. Did he see her no differently than those grasping society women — mocked by Mary Wollstonecraft — whose desire for wealth and status allowed them to tolerate, even thrive, in loveless marriages? Did Lottie see her that way, too? Lottie was so close to Sam, so influenced by him, it was hard to imagine they wouldn't see this the same way.

Defiled. The word raged in her head.

Callandra was only barely paying attention to the tea-time conversation when Norbert announced, without commentary, that Lottie would not be marrying Reverend Blair. There was no reference to this being Lottie's decision (or at least Sam's). The implication was that Norbert was simply correcting misinformation Callandra had presented yesterday.

"In any event, Lottie will be coming with us to Canada — as will her brother," he said, pursing his lips as he came to the important part of the announcement: "Sam has accepted an assignment to build a fine new church for me in Goderich."

———— ✳ ————

The wharf was crowded with well-wishers seeing off the *Christina*. People were embracing, with tearful promises to return some day. Farther down the wharf on a lower level, the steerage passengers — Lottie and Sam among them — were surrounded by sobbing relatives who no doubt knew this was a final parting. Callandra was glad her own mother wasn't there, sparing them both the pain of her departure.

Mrs. Scott, with a dark mesh veil draped over a large hat, clutched Norbert's hand and sounded near tears as she uttered the words: "Safe voyage, dear son." Recovering abruptly, she offered only a stiff "Goodbye" as she nodded to Callandra and Emma.

Mr. Scott and Tommy had said their goodbyes back by the carriage. Mr. Scott simply waved once more before climbing up into the passenger compartment, so that Tommy's cheeky face was the last thing Norbert saw when he turned around the final time.

——— ✽ ———

About a month later, after Nadine Erskine had adjusted to her disappointment over her parents' decision to confine her to Scotland, she heard a rumour that Reverend Blair had proposed marriage to a maid in Norbert Scott's household. It only confirmed what little character Reverend Blair possessed. No sooner had Nadine rejected him than he immediately proposed to the first girl he saw — even a servant girl! How lucky she was to be rid of him.

Chapter Eight

Goderich, Upper Canada, 1836

No doubt about it, Thomas Mercer Jones was pleased with his new home. With its expansive property overlooking the lake, its position above the natural harbour and its fine three-storey structure, it was clearly the grandest edifice in the town. His life had worked well these past few years, split between two worlds. But if he had to make the permanent move to Goderich, he was pleased that it would be to such a commanding perch.

The move was a major promotion, just one more bit of the good luck that had followed him since he'd landed an apprenticeship a decade earlier with Ellice, Kinnear & Company. His rapid rise at the prestigious London mercantile firm hadn't all been luck; his knack with numbers — and for anticipating the needs of superiors — had allowed him to overcome the disadvantages of modest roots. Mr. Ellice himself had spotted Jones's skill in handling complex files and, when he was looking for someone smart and energetic to work for a land development company on the other side of the Atlantic, young Jones seemed the perfect fit.

Jones's good fortune had continued in the New World. Although his father hadn't risen above overseer at a granite quarry, it wasn't much more than a year before Jones was promoted to deputy commissioner of the Canada Company, overseeing more than a million acres of land the Company owned. A young man from a more elevated background might have found life in Upper Canada dull compared to the more sophisticated possibilities in London or Edinburgh. But to Jones, it was an opportunity to rise higher than what would have ever been possible back home, to reinvent himself as a gentleman.

Certainly, as the Company's deputy commissioner, he presented as a person with serious prospects. At social events in York, young ladies had been delighted when he spoke to them or asked them to dance. It wasn't long before he was noticed by Mary Strachan, the daughter of the archdeacon. As Jones prepared to leave the gathering that evening, he was taken aside by William Allan, his boss and the Canada Company's commissioner, who advised him he need look no further for a wife.

Marrying the archdeacon's daughter was another lucky development, as he was now son-in-law to one of the most powerful men in Upper Canada. With the exception of the lieutenant-governor, no man had the stature, influence, or prominence of Archdeacon John Strachan. Some of that pre-eminence derived from his position as head of the Anglican Church in the colony, but it was also due to personal qualities — his impressive intellect, authoritative manner, and dedication to ensuring the development of a young elite loyal to the British Crown. Strachan had become the key figure in the "Family Compact" — the closely connected set of families that dominated Upper Canada politically, financially, and socially, while keeping in check the republicanism and radicalism that surfaced, from time to time, in the common people. By marrying the archdeacon's treasured daughter, Thomas Mercer Jones landed himself in the heart of this privileged little world, erasing any lingering traces of the granite quarry.

As it turned out, Mary was a pleasant woman. And she kept herself well, which was not the same as being pretty, but it would do. Their marriage developed into an agreeable liaison, and they soon had a son and a home on a piece of land adjacent to the archdeacon's mansion on Front Street in Toronto. Jones was obliged to spend five months a year in Goderich as settlers arrived during the warmer weather, leaving Mary and the boy in Toronto where they lived a pampered existence within the comfortable social confines of the Family Compact.

Now Jones was being promoted to co-commissioner of the Canada Company, at the recommendation of William Allan, who was happily moving toward retirement. In Goderich, Jones would simply be referred to as "Commissioner." With this designation, he would truly be a notable person and therefore in need of a grand home overlooking Lake Huron, where he would soon live year-round with his family.

Standing next to Jones surveying the new house was John Longworth. As the two men made their way down the muddy lane that led to Feltie's Tavern, they shared a celebratory mood. With his promotion, Jones would need a bigger staff at the Company's headquarters, which was also moving to Goderich, a key town in the sprawling, wooded Huron Tract where much of the promising land for settlement in Upper Canada was located. Longworth was being elevated to superintendent, a not-surprising promotion, as Jones had always liked the rough-hewn Longworth, whom he relied upon to oversee the Company's agents and their collection of payments from settlers. The agents were extremely unpopular due to their heavy-handed ways, and Jones was happy to leave their supervision in the hands of someone else.

Although it was not yet dark, Feltie's was already crowded. They sat at a table away from the bar and ordered ale and baked pheasant with potatoes, drowned in thick gravy. There were many details to review before Jones headed back to Toronto by steamboat in the morning, and most of the meal was taken up with business. Few of the locals stopped by to wish Jones well before he departed for the winter. Aside from Longworth, Jones had made few friends here. In his position, friendships could be awkward, leading to pleas for leniency on overdue accounts. Jones knew it was more important to be feared than loved.

After business had been dealt with, Jones lingered, enjoying a cigar and yet another ale. He would miss evenings like this. There would be pleasant aspects to being back in Toronto, with his charmed spot in that hierarchical world, but part of him enjoyed being in the backwoods, sharing drinks with a low-life like Longworth. While Jones didn't know all the details, he was aware that Longworth had abandoned a wife and seven children back in Belfast. It would be inappropriate for Jones to go to a tavern in Toronto with such a man, but here in Goderich, looser standards prevailed.

Four years earlier, during his first summer in Goderich, those looser standards had opened a long-closed door in Jones's life. As an ambitious London apprentice, he had adopted a strict code of behaviour, rarely socializing or risking entanglements with young ladies. But that first summer in Goderich, before he was deputy commissioner, he found himself alone in a remote place, far from the rigid social conventions he'd always known. The reticence and reserve that had constrained him in London seemed to melt away when he met Daisy Howard, a servant girl who worked for a family in neighbouring Colborne township. Daisy was a free spirit, completely unlike the girls he had met in London, and she came with him quite willingly to an abandoned cabin in the woods.

By the following summer, having met and married the archdeacon's daughter, Jones realized those carefree days were over.

He returned to Goderich presenting a tightly controlled persona, as an important Company man and rising star in the colonial establishment.

"Daisy is upstairs," Longworth half whispered, meeting up with Jones in the hallway of the adjoining hotel after their dinner.

Jones was jolted by the mention of Daisy. From the look on Longworth's face, it seemed this was meant as a gesture of thanks for the promotion.

Jones hadn't seen the girl in four years, yet she'd remained fresh in his mind.

Now the mere mention of her name sent temptation coursing through his veins, just as it had that first summer. His suite of rooms was at the back of the hotel, with its own stairs, so no one would have to know.

She excited him in a way that Mary never did. There was something enticing about her teasing half-smile, about her catlike way of moving, about her easy nakedness beneath her simple dress. Mary was always stiff and awkward, trying her best to oblige, but easily embarrassed and quick to cover up, ill at ease in anything less than the full armour of womanly garments. Daisy was at home in her own skin, clearly enjoying the effect she had on him.

Daisy was gone without a trace when he woke up. It was still early, so there was plenty of time to get ready for the boat which, he knew, would not leave without him. In the cold light of day, he wondered about his own recklessness. There hadn't been any consequences for him from his involvement with Daisy four years earlier, although there had been significant repercussions for her. As he later learned, she had borne his child. Luckily for Jones, however, no one knew he was the father. Instead, the rumour had taken root that the boy was Longworth's offspring. It helped that Longworth was sometimes seen with Daisy in town after Jones passed her on, and that Daisy's employer had kept her in his service, even with the child. It had all worked out well for Jones, allowing him to extricate himself from the sordid affair and present himself in Goderich as a respectable married man, a devoted husband and son-in-law of the archdeacon.

But now he'd taken a real risk. Jones felt a twinge of regret about his indiscretion, but not the pleasure it had brought. He felt confident he could trust Longworth, even though the scoundrel now had the power to destroy the lucky world he inhabited, commanding perch over the lake and all.

Chapter Nine

1837

Their compartment was spotless and comfortable, one of the few on the *Christina* with two bedrooms and a sitting area. Still, it felt confining to Callandra because it meant constant close proximity to Norbert. There was a pleasant dining room for the roughly two dozen first-class travellers, and a panelled room next to the captain's quarters, where the men from this select group retired after dinner to drink and smoke. Otherwise, there was only the upper deck for walking and viewing the limitless sea.

Callandra had pleaded for Lottie to stay with them, rather than in the crude and uncomfortable steerage quarters. But Lottie had insisted on staying below — no doubt out of loyalty to her brother.

Callandra felt lonely almost immediately — a loneliness made worse by Reverend Blair's decision not to sail on the *Christina*, depriving her of his pleasant, distracting company. Her gloom intensified when it became clear just how strictly the steerage passengers were separated from those in first class. Walking with Emma on the upper deck the first afternoon, she mentioned to a young sailor that she wanted to send for her maid, who was below. The sailor — a pimply-faced teenager with red hair — said that was impossible.

Just before dinner, the gruff, grey-haired captain came to their cabin and explained that no one from steerage was ever permitted on the upper deck. "Don't worry. We have excellent service up here," he said, directing his remarks exclusively to Norbert.

"They're filthy down there, Reverend," he added. "And it will only get worse as the weeks pass."

———— ✽ ————

Callandra spent the first weeks of the voyage in low spirits. She felt queasy much of the time and worried this might be due to more than the ship's motion; increasingly, she felt sure she was pregnant. She told Norbert, who expressed the hope that it would be a boy. It was a measure of their lack of intimacy that they had little to say to each other about the prospect of another child. Her own feelings were mixed; she dearly loved Emma, but had qualms about bringing another child into such an unhappy marriage.

She worried constantly about Lottie. Callandra and Emma got a glimpse of the lower deck by climbing several feet up onto a platform off the main walkway of the upper deck. They were shocked by the wretchedness and suffering visible below. People were crowded like animals in a pen; some were vomiting into open gutters. Yet the orderly world of the upper deck was completely detached from the anguish below.

Emma was the first to spot Lottie, standing against the railing overlooking the sea, Sam next to her. Emma and Callandra called out as loudly as they could, but their voices vanished into the churning wind.

Days later, when they were walking at the back of the upper deck, Emma pointed out to her mother a small, semi-hidden door from which a sailor was emerging. Behind him, there was a darkened staircase leading downward, presumably to the deck below.

Some other passengers came by, prompting Callandra and Emma to move along.

It rained almost constantly for the next few days, making even the short walk to the dining room difficult, and rendering their little world inside the compartment still more confining. Finally, they woke up one morning to find sun streaming through the small windows. Emma went out to see what was happening below, after so many days of rain. She reported to her mother that the lower deck was packed, but she'd been unable to locate Lottie or Sam. At breakfast, the doctor's wife said that her husband had been up most of the night tending to people in steerage, and that three had died, all with high fevers.

"Lottie!" gasped Callandra to Norbert, who sat across the table, beside the doctor's wife.

"There are two hundred people down there, and she's as hale and hardy as any of them," he said dismissively.

"I must speak to the doctor," said Callandra, addressing the man's wife.

"There's no need to wake him," intervened Norbert, then resumed eating, signalling the matter closed. Emma reached for her mother's hand under the table.

They were back in their compartment when the doctor came by to explain that his wife had been mistaken: only one person, an elderly man, had died the previous night.

"I have a friend down there," Callandra said. "She is young, with long, blonde hair. Did you see anyone like that?"

The doctor shook his head, muttering "I don't know ... there are so many ..."

For days, Callandra waited anxiously for news. Finally, late one afternoon, as Emma watched from the platform beside her mother, she began shrieking, pointing to where Sam was sitting on a bench by himself. If he was there alone, Lottie must be sick in the hold, too weak to come outside.

As Emma napped later that day, Callandra made her way to the back of the ship. There was nobody in sight, so she opened the small door and started down the stairs, her heart pounding. She came to a landing, then followed the dark stairs farther down. A sharp bend and then she was at a door. It had a window with bars, and on the other side was the lower deck. With both hands, she slid back the door's large, heavy bolt, and then turned the door handle; it was locked. Confused and scared, she returned up the narrow stairway.

When she got back to the cabin, Emma was there alone. Rummaging through the drawers where Norbert had placed his things, Callandra found a large sack of coins — not the soft, velvet sack of gold coins he carried with him at all times during the voyage — but a cloth sack full of less valuable ones. She grabbed a handful of these lesser coins, returned the cloth sack to the drawer, and rejoined Emma in the sitting room. The coins were still in her hands when, through the window, she could see Norbert approaching. She sat down on the small sofa, putting the coins under the cushion.

Norbert seemed suspicious, as if he knew. She was struggling to think of something to say when Emma abruptly asked him whether it was possible to see land yet, and would he take her out on deck to show her where it would first appear. Emma so rarely spoke to her father that the request seemed likely to further his suspicion. But he took his daughter out on deck as requested, leaving Callandra impressed by the girl's cleverness.

Putting the stolen coins in her purse, Callandra wrapped herself in a shawl and hurried out in search of someone who might have access to keys. Walking toward the back of the boat, she noticed the young red-headed sailor she'd encountered the first day.

"Sailor," she called to him as he organized some heavy ropes. The boy peered up in surprise. He was no more than sixteen.

"Yes, ma'am?" He stood up to face her.

"I once asked you about bringing up someone from below."

"Yes, ma'am," he answered cautiously.

"What about if I went down to see her?"

"No, ma'am," he answered. "That's not allowed, either."

There was no time to waste. She pulled out the coins, which totalled three and a half crowns — an enormous sum to him, no doubt. His eyes grew wide as he looked at the cash displayed in her palm.

"Do you have the keys to the door?" she asked.

Fear flooded his face. While the sum being offered was great, the consequences of such disobedience would be severe.

"I have to see someone below, someone who is not well," she explained. "I will just go briefly to see her, then return. No one will ever know." She opened her hand again, flashing the prospect of instant prosperity to a youngster who had likely only known deprivation.

"Meet me at the door in a few minutes," he said, snatching the coins from her hand.

He was there as promised, a set of keys in hand. He looked frightened as he whispered that he would lock the door after she went through and then return in half an hour. She mustn't be longer than that because he would have to go by then to help with the rigging. If they suddenly hit a storm, he would have to go right away. He didn't explain what would happen to her in the event of a storm, and she didn't ask.

He put the key in the lock, and then abruptly turned around, motioning her silent. Then she heard it, too — a noise on the stairs above them. There was nowhere to hide, no explanation that would satisfy.

As she braced herself, Emma appeared in the semidarkness.

"Good Lord, what are you doing here?" Callandra cried.

"I brought these," said the girl, holding out a blanket and a lemon.

"Oh, yes, yes," said Callandra, grabbing them. Why hadn't she thought of that? The lemon, withered and faded in colour after weeks at sea, seemed worth more right now than gold. How smart of Emma to bring it from the small stash in the cabin.

"Now go back," said Callandra, kissing her daughter.

"No, I want to come."

All of Callandra's instincts told her that was wrong, but there was no time to argue; the sailor would lose his nerve and disappear with the keys.

She motioned for him to proceed. He hesitated; the child represented an added risk.

Then suddenly, he opened the door. Callandra and Emma were barely through it when they heard it clank shut and lock behind them.

Walking onto the lower deck, Callandra held tightly on to Emma. Crowding in all around them were faces that suggested a world of private suffering against which there was no defence. She wrapped the blanket around Emma and pulled her own shawl tightly around her, hiding their fine clothing. She put the lemon in the pocket of her dress — a pocket accustomed to holding no more than a hanky.

Callandra felt off-balance and dizzy as the ship lurched from side to side. She tried to avoid tripping as she searched for the opening to the hold. Finally, she found it, almost falling on a thin, elderly man.

Peering down into the hold, the stench was overwhelming, and she buried her head in her shawl, realizing her pregnancy made her especially prone to vomiting. She pulled her head back up for air. The thought of going down there — of taking Emma down there! — was impossibly wretched, like descending into a latrine.

"Wait here," she said to Emma.

"No, no," cried the girl, clinging to her mother.

"All right," said Callandra. "Use the blanket to cover your face."

Callandra backed herself down through the opening, onto a ladder that was only loosely tacked to the side of the ship. She soon felt the floorboards beneath her. The sway of the ship was even more pronounced down here, and she kept hold of the ladder. Emma followed her down.

The stench, the darkness, the rough rocking of the ship were all overwhelming, but so was the thought that they must be close to Lottie. As her eyes became accustomed to the darkness, Callandra scanned the hold. There were several dozen people scattered throughout the long, low space, but she couldn't see Lottie. The room was cluttered with shelves, strewn with blankets and bedding and decaying food.

"Lottie," she called, but her voice disappeared in the noise. "Lottie!"

A sudden lunge of the ship caused Callandra to fall sideways onto an old woman, whose sickly, sallow face emerged from under a blanket.

"I'm so sorry. I hope I haven't hurt you."

The woman looked close to death, yet no one was caring for her. Rearranging the bedding, Callandra discovered a small pile of silver cutlery, including a large sterling soup ladle. The woman, eyes full of fear and confusion, placed a weak arm possessively over these treasures to prevent Callandra from snatching them.

Feeling for the cutlery, the woman came across the lemon, which had slipped from Callandra's pocket. Then suddenly the lemon — the juice that was to revive Lottie — was in the woman's hand, her spindly fingers closing around it, her hand withdrawing under the bedding.

"No. No. I must have that," cried Callandra, reaching to retrieve it.

Although frail and emaciated, the woman clung to the lemon. As she and Callandra wrestled for it, some of the silver cutlery fell to the ground, with the big soup ladle disappearing under one of the slats in the floor, beyond the woman's reach. Still, she wouldn't release the precious fruit.

"There's Sam!" shouted Emma, pulling her mother. "Over there."

Callandra looked up in the direction Emma was pointing, without giving up her struggle for the lemon. She couldn't see Sam, but Emma had taken off in that direction, scrambling through the semidarkness on her own.

"Emma, Emma. Wait!"

Callandra gave the gnarled wrist a final, sharp squeeze, barely believing herself capable of using such force on a helpless old woman; the lemon finally fell from her hand.

Sam was sitting on the floor at the far end of the hold; Lottie lay next to him. As Emma approached them, Sam looked up in astonishment, and then reached out to her warmly. Callandra arrived a few moments later, and immediately bent down over Lottie. Her forehead was hot, her eyes closed and her face drained of colour.

Callandra gently stroked her cheek, but Lottie didn't wake.

"What's the matter? What does the doctor say?" she asked Sam.

"He hasn't been here for three days," said Sam, his face unshaven. She wondered if he was angry. He hadn't greeted her with the warmth he'd shown Emma.

"What did he say when he was here?"

"He thought it might be typhus. He wasn't sure."

"We brought this for her." Callandra handed him the small, withered lemon. It was hard to believe she had just clawed this treasure from the clutches of a dying woman.

Sam immediately recognized its value. With a knife from his pocket, he cut the lemon, then, gently parting Lottie's lips, squeezed it, letting the juice run into her mouth. The tartness of it made her stir, but still she didn't open her eyes.

Emma placed the blanket on top of the thin one already draped over Lottie.

There was a sudden commotion nearby and Callandra looked up to see that the red-haired sailor had found his way down into the hold, and was being pointed in her direction. He approached with a loud clamping of boots.

"You've gotta come right now, ma'am," he shouted, with breathless urgency. "They're sounding the call early. You've gotta come right now."

Lottie stirred; her eyes opened slightly. She appeared to recognize Callandra, although she barely moved. Callandra leaned forward, kissed her gently on the forehead and squeezed her hand. It seemed like Lottie squeezed back, a faint little squeeze. Emma, too, leaned forward and kissed Lottie. Callandra knew that they could leave now; Lottie would know they had come.

"Ma'am!" shouted the young sailor.

They could still make it back upstairs without the authorities knowing. They could still make it back for dinner.

She took a last look at Lottie and experienced a sudden, calming clarity.

"I'm staying," she said, looking up at the sailor. "Please take my daughter back."

"No. No. I'm staying, too." Emma's face showed an intensity and awareness that seemed impossible for a child.

Callandra turned back to the sailor. "Go without us. We'll never tell anyone how we got down here. Go now, before you're caught."

He left them without another word.

※

By dinnertime, Norbert, realizing where his wife and daughter had gone, was enraged.

His wife's fondness for her maid was hardly news to him, but it hadn't bothered him before. Callandra had never been more to Norbert than a serviceable wife and her attachment to Lottie hadn't interfered with this limited role. But his feelings had changed; Norbert suspected the change was connected to his mother's disappearance from his life, and the huge void it created. He needed someone to constantly, unreservedly, love him. There was no basis to assume that Callandra could do this. But he seized on her dedication to Lottie as the obstacle, the source of her failure to give him his due.

He thought of them down below, laughing and talking, even laughing at him, Lottie smiling and absorbing all the affection that should be his. In his mind, the hold of the ship took on the look of a carnival, the kind of scene he had noticed passing through the countryside on festival days. The carefreeness, the joy, perhaps some dancing — all of it tormented him as he sat alone, unloved.

He decided to have dinner in the cabin rather than risk humiliation in having to explain the situation to the other passengers. After eating, he walked on the deck. Returning, he heard bustling inside the compartment and felt energized at the prospect of expressing his anger. But it was just a maid turning down the beds. Could Callandra possibly be thinking of staying the night below, he wondered, astonished at the boldness of her defiance, of her apparent disregard for her status as a married woman passing the night amid a mob of men. He left the cabin and headed into the captain's lounge; if they came back now, at least they would not find him there waiting.

Callandra awakened as the grey light of dawn became visible through the entranceway of the hold. Emma was pressed up against her mother so that they shared the narrow space normally occupied by Sam, who now sat slumped over, sleeping semi-upright, on the floorboards. Callandra needed to relieve herself, but couldn't bring herself to do what she'd seen others all around her do — squat in full public view over the open trough at the side of the hold.

She became aware of two sailors moving about nearby, no doubt sent by Norbert to retrieve her and Emma. Incredibly, she had barely thought of him and his reaction to their disappearance, so overwhelmed had she been by the immediate struggle at hand.

The sailors found their way to her, assisted by a man who motioned toward the newcomers. The sailors informed her that she and Emma must leave with them at once. Callandra offered no resistance, only delaying to squeeze Lottie's limp hand once more and kiss her again on the forehead, which miraculously felt cooler. Lottie's eyes opened. Was it Callandra's imagination, or did she seem more alert than yesterday? Or maybe, like everything else down here, it was just a question of getting used to it.

Callandra and Emma followed the sailors through the crowded hold and back up the ladder to the lower deck. At the door to the upper deck, one of the sailors, a large burly man, pulled out a set of keys and placed one in the lock. The key turned easily, but the door didn't budge; it was bolted from the other side. The sailor banged on the door loudly, and after several minutes a half-dressed sailor appeared on the other side, visible through the bars.

"These people don't belong here. They're from your side. Open the door, will ya?"

"I've been told never to touch this door," replied the sailor on the other side.

They argued until the upper-deck sailor agreed to seek someone with authority.

But the expectation that he would quickly return soon faded. Callandra sat down on the floor next to Emma, her need to relieve herself all the more acute. As time passed, the sailors became more casual, using foul language as they talked to each other.

The burly sailor began pounding on the door again. Eventually his thumping drew another sailor — this time, the pimply redhead who had made the deal with Callandra. He looked terrified at the sight of her.

The burly sailor demanded the boy open the door.

"I can't," he stammered.

"Just unlock the bolt," said the burly sailor. "They're from your side, these people."

"I don't know that," said the boy. "I never seen them before."

Emma gasped and looked at her mother, who motioned silence. The boy left to seek authorization to admit them, but, after a long while, he still hadn't returned. Callandra overheard the burly sailor suggest to his partner that they take her and Emma back to their bunkroom. She looked away, pretending she hadn't heard this and hoping desperately that Emma hadn't.

It was daylight now, and there were other passengers on the lower deck. She spotted Sam a short distance away. Her heart pounding, she took a last look at the sailors, then pulled Emma with her and ran toward Sam, calling his name.

But it wasn't Sam. When the man turned around, he had a pockmarked face with a strange, drunken look. He smiled at her, making her recoil. Other passengers were watching now. The sailors had followed and were motioning her back.

Abruptly, the big door opened, and the doctor emerged through it, a cloth covering his nose and mouth. He looked at her sternly and muttered something, which Callandra didn't quite catch. He felt her forehead and Emma's, and then motioned them upstairs.

It was another three days before they saw land, and then another day before they were close enough to get an impression of the shoreline.

Norbert had been surprisingly mild in his response to Callandra's misconduct. She apologized and, to her relief, he seemed satisfied. At least, he left her untouched in bed.

More important, Lottie was much better. The doctor reported her fever was gone and she was sitting up most of the time.

"Aren't you glad you didn't spend the rest of the voyage down below," the doctor's wife said to Callandra one morning, as they stood gazing over the railing at the shoreline.

"Yes," said Callandra. "I'm grateful to your husband for his help that morning."

"It was actually a mistake, you know," the woman said, a mischievous look in her eyes. "He was simply going down to do his rounds. He didn't know you were being held down there on the captain's orders."

"Held? On the captain's orders?"

"Yes," said the woman slowly. "It was on the captain's orders, but it was your husband's request that you and your daughter be confined down there for the rest of the trip."

The landing was now only days away. Callandra kept reminding herself of this as she walked with Emma around the deck that afternoon. She was still trying to come to terms with the depths of her husband's cruelty when she pulled Emma over toward the railing, pointing to land. It was the same far-off ribbon of land; there was nothing new to observe. But it kept the girl from watching as several of the ship's officers, at the stern, tied the hands and feet of the young, red-haired sailor, and then tossed him into the sea.

Chapter Ten

Norbert's eyes wandered around the room, alighting on the fine chandelier, a delicately painted vase, some fine porcelain figurines, the crisp linen headrests on the chairs. He hadn't realized how much he missed such refinements until now. The King's Landing Hotel — considered the best place to stay in this grotty little town that fancied itself a city — was rough and rudimentary. In his walks around Toronto over the past week, he had noticed some grand homes along Wellington, John, and Front Streets. But they seemed closed to him; their imposing edifices stern and rejecting. Here however, in the more modest home of William Morris, he felt welcome and immersed in at least some of the elegance of the world he'd left behind.

Morris, a prosperous Toronto merchant with ties to the Presbyterian Church, was keen to make the newly arrived minister feel at home. With his friendly manner, he carried the conversation, allowing Norbert to say little and avoid stuttering. But when his host launched into a diatribe about the Clergy Reserves, Norbert's attention began to stray.

Church politics had never interested Norbert; he was unmoved by the great injustice that Morris insisted had been perpetrated on the Presbyterian Church in Upper Canada. According to Morris, vast tracts of land had been set aside by the Crown to provide income for the colony's clergy, but the Anglican Church had managed to ensure that all this income was directed to its own ministers, with none going to Presbyterian ministers. The name Archdeacon Strachan came up frequently in Morris's impassioned account, and seemed to push his anger level especially high. The archdeacon, it turned out, lived in one of those mansions on Front Street.

After a while, Morris's rant seemed less tiresome, however, as Norbert began to see the implications for his own situation: Anglican clergy in Upper Canada lived extremely well, while their Presbyterian counterparts weren't much better off than struggling pioneers. Norbert didn't fear poverty; he knew he could draw on his mother's resources. But the clearly inferior social status of the Presbyterian clergy was not something he had anticipated.

The arrival of another guest, a businessman named Rupert Ferguson, diverted the conversation onto political matters, notably the growing likelihood of an uprising against the colonial authorities. Once again, Norbert found his interest flagging, until Ferguson mentioned the possibility of unrest "as far away as Stratford — or even Goderich." For some reason, the remoteness this implied came as a surprise to Norbert.

Morris and Ferguson then became involved in a discussion about the road to Goderich, and how the final stretch remained difficult, with dense bush and unstable bridges. Norbert sipped his tea, savouring the delicate taste and the fineness of the china cup.

He managed only a faint smile when Morris turned to him and said how grateful the Presbyterian community was to have "dedicated men, like you, willing to sacrifice your own comfort to serve parishioners living in the bush."

"What a relief after the likes of Turnbull!" said Ferguson.

It was explained that Turnbull, a Presbyterian minister in Toronto, had allowed himself to be lured by the archdeacon from a life of honest poverty in the Presbyterian Church to a life of comfort and plenty in the Anglican one.

Later, as Morris was seeing his guests off at the door, he returned to the subject of defectors. "No doubt, Strachan will manage to lure others. If anyone knows how to buy a man's soul, it is the archdeacon, as he has personal experience in selling his own!"

The insult pleased Morris and Ferguson immensely, and they laughed the hearty but hollow laugh of people who can come no closer to destroying an enemy than to thoroughly disparage him out of earshot.

Norbert took his leave, overwhelmed by the prospect of the difficult and unpleasant life ahead in Goderich, but at least taking comfort in the thought that his brother Tommy likely had no idea how much suffering he was inflicting on his older sibling. Norbert also drew solace from the possibility that the archdeacon might be looking for other Presbyterian ministers with little taste for honest poverty.

---- * ----

Observing Lottie sitting up in bed, Callandra concluded that her recovery was nothing short of a miracle.

She had been diagnosed with typhus upon arrival in Toronto. Now, after four weeks of quarantine, she was completing her recovery in the home of a Methodist widow named Mrs. Tinsdale. It was a modest dwelling, and Lottie, the only boarder, had a very small room. Still, Callandra had been lucky to find it, since most landlords refused to take in those recently quarantined. It had helped that Sam was willing to do repairs to the house. Pleased to have such an able-bodied man around, Mrs. Tinsdale let him sleep in the shed, and fed him, too.

The other miracle, Callandra thought, was that Norbert had been willing to wait around while Lottie recovered. When he had first learned Lottie faced weeks of confinement, Norbert had indicated he intended to move on without her. But, then inexplicably, his attitude changed. Nothing was said, but it became clear he was no longer in a rush to go.

Callandra and Lottie talked about the final weeks of the voyage, about Lottie's quarantine at the military barracks, about Callandra's pregnancy, about their separate lives here in the New World. There was so much to cover after so many weeks apart. After a while, though, Lottie seemed to grow weary and then drifted off to sleep, still propped up in bed. Callandra and Emma sat silently watching over their friend. They were about to go, when there was a gentle knock on the door and Sam came in.

"She fell asleep just now," Callandra explained.

"She does that a lot," he said, arranging the blankets and bedcovers around Lottie. Callandra was impressed with the way Sam attended to his sister. He always seemed to know exactly what she needed.

"Should we leave?" Callandra asked.

"No. I'm sure she'd want you to stay, if you can."

He spoke the words with a gentleness and even friendliness that made her inclined to let go of the animosity she'd long felt toward him. There was now a sense that they had been through something traumatic together — the near death of someone they both loved. Callandra hadn't forgotten how he had insulted her in Glasgow, but things had moved on.

When Lottie woke up again, the four of them chatted with surprising ease, until Lottie mentioned that Sam had been talking about moving to the United States.

"Oh," said Callandra. "What about Goderich?" she said, turning to him. "You're not coming?"

"I'm not sure you're going to Goderich, either," he said. "It's getting too late to make the trek. I've heard the regular coaches don't travel that road after the middle of September. It's already the tenth ... and your husband has given me notice that he'll no longer be employing me at the end of the month."

Callandra hadn't realized any of this — that the coaches were about to stop running and that Sam would soon be released from Norbert's employ. If all this were true, then maybe the plan to go to Goderich had been cancelled, although she hadn't been told.

"Couldn't you find work here?" asked Callandra. "Surely there's plenty of work for carpenters in Toronto."

"Aye, but more down south. I think I could even set up my own business in America."

There was something about the way he said this that made it sound like a plan he had long nurtured — America, his own business.

The comfortable feeling was gone. It now seemed to Callandra that another fierce struggle over Lottie lay ahead, and once again, she had no confidence she could win it.

———— * ————

To his superiors in the Church, Norbert explained his delay in leaving for Goderich by implying his wife's pregnancy made it difficult for her to make the trip on rough roads without her female attendant, who was recovering from an illness. It was suggested that a local woman be hired to accompany them and that they consider the easier but longer trip by boat up the Great Lakes. Norbert explained that his wife couldn't bear more seasickness, and that she would only be comfortable with her long-time maid. Norbert was able to make these expressions of concern about his wife's well-being sound genuine.

In fact, he had put off the trip to Goderich in order to keep an eye on the Turnbull situation. Reverend Turnbull, he had learned, was the minister at St. Andrew's — the large, impressive stone church on Adelaide Street that served the main Presbyterian congregation in Toronto. With a handsome, adjacent stone house for the minister, St. Andrew's seemed part of a princely situation compared to what other Presbyterian clerics apparently had to endure. Yet it was rumoured that Turnbull was being courted by the archdeacon for an even more desirable posting in the Anglican Church.

All of this filled Norbert with optimism. If the archdeacon was courting Turnbull, who had only a degree from an American college, and no oratory powers, what would he think of Norbert, who also lacked oratory talents, but had been trained at Glasgow University? Norbert wasn't upset at the thought of leaving the Church that had nurtured him all his life. He knew that his mother would support his decision if it meant increasing his prospects for happiness; and his father might even be impressed that he managed to advance himself without his mother's help.

The possibility of bettering his situation in this manner gave Norbert an entirely new outlook. He could now envision a life in Upper Canada free from failure, from his father's disdain, from Tommy's mockery, from his dependence on his mother, from the taint of the Barrhead rejection. And he could combine all this with the comforts of the old world. His desire to leave behind the unhappiness of his childhood had never included a willingness to give up luxuries and gentility, the very pleasantness of living.

Norbert had easily resolved to defect to the Anglican Church, but grew discouraged when days passed without an approach from the archdeacon's office. It may have been the harshness of the September winds — a foretaste of winter in Goderich — that finally pushed him to act. One afternoon, he sat down at the wooden desk in his hotel room, brought out some stationery bearing the crest of the University of Glasgow and wrote a note to the archdeacon, introducing himself. It was a clear breech of protocol, and the boldest single act Norbert had ever undertaken.

——— * ———

The response came quickly. By early evening, a messenger arrived at the hotel with a note from the archdeacon's private secretary, Reverend Arthur Potter, inviting Norbert to tea the following Tuesday. He folded up the message after reading it, saying nothing to Callandra, who looked over inquiringly, but knew better than to ask.

In the four days until the meeting, Norbert was full of anticipation. Although confident of a positive outcome, he felt the need for secrecy. It was clear from the way Turnbull was discussed that defections to the Anglican Church were considered base and opportunistic. Should Norbert's visit to the archdeacon become known, there would never be any chance of him replacing Turnbull at St. Andrew's — a fallback position that was at least preferable to continuing on to Goderich.

All of these concerns were in his mind as he dressed for the meeting. He put on his finest jacket, of charcoal-grey Italian wool, and noted with satisfaction that the laundress at the hotel had ironed his dress shirt nicely. Of course, the meeting would make him nervous, increasing his chances of stuttering. But there was every reason to believe that the archdeacon would do most of the talking.

Fortunately, Callandra and Emma were out visiting Lottie, so Norbert faced no inquiries as he left the hotel in a carriage. The office of the Archdiocese was an imposing stone building with a circular driveway that allowed Norbert to be deposited right at the front door, which was removed from the street. He entered through the heavy wooden doors. The inside was grand with marble columns, reminding him why he preferred to be associated with this Church.

The doorkeeper took Norbert's hat and coat and ushered him into an elegant room, with large-cushioned chairs, thick carpets, and heavy, velvet curtains. He was early but was pleased to wait, enveloped by the room's grandeur and opulence. He declined an offer of tea, preferring to await the arrival of his host. He had a rough sense of what Archdeacon Strachan looked like — silver-haired and distinguished, slightly rotund. But when the doors opened fifteen minutes later, a very different sort of man was ushered in.

"This is Reverend McAndrew, recently arrived from Scotland," the doorkeeper said to Norbert, and then introduced Norbert to the new guest as "Reverend Scott, also recently arrived from Scotland."

Reverend McAndrew was tall and appeared to be in his mid-thirties, with a head of curly, reddish-brown hair; he was also clearly a Presbyterian clergyman, and therefore as unhappy to meet Norbert here as Norbert was to meet him. What sort of preposterous joke was this to bring them together — two would-be traitors to the Presbyterian faith, in full view of each other?

They spoke little, restricting themselves to the weather. From McAndrew's accent, Norbert judged him to be from Edinburgh, and likely the holder of a degree from that city's prestigious university.

Was it possible that the archdeacon had done this deliberately, to ensure that they both, out of embarrassment, accepted positions in his church? Although Norbert knew he wanted to defect, he was alarmed at Strachan's indelicate, high-handed manner.

The door opened again and both men rose, this time to be introduced to the archdeacon's secretary, Reverend Potter, a thin, proper-looking man who immediately rang for tea. When it was served, Norbert declined, saying politely that he would wait for the archdeacon. Only then was it stated that the archdeacon would not be joining them. Indeed, it became clear that Strachan had never intended to be there, and that even his secretary was pressed for time.

Before finishing his tea, Reverend Potter reported that the Church had no openings for ministers, but would keep both gentlemen in mind for the future. It seemed futile to deny that they were interested in such employment, so both men remained silent, looking anywhere but at each other. It was even more awkward after Potter excused himself, leaving the two Presbyterians waiting together in the hallway for carriages.

By the time Norbert got back to the hotel room, he felt a resolve not unlike the one he'd felt the day Tommy had mocked him on the back lawn.

When Callandra and Emma returned, before they even had taken off their coats, he declared: "We've dallied here far too long. We must leave for Goderich at once."

It was early morning when Callandra and Emma made their last trip to see Lottie. Callandra clung to the faint hope that her friend might be recovered enough to come with them to Goderich after all. But she agreed with Sam that Lottie was in no shape to make the trip.

That was about all they agreed on. Indeed, it was a great disappointment to Callandra that this last visit to Lottie was marred by Sam's presence. He no doubt felt the same; it turned out that this was to be his parting from Lottie as well, although he was not going to America. Norbert's decision to leave for Goderich now, in the third week of September, meant that travel by regular coach was impossible; they would need their own carriage. Callandra was surprised to learn that Norbert had sent a note to Sam the previous evening informing him that his employment was not cancelled; he would be needed in Goderich.

"Why don't you just say you can't come?" she suggested.

"Your husband has offered me a generous settlement if I stay long enough to ensure the construction of his church," said Sam.

The contentiousness continued after that, as Sam promised Lottie he would be back by spring and then they would move to the United States. Callandra, on the other hand, insisted that she would return as soon as the coach started running so she could personally accompany Lottie to Goderich.

After bidding a tearful farewell to her dear friend, Callandra went to make final arrangements with Mrs. Tinsdale.

Then Callandra and Emma, followed by Sam, walked out of the little house, leaving behind the one person they all felt deeply connected to.

Callandra recognized the face immediately; his energetic eyes latched on to hers as well.

"Oh, Reverend Blair, how good to see you," she said, anxious to dispel any lingering embarrassment he might feel. "You remember Emma?"

Blair had only been in Toronto a couple of days, having just arrived from his Atlantic crossing. As they discussed the voyage — his third trip across the ocean — Callandra became conscious of him looking around the hotel lobby. She realized he was of course looking for Lottie, although it wasn't clear whether he hoped or feared to see her.

"You must come and see us in Goderich," she said. "In fact, we're leaving this morning. Perhaps you could take tea with us here before we leave."

"I would like that very much, Mrs. Scott, but I have to get to a meeting …" his voice trailed off, distractedly.

"Please just call me Callandra."

She sensed sincere regret on his part; it was clear they liked each other. He turned to go, then hesitated and, blushing slightly, asked, "And Miss Lottie … is she well?"

Callandra explained how sick Lottie had been onboard the ship, and how much better she was now, although still in bed and not well enough to travel. Blair's eyes widened as he listened. He stopped looking nervously around; the news of Lottie's brush with death had clearly affected him.

"And where is she?" he asked.

"She's staying here in Toronto — at Mrs. Tinsdale's house on Metcalfe Street. I would be grateful if you could look in on her from time to time, until I can come back for her."

Only then did Callandra realize she was asking a rejected suitor to make courtesy calls on the woman who had rebuffed him. Somehow, it seemed all right to do so however, given the seriousness of Lottie's condition, Blair's generous nature, and the more relaxed customs of the colonies.

"Yes," he said. "I could do that … if it would put your mind at ease … and if you think it would be helpful to Miss Lottie."

"Absolutely, I do," Callandra said. How sad that Lottie hadn't married this thoughtful and pleasant-looking man!

"I will then," he said. "Mrs. Tinsdale's, on Metcalfe Street?"

"Number 22 Metcalfe. It's a small house — a little porch at the front. Perhaps I'll send Lottie a note saying that I've asked you to look in on her?"

"Aye, that would be good."

"I'm so glad I ran into you," she said. The thought of a renewed courtship as Lottie recovered was already taking shape in Callandra's mind.

"Me, too," he said. "I only wish I'd run into you yesterday."

She looked at him quizzically.

"I didn't realize you hadn't gone to Goderich yet. There is an opening for a minister here." Then lowering his voice, he added: "Perhaps you haven't heard. It only happened yesterday, but Reverend Turnbull has left our Church to join the Anglicans."

Callandra looked surprised; things like that never happened, as far as she knew.

"So I suggested a minister whom I'd gotten to know on the boat coming over: Reverend McAndrew, a fine fellow, to replace Turnbull at St. Andrew's. Of course, the congregation will decide … it's just that, if I'd known you were still here, I would have put forward your husband's name instead. I so admire him."

"Oh," said Callandra, realizing her disappointment. "I would have liked that." Then, as much to herself as to Blair, she added, "But it wouldn't have mattered, you know. My husband seems to have his heart set on Goderich."

Chapter Eleven

Nothing had prepared Callandra for the darkness and desolation of the forest.

The first two days had seemed bleak enough, but they'd been close to Lake Ontario, even if trees sometimes blocked it from view. In Hamilton, at the inn where they'd spent the night, they'd heard reassuring things: the driest autumn in years, conditions couldn't be better. The only jarring note was the answer to the question of how many days to Goderich. Nobody had heard of it.

But Norbert had acquired a map that clearly showed a place called Goderich situated on the shores of Lake Huron, at the end of a string of settlements. They also had the well-built carriage that Norbert had purchased in Toronto. With two sturdy horses, and Sam driving, everything felt secure. Leaving Hamilton in the morning, the day was pleasant and sunny. They passed a large sign pointing to the road that ran southeast to the United States. Callandra wondered how Sam must be feeling as he instead directed the horses westward into dense woods.

The road beyond Hamilton was crude, and there was almost no one else on it. In an hour, they encountered just three farm wagons on shaky wheels. Only one of those, piled high with bundles and pulled by an ox, was going in the same direction, and they passed it quickly. A dozen or so people walked beside it, including children.

Occasionally, there was a small clearing stretching back from the road; after a while, there was only forest. The trees blocked the sky. Even though it was morning and the sun was out, it was dark and chilly. Occasionally, there was a break in the arch of trees, letting through an intense shaft of light, then back to semidarkness.

The fierceness of the forest was increasingly difficult to ignore. The road became slower and bumpier, too. It had been uneven since Hamilton, but now the ruts were deeper and more frequent.

Norbert and Callandra faced frontward with Emma between them in the compartment. Given the ominous surroundings, it would have seemed normal for husband and wife to talk to each other, offering up mutual support just through the sound of their voices. But they had nothing to say to each other.

The carriage stopped. They were in a small clearing, with sunlight streaming down. The carriage frame shook slightly as Sam climbed down from the driver's bench and appeared on Norbert's side.

"I need the map," he said, as Norbert opened his door. Callandra noticed that Sam didn't say "sir."

Norbert opened the cubbyhole in the interior carriage wall beside him, where he kept his valuables, and produced the map from inside a leather case.

Sam explained that the road divided into two at this point, but there was no sign indicating directions. Everyone got out to look. There were bushes and undergrowth, except where the narrow road cut through. No wonder the ride was so bumpy; they were driving over rough-cut logs, laid tightly together in parallel fashion. It was hard to even stand on them without slipping on the moss.

The road didn't actually divide into two. Rather, it continued more or less straight ahead. But another road went off on an angle to the left, and seemed, if anything, to be the more "major" road. At the side was a crude, windowless shack that appeared to be abandoned.

Sam got down on his knees and spread out the map in a patch of sunlight. It was clear that they had to take a road to the left, but it wasn't obvious if the correct road was this one or one up ahead. Norbert studied the map, too, from a standing position, and pronounced that they should take this path to the left.

"I'm not sure," said Sam. "If that's the road we're looking for, then the scale on this map is all wrong."

"Let me see," said Norbert. Sam passed the map to him, and Norbert held it up awkwardly, having trouble balancing on the logs beneath his feet.

"This is the road that we want," Norbert concluded. "See how it breaks off to the left."

"We shouldn't hit that road for another couple of hours at the pace we're going," Sam said. "We should just keep going straight. That was my first instinct, but I wanted to check with the map. Now I feel more certain."

"No," said Norbert. "It's clear that we should turn here."

Sam started folding up the map. "Well, I'll go back on foot about a mile or so," he said calmly. "There was a sign with some town names on it."

"You should have paid more attention to that sign at the time," Norbert shot back angrily.

"Yes, I should have," Sam replied. "But the names meant nothing to me. I didn't have the map. Now I do."

Before Norbert could reply, Sam tied the carriage reins to a tree and started heading back toward Hamilton.

Norbert said nothing, even though he clearly didn't want Sam to go. Callandra also wanted to stop him, but stayed silent. Only Emma, wide-eyed, blurted out in a voice that echoed and then evaporated into the cavernous arc of trees above, "Don't leave us!"

It would be impolite for Blair not to visit Lottie.

Walking from the hotel down to the lake, the arguments tumbled easily into place in his mind. Callandra had asked him to visit her dear friend because she couldn't be there herself. Furthermore, tending to the needs of the sick was an act of charity, part of his obligation as a clergyman. Framed this way, the visit could be seen as a duty.

Walking in this bustling stretch of town, he surveyed the faces of those around him, realizing that they had all likely experienced something akin to this in their lives. Blair, however, had never had feelings like this before.

It had been his need to get such feelings under control that had led him to change his travel plans and return to Canada on a later boat where there was no chance of seeing Lottie. Yet onboard ship, he spent hours staring at the ocean and seeing only her.

There was also the problem of the nature of his thoughts. It was normal for a man to feel desire for a woman he intended to make his wife. And in those first days after meeting Lottie, it had all seemed fine, a lovely blending of the human and the sublime, surely part of God's plan. But after she rejected him, these thoughts didn't end. It struck him now that all the time she had been deathly sick crossing the ocean, he had been thinking about her in an ungodly way. In fact, these sorts of thoughts — of undoing her clothing, touching her pale, soft skin — had intensified after she had rebuffed him, as if he were punishing her by degrading her in his mind.

In a way, he understood her rejection, even found it appropriate. It was inconceivable to him that a delicate creature like Lottie would be capable of thinking of him in the way he sometimes — indeed all too often — thought of her. The kind of woman who would marry a man she barely knew would likely be motivated by material considerations, which Lottie clearly wasn't. Her rejection only proved the validity of his feelings for her.

He walked to where the road ended and the wharf began. There were many things he did not miss about Glasgow, but he did miss the sidewalks. The informality of the New World pleased him when it came to people; it meant less artifice. But there was much to be said for well-maintained sidewalks, rather than the rutty, earthy walkways here that virtually blended into the mud-covered streets. Even after a stretch of dry weather, like now, the ground everywhere still seemed soft and mucky.

He walked back to the hotel. The sun was edging out, its mild rays warming his black cloak. At the concierge's desk, he ordered a hackney.

Yes, he would visit Lottie. He had a duty. He had made a promise to Callandra.

———— ✳ ————

They got back in the carriage, almost as soon as Sam had disappeared from view. For a long time, they sat silently, as they had for the previous two days. But it was more awkward now, without motion to distract them from their awareness of each other. Emma was crying, but silently so as not to provoke her father. The horses pulled on the reins every now and then, rocking them. A squirrel scampered across Norbert's door, giving them all a jolt.

Callandra couldn't stop thinking about the ox-driven wagon they'd passed, full of hungry, desperate-looking people. With each minute, her fears grew that the slow-moving ox would reach them before Sam returned — if he was in fact coming back. He could be on his way back to Toronto by now, or heading toward the American border.

She got out of the carriage to look down the road behind them. It was hard to see very far, under the darkened arch of trees. There was no sign of Sam — or, for that matter, the ox caravan.

"Why don't we turn back?" she said, climbing back into the carriage.

"Yes, yes!" Emma said, raising her tear-stained face.

Callandra had sensed that Norbert, too, was growing more fearful, but now that she and Emma openly favoured returning, he seemed incensed by the very suggestion.

"That worthless servant!" he said.

Callandra liked the way Sam had defied Norbert, given her husband's childishness in refusing to relinquish the map to the person actually driving. It was satisfying to see someone put Norbert in his place — not ridicule him for his stutter, but ignore his commands because they were foolish and self-centred.

"I'm going to cut his pay in half!" declared Norbert.

"You may not have a chance," she said. "I suspect he's not coming back."

"Then I'll have him wh-wh-wh-whipped," said Norbert, his hands shaking erratically.

After that, there was silence again between them. Norbert continued to shift restlessly and make guttural sounds of exasperation, as if his keenness for Sam's return was motivated solely by his desire to begin a stringent round of punishment. Emma put her head back in her mother's lap and her quiet but persistent sobs presented a further rebuke to the notion that, with Sam gone, there was still a man to protect the family.

Callandra descended from the carriage again, hoping to spot Sam approaching in the distance. She scanned the road and was startled to detect some motion. But the next moment she couldn't see anything at all. She stood riveted, watching for movement. Emma opened the carriage door and muttered, "Momma, Momma."

This time she was sure. There was motion in the distance, but the longer she looked, the more it seemed unlikely it was Sam. In fact, there was more than one of whatever it was.

She got back into the carriage, putting her arm around Emma, trying to suppress her own surging fear. One possibility was to climb up to the driver's seat and drive the carriage forward herself. Surely she could manage, at least enough to escape the ox caravan that she was convinced was approaching. She looked over at Norbert; he was sitting bolt upright in the far corner of the carriage, still apparently fuming over the misbehaviour of his underling, offering no comfort to their terrified daughter. It seemed pointless to consult him about the possibility they were in imminent danger.

For a while she just sat there, cradling Emma in her arms, paralyzed by indecision. If she were going to move the carriage, the time to act was now, rather than be trying to figure out how to work the reins as the ox cart and potential marauders closed in on them.

At the very least, Callandra felt she should lock the carriage doors. But then there was no way to lock those people out if they were determined to break in. Better to look calm and unafraid, like fellow travellers trying to make their way through the bush — the common foe. So she just sat there immobilized, stomach knotted in fear, wondering how much time was left. Maybe fifteen minutes, maybe ten.

It seemed like less. First, there was a man's voice, yelling in the distance. There might still be time to get the carriage moving. But it had to be right away. Instead, Callandra simply tightened her embrace around Emma and tucked her own head down, burying her face in Emma's hair.

Norbert finally locked the doors, reaching across to secure the bolt beside her. His lips were trembling; his anger replaced with fright. There were sounds nearby, voices.

"Shhh," he whispered urgently to Emma. "Shhh."

They sat in stone silence, aware of people approaching. Norbert rechecked the locks.

There was movement directly outside the carriage, someone on the step on Callandra's side, and then Sam's face suddenly visible. Emma let out a scream of relief.

"Oh, Sam," Callandra exclaimed, "You're back!"

He seemed surprised by the warm reception, and apologized for his tardiness. He had stopped to help the family with the ox cart after it had become stuck in a rut.

"They're from Dundee. Just got here three days ago. They're on their way to Flamborough, not far from here," Sam said. Behind him, Callandra could see the faces of some of the children, all curiosity and hunger, with clothes inadequate for the brisk weather. Callandra caught a glimpse of a young woman with a baby, and two men, one likely a grandfather. There was nothing frightening about them.

"So, is it straight forward or to the left?" snapped Norbert, as if nothing had transpired in Sam's absence except frustration over the delay.

"Straight ahead," said Sam matter-of-factly, avoiding the obvious point that his reading of the map had been the correct one.

"Well, we're now an hour or two behind schedule," replied Norbert, pulling his watch purposefully from his breast pocket. "Next time, pay attention to the road signs!"

"Could we give the children a ride?" Callandra asked.

"No, we must move on," Norbert said to Sam, who hadn't moved.

"Perhaps you might want to at least give them some words of encouragement," Sam answered. "I told them you were a pastor."

"Get going!" Norbert answered sharply. "And give me back the m-m-m-m-map."

Sam handed him the map and then went to the back of the carriage to say goodbye to the family with the ox. He patted one of the small boys affectionately on the head, and then climbed up onto the driver's bench. He wasn't exactly lingering, but he wasn't rushing either. Callandra heard Norbert mutter, "Such impudence!"

The trip resumed in silence. Callandra and Emma watched the children outside the window stare blankly up at them as the carriage pulled away. The family, and all its neediness, quickly receded from view.

———— * ————

Norbert's sullenness pervaded the carriage the rest of the day. He kept pulling out his watch amid groans of irritation. When Sam stopped to water the horses at a stream by the road, Norbert tapped his cane to signal frustration. By the time they approached the village of Gulliver, Norbert declared they were too late to stop for tea, as had been planned the night before. It didn't matter; despite its relatively prominent marking on the map, Gulliver turned out to be little more than a clearing in the woods with a beer parlour, a silo, and a bunkhouse where a few drunken men sat out front on a bench. Nobody was disappointed by Norbert's insistence that they continue.

But as the afternoon wore on, it became clear why Gulliver was relatively prominent on the map; it was about as big and civilized as things got in this part of the woods. There were some alehouses, but establishments selling anything other than alcohol were rare. And while women were occasionally visible in passing wagons on the main road, these small villages — outposts, really — were mostly a man's domain.

The relief Callandra felt on entering the town of Shade's Mills would have been inconceivable only a day earlier. Although a small and unsophisticated place, it had a reassuring respectability about it: a clapboard church, several streets lined by modest but well-kept homes, women and children walking about, men on the street who weren't drunk. There was even a small two-storey hotel, and they were able to get the front room on the second floor. The furniture in the room was sparse, but the bedding was fresh and there was a clean washbasin and towels. Dinner, which they ordered to the room, was the standard fare of barley soup, pork with gravy and potatoes. Tonight, it tasted good.

After dinner, Callandra felt sufficiently comfortable to venture downstairs with Emma. It was an opportunity to get away from Norbert, even just briefly. But opening the front door, she realized it would soon be dark, and there were no longer women or children on the street. Freedom to walk about, even in Shade's Mills, was apparently a daytime privilege. To the side of the hotel, just then, she noticed Sam brushing down the horses.

It was the second time that day that the sight of Sam had made Callandra feel suddenly safe. She called to him, and then realized that she had nothing really to say.

He came over, brush in hand.

"Will you come for a walk with us?" asked Emma.

"Of course," he answered, before Callandra could intervene to override such an inappropriate request. "Just let me tie the horses."

He quickly reappeared from the side of the hotel, an easy smile on his face. It seemed silly to protest; walking through the town would be safer with him.

With Callandra holding Emma's hand and Sam beside them, they walked a short distance beyond the hotel, past the post office, a dry goods store, a cluster of houses. That brought them to the little Anglican Church, clearly the town's central landmark. It was made of wood and painted white, and he stopped to examine it more closely. Callandra motioned that she was happy to wait, so he walked around, looking at it from different angles, presumably getting ideas for the church he was planning to construct in Goderich.

After days in the carriage, it was truly enjoyable to be out walking like this, and on a fine September evening.

Next to the church was a graveyard filled with heather bushes, and Emma wandered over to pick some of the purple flowers. Sam returned to where Callandra was standing watching her daughter.

"Thank you for the walk," she said.

"It's my pleasure." He sounded sincere.

"— and for coming back this morning," she added.

"I would hardly abandon a pregnant woman and child in the middle of a forest!"

"I guess I just meant ... I'm sorry you were treated badly today," she said.

Sam's eyes met hers. "It's not your fault. Your husband seems just as mean to you as he is to me."

"Meaner!" she said, and then realized it was wrong to be revealing such intimate details of her marriage.

"Meaner? Really?" he asked, his eyes intently surveying her face.

She looked away, not wanting to elaborate.

"We should go, really," she said. Emma joined them, bringing the conversation to an end.

They walked back in silence. At the hotel, Sam opened the door for her, and she glanced up at him fleetingly.

"Just don't let on that you've been with me," he whispered, as she moved past him.

"Good night," she said, trying to appear unfazed as she ushered Emma up the stairs.

Norbert was engrossed in studying the map when they got back to the room, and seemed to barely notice, or care, that they'd been absent. He was also drinking Scotch, which generally made him more mellow.

✢

In bed that night, she lay awake long after Norbert and Emma had gone to sleep. She regretted her openness with Sam; she hadn't meant to divulge so much. He had caught her off guard. She recalled that he had looked concerned — or had he just been curious? No doubt, he must have been surprised that she so readily responded to his probing questions. She also now recalled that he had referred to her as a pregnant woman. But how did he know that? Her pregnancy was barely noticeable. It suggested that he'd been surveying her very closely, even below her neckline. She decided that he wasn't being disrespectful, but there was something overfamiliar in his behaviour.

After Shade's Mills, the road narrowed and became more uneven, making the ride bumpier still. The weather also got colder. It now seemed impossible to get warm, even inside the carriage with several blankets over them. It was worse for Sam, of course. Callandra thought of him sitting outside, unprotected from the wind. It occurred to her that he probably knew about her pregnancy because Lottie had told him. Perhaps his presumptuousness was mostly in her imagination.

They had been told about a hotel in Stratford, but arrived late in the afternoon to find it closed for the winter. It soon became clear that the only accommodations still open, from there to Goderich, were grim little roadhouses — essentially one-room log cabins where guests slept alongside the owner's family in front of the fireplace.

They stayed in such a place just beyond Stratford. Dingy as it was, Callandra was struck by how pleasant it was to be separated from Norbert. She and Emma undressed behind a partition, along with the owner's wife and daughter, and then found a spot alongside them in front of the fire. Norbert bedded down, fully clothed in his suit, near a small group of men, including Sam. He was clearly uncomfortable in these undignified quarters, sleeping not just next to his underling, but next to other men who looked even less refined.

Sam negotiated easily among these men and they signalled their acceptance by asking him to join them at a tavern down the road. One of the men mentioned there would be women there. Sam declined the invitation, reinforcing Callandra's image of him as Lottie's responsible older brother, the kind of man who would find drunken carousing distasteful. But she suspected another possible factor: the owner's daughter.

Callandra's first impression of her as pretty was certainly correct. She looked about sixteen and was even prettier upon closer examination — a slender slip of a girl with small, delicate features and long, light brown hair. Her appeal was probably heightened by the fact that, in her simple gingham dress and frayed sweater, she appeared to have gone to no trouble to enhance her attractiveness — indeed, conceivably had gone to some effort to conceal it, in which case her efforts had failed. She moved around the cabin, gathering up dishes and scrubbing down the long table where they'd all eaten.

Her slimness made Callandra conscious of her own swollen waistline, and embarrassed at the thought that she had lain awake the other night thinking Sam had been watching her in the way he was undoubtedly watching this girl.

The girl struggled to move the butter churner, and Sam came quickly from across the room to help her, providing what seemed to Callandra to be definitive proof of his keen interest. He lifted the large churner effortlessly, placing it where the girl pointed. Then there were barrels she wanted reorganized against the wall, which involved more lifting of heavy objects. As she directed him through these tasks, she smiled at him.

The girl slept next to Callandra and Emma that night. Callandra never learned her name, although she lay awake, thinking about her, remembering back to when she herself had felt the kind of excitement that this girl must have felt in the presence of Sam.

In the morning, the girl helped her mother make a breakfast of porridge and hotcakes for everyone. Sam went out to ready the horses. The girl helped carry bags to the carriage. There was no reason for her to then linger by the front door of the roadhouse, as she did.

Callandra was already in the carriage when Sam climbed up to the driver's seat, so she couldn't see him. But it seemed from the expression on the face of the owner's daughter that something had happened between them.

———— ✶ ————

It was late afternoon when they stopped in a small clearing in front of a particularly bleak roadhouse. This one had no windows or porch, and it looked like a heavy tree branch had fallen on the roof. That branch now lay beside the cabin, but the damage it had done to the roof had only been partially repaired.

Sam climbed down and came around to Callandra's side, where there was more space on the road. Opening her door, she wondered if it wasn't obvious what kind of thoughts she'd been having about him. But he barely looked at her, directing his comments past her to Norbert.

"This may be the last place for a brief rest and something to drink," he said. "I don't think there is anything else before Clinton."

Norbert instructed Sam to move on, without consulting Callandra or Emma.

Sam asked to see the map, which Norbert passed to him.

"I'll just check how far it is to Clinton," said Sam, heading into the roadhouse.

Callandra knew from her own perusal of the map that Clinton was the last stop before Goderich; the trek was almost over. Her expectations of Goderich had not been high when they set out, but the town now loomed like a beacon of civilization.

Sam returned accompanied by a stocky, middle-aged man with a grey-flecked beard, whom he introduced as the innkeeper. The door of the roadhouse remained open, allowing Callandra to catch a glimpse of a darkened room with a number of men inside.

"There's nothing between here and Goderich," the innkeeper said to Norbert, who remained in the carriage.

"What about Clinton?" asked Norbert.

"This is Clinton," the man replied, half smiling, revealing a mouth full of crooked teeth.

"How far is it to Goderich, then?" asked Sam.

"I don't know. Never been there. Heard of it, though."

"It looks like we'll have to stay here, then," said Sam to Norbert.

"Hmm," the innkeeper said, glancing at Callandra and surveying the fineness of the carriage, but speaking to Norbert. "There's a road crew in there. We're not really set up for ladies ... but I guess we can make do for one night."

Norbert looked displeased. He got out of the carriage and headed into the roadhouse. The innkeeper followed.

Sam leaned against the side of the carriage, his face turned to the door of the inn in anticipation of Norbert's return. It gave Callandra an opportunity to survey him silently, to see him in a new light. Most of the time she'd known him, he'd been cold and mistrustful of her, although she'd occasionally seen another side of him that she'd liked.

But this wasn't just about liking or disliking him.

Norbert reappeared by himself. "No. There's no possibility we can stay in this place," he said firmly. Callandra didn't like the idea of staying there, either, although Sam must have a reason for suggesting they stay. But now that Norbert had decided they should move on, he would be loath to reverse himself.

"It is a rough place, I agree," said Sam to Norbert, "But it will be dark in an hour, and I doubt we can make it to Goderich by then. Either we spend the night here or risk being stranded in the woods ... I don't think that would be very comfortable for your wife and daughter. At least here, they'll have a bed."

"It's not safe in there ... for women and children." Norbert scowled as he grabbed the map from Sam. "We're wasting time. Let's get going."

"Don't worry. I'll protect your wife and daughter," said Sam.

Norbert looked at him with withering scorn.

"Oh, Norbert," said Callandra, trying not to sound as if she were challenging his authority. "I wouldn't want to end up in the woods overnight."

"I'd be afraid in the woods!" Emma chimed in, addressing her mother.

"We're better off here," Sam said with a quiet resolution that was all the bolder in its insubordination because of the calm, authoritative manner with which he delivered it.

"I'll make the decisions," Norbert snapped, jutting out his lips. Callandra was struck by how small and frail he looked, glowering up at Sam. Not a good situation: it was when Norbert felt humiliated that he became mean.

"No disrespect, sir, but I doubt we can make it to Goderich by nightfall," said Sam with a breezy confidence that suggested "sir" was not said in deference, but to avoid provoking a frightened child. "This is our best option."

Norbert said nothing. He, of all people, would be frightened in the woods after dark.

Sam asked Callandra if she'd like to see the tiny room where she and Emma could stay the night, and then held the carriage door for her. Slowly, she stepped down.

"And where am I to sleep?" demanded Norbert, before Callandra even had a chance to enter the roadhouse.

"With the men, by the fire."

"With those brigands and thugs?"

"They're road workers, not criminals. You'll be fine," said Sam. "And if you're worried about your gold, give it to your wife. I'll sleep outside her door. No one will bother her."

The mention of gold was jarring. It wasn't clear how Sam knew about the small sac of coins which Norbert kept in the breast pocket of his waistcoat.

"Ha! So you'll protect the gold and the woman! I suspect you'd like to get your hands on both!" cried Norbert, gesticulating. "You impudent b-b-b-b-bastard. Get into the carriage. Do as I say, b-b-b-b-b-both of you!"

Callandra climbed back into the carriage. Then Norbert got in on his side and began tapping the inside of the vehicle impatiently with a cane.

Sam said nothing, standing with his arms crossed, surveying the scene with a look of detachment. The horses began stirring in confusion from the noise of the cane-tapping, and Sam went over to calm them. The delay and Sam's apparent nonchalance further infuriated Norbert, who tapped more loudly and furiously.

A cluster of men stood in the doorway of the roadhouse, watching and laughing.

Then Sam, relaxed and unfazed, opened the door on Norbert's side. "Now, why don't you stop all that tapping?"

When Nobert kept tapping, Sam seized the cane from his hand.

"G-g-g-give that back!" he ordered, but Sam declined to yield the cane as Norbert tried in vain to snatch it back.

"You don't want to upset the horses," said Sam, with a continued composure that highlighted Norbert's helpless rage.

Sam walked around to the back of the carriage, checking the transom and wheels. Inside the passenger compartment, Callandra could see the outline of Norbert's face, frozen in fury, staring in front of him.

Tense moments passed before Sam reappeared at Norbert's open door. Lowering his voice, he spoke directly to Norbert: "And, just to be clear — if I'd had a mind to take either your gold or your woman, I'd have done so by now ... Out here in the forest, you have no power over me."

With that, Sam made a point of throwing the cane deep into the woods, prompting more laughter from the men in front of the roadhouse.

"I'll let you know when we get to Goderich," said Sam, taking the map from Norbert. He climbed up to the driver's seat, gave the horses a signal, and the carriage lurched forward.

The focus turned to making it to Goderich by nightfall. It was dark enough already in the forest. As they proceeded, the horses sped up and the jerking motion of the carriage got more intense. Norbert's sullen withdrawal allowed Callandra to remain withdrawn, too. She pondered what Sam had said about Norbert having no power over him in the forest, how he could have taken the gold — and her — if he'd wanted to. That was surely true. They were captives of a pirate, but one who chose to do them no harm, and indeed was protecting them. She found the thought strangely exciting, even more so because of the speed of the carriage, which frightened and thrilled her.

Just as darkness was taking over, there was a loud cracking sound. Then the carriage lunged to the side, hitting something and plunging downward. They were all jolted out of their seats, and there was a strange, pained cry that came from a horse, but was otherwise unrecognizable. That was the last thing Callandra remembered before the shock of the cold water.

Chapter Twelve

The sitting room was a comfortable size for two but, with Mrs. Tinsdale, it felt cramped.

Blair had sent a note clearly indicating he was a pastor visiting an ailing parishioner. If there was something else to his visit, it was none of Mrs. Tinsdale's business. He was vexed at how quickly she seemed to grasp that there was, indeed, something else.

The skin on the old lady's face sagged, but her eyes were eagle-sharp. She sat upright in her wooden chair, watching. A pile of knitting lay untouched in her lap.

Blair was struck anew by what a lovely-looking creature Lottie was, how very soft and feminine. She also appeared more receptive to him in her weakened state, making him glad that he'd come and not embarrassed by what had transpired between them.

She explained that the doctor told her to expect a long recovery. "The Scotts will have to find someone to replace me."

"I'm sure they could never replace you," he responded, realizing that this sounded like an expression of his own feelings. "You know how devoted Mrs. Scott is to you."

Mrs. Tinsdale seemed to have picked up on his keenness, even if Lottie hadn't.

"Yes," said Lottie, looking off wistfully. "I miss them all so much."

There was something so sweet and sincere about her. Blair regretted he'd charged in so quickly with his marriage offer, rather than letting things develop more slowly.

Lottie asked about his work in the Church, and he told her about the controversy over the Clergy Reserves, and the unfairness of colonial authorities toward the Presbyterian Church. She appeared attentive.

"May I call again?" he asked, as he took his leave. This came out effortlessly, and her face looked particularly radiant as she replied, "Yes, please. Do come again soon."

Soon. She had added that word, upping the ante considerably. He hadn't mentioned a time frame at all. "Soon" gave his next visit almost a sense of urgency. And "please," as if it were something he was doing for her.

Mrs. Tinsdale's rickety wooden gate didn't quite close, so he fidgeted with it for a few moments before stepping up into his waiting hackney and heading back to his office. He felt a frisson of excitement at the thought that, when Lottie got a little better, he could take her to church, where they'd be free of Methodist supervision.

Arriving back at his office, Blair found a parcel with a note attached:

> My dear Reverend Blair, would you be so good as to offer your opinion on this draft of my sermon for St. Andrew? I appreciate your kind efforts on my behalf. Sincerely, James McAndrew.

Blair found the sermon surprisingly good. McAndrew showed an appreciation of complexity — of Christ's thorny offer of love and temptation. There was also an impressive command of language. "All the wheels of God's dispensation, sweet and bitter, are rolled upon his axletree of love." Blair tossed the image "axletree of love" about in his mind, considering it good, even splendid.

Looking through the rest of his mail, he discovered a letter from an official of the Glasgow Colonial Society, reporting that fundraising had been disappointing, with the exception of the "generous donation of Mrs. Thomas Scott of Glasgow, who not only pledged sixty pounds, but committed to do so on an annual basis." Clearly Norbert must have inherited his big-hearted tendencies from his mother.

As Blair put on his coat, with the intention of visiting McAndrew, there was a knock at the door. It was William Morris, his longtime ally on the Clergy Reserves issue. In addition to being a prosperous merchant, Morris was an elected member of the Legislative Assembly where he was instrumental in passing bills ensuring the Presbyterian Church a share of the proceeds of the Clergy Reserves — only to have the bills overturned by the lieutenant-governor's Executive Council, on which Archdeacon Strachan was the leading force.

"Strachan is at it again!" said Morris, pulling from his satchel a printed copy of a sermon the archdeacon had given the previous month in Kingston. It included scurrilous, unfounded attacks on Presbyterian ministers in Upper Canada, accusing them of disloyalty to the British Crown.

"How dare Strachan speak of loyalty!" responded Blair.

Trained as a Presbyterian minister in Scotland, Strachan had been rejected by a Presbyterian congregation in Montreal, prompting him to switch to the Anglican Church.

Blair was glad to see Morris freshly fired up about the need to defend Presbyterian ministers. Recently, Morris had begun arguing that the proceeds of the Reserves should be shared not just with Presbyterian clergy but with all Christian clergy in the colony — or even be used to pay for public education! Surely there was a limit to how far equality could be pushed, Blair felt, before it became self-defeating.

"Oh, and something else you'll be interested in," said Morris, as he prepared to leave. "When I was picking up that sermon, someone I know in the archdeacon's office told me that a couple of our ministers were over there last week ... looking for work!"

Blair scoffed dismissively. "Strachan would like us to imagine that our people are as disloyal as he is."

"Sometimes I worry there's truth in that," said Morris, dropping his voice. "It's sad, but the defections do seem to come from our Church. You never see Methodists or Wesleyans going after the Anglican riches!"

"These sorts of rumours are meant to demoralize us," said Blair. "Until I hear something specific, I ignore them."

They walked down two flights of stairs together in silence. In front of the building, Morris offered Blair a ride in the hackney he had waiting. Although not far to his flat, Blair accepted, glad for an opportunity to strategize further about the Clergy Reserves.

"I should tell you, Jonathan," said Morris. "What I heard was specific."

"Well?" said Blair.

"According to my friend at the Archdiocese, two Presbyterian ministers called on the archdeacon last week." Morris looked around, ensuring they were out of earshot of passersby. "One of them appears to have been that new chap, McAndrew. And there was a shorter fellow with him."

"Really?"

"Imagine that!" scoffed Morris. "The fellow is barely off the boat and he's ready to defect! Have you met this McAndrew?"

"Uh, no ... I don't believe so ... I'm sure I haven't."

"So where can I drop you?" Morris asked, opening the door to the carriage.

Blair hesitated. "You know, I think I feel like walking."

———— ✻ ————

Blair spent the evening alone in his room on Adelaide Street, not even going down for supper. He was never one to enjoy idle conversation, and certainly not tonight. He reminded himself that he was not guilty; he had not tried to defect. Still, if Morris's informant was correct, there had been two men petitioning Strachan and people might suspect Blair to be the other man, because he'd been openly friendly with McAndrew since meeting him on the boat, and McAndrew was indeed taller than Blair.

He picked up the book of psalms he'd been reading, and tried to lose himself in the rhythm of the lines. It was too early to go to bed and he was hungry, so he went downstairs and asked his landlady if there were leftovers he could take up to his room.

"Oh, I didn't realize you were here, Reverend," she said. "A gentleman was looking for you just now — another clergyman, a tall, young man — but I said you were out."

Blair retired to his room with boiled beef and potatoes, and felt better as soon as he began eating. The thought occurred to him that perhaps he should consider discussing these developments with Lottie. He had nothing to hide, after all, and she had listened with interest to his tales of the goings-on with the Church. Divulging more details might allow him to develop a feeling of intimacy with her.

He felt restored by the end of his meal, and resolved to share all of this with Lottie — all but the sermon, which reflected rather too well on McAndrew. Blair knew little about women except that they were unpredictable in matters of the heart. It seemed hard to imagine, though, that a flair for poetic language and a sensitive understanding of the struggle for faith wouldn't be among the things they'd find most attractive in a man.

---- * ----

The first few moments, right after waking, were the most unsettling. Of course, it was just a dream — convoluted, blurred, nonsensical. But segments were too powerful to comfortably dismiss: he and McAndrew in front of the archdeacon's residence, trying to leave, but being unable to move. It was no longer clearly the archdeacon's residence, nor was his companion still McAndrew; the person had changed into someone he couldn't identify. Still, the feeling of trying but failing to flee persisted.

The fire had gone out and the room was cold. Blair had no desire to get out of bed; he only wanted the dream to disappear. Or at least that part of the dream. There was another part he desperately wanted to retrieve, but couldn't. Only the sensation of it came back to him — a sensation of intimacy with a woman, undoubtedly Lottie. There had been a closeness, an understanding, a familiarity. He couldn't bring any of this back into focus, but the feeling that something had happened between them was unmistakable. It had felt natural to touch her, to hold her, and she wanted him to do these things.

Blair lay awake a long time, keenly trying to reconstruct his dream out of fragments of feeling. But while the first part came back vividly — Nadine's father; that's who McAndrew had metamorphosed into! — the other part remained elusive.

The images were gone, irretrievable; only the feeling of elation remained.

———— ✤ ————

"Soon" was a vague concept. It could mean a matter of hours, days, or months, depending on the context, but seven days seemed an appropriate time to wait when one had been asked to come again "soon." On the sixth day, Blair sent a note to Lottie, inquiring if he might visit the following day at three o'clock. The messenger had been instructed to wait for a return note. The reply came back affirmative.

Although still pale, Lottie looked more alert this time. She smiled sweetly up at him from the love seat, reviving momentarily that elusive feeling of familiarity from the dream. Mrs. Tinsdale had positioned her chair farther back than the last time, without relaxing her vigilance. It was as if she knew what went on in his dreams.

As soon as he sat down, he brought out a book of English poetry that he had purchased for Lottie. As she fussed over the fine volume, he surprised Mrs. Tinsdale with a collection of Methodist sermons.

The conversation flowed easily after that; Mrs. Tinsdale even left them unattended as she prepared tea and biscuits. His initial impression that Lottie was healthier was confirmed; her voice was stronger, and she said she felt much better. It seemed her improved state might have something to do with his attention. Heartened, he decided to follow through with his plan to confide in her about the archdeacon's attempt to lure Presbyterian ministers into the Anglican fold.

"He's shameless in his efforts to recruit our pastors, and sadly, with his ample resources, he has occasionally succeeded," said Blair.

"Aye, but you don't see none of that in my Church," Mrs. Tinsdale proudly intervened, trampling on the intimacy of the moment.

"Are there many in our Church who have defected?" asked Lottie. It was thrilling the way her eyes looked into his.

Blair pointed out that the most notable defector was Strachan himself. He described this story in detail, confident in his ability to recount it.

"There have been a few other defectors, as well," continued Blair. "Recently, there's been a report of two Presbyterian ministers paying a visit to the archdeacon."

"Perhaps that wasn't about defecting," said Lottie. "Could there have been another purpose?"

"Well, I suppose," said Blair, embarrassed he hadn't thought to give these suspected traitors the benefit of the doubt.

A moment of silence fell between them, and then Lottie cast her eyes down, apparently shying away from the intensity of their interlocking glances. This was natural in a woman, of course, and had the effect of making their interaction feel all the more profound. With her gaze downward, he was able to study her face more freely. His eyes feasted, taking in the softness of her brow, the graceful lines of her lips.

"And do they know who these men were?" asked Mrs. Tinsdale.

"Well, one of them is reported to look like Reverend McAndrew, whom I met very briefly onboard ship during my last crossing," said Blair.

"Oh, my goodness," said Lottie, her bright green eyes looking up again. "Did he seem, uh, like someone who would do that sort of thing?"

"It's hard to say," said Blair. "I barely spoke to the man."

"So has he defected?" asked Lottie.

"Not yet. These things take time to arrange, I imagine," said Blair. "It's odd because Reverend McAndrew is to give the sermon at St. Andrew's a week Sunday. I believe the congregation is considering him for a position there."

"So if he defects right after that, it will be all the more scandalous!" exclaimed Lottie.

"I suppose you could say that." He would have downplayed the suggestion of scandal from anyone else. But coming from Lottie, it was a welcome sign that their intimacy was growing, that she felt comfortable making such a delicate comment to him.

The visit lasted longer than the last one, and it seemed obvious he would be expected to call again. But he still wasn't prepared for what Lottie said as he rose from his chair.

"Perhaps I could accompany you to Reverend McAndrew's sermon? I would enjoy that."

Blair almost tripped as he walked down the front steps of Mrs. Tinsdale's house, and then jubilantly plucked a bloom from the lady's garden and fitted it into his buttonhole. Other than the possibility that Lottie was fascinated by Church politics, it seemed hard to avoid concluding that she was rethinking the hasty decision she'd made back in Glasgow.

It happened so quickly. All of a sudden, the carriage was in the river, partially submerged and sinking, with bitingly cold water pouring in the sides and through the floorboards, splashing against their legs as they scrambled to climb on top of the bench. Emma was screaming, her piercing cries enhancing the panic in the semidarkness.

Sam appeared in the river alongside the carriage. "Push open the door!" he called up to them.

"You scoundrel, look what you've done!" cried Norbert.

"Push open the door!" Sam repeated. "The carriage is going down. You've got to get out while you can."

The horses, struggling to keep their heads above water, jolted the carriage back and forth, causing Norbert to fall from the bench and end up on the floor.

"You've got to get out now," Sam repeated, more urgently. "The carriage is sinking."

"Norbert, help me push the door!" cried Callandra. "We've got to get out!"

"No. We're safer here than in the water," Norbert insisted.

Sam climbed onto the step of the carriage and forced the door open. A surge of water poured in, flooding the floor, and prompting Norbert to scream like a terrified child.

"You see, he's trying to drown us," yelled Norbert.

"No! We're going to drown if we stay," Callandra shot back, desperately holding on to Emma as the carriage tilted back and forth, more water pouring in.

"It's not far to shore. I'll get you there," Sam called to Callandra. "Pass me the child."

Callandra jumped down from the bench, Emma in her arms, into the rising pool of water. She tried to balance herself as she moved toward the open door, but the carriage kept swaying back and forth in the roiling water. Norbert scrambled to get back up onto the bench, too focused on his own safety to interfere with Callandra as she tried to transfer Emma to Sam's outstretched arm.

Emma reached for Sam, and he easily took her in one arm, then reached back for Callandra. "Now you, too," he said. "Grab on to my arm."

"No, d-d-d-d-d-d-don't leave me here alone!" cried Norbert, pulling at her shoulder and causing her to slip backward into the water on the floor.

Sam reached in to grab her, but Norbert latched on to her woollen cape.

"Take the cape off!" Sam yelled.

Callandra struggled to unclasp the cape from around her neck, but her shaking hands couldn't get it free. Norbert tightened his hold on it.

Emma screamed for her mother, but as Callandra tried to move toward Emma and Sam, Norbert yanked on the cape, choking her, and pulling her back from the door.

"Don't leave me here!" he cried, as the carriage continued to sink.

"Let her go!" demanded Sam.

Norbert held on to the cape more tightly. Sam forcefully extricated Norbert's hand from the cape, pushing him back against the far side of the carriage to free Callandra. But, as Emma reached out for her mother, the girl slid out of Sam's hold, falling onto the floor.

All of a sudden, Emma was slipping out the door into the river. Then she was gone. Sam immediately dove in after her. Callandra watched, screaming, transfixed in horror. It was so hard to see in the gathering darkness. The water was darker still, and moving rapidly.

Sam resurfaced a short distance from the carriage, but without Emma. He immediately dove back down.

Callandra had no idea how to help but jumped in anyway. Her cape, now sodden, weighed her down as she dove under the brutally cold water, feeling a desperation she'd never felt before. Somewhere in that dark, churning water was her beloved child. If they didn't find the girl right away, she would drown or be swept down the river, gone forever. But the more Callandra struggled to move through the water, the more she became entangled and trapped in her cape, adding to her terror and helplessness. Surfacing for air, she struggled again to get it off her neck, but couldn't. There was no time left. She had to dive down again, but the cape was choking her.

Suddenly Sam surfaced again a short distance away. Callandra could barely see in the splashing water, but it looked like he was holding something. Then, joy of joys, she heard what was unmistakably the sound of Emma gasping and coughing.

Then Sam was beside Callandra. He had Emma firmly in his grip and now held her as well. She finally managed to unclasp the cape and get free from it.

"Just lie on your back and let me pull you," he said, trying to calm her down so he could concentrate on reassuring Emma, who was grabbing him tightly around the neck.

Callandra did what he said, letting her body go limp. She could feel his strength pulling them through the water, despite the current against them. Even Emma was calming down as they moved toward the far shore.

Then, before long, Sam was no longer swimming, but walking on the river bottom. Callandra let her legs go down, too, and discovered she could touch the bottom, just barely. She could see the shoreline, with the forest behind it. A little farther, and she could now easily touch the bottom. Thick weeds entangled her legs under the water. Sam was beside her, Emma safely on his shoulders, shuddering from the cold, still coughing, but very much alive.

And then they were on the rocky shore. Callandra just huddled there, holding tightly on to Emma, shivering and wet under dripping clothes, feeling stunned and barely able to comprehend what they'd just been through. She looked up to see Sam wading back into the river, swimming toward the carriage. In the fading light, she couldn't even see if the carriage was still there.

He was gone for what seemed like a very long time. Emma, with trembling lips, asked if he was coming back. Callandra said yes, but once again, she wasn't sure.

The outline of a shape became detectable in the river. As it came closer, she could see it was a horse, swimming toward shore. Finding its footing in the shallow water, it came up on the bank a short distance from them.

Then, a few moments later, she spotted Sam in the river, swimming in their direction. He was pulling something that looked like a plank behind him in the water.

He got to shore, immediately secured the horse, then returned to Callandra and Emma.

How could she have doubted him? He had just saved their lives. "There was no sign of your husband" was all Sam said.

Chapter Thirteen

It had started to rain, the drizzle compounding the dampness and cold. Thoroughly soaked, Callandra tried to control her shivering to present a more reassuring image to her daughter.

"We can't stay here," Sam said. "We've got to find shelter."

But where? They'd made it to the far side of the river, the Goderich side — or so it seemed — but a black forest loomed in front of them.

"What about Norbert?" said Callandra, feeling suddenly aghast at the thought of just abandoning him. He had probably drowned by now. She wasn't sure how she felt about that. Certainly, he was cruel right up to the end, showing no concern for anyone but himself. He had almost pulled her under. Still, could they just move on without him?

"We need to find shelter," Sam repeated, motioning toward Emma.

Of course, he was right.

Sam helped Callandra and Emma up onto the slippery back of the horse. They grasped his mane to steady themselves as the animal moved forward nervously, evidently still traumatized by the river. Sam had salvaged a canvas bag of Callandra's from the top of the partially submerged carriage and transported it across the river on a broken piece of floorboard. She was relieved when she saw it, realizing there would be dry clothes inside. He slung it over the horse in front of Emma, and then pulled himself up behind Callandra.

Having Sam on his back seemed to calm the horse, and soon they were moving slowly through the darkened, shimmering forest, as the horse's footing became stable and steady, even on the slick logs beneath. Sam held the reins, his arms enveloping Callandra and Emma. Holding on to the mane helped them balance, but Callandra knew it was Sam who was preventing them from falling off. She felt her heart speeding, pressed up against him like that, enclosed in his arms.

It seemed like a long while that they clomped through the forest, their eyes adjusting so that, in only the dim glimmer of light from the moon, they could distinguish leaves and branches on either side of the road. Beyond the drizzling rain, there were occasional animal sounds far off in the forest that should have been intimidating, but somehow were not. When the horse occasionally stumbled, Sam's arm pulled Callandra and Emma in closer to him, steadying them and leaving Callandra feeling strangely safe and protected.

Perhaps she was still too stunned, too overwhelmed by everything that had happened for Norbert's death to really register. She felt some pity as she imagined his last struggle against the river, alone and frightened, probably calling for his mother. Certainly, it was wrong of her — wrong in every way — to be enjoying the sensation of closeness to Sam. But then Norbert had surely caused the accident with his stubbornness. He had endangered Emma's life.

——— ∗ ———

It was Callandra who spotted the outline of the small cabin in the woods just off the road.

Inside, the windowless cabin was cold and dark but dry. Searching in the darkness, Sam found some flint on a shelf and got a fire going in the woodstove. The cabin appeared to be an old shelter, perhaps used by men reconnoitering in the woods. There were blankets, cushions, and a straw rug on the floor. Under the circumstances, it felt luxurious.

The fire soon took enough of the chill out of the air that Callandra was able to remove Emma's wet clothes and wrap her in a blanket. There was a small stack of logs, but not enough to last the night. Sam went outside searching for branches that weren't thoroughly drenched from the rain. Callandra undressed and switched into a soft muslin dress that was at least partly dry, even after hours in the canvas bag in the rain. She huddled with Emma under blankets on the rug in front of the stove.

Sam returned with an armful of birchbark and wood, feeding some of it into the fire. At first, the flames flickered, but when the wood dried out, they grew stronger and warmer. He went out several times to get more, until there was a substantial pile on the floor by the stove.

He took off his soaking jacket and started looking around the cabin. There was a container of water, and they all had some to drink. Other than that, there was little of use — a bottle of vinegar, a jar of salt, some plates, cups, and spoons. Not a scrap of food. But oddly, in a partially hidden panel in the wall, Sam found a flask with a fine leather covering. Removing the top, he sniffed it and took a swig, then offered it to Callandra. She declined but thanked him, reminding her that she hadn't yet thanked him for saving their lives.

They clustered by the fire trying to get warm, Emma curled up against her mother, with Sam a few feet away. They sat a long while in silence, as Emma drifted off to sleep.

"By the time I saw the bridge, it was too late to slow the horses ... I shouldn't have been going so fast," Sam finally said, putting his face down into his hands.

"No," said Callandra soothingly. "You were just trying to get us to Goderich before dark. We shouldn't have been on that road so late." She felt so deeply grateful to him for saving Emma that she wanted to alleviate his feelings of guilt, even though she realized he was right; he had been going too fast.

They returned to silence. After a while, Sam fished something out of his pocket. It was Norbert's velvet sack of gold coins, soaking wet, with the string still drawn tight. He handed it to Callandra.

"This was in the breast pocket of his coat, which was inside the carriage," he said. "He must have taken off his coat to swim."

Callandra was stunned. Why hadn't he mentioned this earlier, when he'd said there was no trace of Norbert?

Sam passed the flask to her again, noting that it was fine silver and that the brandy seemed of very high quality. She was tempted, but again declined. She had only had liquor that one time with Lottie, and it reminded her of a party, which now seemed inappropriate.

"It will warm you up. You're still shaking."

That was true, and it seemed silly to resist. Despite Norbert's death, they were alive. Emma hadn't drowned. She took a swig.

"Take it slow. It'll burn your throat."

The stinging gave the sensation of warmth. Besides, it tasted good.

"I'm impressed. You didn't even choke," he said, a smile passing over his face. He was sitting on the floor near her.

"Do you think Norbert just stayed in the carriage?" she asked.

"He wasn't in it. I swam around and couldn't find him. I suspect he tried to swim, but was pulled along by the current."

It wasn't clear how hard Sam had looked for Norbert, and Callandra didn't ask. He was probably dead by the time Sam got back to the carriage.

"I guess he drowned" was all Callandra could say. "I don't think he knew how to swim."

Sam just looked away.

"Thank you for saving Emma — and me," she said.

Sam brushed off the compliment. "I wasn't able to save the other horse. It was awful watching that and being unable to help."

It struck her that the horse's drowning upset him more than Norbert's. But then he'd witnessed the horse's death; Norbert had simply vanished without a trace. Or so he said.

Of course, it was possible that Sam had forcibly taken the gold from Norbert — letting him drown or even pushing him under. But she didn't believe that. If there was any doubt about his intentions, there was the fact that he'd just given her the sack of coins.

"But I mean what I said — without you, Emma would have drowned," she said.

He looked over at her with serious eyes. "Well, thank *you* for what you did for Lottie. It really helped when you came down into the hold of the ship. That was brave."

Now it was her turn to slough off the compliment, although she was happy to hear it.

They sat in silence for a long time.

"Are you getting any warmer?" he said eventually.

"The brandy is helping." Mostly, however, she was feeling light-headed.

He threw a damp piece of wood into the fire, and it crackled loudly. "I'm amazed how well you're handling it."

"I've actually had it before," she confided, "one night, with Lottie. We had quite a lot."

"Really? You and Lottie got drunk together?" He looked at her now with soft, curious eyes. They smiled at each other.

Callandra told him about that night, about how close she'd felt to Lottie and how much that closeness had helped her survive those dreadful, unhappy years in Glasgow. *Which were behind her; now, more than ever, behind her!* She could feel the brandy doing strange things to her; her head was buoyant, almost floating. Sam seemed to be listening to her with great interest, the drowning horse gone from his mind. Talk of Lottie had changed things, but not in a contentious way, as had often been the case between them. Now Lottie was like a reference point between them, a bond that existed beyond being stuck here in the woods together.

Emma had slumped over in her sleep, and Callandra laid her down on the rug, arranging the blankets into makeshift bedding around her.

"She seems warm now," said Callandra.

"But you're still shivering."

"A little."

Sam offered her more brandy and her wooziness grew as she sipped it slowly. She wasn't sure if she really was warmer than before, or if the brandy had simply numbed her to the chill. Either way was fine. She was still shivering, but it didn't seem to matter. Norbert's death now felt unreal, as did their precarious situation here, which didn't feel all that precarious anymore. She felt giddy, whimsical, her head spinning.

"I didn't realize you were such a bad influence on Lottie, getting her drunk and all," he said playfully.

"It was just once!" she protested, laughing.

"I should have intervened to save her from your corrupting influence!"

"You tried. Remember? It didn't work." It was wrong to be cavorting with him like this, but it felt so good.

"I didn't really try. I was being nice," he said. "I felt sorry for you, all alone there in your castle. The beautiful, unhappy princess."

She knew he was teasing, but did he really consider her "beautiful"?

"You're still shivering. Your lips are blue." He tilted the spout of the flask against his fingers and then touched his moistened forefinger to her lips. Just like that. He was touching her, his finger tentatively on her lips.

She should have stopped him. But she didn't, and he moved closer. He poured more brandy onto his fingers and ran his forefinger back and forth on her lips, gently, but less tentatively.

"They're still blue," he said softly, offering up a facade, in case she wanted one, that his gesture had something to do with making her warm.

Again, she didn't stop him. Her head kept spinning; round and round it went.

He moved closer still, looked straight into her eyes, as if waiting for a hint of resistance that didn't come. He let his finger wander beyond her lips, onto the rest of her face. It was, of course, outrageous that he was doing this, downright disrespectful.

She touched his finger to stop him. But she didn't stop him. She just let her finger rest on his. Her hand was cold, and he took it in his and gently kissed the back of it, blowing warm breath on it. Then his arm was around her, and he was pulling her close to him.

Everything about this was wrong. Except that here, now, it didn't matter. Or at least she didn't care. Nothing mattered but this.

There was a sound outside, a rustling of branches, close to the cabin. They stopped, and then heard it again.

"My God," she whispered.

More rustling.

Sam went outside to investigate. She could hear him moving about out there in the dark, whacking at branches and bushes. Norbert would have every right to kill them if he caught them together like this.

Then Sam reappeared in the doorway. "Whatever it was, it seems to have gone."

He put more wood on the fire and then sat back down beside her.

He reached over and put his arm around her again. But this time, instinctively, she turned her face slightly away. She didn't mean to rebuff him. But there was something a little too familiar, a little too certain, about the way he'd approached her just now. She wanted to talk about the noise in the woods, not just resume where they'd left off, as if it were clear where they were going. She was not at all sure where they were going.

After that, Sam backed off. She had expected him to simply slow down, approach her more tentatively, more respectfully. She wanted him to recognize the difficulty, even impossibility, of her situation, which he'd implicitly acknowledged with his initial cautiousness. But now he seemed to take her slight hesitation — surely reasonable under the circumstances! — as rejection. At least, he didn't try again.

He didn't seem angry, however. It was as if he saw the wisdom in her rebuff. She lay down next to Emma, and he came over and arranged the blankets around the two of them. It was an affectionate gesture, but no more than that.

He went back outside and returned with more wood, then tended to the fire. She wanted to say something to him, something that would revive the playfulness that had sprung up so effortlessly between them only a short while ago. But he was farther away now and wasn't looking at her, no longer consuming her hungrily with his eyes.

After a while, he wrapped himself in a blanket and then lay down on the other side of the room.

There was so much to relive in her thoughts — the panic as the carriage went off the bridge, Emma disappearing into the river, Norbert's desperate thrashing, the water, the cold ... Sam's caressing finger. He had touched her, sending a charge through her, like nothing she'd ever experienced. Despite the horror of everything that had happened, there was the thrill of Sam's touch. She relived the memory of it over and over and over.

Callandra awoke feeling feverish, with a throbbing headache and sharp pain in her throat. The fire in the stove had gone out overnight and the cabin was cold again.

"I should go back and look for Norbert's body," said Sam, working to restart the fire. "It may have washed up on shore overnight."

"Yes … of course," said Callandra.

Even in the light of morning, she couldn't summon any grief over Norbert's death, if indeed he was dead. For the first time, however, she pondered the word "widow." That's what she probably was now — a widow, and a pregnant one.

"Did Father drown?" asked Emma softly, from her nest in the blankets.

"Yes … I think so," said Callandra, rocking her daughter, unsure of what the girl was feeling.

"Will we have to go back to Glasgow and to Grandmother?" asked Emma, her voice heavy with emotion.

"I don't know. First, we have to make it to Goderich."

Sam went to ready the horse, and Callandra, wrapped in a blanket, followed him outside.

"I apologize for my behaviour last night," he said.

"Oh no," she stammered. "No need to apologize. You saved our lives."

"My driving was reckless," he said. "I take full responsibility for what happened. I endangered us all."

"No —"

"But that's not what I mean," he continued. "I mean, I'm sorry about my behaviour *here* last night.

"You needn't be."

She felt crestfallen. She wanted him to share her excitement about what had happened between them, not be full of regrets.

"I got you drunk and then took advantage of you," he continued.

"No — I was cold and you made me warm."

"And how are you feeling today?" he asked, ending the topic of their intimacy.

"My throat is terribly sore."

He felt her forehead. "Oh, you're sick," he said. "We've got to get you to Goderich right away."

He insisted they press on, saying he would return later to search for Norbert's body. He estimated it was ten or fifteen miles to Goderich. It would be a difficult trek in the rain, which had just resumed with considerable force.

He helped Emma and Callandra onto the horse's back, their clothes already wet from the rain after drying overnight.

"The logs are really slippery," he said. "I'll walk, so I can better guide the horse."

Without him up there, it felt precarious on top of the horse — too high off the ground — especially when the animal started moving. Callandra held on to the mane and tried to keep Emma in place. There was none of the exhilaration she'd felt the night before. She began wondering if he was anxious to get them to Goderich so that he could then leave for Toronto. Suddenly, the prospect of him departing loomed huge in her mind, crowding out thoughts of Norbert's death, of her widowhood, of her pregnancy.

There was no one else on the road. Callandra's headache was getting worse, and it was sharply painful to swallow. She felt feverish and nauseous as well. Trying to steady herself, she felt more and more that she needed to lie down.

The rain had stopped, so they pulled up by a stream for water and rest. Sam helped them off the horse, and laid Callandra gently on the ground. She fell asleep for a while and then woke up, feeling worse, with sharp pains now in her stomach.

"I think I should go for help," he said. "On horseback, I can probably get to Goderich and back in an hour."

Emma vetoed that idea so emphatically that it was unnecessary for Callandra to express her opposition as well.

There was always the possibility that someone would come by in a wagon but, as the day wore on, that seemed less and less likely. The air was getting colder. And with a wet blanket around her, she felt thoroughly chilled. In the strongest voice she could muster, she announced she felt able to continue the trek.

"Can you sit up on the horse alone?" Sam asked Emma.

She nodded that she could.

"Then I'll carry your mother."

The rain began again as he put Emma back up on the horse. Then he lifted Callandra, cradling her in his arms, and continued down the road.

They walked a long time. It was dark when Emma noticed the farmhouse with a curl of smoke rising from the chimney. She ran up and knocked on the door. Everything happened quickly after that.

"My mother is very sick," she said to the wispy-looking man who was shocked to find a little girl, soaking wet, standing in his doorway.

"Can you help us?" called Sam as he approached the house, still carrying Callandra. They, too, were drenched.

"Aye! Come in, come in," said the man, as a woman appeared behind him, straining to see over his shoulder. "I'll go for the doctor."

Callandra had been drifting in and out of a fevered sleep the whole time she had been in Sam's arms. All she would later remember was the feeling, as he carried her into the house, that everything would be all right now that they had made it to Goderich.

Emma watched as Sam laid her mother out on a bed, with the family crowding around to help.

The house smelled deliciously of roast chicken, and Emma allowed an older lady to take her into the kitchen, with the promise of hot soup.

The woman took off Emma's wet outer clothing, directed her to a little seat by the woodstove and wrapped a knitted shawl around her shoulders.

"Don't worry, dear, your mother is going to be all right. Everything's going to be fine now," she said.

Emma just sat quietly by the stove, wary, but enjoying the heat.

"What's your name, dear?" said the lady, who spoke in a thick Glasgow accent and reminded Emma of her grandmother, although this lady was nicer.

"Emma ... Emma Scott."

"I'm just going to heat this up some more," said the woman, moving a pot to the front of the stove and stirring it with a large spoon. There were three children, all smaller than Emma, playing on the floor nearby.

"Scott? Scott!" the woman suddenly exclaimed. "The preacher from Glasgow? You're not the preacher's daughter?"

"Yes," said Emma.

"Oh, my heavens!" the woman exclaimed. "Whatever happened? We've been expecting you — but not like this!"

"Well, the horses were going so fast," began Emma, "because Sam was trying to get us to Goderich by nightfall."

"What? Who's Sam? The carriage driver?" asked the woman.

"Yes. And then the carriage fell off the bridge."

"Oh, my Lord!" The lady stared at Emma with horror.

"And we were all in the water."

"No!"

"Yes," said Emma, pleased to be able to report what they'd been through. "And then we spent the night in a cabin in the woods."

"You stayed the night in the woods?"

"Yes, in a cabin."

"Oh, gracious," said the lady, as she ladled soup into a cup and passed it to Emma. "The important thing is at least you're all safe now."

"Yes, we're safe now. Sam rescued us. But he couldn't rescue one of the horses. He drowned."

"Who drowned?" the woman asked, confused.

"The horse."

"Oh dear."

"— and my father drowned, too."

"What? What do you mean? You said you were all safe?"

"No."

"Child, what are you saying?" She sounded suddenly reproachful.

"My father drowned," Emma repeated.

"I should think you'd be more upset if your father had drowned!" The lady now seemed very much like her grandmother. Her face had the same stern, sharp, disapproving look.

Emma, afraid to say more, remained silent.

"It's naughty to make things up, you know," the lady continued. "Your father seems fine, just upset about your mother's sickness."

Emma still said nothing, didn't know what to say.

"You meant the carriage driver drowned. Is that what you meant?" the lady asked.

"No."

The woman looked at her harshly. Emma paused for a few moments, then changed her answer: "I mean, yes."

She wasn't quite sure why she lied, except that the lady was angry, and that was what she wanted to hear.

While the woman tended to the other children, Emma quietly got up and went into the bedroom. She watched in silence as a younger woman applied a damp cloth to her mother's forehead, then put the cloth back in a basin of water, squeezed it tightly and reapplied it. Her mother was groaning. Sam stood silent at the end of the bed.

The young woman passed him the damp cloth as she left for the kitchen to prepare a hot drink for her patient. "Just keep applying it. I'll be back shortly."

Sam took over, doing as instructed. Emma went and stood beside him, looking down at her mother, whose eyes were closed. Despite the attentive care, she didn't look any better. Her moaning continued, and she reached out her hand. Both Sam and Emma held on to it, reassuring her.

After her mother seemed to drift back to sleep, Emma said to Sam: "That lady with grey hair thinks you're my father."

"You should have told her your father is dead," he said.

"I tried to. But she wouldn't listen."

"All right. Don't worry. I'll tell her," he said. "Run over and get that blanket there."

Emma retrieved the blanket and helped Sam put it over her mother, then wiped her brow.

"Sam?"

"Aye?"

"Please don't tell."

"Don't tell what?"

"That you're not my father."

He looked down at her. "But I'm not your father, Emma."

"But we could say you were, couldn't we?"

"No." His tone was firm.

She said nothing.

"You can't pretend about things like that," he said, softening his voice. She was only five, after all. "It's too important."

"But nobody would have to know," she said, reluctant to give up. "We could keep it a secret."

"No. We can't do that."

"Why not?"

"It's wrong. Besides, people would find out."

"Not if we don't tell them. Please." She looked up pleadingly. "Otherwise, they'll say I lied. And they'll send me and Momma back to Scotland. I know they will. I don't want to go back there. I hate it there. Please."

"Emma, it's impossible."

The thought of returning to live in her grandmother's house in Glasgow brought a rush of tears to her eyes.

"Ple-ease."

"No."

There was a knock on the bedroom door, and Sam opened it to find the young woman excitedly ushering in the doctor, a balding man with a medical bag.

"Thank you for coming so quickly," said Sam, moving to get out of his way.

"How is she?" the doctor asked, proceeding directly to the bed, followed by the young woman and her mother.

"She seems to be in a lot of pain. And we can't get her fever down," said Sam.

"How long has she had the fever?" asked the doctor as he began examining her.

"I didn't notice it until this morning ... but it may have started in the night. We had a terrible accident yesterday, and ended up in the river. We were all soaking wet."

"You spent the night in a cabin?" asked the older woman.

"Yes, we were out of the rain. But it was still cold in the cabin. She was shivering badly all night. Early this morning she complained of a sore throat."

Sam stood back from the bed. His glance met Emma's. Her crying had stopped and she looked at him with huge, hopeful eyes.

"She's pregnant, right?" the doctor asked Sam.

"Uh, yes."

The doctor began undoing the buttons at the top of Callandra's dress.

"Perhaps the child should leave the room," the doctor said softly.

Sam took Emma by the hand and together they left the room, retreating to the little parlour, where they sat alone. He couldn't stand to look at Emma, couldn't face those pleading eyes. They sat there like that for a long time.

Finally, the doctor came out, followed by the two women. They were joined in the parlour by the older man who had first greeted them at the door.

"I am sorry to be the bearer of tragic news," the doctor announced grimly. "But your wife has just miscarried, Reverend."

The older woman sighed heavily, and her daughter turned to Sam and said how deeply sorry she was.

"Her fever has broken, and I don't think she has pneumonia," the doctor continued. "She'll need lots of rest and care. But I do believe, God willing, she'll be well again."

"Thank you, Doctor," was all Sam said.

The doctor gave further instructions for Callandra's care and then took his leave.

"You'll stay with us here, of course," the young woman said to Sam. "We're Presbyterians, you know."

"Oh."

"In a few days, if your wife feels up to it, we can move you to your new house. It's modest, but cheerful. I helped with the preparations. My husband's gone to let everyone know you've arrived. In the meantime, let's get you something to eat."

Then, taking Sam's hand and squeezing it warmly, she added: "I'm so sorry about your loss. But I do want to tell you, on behalf of the Presbyterian community of Goderich, how happy we are that you're here."

--- * ---

Callandra woke up, drenched in sweat.

"How do you feel?" Sam asked.

"Not so good," she answered. "Where are we?"

"Goderich," he said. "You've miscarried."

"Yes," she mumbled. "I know."

She was too weak and exhausted to even begin to think of how she felt about that.

"These are very kind people who are taking care of you," Sam continued. "But there's been a big misunderstanding …"

"About what?" she asked.

Emma leaned over her mother and whispered enthusiastically, "We're going to pretend Sam is my father."

"No, we're not going to do that," said Sam calmly. "But that's the misunderstanding. They think I'm Reverend Scott."

"What? Why do they think that?"

"They just assumed it … the way we were behaving, like a family. And they knew we'd spent the night in the cabin together. Then the doctor asked me if you were pregnant … and I said yes."

"Why can't we pretend?" interjected Emma, her voice rising above a whisper in her excitement. Both Callandra and Sam simultaneously said, "Shhhhh."

"They really believe he's my father," Emma continued, dropping her voice. "They keep calling him 'Reverend.'"

"I better clarify this right now," said Sam with resolution. "I'm sorry I didn't do it sooner. It just seemed like the wrong time. I'll tell them there's been a misunderstanding."

"But isn't it too late for that?" asked Callandra, as the pieces started falling into place in her mind. "What are you going to say — that you're not my husband, but we spent the night together in a cabin?"

"We needed shelter. Your husband had just died. Surely no one would imagine anything happening under such circumstances," Sam protested.

They looked at each other. Last night seemed impossibly far away.

"I should leave," he said.

"No!" she said instinctively.

Even in her confused state, Callandra sensed the worst of all possible options would be Sam's departure. Not only would she be a destitute widow, but she'd be a woman who had stayed with a man in compromising circumstances only hours after her husband's death.

"Should I stay then? Do you want me to stay?" he asked.

"I don't want to hold you back, if you'd like to go. I know you don't want to be in Goderich ... You've helped us enough already."

"Oh, please, please don't go, Sam," said Emma, her voice rising again and tears welling up in her eyes.

They were silent as Emma cried, her little body clamped onto her mother.

"I'll stay," Sam said to Callandra, "at least until you've recovered and we can figure out what to do."

"That's probably the best — for now," she replied, sounding exhausted and considerably more indifferent than she felt.

Chapter Fourteen

Dressed in coat, hat and muff, Lottie was sitting in the parlour when Blair arrived. She still looked pale, but there was no disguising the natural beauty of her face. Walking with her toward the carriage, even with only Mrs. Tinsdale watching, he felt proud.

That feeling was amplified as they descended from the carriage at the main steps of St. Andrew's Presbyterian Church. There was always a good turnout at St. Andrew's on Sunday morning, but this crowd was bigger than usual, no doubt because of the congregation's keen interest in getting a good look at one of the candidates for the minister's post.

Virtually everyone Blair knew was there. He had told some acquaintances that he'd been making visits to a convalescing young woman at the request of a fellow clergyman's wife, but he was sure that none of them had imagined he would bring her to church, or that she would be so pretty. As they walked up the aisle and found seats in a pew near the front, Blair nodded to a few people, pleased that their eyes were straying onto the fetching creature at his side, so comfortably perched on his arm.

Was such vanity not an insult to God? Blair felt confident that it wasn't; his certainty rooted in his belief that his feelings toward Lottie were honourable and in keeping with his service to the Lord. Blair often felt uncomfortable in church, unnerved by his failure to focus sufficiently on spiritual matters. But, with Lottie beside him, her gentle voice audible to him during the reading of scripture and singing of hymns, he felt a oneness with the church. As he looked around, he was struck anew by the majesty of the sanctuary, the glory depicted in the stained glass, the grace of the vaulted ceilings.

He even felt a twinge of sympathy for poor McAndrew who, despite a composed exterior, was almost certainly nervous as he waited to be called upon to give his sermon. Blair noticed that McAndrew's head seemed slightly too large for his body — a discrepancy particularly evident in the religious frock he was wearing.

Lottie leaned in Blair's direction. "He doesn't look much like a defector," she whispered, the brim of her hat brushing against his head.

Her gesture was at once exhilarating and worrying. It suggested a thrilling intimacy between them, but the word "defector" — even if only whispered in that gentle voice — was unsettling, here in church of all places. He discreetly looked around. Surely he was fretting needlessly. There was no evidence that the rumour about the two Presbyterian ministers visiting the archdiocese had gotten around; certainly none that he was implicated in it.

Lottie smiled at him. Was there a touch of the coquette in that smile? he wondered.

McAndrew presented his sermon. Blair was reminded once again what a gift the man had with words.

On the carriage ride home, it was clear to Blair that the outing had been a success. Lottie said she was tired but happy that she had gone. And she perked up when Blair mentioned that Reverend Joshua Stephens would be giving a sermon next week, and then the congregation would vote the following week.

"Have there been any rumours of Reverend Stephens defecting?" she asked.

"Oh no," said Blair, wondering if it had been a mistake to mention the defections to her. "Would you like to come to Reverend Stephens's sermon?" he asked, astonished by his comfort level.

"Yes," she said softly, and then, again, flashed that coquettish smile. "I don't think Reverend McAndrew is a defector."

"No, I'm sure he's not," said Blair, anxious to disassociate himself from such a malicious rumour. "What did you think of his sermon?"

"It seemed a little flat," she said.

His relief that she hadn't been overly impressed by McAndrew was mixed with a feeling of deflation that she didn't share his appreciation of the beauty and power of the sermon.

"Except for the part about the axletree of love," she continued. "I liked that."

The caring and attention of the Presbyterian women of Goderich was considerable. Half a dozen of them showed up to transport the new pastor, his family, and their horse to the cottage that had been made ready for them. Bundled in blankets as they drove through the town, Callandra was struck by the decent, respectable feeling of Goderich, despite its primitive roads and humble dwellings. Certainly, the presence of these reputable women gave the place a very different air than the grungy outposts they'd encountered on the journey here. The cottage was small and rustic, but the women had made it clean and comfortable. A kindly lady called Mrs. Talbot ensured that everything was taken care of, and made it clear she wanted nothing in return but Callandra's recovery. Amid the warmth, Callandra was tempted to forget the situation was steeped in duplicity.

It was surprising that Sam had been so easily mistaken for the new minister. The misunderstanding was based on nothing more than the confused conversation that first evening between Emma and the grandmother. The next morning, Sam had confirmed Emma's story that there'd been an accident and the hired man accompanying them had drowned. This then was the account the town heard, and people simply believed it. A small group of Presbyterian men had gone back to the site of the broken bridge to look for the body. When they'd found nothing after searching up and down the riverbank, that was the end of the matter. It was a testament to how little attention was paid to the lives of workers that there were few follow-up questions about the hired man. Mrs. Carmichael, the young woman who had cared for Callandra the first night, asked if he had had a wife and children, and was assured he'd had no dependents. Beyond that, there seemed to be little curiosity or concern about him, nor grounds for questioning the basic story about the accident.

Even if the townspeople weren't suspicious, there was still much to fear. Callandra was haunted by the thought that Norbert had somehow survived and would show up in Goderich sooner or later. And Sam was deeply uncomfortable posing as Norbert. He was adamant that, once she was settled and well, he couldn't stay on in Goderich, that, even if he were willing to be so dishonest, he'd almost certainly be caught and the consequences would be severe — for all of them. Callandra didn't argue with any of this.

It occurred to her, however, that Sam could take her and Emma with him when he went. There was nothing to keep any of them in Goderich now. She felt sure that if she asked him, he would agree to escort them back, but he never mentioned this possibility. He simply talked about how he had to go. All this led her to conclude that he didn't feel as strongly about her as she did about him.

As she drifted in and out of sleep those first few weeks, she worried about the possibility that Norbert might suddenly appear, and how enraged he would be that they had abandoned him. His retribution would be brutal.

But, despite her fears, mostly she thought about those fleeting moments when Sam had placed his finger so tenderly on her shivering lips. Why didn't he try to revive their physical intimacy? She wanted to believe his reticence stemmed from a reluctance to impose himself on her now that circumstances had bound them together, ostensibly as husband and wife. He slept alone in the tiny extra bedroom; Mrs. Talbot had decided that was best until Callandra recovered. Most men would have taken advantage of the situation, forcing themselves on her and then departing, likely with her gold. When she thought about it this way, Sam's reserve was admirable, even chivalrous, and fit well with her new sense of him as honourable. It was she who yearned for something dishonourable.

For now at least, it seemed she would have to settle for him being warm and supportive, which was at least comforting. He and Emma would often sit by her bed. He'd read to her from a newspaper that he'd bought in town or sometimes from *A Vindication of the Rights of Woman* — one of her few personal belongings to survive the accident.

She was impressed by how well he read — just as Lottie said — and it was to his credit that he willingly read material that he probably found uninteresting or even silly. Callandra wondered what he thought of the book's negative depiction of female behaviour aimed at pleasing men. It was hard to tell from his expression.

> Gentleness, docility, and spaniel-like affection are, on this ground consistently recommended as the cardinal virtues of the sex; and disregarding the arbitrary economy of nature, one writer has

declared that it is masculine for a woman to be melancholy. She was created to be the toy of man, his rattle, and it must jingle in his ears whenever, dismissing reason, he chooses to be amused.

Emma interrupted, asking him to read that part again, apparently pleased by the references to things she could understand — "toy" and "rattle."

He obliged, shaking his head when saying "rattle," to her amusement.

This was another aspect of his new identity; he had stepped into the role of Emma's father with ease and believability. The girl told her mother about how Sam took her for walks around town on his shoulders, how he was teaching her to ride the horse and to stack wood after he chopped it. She had taken readily to calling him Papa, and clearly lapped up the fatherly attention he bestowed on her, having never experienced any before.

"What is the toy of man?" asked Emma.

"Women are created to be the toy of man ... at least that's what the book says," he replied. "But the lady who wrote it doesn't think they should be the toy of men."

"Do *you* think they should be the toy of men?" asked Emma.

"If they want to be ..." he said.

Callandra wasn't sure what to make of this answer. He seemed to be disagreeing with Mary Wollstonecraft, but perhaps he was just trying to humour Emma.

He continued reading, and soon Callandra fell asleep. When she awoke, he and Emma were still sitting there, watching over her.

"How are you feeling?" he asked.

"A little better."

"Good."

They fell into silence.

"The suit looks good on you," she said eventually. It did.

"It's the third one. I told him that's enough." The local tailor was a Presbyterian who insisted on making complimentary suits to replace the ones the town's new pastor had lost in the unfortunate accident.

"You're looking like a minister."

She regretted her words, knowing how much he disliked the pretense, even if he hadn't done much pretending. Although his accent suggested humble roots, he displayed sufficient command of English grammar and vocabulary that it seemed plausible that he'd been educated for the clergy. He didn't wear a clerical collar, but they were optional for Presbyterian ministers, even back in Scotland. Altogether, he was presenting himself convincingly as a Presbyterian minister without altering his look or behaviour much at all.

"I don't feel like a damn minister," he said. His tone was light and they both smiled.

"And I don't feel like a minister's wife. I'm sorry my recovery is taking so long," she said.

"You can't help it," he said. She wanted him to say something like "I just want to be here with you, no matter what." But he didn't.

"I was thinking we should write to Lottie," she said.

"Yes, I've been thinking about that," he answered. "But I don't know if we can trust the mail here."

"Well, we wouldn't have to tell her everything in the letter."

"I could never mislead her."

"Of course not. I wasn't suggesting that ... we could just let her know we're safe."

"I suppose."

He urged her to get back to sleep. He moved closer and, for a moment, she thought he might lean down and kiss her. But he only adjusted her coverlet and then went out, leaving her feeling upset about what he'd said. He seemed to be suggesting she was comfortable with dishonesty, when it was he who was proving truly good at deception.

―――― ✦ ――――

Had settlers arrived in the Goderich area to find viable roads, sturdy bridges, and a functioning mill, it's unlikely that the lack of a local Presbyterian minister would have been regarded as an undue hardship. But Thomas Mercer Jones, commissioner of the Canada Company, had no intention of fixing the real problems settlers faced trying to survive on the land the Company sold them; that would have been costly for the Company, annoying the directors back in London. By comparison, providing a small subsidy for the upkeep of a local Presbyterian clergyman was a cost-effective gesture.

But what was to be done with a clergyman who didn't preach? It was at least three weeks after Sam's arrival in Goderich before Jones even became aware of this situation. The commissioner knew that the new minister and his family had been involved in a bridge accident on their way to town. Indeed, the accident had necessitated repairs to the bridge and revived complaints about the poor quality of many bridges in the Huron Tract. Now reports that the new pastor seemed to have little interest in preaching threatened to arouse further local dissatisfaction. Accordingly, Jones had him summoned.

Sam arrived at Jones's imposing house — a mansion by Goderich standards — in his newly tailored suit and was ushered into a book-lined study. The room had a window overlooking an ample stretch of property and, beyond that, the lake. Sam was directed to sit in a chair that faced away from the window so that only Jones, seated at a fine oak desk, could see the spectacular view.

The commissioner was in his early forties, but with his officious and petulant manner, he seemed older. He had thinning dark hair and wide sideburns that covered much of his lower face, framing his mouth. His eyes were overshadowed by heavy, dark eyebrows that grew almost together. He had a slim build, and his suit was immaculate, set off by starched white collar and cuffs.

"I'm sorry to hear that your wife isn't well. I trust she's recovering," said Jones, glancing up from his papers at Sam with minimal interest. A Presbyterian clergyman was a lowly paid employee of a secondary church, although the "man of God" designation bestowed some stature.

"Yes, there's progress, but the doctor said that it would take a while."

"Where were you educated, Reverend?"

"University of Glasgow."

"Hmm," replied Jones, looking Sam over with more curiosity. The sheer size of the man was notable, unusual in a clergyman.

"I spent a lot of time as a pastor at the orphans' mission in Glasgow. After a while, I started to talk like them, I guess."

"Hmm," Jones repeated, knitting his eyebrows together. "I'm sure your people would like to know when you'll begin preaching."

"Well, sir, I'm keen to begin, but there's nowhere to do so. As you know, this town lacks a Presbyterian church."

"Ah, that doesn't matter," Jones said, waving cigar smoke away from his face in a dismissive gesture. "There are plenty of barns — or even a tavern — that could double as a church for the time being."

"They seem unsuitable, sir."

"You'll recall, Reverend, that our Lord was born in a stable."

"Aye, and lived in poverty, but he was a special case, you must admit. We haven't always followed his example perfectly," said Sam, looking around the ornate room. This bordered on impertinence, and the commissioner's stern features tightened.

Sam added, "I see the Anglicans have a fine church in Goderich."

This struck Jones as a contentious comment, given the Clergy Reserves controversy.

"I propose to build as fine a church for the Presbyterians here," Sam continued.

"Reverend," Jones said. "You are aware that the Company contributes to your salary?"

"Yes, sir."

"How would you like it if the Company were to withdraw that support until you begin preaching?"

"I wouldn't mind, sir," said Sam. "That seems like a fair solution."

Jones returned to his work as soon as Sam had been ushered out. The pastor's acceptance of his pay cut meant that the meeting had ended cordially, if a little abruptly. Still, Jones felt displeased that the clergyman, when confronted with power and authority, hadn't become more clearly submissive.

---- ✱ ----

On his way home, Sam encountered a small gathering of men milling about outside Feltie's Tavern. They crowded around him, keen to find out what had happened at his meeting with the commissioner. He had met some of them already and found them welcoming, but he now wondered if they had been complaining about his failure to preach, prompting the summons from Jones.

"I told him we needed a Presbyterian church here in Goderich, but he made it clear the Company won't be helping build the church — or contributing to the minister's salary," said Sam.

This provoked grumbling against the Company. The men knew that the Company had pledged to subsidize the minister's salary — even though Sam hadn't known — and they now regarded the cancellation of that pledge as an insult to the Presbyterian community. Sam did not mention the reason why Jones was refusing to pay him.

"But that shouldn't stop us," he continued. "We can build the church ourselves."

The men looked skeptical; it sounded as if Sam expected them to build him a church.

"Actually, I'm going to build it myself," he said. While the notion of a pastor constructing his own church was far-fetched, Sam was no ordinary-looking pastor. With his strapping physique, he looked capable of realizing such an ambitious plan.

"Of course, I'd be grateful for any help," he added. "I propose to start right away. We should be looking for a site."

Whatever hostility might have been building toward Sam, he easily shifted to the usual targets of resentment — Thomas Mercer Jones and the Canada Company. The men offered their new pastor sympathy for the unfair way the Company was treating him. Just about everybody offered to help build the church, leading to a great deal of camaraderie. After several rounds of drinks at Feltie's, Sam led the group to a magnificent spot on the hill overlooking the lake — a spot he had noticed a few hours earlier on his way to see Jones. He told the men, with the air of a declaration, that this was the perfect site for their new church.

Jones was notified by his butler that a rowdy crowd was passing by on the road in front of the house. From an upstairs window, he watched as the troop of Presbyterians hooted and caroused on a nearby stretch of the bluff. Like his own property, it was one of the choicest pieces of land in the Huron Tract, if not the entire colony. Without giving it much thought, Jones had assumed that this prime spot would someday be part of a fine estate belonging to a distinguished family of Anglican stock.

He certainly had no intention of allowing a squalid Presbyterian church to be built there. But the intensity of emotions displayed by the boisterous crowd convinced him that it would be best if the

Presbyterians had a church. And since the Company owned all of the land in the Huron Tract, Jones decided to let them have a tiny plot on the outskirts of town, near where the Company planned to build a jail.

———— ✱ ————

Sam's plan for the church would have to be scaled back, given the limited building materials the Company was willing to provide. Even so, there was lots of enthusiasm for the project among the Presbyterians and work began almost immediately.

Sam was the first to show up at the construction site every morning, having figured out plans for that day's work before the others arrived. He quickly assessed the abilities of the other men and assigned tasks accordingly, always taking the most difficult or arduous tasks for himself. Before long, they had abandoned the formality of "Reverend" and were just calling him "Bert" — which, everyone agreed over ale at Feltie's one night, suited him much better than "Norbert."

It was common for a small group of Presbyterian onlookers to gather at the site, watching the progress. So Sam hadn't noticed one afternoon, a couple of weeks into the project, that the group was bigger than usual.

"Would you just say a few spiritual words to us?" asked a middle-aged woman wearing a red woollen cloak on this brisk but bright autumn day.

Sam hadn't seen her approaching. Surprised by the request, at first he just smiled.

"Not a sermon," she continued. "Just a few words of spiritual guidance."

"Oh, uh, uh, yes ... yes, of course," he said awkwardly.

"That would be wonderful," said the woman. She had soft grey eyes and a warm look of anticipation.

Sam finished packing up his tools, hoping the woman would leave now that she had extracted a commitment from him. But she stayed, along with the dozen or so men and women arrayed behind her, as well as his co-workers.

"When would you like me to do that?" asked Sam.

"Well ... now?"

"Now?"

He soon found himself being led by the group a short distance down the road to a small farmstead, where they were met by another couple dozen enthusiastic Presbyterians. In the modest yard, wooden chairs and benches had been arranged in a fashion designed to resemble the pews of a church, with bundles of hay providing additional seating. A small table with a toolbox, wrapped in a ribbon, served as a makeshift pulpit. Everyone was smiling.

"We're so grateful you're building a church. But in the meantime, please accept our modest outdoor church," said the woman in the red cloak, with chickens running loose at her feet. "We want you to feel at home here."

Sam stood among the enthusiastic Presbyterians, smiling back at them. "This is very thoughtful of you," he said.

There was an awkward silence, prompting him to repeat his appreciation.

"Thank you for coming to Goderich," said one of the men, whom Sam recognized to be from the Carmichael family, who had taken him in the first night in Goderich.

"I'm glad to be here," he said. "And thank you for all the help you've given Callandra. Now I think I should go and attend to her."

"Oh, please, Reverend," said the woman in red. "Could you just give us a few spiritual words? It would mean so much."

To underline the entreaty, the parishioners started sitting down on the benches, chairs, and bundles of hay. Soon all were seated.

Then the woman with the red cloak hummed and, at the stroke of her hand, they all rose and began to sing.

"Holy, holy, holy ... Lord God Almighty ... early in the morning, our song shall rise to thee ..."

They had clearly practiced for this moment. Sam stood listening to their gentle harmony, feeling increasingly trapped.

"Holy, holy, holy! All the saints adore thee; casting down their golden crowns around the glassy sea; cherubim and seraphim falling down before thee, which wert, and art, and evermore shalt be."

The parishioners grew more animated with each verse, thrilled to be singing this rousing hymn for their new minister, sheer joy evident on their faces.

"Holy, holy, holy! Lord God Almighty!" they pealed out the words, moving toward a rapturous crescendo.

"All thy works shall praise thy name, in earth and sky and sea. Holy, holy, holy! Merciful and mighty, God in three persons, blessed Trinity."

The hymn was over and they all took their seats. Now only the gentle chirping sounds of the barnyard could be heard.

Slowly Sam went to the front and stood behind the pulpit, looking out at his congregation. He didn't recall much about the Presbyterian services he'd attended as a ward of the Glasgow orphanage, except that he'd been impatient for them to end.

"The Lord is thy shepherd," he said, dredging up the words from his memory. "Thou shall not want."

But he couldn't remember what came next. He stood speechless, all eyes upon him.

"Actually, that's not correct," he said. "The Lord is your shepherd. But you *do* want."

They stared at him, blank-faced.

"Yes, that's the truth: you *do* want. I mean, there are many basic things you are in need of, and that you should have," he said, a train of thought forming in his mind.

"Here we are in the New World, in a land where the earth yields much bounty," he continued, finding his words as he went. "But, already, so much of that bounty has been claimed by a small group of people — just like in the old world."

These thoughts were a variation of what he'd read in pamphlets put out by the radicals in Toronto, and in keeping with themes from the workers' journals back in Scotland.

The crowd looked at him with curiosity. Nonetheless, he was saying something he believed in. And so, at this makeshift pulpit before this adoring makeshift flock, he began to feel a certain rhythm, even a conviction, his voice gaining strength and resonance as the moments passed.

"You, who work with your hands, to till the soil — its bounty belongs to you," he said. "When Jesus came to earth, he didn't live in riches and splendour — like some people do, even right here in Goderich!"

There were muffled sounds as members of the congregation whispered to each other.

"Ya!" yelled out one boy, who looked on the verge of manhood.

"Can you lead us in prayer?" said an older man, toward the back of the gathering.

"Yes … of course," said Sam, wondering if he could remember the words of the prayer he used to recite every morning at the orphanage. *Our Father, who art in heaven, hallowed be thy name …* But he wasn't confident he could remember it all.

"But first, let's hear another joyful song," he suggested.

"We've only practised that one," said the woman in red.

"Well … then, please, sing that one again. It was so beautiful."

The woman hummed, and the parishioners stood and began singing again, led by her strong, tuneful voice. They sang even more robustly than the first time, apparently delighted to be giving a repeat performance at the request of their new minister.

As their voices rang out, Sam could see a man on horseback approaching from down the lane. He wore dark clothes and a leather vest. When he pulled up at the front gate, people seemed to recognize him, but they kept singing — except for a middle-aged man who rose and started toward the gate to speak to the visitor. A girl, about fifteen or sixteen, also rose, and assisted him, as he walked with a pronounced limp.

"Holy, holy, holy! Though the darkness hide thee, though the eye made blind by sin thy glory may not see …"

Sam's hope that the visitor would distract everyone and bring an end to the proceedings quickly faded. The singing simply continued, as the man with the limp stood at the gate speaking with the man on horseback, while the girl watched. The hymn would soon come to an end and then, presumably, there would be fresh requests for a prayer. *Give us this day our daily bread … and forgive us our trespasses …* but what came after that?

The visitor got down from the horse and came through the gate. He was tall, with dark wavy hair, and as he moved closer, the man with the limp backed up awkwardly, tripped, and ended up on the ground. The girl bent over to assist him. At that point, a boy of about twelve bolted from the ranks of the singers and headed to the gate, calling "Papa!" He was followed by a few other smaller children.

The visitor made no effort to help the man to his feet.

Some of the singers looked over now, as the girl tried to help the man up from the ground. Then the visitor pushed the girl aside and leaned over the man on the ground, shouting something at him. The singing stopped and all eyes turned toward the scene by the gate.

Sam strode over and helped the man on the ground to his feet.

"Who the hell are you?" asked the visitor in a broad Irish accent. Although not quite as tall as Sam, he looked tough and menacing.

"I was going to ask you the same question," said Sam, in a more mellow tone.

"I'm Seamus O'Reilly, agent for the Company. Who the hell are you?"

"I'm the new Presbyterian minister."

O'Reilly chortled dismissively. "Well, return to your hymns. You have no business here."

"One of my parishioners seems to need some assistance."

"This man is four months overdue in his payments to the Company," said O'Reilly.

The man with the limp turned to Sam to explain himself: "I hurt my leg. It's taking me longer to get the harvesting done —"

Sam turned to the boy who had run over to help. "Go fetch a chair for your father."

The boy quickly retrieved a rickety wooden chair and helped his father into it. The younger children gathered around him.

Sam then turned to O'Reilly and said calmly: "This man clearly has a family to support. Given the circumstances, I'm sure the Company can make allowances."

By this point, the other parishioners had moved closer to observe what was going on.

O'Reilly looked impatient. "If he wants to get himself hurt, that's his problem. Not mine."

"I'm sure the Company won't go under if they have to wait a little longer for an injured man to make his payment," said Sam.

"That's not the way business is done," snapped O'Reilly. "All I know is the rules of business ... I suppose you think you know the rules of God."

"No, not really," replied Sam. "Just the rules of human decency."

O'Reilly stepped closer to Sam, staring at him fiercely. "Those rules don't interest me, either."

"I can see that," said Sam, stepping back to signal he didn't intend to push things further.

Satisfied by Sam's retreat, O'Reilly turned back to the injured man. "I'll be back, and you better have that money," he said, a half-smile creeping over his face. "You know I don't like to wait."

At that, he kicked the legs of the chair, knocking it over and sending the injured man back onto the ground. The parishioners gasped, but no one moved forward to interfere.

"Leave my father alone!" cried the boy, stepping forward as if to take on the Company agent himself.

"You stupid kid —" said O'Reilly, grabbing the screaming boy and putting his head in a rough chokehold.

Sam moved immediately to extricate the boy. When O'Reilly resisted his intervention, Sam grabbed him with both hands by the collar and shook him hard until he let the lad go. Then Sam pushed O'Reilly through the open gate so forcefully that the agent hit the ground, bumping the back of his horse as he fell. The horse started off down the lane.

O'Reilly lay on the ground for a few moments, apparently stunned by the strength and audacity of the new pastor, then took off down the lane after his horse.

The parishioners looked shocked; nobody had ever challenged the Company like this before.

"I think we'll leave the prayer for another time," Sam said eventually, walking out the gate and closing the latch behind him.

"Aye, of course," said the woman in the red cloak.

All was silent as Sam walked away. As he turned down the narrow path toward his house, the crowd at the gate let out a boisterous cheer.

Chapter Fifteen

"I'm quite astonished by the decision," said Blair. This implied he felt McAndrew's rejection by the St. Andrew's congregation was undeserved, and therefore revealed nothing — he hoped — about the pleasure he took in it.

They were sitting in Mrs. Tinsdale's parlour, which, despite the best efforts of a wood stove, felt cold in the November chill that had set in. Lottie, wrapped in a quilt, showed only limited interest in McAndrew's defeat.

This allowed Blair to dismiss his fear that she fancied McAndrew. He had even wondered if her interest in the notion of McAndrew as a defector had been based on some attraction to the possibility. Blair had heard that a dash of unscrupulousness in a man sometimes attracted the interest of women. So it was a relief for him now to conclude that Lottie was not like this; there was a moral depth to her that, he was sure, was the main source of his attraction.

He had reported the news about McAndrew first. His next bit of news would undoubtedly disappoint her: there had been mail from Goderich that morning, but, once again, nothing for Lottie.

Unlike her reaction to the news about McAndrew, her disappointment this time was palpable. She bit her lip and looked out the window, struggling to compose herself. He felt like a fool for failing to appreciate that McAndrew's employment prospects would rank low in importance compared to the fact that it had been almost two months without word from her brother and her dearest friend.

He quickly pointed out that he could at least confirm that they had arrived safely in Goderich, since he had received a letter that morning from a Goderich parishioner, with references to the new minister. He pulled it from his pocket and passed it to her.

> My dear Reverend Blair:
>
> I trust that this letter will find you well and recovered from your ocean crossing. I write to tell you that the splendid minister you have found for us has brought hope and joy to our community.
>
> I trust also that you will indulge me once again if I remind you, however, of our difficulties here. Many of the families have cleared only an acre or two, and lack sufficient supplies to get through the winter. Our roads are all but impassable for most of the spring and fall, and our bridges in a precarious state. As you know, we have made our complaints countless times to the Company, to no avail. The indifference of the commissioner is the source of much of our discontent.
>
> I particularly want to inform you about one matter. While your colleagues at the Glasgow Colonial Society have been most gracious to provide us with a minister, the Company, through ill will and stinginess, has reneged on

its commitment to contribute to his upkeep. Not even a farthing for himself and his family! I trust you can appreciate how much heavier this makes the burden on the Presbyterian community here.

Our ladies have contributed greatly, especially given that his wife was very sick for several weeks after their difficult trek here. Reverend Scott has not complained, revealing himself to be a true servant of God. Indeed, he has embarked on the building of a church.

We do appreciate that the Society must serve the needs of many congregations. But, given the direness of our circumstances, we humbly submit this request for more assistance.

Your obedient servant,
Wm. J. Cosgrove

"I wonder what happened to Callandra," said Lottie. "It seems she was very sick, but there's so little detail."

"Yes, and no mention at all of your brother," he said.

"Well, that's no surprise," said Lottie, pulling back slightly. "The help is rarely mentioned."

There was an awkward moment, as their different stations in life suddenly created a gulf between them. But, like so much about Lottie, this slight pulling away only made Blair all the more eager to make the connection, to show that he regarded her not as a servant but as his future wife. For one impetuous moment, he contemplated reaching out for her hand, but then realized it was too soon for such intimacy. Besides, the presence of Mrs. Tinsdale, fussing nearby with a tray of biscuits, ruled it out.

It was Lottie who broke the silence. "In fact, the letter tells me everything I need to know about my brother," she said, more cheerful than she'd sounded so far that afternoon. "Reverend Scott may be getting the credit, but it's Sam who's actually building the church."

---- * ----

After weeks convalescing, Callandra was thrilled to be out of bed, feeling significantly better and realizing, with only a touch of guilt, that her prospects for happiness had improved immensely since Norbert's death.

She'd heard that newcomers to the Huron Tract were often disheartened by the roughness of life in the backwoods, but Callandra felt none of this. She was delighted to be free of all the opulence and splendour of the Glasgow mansion. Here, in this crude wooden cottage, she felt a sense of possibility she'd never felt before. She had come to love their little house, with its rudimentary kitchen where they ate together every night, like a family. She had rearranged the simple wooden furniture and brightly coloured cushions in the sitting room, making the room cozier than the way Mrs. Talbot had organized it. She imagined creating a flower garden outside in the spring. She knew she could be happy here, and that this could be home.

It was unnerving, however, to realize that any future happiness she could envisage included Sam. She yearned to be close to him again, to relive the intimacy that had happened so magically between them the night in the cabin. The memory of it was exquisite. No matter how many times she thought back on those moments, they never lost their freshness, their sweetness. They had transformed her life.

Or had she actually been in love with him for years? When she looked back now, it was difficult to imagine she hadn't always appreciated what a striking figure he truly was — so tall and strong and fearless. And, with rugged features, a wide brow, and clear blue eyes — so handsome, too. Not in a standard way. But, yes, handsome.

Maybe she had always seen him that way, but had never let herself indulge where those thoughts would lead. How could she? She'd been married. Beyond that, she and Sam had been rivals over Lottie, and there had been such mistrust and animosity between them. How wrong and unnecessary that all seemed in retrospect! She trusted him now — perhaps more than anyone. He had saved her and Emma from the river. It was only because of him that they'd survived the night in the woods. And with him there that night, even in that isolated cabin, she hadn't felt scared, only protected and safe — and desired. Yes, that was the source of the joy: desiring him and feeling desired by him.

Or had she misread the situation? The physical distance between them now seemed enormous and baffling. In some ways, this was for the best, since it meant that she didn't have to worry about becoming pregnant again. Still, she yearned for his attention, and was saddened that he didn't seem to feel the passion that she did.

She believed that he did, however, and, at times, was sure of it.

One evening, they had an upsetting conversation about how they were deceiving the people of Goderich. It revived her own feelings of guilt, as well as her disappointment that the deception remained his central focus. She withdrew from the conversation to put Emma to bed, and then went about doing household chores. When she climbed onto a chair to reach a bowl, he came over and reached it for her. Then he took her hand to guide her down, holding it just a little longer than necessary, as they both stood facing each other. Their eyes met, and she felt sure in that moment that he wanted her as much as she wanted him.

"We can't do this," he half whispered, withdrawing his hand and moving back a step.

She felt a strange thrill that he was acknowledging there was something compelling between them, something that must be resisted.

She tried to meet his gaze again, but he was no longer looking at her.

"I can't stay," he said.

She had heard him say this many times, and she felt an urge to blurt out that she would go with him, wherever he was going, that she and Emma just wanted to be with him. But this seemed too much to divulge.

"I know," she said. "We can't go on with the deception."

He kept looking away, and she could feel him disengaging.

"There's no reason to stay in Goderich — for any of us," she continued, feeling emotion rising in her voice. "I hate the dishonesty, too."

"I know," he said, looking over at her, "... there are some things I should tell you."

She felt wild with curiosity, but he went silent.

"Please tell me," she urged. But he moved farther away, leaving her feeling completely cut off from him.

After a while, he said: "There's talk of a rebellion against the colonial authorities in Toronto ... if so, I've pledged to join it."

She recoiled in shock, with so many questions crowding into her mind. Was this just a possibility, or was a rebellion actively being planned. If so, when?

Could this be what was holding him back from intimacy with her? Was it possible that he resisted such indulgence, knowing the consequences would fall hardest on her?

One thing was clear: if this was his plan, it would be hard to talk him out of it. A rebellion fit with his radical leanings. He would probably regard rising up against the colonial government as a noble deed — even a duty. She felt grateful at least that he was telling her all this. Joining a rebellion amounted to treason, but he evidently trusted her enough to confide in her.

"Must there be a rebellion? I mean, are there not other ways to bring about change?" she asked, although she realized, from reading the workingmen's journals back in Scotland, such a question might be considered naive.

"Possibly," he said, "but the authorities are completely unresponsive to the people. They routinely reject the reforms passed by the assembly."

She was glad he had treated her question seriously and was formulating a follow-up when he continued.

"Believe me, I want no part of any fighting, if it can be avoided … My father died in an uprising."

"I didn't know that," she said. "Lottie never told me."

"She never knew him. She was so young when he died."

"What was the uprising?" Callandra asked, sensing he wanted to talk about his father.

"It was a labour battle … have you heard of the Radical War?"

She confessed that she hadn't, and regretted not paying more attention to the articles about labour struggles, which had never interested her as much as the ones about the rights of women.

"I was only eight at the time, but I read about it later. My father was a weaver, and there was a big strike after their wages were cut. He was in a march and the police ambushed them near Bonnymuir … I remember the funeral."

"That's awful."

"My mother was already dead. So, after that, I was an orphan."

The story raised so many questions in Callandra's mind. Had his mother died giving birth to Lottie? Did Lottie even know any of this?

"My father was a hero," he continued.

Suddenly Callandra felt that she understood Sam in a whole new way. His father had been on strike, fighting for his rights, when he was killed by police. No wonder Sam had become a radical. No wonder the quest for women's emancipation seemed to him a lesser cause.

Callandra wanted to return to the subject of a possible uprising. But Sam evidently didn't want to talk more about any of this now and went outside to cut wood, leaving her alone with her thoughts.

She wondered if she should just tell him the truth about her feelings for him. There was something blocking her — perhaps a girlish notion that she shouldn't look too eager, that it was up to him to take the initiative in their strange, complicated relationship. Mary Wollstonecraft would surely disagree, dismissing any role for feminine coquetry, insisting a woman openly declare what she wanted.

In principle Callandra agreed, but she wasn't sure she trusted Wollstonecraft on this one. More importantly, she doubted it would make a difference.

---- ✣ ----

Sam's confrontation with the Company agent consolidated his popularity among the Presbyterians of Goderich. Another consequence was Rosalee Calhoun coming to work for Callandra. Rosalee was the girl who had helped her injured father when he was accosted by the Company agent, and she had appeared the next morning to thank Sam for his intervention, offering to help him in any way she could. Mrs. Talbot came up with the idea that Rosalee should become Callandra's housekeeper, for which the Presbyterian community would pay her a small stipend, helping the Calhouns with their financial problems. It seemed an advantageous situation for all.

With Rosalee taking charge of the housekeeping, Callandra had time to indulge in something she truly enjoyed — writing a diary. It wasn't so much a diary as a notebook where she jotted down thoughts and observations that she planned to develop into an essay. Perhaps it was far-fetched, out here in the bush, to dream of being published in one of those fine political journals like *Tait's*. Yet it was part of her sense of emancipation following Norbert's death that she felt free to nurture such a wild, enchanting dream. Living as a family with Sam and Emma — and writing for *Tait's* — was her treasured secret thought, the favoured grove where her mind ended up when she let it wander.

Given the significant help that Rosalee provided, Callandra felt favourably inclined toward her. Even so, she was surprised one afternoon when Rosalee, after mentioning she'd been invited to a barn dance, asked about a dress hanging in Callandra's closet. She had never seen Callandra wear it and wondered if she could try it on.

It was the muslin dress Callandra had switched into the night of the carriage accident. She hadn't worn it since, perhaps because of its jumble of happy-sad memories. Unable to think of a reason to deny Rosalee's request, Callandra said yes.

The pale pink colour didn't go well with Rosalee's reddish hair, but, as she fastened the little buttons through the bodice, it highlighted her fullness of bosom — a fullness that wasn't evident under her usual formless clothing. Rosalee beamed as she pranced around in the dress, catching glimpses of herself in the small mirror on the bedroom wall. Although her face seemed rather ordinary-looking most of the time, when her features were rearranged into a smile, they aligned in a way that made her really quite pretty.

Callandra wanted Rosalee to put the dress back in the closet, but was reluctant to make such a mean-spirited request.

"Oh, it's so beautiful," said Rosalee.

After parading a little longer, Rosalee took it off. She ran her hands lovingly over the soft muslin fabric, hung it back in the closet, then returned to chores in the kitchen.

Callandra sat down to write in her diary, but felt too upset about what had just happened. She, who had so much, had taken umbrage over the wishes of a deprived servant girl! A Wollstonecraft quote intruded into Callandra's thoughts: "The grand source of female folly and vice has ever appeared to me to arise from narrowness of mind." Callandra felt she had exhibited a narrowness of mind toward Rosalee, who had dared to yearn for a dress and then dared to look so sweet in it.

It was getting dark outside when Callandra put away the papers on her small table. Rosalee was preparing dinner, and the smell of roast duck filled the cabin. The poor girl. She had to work so hard, and it took so little — trying on a dress — to delight her.

"I was thinking about the dress," said Callandra as the girl put on her coat. "I was thinking maybe you'd like to wear it to your dance."

Rosalee let out a shriek of joy, leaving Callandra pleased by her own generosity, and prompting her to realize that she, too, needed the affirmation of something pretty.

――― ✽ ―――

Sam and his men were building a scaffold at the construction site when word reached them that the rickety bridge just south of town had collapsed and a boy had been hurt. They rushed to the little creek, where a crowd from town had already gathered, and soon learned that the boy, just a toddler, had drowned, trapped under a cart in the shallow water.

A large man in overalls yelled angrily in a foreign language, even as he stacked potatoes and squash that had fallen from his cart into the water. The crowd stood back, unsure of how to deal with him in his grief and rage.

Sam went straight to where the boy's tiny body had been laid by the creek, and removed the sack covering it. The thin little corpse was pale and cold. While the townspeople watched, Sam took off his own coat and put it around the farmer's shoulders, then helped the man stack his produce.

An adolescent yelled something about marching to the commissioner's house with the dead boy's body, demanding that the Company fix the bridge. A few supportive comments followed, but most of the crowd remained silent.

It was shortly after this outburst that a fine carriage came down the road where the crowd had gathered on the flats near the creek. Whether it had come by chance or design was unclear, but there was brief speculation in the crowd that it contained Mr. Jones himself, since it certainly looked like his carriage and there were few like that in the whole Huron Tract.

The youth who had urged marching to Jones's house spotted this opportunity and walked toward the carriage, yelling about the dead boy and the bridge. The driver quickly manoeuvred to turn the carriage around on the narrow, boggy roadway. As he tried to back up the horses, one of the rear wheels slipped into a rut and became lodged there. By this point, the focus of the crowd had moved from the tragic scene by the creek to the drama unfolding on the roadway. The youth moved closer to the carriage.

"Look what the Company has done!" he shouted. Inside, two ladies appeared frightened. Jones was nowhere to be seen.

"There's a dead boy over there, because the Company wouldn't fix the bridge," shouted the youth, his loose, dishevelled hair flying about his ruddy face.

A few others from the crowd joined him at the carriage, which pivoted back and forth as the driver tried unsuccessfully to free the wheel from the rut. One of the horses reared up on his hind legs. A high-pitched scream from inside the carriage pierced the air.

The crowd continued to gather around, with others yelling about the bridge and the dead child. The youth began rapping on the side of the carriage, prompting the driver to turn around and threaten him with a horsewhip.

Suddenly Sam grabbed the whip from the driver, tossing it on the ground.

"There'll be no whipping. There's been enough suffering here today," Sam said. From inside the carriage, the muffled sound of a girl crying was audible.

"The Company bears responsibility for the tragedy," Sam continued. "But this isn't the way to deal with it."

The townspeople, who had fallen under the spell of the boy with the wild hair, now became quiet again. They watched as Sam walked around to examine the back of the carriage.

"I need some help here," he said.

A few of the men who were helping build the church came forward. Along with Sam, they lifted the vehicle, freeing the wheel from the rut. Sam walked back to the front, guiding the horses as they made the turnaround. Then he picked up the horsewhip from the ground and gave it back to the driver.

"Take the ladies home safely," he said, "and tell your master to fix that bridge."

As the carriage sped off up the hill, the townspeople stood, riveted, unsure whether to feel defeated or relieved.

"On second thought," Sam said to the crowd, "if we really want that bridge rebuilt, there's only one way to do it … we can do it ourselves!"

———— ✳ ————

For most of the next week, Sam and the Presbyterian men who'd been building the church applied themselves to the task of repairing the small bridge. Their dedication was impressive. They had their own farms to cultivate, but now were devoting significant time not just to building a new church, but also to fixing a bridge that was clearly the Company's responsibility.

Their selflessness inspired others beyond Presbyterian ranks. The rebuilding of the bridge soon became the central focus of the town: a source of communal pride. One day, despite rain and cold, there were twelve men working on it. And when the sun came out the next day, a small crowd from the town came to watch and cheer as an ox-driven cart made its way safely across the solidly rebuilt structure.

Looking out over a majestic expanse of lake from the window of his study, Jones quietly celebrated the fact that the reconstructed bridge meant there would now be one less grievance to manage in a town full of people unappreciative of his efforts.

It also might help quash grumblings back in London about the Company's poor rate of return on its Huron Tract investment. The directors had not been pleased by the lavish spending on the commissioner's new official residence in Goderich. So the free labour of the townspeople in rebuilding the bridge was a timely bit of help, sparing Jones from having to worry about coming up with more money for bridge repairs.

None of this good fortune caused Jones to look more favourably on the town's new minister, despite his role in masterminding the bridge reconstruction. Nor did Jones show any gratitude toward the clergyman for intervening to spare his wife and niece from a great deal of discomfort, if not more.

The commissioner poured himself a brandy as he contemplated the downside of this good fortune — a growing mythology in town about how the new pastor was exceeding all expectations, even renewing people's faith in religion.

---*---

As part of his growing popularity in Goderich, Sam was invited to the barn dance that Callandra had heard about through Rosalee.

It was held on the eastern edge of town in a barn belonging to a prosperous farmer and prominent Presbyterian. Although the late November wind was cold and sharp, the interior of the barn had been decorated with scatter rugs and embroidered wall hangings, making it look warm and welcoming.

Callandra enjoyed walking in with Sam and Emma. With her arm looped through his, they looked like husband and wife, and she relished the feeling. He was, after all, not just a much-admired figure, but also easily the town's most dashing character.

She was conscious of trying to look eye-catching herself. Gone was the overly modest look that she'd embraced back in Glasgow, when she was happy not to draw her husband's attention. Now she keenly wanted Sam's. She no longer wore her hair pulled back or gathered under a cotton cap as she often had in the Scott mansion. She now let it flow freely, allowing it to tumble down in all its fullness. Tonight she wore it swept back loosely into a chignon, with some strands cascading down her back. And she was wearing a flattering new dress, which had been made for her by the local seamstress as a welcoming gesture to the new clergyman's wife. Made of light blue cotton with a slightly scooped neckline, it cinched her in tightly at the waist, making her look and feel again like a slim, young girl.

The barn was crowded, mostly with teenagers dancing the quadrille, or a truncated version that Callandra recalled from her own girlhood in Ayrshire. The adults, acting as chaperones, stood around the edge of the well-swept dance floor while a fiddler played lively tunes, creating a mood of joviality. Rosalee was dancing, swooping around with a theatrical agility that set her apart. She looked comely in Callandra's pink muslin dress, even with a knitted brown sweater over it. Callandra was certain that, after a good bit of dancing, the sweater would come off.

Still, she felt comfortable and proud on Sam's arm, as everyone expressed excitement about the rebuilding of the bridge and the construction of the church. So it came as a shock when an adolescent girl came over and asked Sam to dance. Even by the lax social standards of Goderich, this seemed brazen. The girl wasn't comely or nicely attired, and her overture appeared more gregarious than flirtatious. Before Sam had a chance to respond, he was being led away by the girl to smiles of approval around the room.

On the dance floor, Sam was an arresting figure, so tall and broad-shouldered. He didn't know the steps, but none of them knew more than a few, giving the dance a chaotic quality that suited the rough surroundings. Sam stepped easily about, bowing, twirling, and moving effortlessly between partners. He was clearly enjoying himself. Rosalee flashed her eyes teasingly in his direction, and she seemed to move with even more lithe animation now that he had joined in. Whenever the two of them ended up partnered together, as the dance required, she looked up at him with that full smile that lit up her face, transforming her into a fetchingly pretty girl.

Watching from the sidelines, Callandra suddenly felt less sure of herself. Perhaps it was too obvious that she had been seeking his notice, and worse, that her efforts were failing. In just minutes, she had gone from the bliss of feeling physically close to him to the pain of watching him drawn in by Rosalee's flagrant flirtation. After weeks of yearning for his attention, she was now obliged to watch as he showered it on someone else.

"And how are you adjusting to life in Goderich?" asked a kind-faced, older woman who had approached Callandra from behind.

"I like it very much, thank you," replied Callandra, straining to conceal the emotions flaring inside her.

"I'm having a quilting bee next week, and would love you to come," the woman said. "We're almost finished the quilt. I'm thinking it could be used in the new church."

"Oh, thank you," said Callandra.

The woman proceeded to explain that she was one of the earliest settlers in Goderich, and then launched into a description of what the town had looked like when she arrived. Callandra listened politely, turning her head slightly to survey the dance floor.

Sam was still dancing, but Callandra couldn't see Rosalee.

"That is kind of you to think of the church," said Callandra.

They were joined by two more women who had worked on the quilt and were keen to talk about it. Callandra nodded and then turned her head again, just in time to spot Rosalee returning to the dance floor, having removed her sweater. She had clearly altered the dress: it now tapered in tightly at the waist, further accentuating her shapeliness.

"Satin makes such a nice highlight in a quilt," one of the women continued.

As Callandra looked over again at the dance floor, she couldn't see either Sam or Rosalee. She tried to disengage from the conversation without appearing rude, even as her eyes darted around in search of the missing pair. She felt dizzy, like she might faint.

Emma asked if she could have some punch, allowing Callandra to excuse herself to take her daughter to the refreshment table.

After a while, the fiddler took a break and the dancing stopped. Then, out of nowhere, Sam appeared beside Callandra and Emma. They were joined by a few parishioners eager to compliment the minister on his dancing. Sam put his hand on Callandra's shoulder in a husbandly gesture, but she resisted his gentle pull. As he glanced down at her in surprise, she looked away.

"That's my daughter, Philomena, who asked you to dance," said a big-boned woman who shared her daughter's rather unattractive facial features as well as her friendly exuberance. "I hope you don't mind her boldness."

"Not at all," Sam replied with a smile. "Boldness is a good quality."

"Even in a woman?"

"Especially in a woman."

"The young people adore you — as I'm sure you know," said the woman. "Philomena is good friends with Rosalee, and we hear from Rosalee about what a fine employer you are, how well you treat her."

"That would be Callandra who treats her well. They're together all day. I haven't had much interaction with Rosalee."

As Sam said this, he gently took hold of Callandra's hand, but she instinctively pulled it away. How could he claim to have had little interaction with Rosalee right after their flirtatious interaction on the dance floor!

But displaying her annoyance — to him and possibly to others — only heightened her humiliation. She tried to get control of herself.

The music started up again, and Sam and Callandra found themselves alone, along with Emma, slightly apart from the gathering.

"Are you angry at me?" he asked in a low, almost whispered voice.

"No," she said, still struggling for composure, then continued, sounding more resentful than she meant to, "No, I don't mean to spoil your fun. I just fear you will give us away."

"Give us away?"

"You are supposed to be married, yet you devote your attention to someone other than your wife," she said, half under her breath, wishing she hadn't started down this road.

He paused, taking that in. "Well, married men are known for chasing females other than their wives, so if anything, I am increasing the credibility of our marriage," he said, with a slight smile.

But it sounded as if he were confirming her worst fears, that he was chasing Rosalee.

"That's very insulting to me, as your wife." She realized immediately how silly as well as jealous this sounded.

"I certainly didn't mean to insult you ... I guess I don't think of you as my wife."

"No, it's clear you don't. I'm sure if you had a wife it would be someone more fawning and docile ... someone with 'spaniel-like affection.'"

That phrase from Mary Wollstonecraft had just popped into her mind and she couldn't resist using it; it was the perfect description of Rosalee. Besides, there was something comforting about invoking Wollstonecraft, even though he wouldn't recognize the reference. Callandra reminded herself how uninterested he'd been in Wollstonecraft and the rights of women.

"You mean someone who was more like a toy ... a rattle?" he said softly.

He was being playful and teasing. She wished she could be lighter, but felt trapped in her jealousy.

"I'm sure you think that's the role a wife should play," she said.

"I have no such thoughts ... but if you're worried about being my toy, you'll be pleased to hear that you're not doing a very good job of it."

This was delivered again with a gentle smile, but it hurt, especially since Rosalee joined them moments later, her bodice unbuttoned as low as possible without drawing censure.

"Will you come dance again, Bert?" she said, effusively. "Everyone wants you to."

"No, thank you very much," he said courteously but without flirtation. "I want to spend some time with my wife."

The use of the word "wife" had a clarity to it, and Rosalee returned to the dance floor alone. After that, Callandra managed to compose herself and they rejoined the party. By the end of the afternoon, as they were saying their goodbyes, Sam slid his hand behind her back, and she let him guide her around. She even took his arm again, although with less confidence and pleasure than before.

"That was very clever of you to appear jealous," he said to Callandra, as they walked home in the dusk with Emma. "It definitely helps our cover."

---   *   ---

The next day, Callandra decided that Sam's actions had not been inappropriate. Rosalee, on the other hand, had had the audacity to openly flirt with him in front of Callandra, while wearing her dress, no less!

Still, Callandra felt that it was better to appear unfazed and confident in her role as Sam's wife. So they sat down together for their usual mid-afternoon tea, and Rosalee began talking about the party. Callandra listened while Rosalee provided an assessment of all the young girls — how each one looked and how much attention she'd attracted on the dance floor. One who looked nice but didn't dance, she said, was Daisy Howard.

Then, in a more confidential tone, Rosalee explained that the girl had had an affair with Mr. Longworth, the Company superintendent, meeting him for secret assignations in the Company's cabin in the woods — and then bearing his child. Rosalee had befriended Daisy and thought it was unfair that many of the townspeople shunned her. Fortunately, Daisy hadn't been crushed by her misfortune; it helped that Mr. Jones arranged to have money delivered to her from time to time, which Rosalee understood was to keep the girl quiet about the misconduct of his top employee.

Rosalee obviously enjoyed imparting this gossip. Callandra didn't know whether to believe any of it, but she wondered whether the cabin in the woods where Daisy and Mr. Longworth had apparently met was the same one where she, Sam, and Emma had spent the night. If so, had that been Mr. Longworth's brandy they'd been drinking? It was an intriguing possibility, but Callandra didn't want to speculate about any of this with Rosalee.

"Well, it was a nice party," said Callandra, switching topics.

"Aye," said the girl.

"It seems there are lots of fine young people in Goderich," said Callandra, blandly.

"Aye, but none I'd marry."

"No?"

"No," repeated Rosalee, and then her look grew whimsical. "When I marry, I want someone wonderful."

"Well, you're right to aim for that," said Callandra.

"— someone like your husband," Rosalee continued. "He's grand."

"Yes," said Callandra, rising to end the conversation.

"He surely is," replied Rosalee. "And, if he were my husband, he wouldn' be sleepin' all by himself!"

——— * ———

That evening, Sam confided in Callandra what he'd learned from rebel sources in Toronto: that plans for an uprising were well underway. Virtually the entire garrison of Upper Canada had been sent to Lower Canada to quell a rebellion there, indicating that the unrest was widespread, and that colonial authorities in Toronto were largely unprotected.

Sam also disclosed that he was involved in a small group in Goderich, including some of the men helping him build the church, who were preparing to take part should a rebellion occur in Upper Canada. The men all understood that if they were caught taking up arms against the colonial government, the consequences would be severe. The sense of danger had been heightened when Allan Grayson, whose brother worked in the Company store, started showing up to help with the church construction. Grayson was an Anglican, making his willingness to help build the Presbyterian Church suspicious, and leaving Sam and his cohorts worried they were being watched.

Callandra remained pleased that Sam was entrusting her with all this sensitive information, even as she was alarmed to learn how far the plans for a rebellion had advanced. If he joined it, he could well end up dead, injured, or imprisoned, with his false identity exposed. At the very least, he would surely end up separated from her. She was upset that that didn't seem to deter him. But then, he had made no commitment to her; she wasn't even sure how he felt about her. So it seemed futile to try to discourage him, to follow her heart and plead with him not to go.

She had also noticed a transformation in him. He was less concerned about the dishonesty of his life in Goderich. She suspected this was because he now felt his deception served a larger purpose, an important political end. By posing as a Presbyterian minister, he was providing cover for the risky preparations needed for a rebellion. Political authorities would be less likely to suspect a man of the cloth of involvement in an armed uprising. A group of Presbyterian men could therefore get together, ostensibly to work on building the church, without arousing suspicion.

One afternoon in late November, Callandra agreed to allow the group to meet at their home. When the men arrived — seven in all — they sat around the kitchen table, talking quietly. Callandra was surprised that among them was Colonel Van Egmond, a distinguished-looking gentleman whom she'd had met at the barn dance, as well as Dr. Drummond, the doctor who'd cared for her that first night in Goderich.

Callandra watched from the little alcove where she was putting Emma to bed, alarmed to hear them talking about taking up arms. Evidently, rebel leaders had called for five thousand men to gather north of Toronto.

The voices began to rise, as disagreement developed over whether a rebellion had a chance of succeeding.

"With Colonel Van Egmond leading it, yes," said a heavy-set man. The colonel appeared pleased by this confidence in him.

He also seemed old to Callandra, but the men agreed that, with his credentials from the Napoleonic wars, he had the kind of battlefield experience the rebels needed.

"That won't make much difference if we end up facing a flank of trained soldiers," said a man smoking a pipe. "We don't know how many have been held back."

"There are credible reports their forces are very thin," said the colonel. "As of last week, Fort Henry was empty; almost the entire garrison was hunkered down in Lower Canada."

Dr. Drummond noted that could change by the time a rebellion begins in Toronto.

"Besides, let's not forget that we've made progress in recent years. We shouldn't assume the only way to bring about reform is through force," the doctor continued.

Then she heard Sam's voice, clear and strong. "We also shouldn't forget what Joseph Hume said — that without a display of physical force, the Reform Bill would never have passed in Britain," he said, giving the call to arms a moral underpinning that made it sound more compelling to Callandra, despite all her doubts and fears.

After that, the talk switched to logistics. If the colonel was going to lead the rebels in Toronto, it was agreed that a band of men from Goderich should accompany him there. Two young men, barely out of their teens, named Randall and Joe, enthusiastically offered to be in that band.

Callandra's heart sank as she looked down at her daughter sleeping peacefully; Sam would certainly be among those men.

The meeting appeared to have ended, but Callandra felt too dispirited to bid the men good night.

"Can we hide them here?" she could hear one of the men ask in a low voice.

"Yeah, they're less likely to check here," said another.

"No," Sam responded. "We'll hide them at the church, under the boards at the back."

"But what about Grayson? He could find them there."

"I can't endanger my wife and child —"

At that, Callandra began humming quietly, in case Emma was still awake. The possibility of a cache of guns right in the house — so close to Emma — left her freshly alarmed.

There was more talk between the men in lowered tones, and then Callandra could hear Sam saying good night to them in front of the house. She continued to gently hum lullabies, in part to calm herself.

When Sam came back in, he joined her, crouching at Emma's bedside.

"Don't worry," he said. "Nothing will be stored here. Everyone agreed they can be hidden at the church."

"But what about Grayson? He could find them."

"Well, if we hide them here, Rosalee might find them. I certainly wouldn't trust her either."

Chapter Sixteen

The next day, there was a knock on her door and Callandra opened it to find Mrs. Cameron, the kindly old woman from the barn dance, and a young man. He lived on a farm northeast of Goderich, Mrs. Cameron explained, and had come to town that morning to fetch the local midwife as his wife was ready to give birth. But the midwife was sick, and Dr. Drummond had been called away on an emergency. The young man had sought Mrs. Cameron's help, and she was now bringing him to Callandra who, she'd heard, had experience as a midwife back in Scotland.

"Oh no," Callandra said, inviting them in. "My mother does midwifery, but not me."

"Did you ever accompany your mother to a birth?" asked the older woman.

"Yes, a few times. But that was long ago. I don't remember much."

The young man, dressed in a flimsy jacket despite the chilly weather, had a slender build, flattened-down dark hair, and a doleful look about the eyes. He left it to Mrs. Cameron to explain that there was no woman at home to help with the delivery, as his mother had passed on last summer.

"I can't leave my daughter," Callandra said. "My husband isn't home until —"

"I can stay and care for Emma," interrupted Rosalee, appearing from the kitchen. "Really, I can stay as long as I'm needed."

The quickness with which Rosalee offered her services made her appear big-hearted while Callandra looked uncaring.

"It's a good Presbyterian family," Mrs. Cameron noted. "They contribute to the fund."

The fund, Callandra knew, paid Sam's salary.

"I'll make sure everything here is all right," insisted Rosalee, looking straight at Callandra. "You needn't worry at all."

His name was Ethan and he had come to town in a small, uncovered cart pulled by a weary horse. The wooden bench in the cart tilted downward on one side, making for a most uncomfortable ride in which Callandra couldn't prevent herself from slipping in his direction as he encouraged the horse onward.

She directed Ethan to go by the church site, so she could tell Sam where she was going. It was only a small detour, and even though they were pressed for time, she felt no qualms about insisting, and he offered no resistance. As they pulled up alongside the scaffolding, she was struck by the progress of the construction and the buzz of industry at the site. One of men called to "Bert" that his wife was outside.

Sam appeared from the back and walked directly to the cart.

"What's going on?" he asked, as she shifted as far away from Ethan as she could.

"I have to help with a baby delivery," she began explaining, her saddened look meant to convey that this mission was being undertaken with great reluctance. "This is Ethan. His wife is in labour."

"Hello, Reverend," said Ethan, extending his hand.

Sam took his hand but looked skeptically at Callandra. "How do you know Ethan?"

"Mrs. Cameron brought him to our house."

"Mrs. Cameron?"

"You know — that nice lady who did the quilt for the church."

Sam's expression eased a bit, but he remained skeptical.

"I said I would go," said Callandra.

"No," said Sam firmly, and reached in to pull her out of the carriage.

"But I told him I'd help …" she protested.

"If you're going, I'm going, too." Sam was standing directly opposite her, after lifting her from the carriage. His hands lingered on her waist for a moment.

Apologizing to Ethan for the delay, Sam dispatched one of his men to borrow a cart in town. He then ran home to their cottage and, after a short while, returned on horseback with Emma. A sturdy-looking cart, provided by a kind parishioner, had already arrived, and Sam quickly hitched it to the horse. As they followed Ethan's cart along the main road out of town, Callandra marvelled at her suddenly improved circumstances.

Thomas Mercer Jones looked up from his desk with irritation. Rather than satisfying the people of Goderich, the reconstruction of the bridge by Sam and his crew only increased demands that the Company carry out other long-overdue improvements. In particular, there was renewed pressure from the farmers in Colborne township, immediately north of Goderich, to have a bridge built over the Maitland River.

"If that clergyman can build a bridge in less than a week, then surely the Company can construct something across the Maitland after all this time," said Daniel Lizars, in a suit with high collar and necktie, his wavy white hair and beard framing a broad, well-weathered face.

"Well, the Maitland bridge is a more challenging project," replied Jones from behind his desk.

"Yes, but you have the resources," insisted Lizars, "and we've paid good money for our land."

This was true. Lizars and other relatively well-to-do members of the "Colborne clique" had been among the first Scottish settlers in the Huron Tract, and, unlike more recent arrivals, had paid in full for their properties in advance. This gave them a certain stature with the Company. At the same time, since there was nothing more to collect from them, the Company didn't have to worry about placating them, which was why Jones largely ignored their demands for a bridge.

"Well, we are looking into it," he said.

"Why don't you just hire that clergyman to build it for you?"

This was meant as a jest, but it annoyed Jones and made him even less inclined — if this were possible — to build the bridge. Besides, it was already late November, and the Maitland would soon freeze over, retiring the issue until spring.

After Lizars had taken his leave, Jones decided to depart from his regular morning schedule and take a stroll on his land above the lake. It was a brisk, clear day with whitecaps dancing on the vast stretch of water, reminding him that, as isolated and undeveloped as the Huron Tract was, there was a stark beauty about it.

Since moving his family here, he had been determined to make things work out well. But getting the Company's finances under control turned out to be more difficult than expected. It had crossed Jones's mind that his marriage to the archdeacon's daughter might explain the patience of the Company's notoriously demanding directors back in London.

This highlighted another aspect of Jones's anxiety — the need to impress the archdeacon. John Strachan certainly wouldn't be happy that his cherished daughter had moved all the way to Goderich, only to be embarrassed by her husband's performance in his post there. Thus, satisfying both the directors and the archdeacon hinged on getting the Company's financial house in order. Clearly, Jones had to intensify his efforts, regardless of how unpopular that made him in the town.

Above all, Jones was a pragmatist, and it had made sense to him to advance small amounts of seed to get the settlers started, enabling them to develop functioning farms so they could eventually pay off their mortgages. But the directors disapproved of such largesse. Their penny-pinching — and the archdeacon's well-known impatience for results — left Jones in a bind, pushed in one direction by short-sighted directors and an exacting father-in-law, and in the other by a local crowd lacking the slightest understanding of the business world.

Mary and her niece, Annabelle, dressed in warm wraps and bonnets, emerged from the house arm-in-arm and spotted Jones by the hedge overlooking the harbour.

"What a fine day for a walk," he said as they joined him, with Mary's French perfume detectible even with the brisk wind.

Mary seemed to be adjusting to Goderich. It helped that Annabelle was visiting from Toronto, with plans to stay till spring. Annabelle was only sixteen, but still good company for Mary who, with a small child and few acquaintances in Goderich, was isolated and deprived of female companionship.

Just how Annabelle would fare in a Goderich winter was less clear. But her stay had been considered a good idea by the archdeacon after Annabelle had developed a regard for an American traveller — in his early thirties — who had visited Toronto while selling medicinal oils. The archdeacon was known to be particularly fond of his granddaughter and was inclined therefore to blame the budding liaison on inadequate supervision. The situation made the case for a sojourn in Goderich all the more compelling, and Mary had reported to her father that it seemed to be working out well.

On this fine day, both ladies seemed in good spirits. Mary had been planning a dinner party — always a challenge in Goderich, given the limited number of suitable guests. It was unfortunate that relations with the Colborne clique were so strained, since their ranks included some of the most educated and well-mannered people in the Huron Tract.

"What about Mr. Longworth?" asked Mary. "You see him a great deal. Should we include him at the dinner table?"

Jones had been looking out over the harbour, idly noting the fresh build-up of sand in the bay and realizing there'd be renewed demands for the Company to clear it. But Mary's suggestion gave him a jolt. Longworth was far too coarse to be around Mary in a social setting. Besides, he knew too much.

"Oh, no ... he's not really suitable," said Jones. "He doesn't have a wife."

"I understand he has a ... a ... young lady friend. He could bring her."

"Well," Jones said, shocked that Mary had learned this much detail. "She wouldn't be appropriate ... I believe she's a servant."

"I don't mind having a servant at our table," said Mary, with a pleasant smile. Jones never ceased to be surprised by his wife.

"I don't think you would want such a girl at our dinner table," he said uncomfortably. "I've heard she has a disreputable past."

Jones was conscious of Annabelle listening intently, intrigued by this turn in the conversation.

"Oh, nonsense," said Mary. "I would think Mr. Longworth's past would be of more concern. Surely abandoning a wife and children should be regarded with more disdain than whatever that poor girl may have done. No doubt she thought it would lead to marriage."

It unnerved Jones that Mary knew about Longworth's unsavoury past, and that she was aware of Daisy Howard at all, even though she hadn't mentioned the girl's name.

"I don't know details about Longworth's past," Jones continued to his wife, "but I suspect it makes him unsuitable to have at our social events. I appreciate him only for his business acumen …"

They walked on in silence for a while, with Jones growing increasingly uncomfortable.

"Ahh, I've got an idea," he said. "Why don't we instead invite Daniel Lizars and his wife to dinner! … Yes, I think it's time we tried to patch things up with the Colborne clique. Perhaps this could be a start."

Although Jones disliked the thought of further pressure about the Maitland bridge, the prospect of Lizars stepping in for Longworth was a relief.

"Well, that sounds fine," said Mary amiably. "And Annabelle had another idea — perhaps we could also invite that nice clergyman who rebuilt the bridge."

"Good Lord!" replied Jones.

He looked at Annabelle. She had an oval face, with small, attractive features. But he now concluded there was something insufficiently demure in her expression, which perhaps hinted at a taste for troubled liaisons.

"That would be unseemly," replied Jones, directing his comments to his wife. "He's a ruffian."

"But he saved us the other day," continued Annabelle, displaying the kind of spunk that a long winter in Goderich would surely squelch.

"Quite out of the question," said Jones, shutting down the subject while marvelling at how some males, even though uncouth and unpropertied, had a knack for winning the favour of females.

The slow and irregular mail service to Goderich — always an annoyance — was particularly a problem now, thought Jones as he read through letters just arrived from Toronto. Most of this batch had been written three weeks earlier, in late October; clearly the situation was becoming ominous, if things hadn't already boiled over.

His co-commissioner, William Allan — close friend of the archdeacon and well positioned near the top of the colony's business and political elite — wrote to describe the growing unease in Toronto over reports that William Lyon Mackenzie was attracting large crowds at Reform meetings in communities near the city:

> I have certainly been surprised by the size of the gatherings, numbering well into the hundreds. At one meeting in Bolton last week, close to five hundred people were said to attend. And then the next day, he drew a similar crowd in Caledon, and then a few days later an even bigger and rowdier one in Hamilton.
> What is alarming is not just the apparent popularity of this knave, but his increasingly open defiance. The resolutions passed at the gatherings go beyond his usual cry for self-government (as if Upper Canada were ready for such a thing!). They now call for the formation of "Local Vigilance Committees." And many attending the rallies carry pistols, pikes, muskets, and clubs. Mackenzie admits to meeting with the agitators in Lower Canada, and he expresses open admiration for the rebel Papineau. There are reports that

Mackenzie and his inner circle are actively planning a rebellion in Upper Canada — as early as January, possibly even December.

Should they be so foolish, I have no doubt that the hooligans will be quickly and harshly dealt with. But there are concerns about the possibility of uprisings farther away, beyond the reach of a garrison. The Huron Tract has even been mentioned as an area of possible agitation. As you probably know, the radicals held meetings last month in Guelph, London, and Stratford. A report about the Stratford meeting identified Colonel Van Egmond, touted by some as a possible rebel commander. It is hard to believe that this is the same gentleman who made tidy sums from us on that road-building contract, but it is apparently so.

The possibility of unrest — even as far away as Goderich — is not being ruled out. I have been informed that a small contingent, totalling two dozen soldiers, is being transferred to Goderich as an additional security measure. I am grateful to Sir Francis for this, given that he has responsibility for the whole of Upper Canada. But he is well aware that the Company has been a favourite target of the radicals, and that their message has resonance — unfairly — with some of the Huron Tract settlers. The soldiers will provide security around the Company offices and of course your personal residence.

If you are aware of anything that might suggest possible rebel action, please do forward any intelligence forthwith, as I am in close touch with Sir Francis and his advisors.

With my warmest regards,

Yours,
William Allan

The prospect of an uprising seemed suddenly real, and Allan's assessment of the danger to Jones and his family made it particularly alarming. He was aware that a local militia was being organized by Tiger Dunlop, a prominent Goderich figure who had helped the Company get started in the Huron Tract. Although Dunlop was still employed by the Company, he was his own man, and Jones considered him unreliable. It was good to know, therefore, that Sir Francis would be providing security with actual soldiers.

Jones immediately summoned Longworth, and within an hour, a meeting was arranged with Allan Grayson.

It had been Jones's idea to have Grayson spy on the Presbyterian Church-building crew. He had wondered if his personal animosity toward Norbert Scott had made him overly suspicious, but today's mail removed that doubt. If there was a plan being hatched for a rebellion in Goderich, he now felt sure that Norbert Scott was mixed up in it; perhaps even its ringleader.

Grayson, in his mid-thirties, was well spoken by local standards, and understood the need for discretion. He reported that there was a strong sense of camaraderie among the men working on the church. Norbert was a natural leader among them. This was very much his project and the men were drawn to his sense of purpose and the pride he took in his workmanship. Proof of the respect he commanded could be gleaned by how quickly they all fell in line when he intervened to protect Mrs. Jones and her niece the day the boy drowned in the creek.

"Well, let's not exaggerate his intervention," said Jones, knitting his eyebrows in mild irritation. "I've heard from my wife that the crowd was in fact not so unfriendly."

"With all due respect, sir," said Grayson. "I believe Mrs. Jones may have misread the situation. People were quite worked up about that boy drowning. There is, as you know, a lot of bad feeling against the Company. Reverend Scott definitely calmed the situation."

"Hmm," said Jones.

"In any event," said Grayson, "it was odd the way Norbert seemed to be on the side of the Company that day. Normally he's not."

"Tell us about that," said Longworth, seated in a fine leather chair.

"Well," Grayson continued, shifting in his wooden chair. "He has had little good to say about the Company, sir. I've heard him say how unfair it is to the settlers, demanding payment when people have no money. I believe he used the word 'tyranny.'"

"Tyranny! That's ridiculous, for God's sakes!" scoffed Jones. "Does he have no idea of the costs of running a business?"

"I'm just telling you what he says, sir. I'm not meaning to say it's true ... but I guess he does talk to quite a few people around here about their problems, being a clergyman."

"A clergyman!" sneered Jones. "Just what kind of clergyman is he? Does he ever perform any religious services?"

"He presided at a service on the Calhoun property last month," said Grayson, prompting audible jeers from both Longworth and Jones.

"What about rebellion? Has he talked at all about the need for a rebellion?"

"Yes, I have heard him talk about that."

Jones leaned forward, impatient to hear more.

"He likes the idea of a rebellion. He speaks with admiration about the way the Americans stood up to the British."

"Does he talk about that sort of thing happening here?" asked Jones.

"You mean here — in Goderich?"

"Well, yes."

"I haven't heard anything like that," said Grayson. "But he does talk about the Reformers in Toronto."

"What about them?" asked Longworth.

"That their cause is just. Apparently, Mackenzie said that if a rebellion happens, anyone joining it will get free land afterward."

"Ha! That's pure theft," remarked Jones. "Others have to work hard to pay for their land."

"But some get it for free — according to the pastor. He says the 'Family Compact' live like noblemen by stealing what belongs to the people," said Grayson. "I don't know where he gets that idea, sir, but I've heard him say it."

"It sounds like he's spreading seditious lies, verging on treason," said Longworth, addressing his comments to Jones. "You might consider arresting him."

"Hmmm, possibly," Jones mumbled in reply. But arresting the popular new minister would cause bad feelings in the town, which wouldn't be helpful.

Then, turning to Grayson, Jones continued, "You're sure there hasn't been any talk of an uprising here in Goderich, or destruction of Company property — anything like that?"

"Well, I can't say there's been no talk of that sort. All I can say is I haven't heard it. I think there may have been a meeting one evening at Norbert's house. I wasn't invited. I only know about it because I heard about it from his servant girl."

Jones looked at Grayson with interest.

"She wasn't there, either, but she saw a few men arriving when she was leaving that night. They were men who are building the church. And she says Colonel Van Egmond was there, too … she knows his granddaughter."

"How many were there?" Jones shot back. "Why didn't you report this immediately?"

"I guess I didn't … didn't realize … it was important."

"When was this meeting?" snapped Jones.

"Just last week. I'm not sure which night. I can find out."

"You know this girl? Can she be trusted?" asked Jones, rising from his chair and walking around his desk, so that he was standing directly in front of Grayson.

"I believe so, sir. I think she could be quite useful to us. It would probably help if we could give her something — perhaps some flour or beans from the Company store. I know she is helping support her family …"

"That could be arranged," said Jones. "She could tell us if she hears of another meeting."

"Yes, sir. And more than that. She knows a lot."

"Like what?"

"Well," said Grayson. "She says that Norbert and his wife have separate rooms, and they never sleep together."

Jones began pacing around the room, not sure how to react to this odd but mildly interesting tidbit. "So?" he responded finally, from the far end of the room. "We're not interested in the fine points of his marriage. I'm sure his wife has her reasons." He resumed pacing. "What else does this servant girl know?"

"She took his wife's diary and showed it to me."

"Did it say anything important — you know, about the politics?"

"Well, I only read part of it, because she had to return it before the wife got home. It's mostly about her feelings and her views on women's suffering."

Jones rolled his eyes.

"But I remember it said something like 'Everyone loves him, and no one seems suspicious.' Or something like that. The word 'suspicious' was definitely used. I remember that."

Jones walked back to resume his spot in front of his desk, directly facing Grayson.

"Was it referring to Norbert?"

"I think so."

"The reference in the diary was about Norbert? He's the one whom everyone loves and no one is suspicious of?"

"Yes, that was my impression."

"Meaning everyone in Goderich?" asked Longworth.

"That was how I read it."

"Curious indeed," said Jones.

The interview lasted another two hours. By the time Grayson left, Jones felt they had learned enough to take seriously William Allan's concerns about the possibility of a local uprising in Goderich.

"There was another interesting missive in the mail today," Jones said to Longworth, walking over to the liquor table and pouring two brandies. "I've saved the best for last."

He clinked glasses with Longworth and then produced a letter from the top drawer. "This came today as well. It's from the archdeacon's office."

"Oh."

"A few weeks ago, I wrote to Arthur Potter, the archdeacon's secretary, asking him if they knew anything about our new clergyman," Jones began. "I didn't think they would, but I was wrong. In his reply today, Potter says that Reverend Norbert Scott applied to them about joining the Anglican Church."

"What! Really? You mean defecting from the Presbyterian Church?"

"Precisely," said Jones, savouring the brandy and allowing a smile to spread across his face, emphasizing his large dark sideburns.

"And he kindly enclosed Reverend Scott's letter of application to the archdeacon."

"My, my!" said Longworth, reviewing the letter handed to him.

"I can't imagine how long he'll remain a hero among the Goderich Presbyterians once they hear he tried to defect to the Church of England," said Jones. "So much for his pretense about being a man of the people. He clearly wants to feather his own nest!"

"And live off the spoils of the Clergy Reserves, no less! That should impress his rebel comrades," Longworth said with a laugh.

"He's effectively pledged support for the Family Compact," said Jones, raising his glass in a toast. "To Reverend Scott, beloved hero of Goderich — although not for long!"

---- * ----

It was almost dark by the time they arrived at Ethan's farmhouse, which was deep in the bush, miles from the last homestead. There was a light flickering inside as they approached the front door. Callandra wondered if, by the grace of God, the delivery had already happened, making her duties that evening considerably lighter.

As they followed Ethan into the house, a young girl — not much older than Emma — came running to her father, oblivious to the strangers.

"It hasn't come yet," she half sobbed, grabbing her father's leg. Ethan put his hand on his daughter's head.

"It's going to be all right," said Callandra softly, not bothering with introductions. "The baby will come when it's ready. I'll help your mother."

An older man appeared, clearly heartened by the arrival of the strangers. He was stooped over and walked haltingly.

"This is our new minister, Reverend Scott," Ethan said.

"Ahh, very nice to meet you, sir," said the old man, surveying Sam with great interest. "You're the one building the church? It will be grand to have a Presbyterian Church in the tract."

The old man, lantern in hand, showed Sam, Callandra, and Emma to a room at the front of the house. It was a pleasant room with a fireplace, rocking chair, and a large bed covered with a heavy quilt. A Bible lay on the bedside table.

"But this is your room, sir," objected Sam.

"I want you to have it tonight," insisted the old man, motioning to Ethan to bring the small cot in for the child. "I'm honoured to have you and your family in my home, Reverend."

Callandra hoped Sam wouldn't protest too much. She liked the idea of being together in this room — even if there would be three of them and she would be up all night delivering a baby. The cart ride had left her happy. There hadn't been much talk, but it had felt wonderful being together in the wagon.

"Can I see your mother?" Callandra asked, and the little girl took her into the back room. Emma followed.

This room was smaller, but cheerfully decorated, with a warm rug on the floor. The little girl stoked the fire. Her mother, Deirdre, was asleep on the bed, her face drained of colour. As Callandra prepared for the ordeal ahead, she was impressed by the tidiness of the room, the orderliness of the towels, sheets, and unguents on the bedside table, along with a large bowl of water, gauze, and scissors.

"You've done a very good job of organizing here," said Callandra.

"This is wild cherry balsam," said the girl, picking up a bottle from the table. "If you put some on her tongue, it helps."

Deirdre began stirring, and then was suddenly wide awake, letting out a sharp cry.

Callandra could see that her arrival was a great relief to the little girl. Her name was Una, and she watched with hopeful eyes as Callandra wiped her mother's brow, massaged her back, and dropped wild cherry balsam onto her tongue.

The screaming grew more intense, more piercing. Callandra had been through the brutality of childbirth herself, witnessed it with other women, yet somehow the terror of it was fresh and startling in this room. Emma should not be witnessing all this suffering. Nor should Una be watching her mother writhe in agony, as if being torn apart by wild animals. Callandra urged them to leave the room, trying to make it sound as if she had the situation under control.

But Una, transformed from the terrified little girl Callandra had first encountered, now insisted she'd stay and help with the birth. Emma stood behind her, silently taking everything in, too overwhelmed to talk.

In one of the lulls between Deirdre's screams, there was a knock on the door. "There's hot stew," said Sam from the other side.

"Yes, these girls need to eat, thank you," said Callandra, opening the door and ushering them out to Sam's care. The smell of cooked rabbit wafted into the room, making Callandra feel hungry. Behind Sam in the doorway, she could see Ethan and his father at the kitchen table.

"You'll need some, too," Sam said to Callandra.

"Thank you but I'll eat later," she replied, closing the door as Deirdre began to scream.

Callandra decided she would eat when Deirdre slumped back into another lull. But that lull never really came. The contractions grew more intense and more frequent, with little break between them. Una tried to come back into the room, but Callandra discouraged her, remembering one delivery back in Scotland where the mother had died. Summoning every bit of composure she could, Callandra insisted that it was best to have only one person present at this stage. She promised Una that she'd apply the wild cherry balsam to her mother's tongue, and then gently, firmly closed the door.

After that, she was alone with Deirdre. Callandra found inner resources that surprised her. Or maybe she just eventually became numb to the pain she was witnessing. Her mind kept looping back to the carriage ride, sitting close to Sam, with Emma between them, puzzling over why he had insisted on coming — protectiveness, concern, possibly jealousy? The *clomp, clomp, clomp* of the horse's hooves over the warped wooden road, the darkness of the forest around them, the unknown destination ahead.

It was well into the night when the baby arrived. Callandra was enormously relieved, and strangely capable of handling the earthy reality of childbirth: cutting the cord, cleansing the newborn, and delivering him into the arms of his depleted — but living — mother.

Ethan was asleep on the floor in the kitchen when Callandra woke him and told him the news. In the candlelight, she could see a smile spread across his face.

"A boy! That's terrific!"

"Shall we tell your father he has a grandson?"

"He'll be happy, but it can probably wait till morning."

"And your wife — she's weary, but doing well now," continued Callandra. "You can go in and see her."

Ethan got up from the floor.

"Just don't wake them," added Callandra. "They're both asleep."

"Oh, well then, why don't I leave it till morning — if they're asleep now."

"Well, no, someone should be with them, watching them, to make sure they're all right. I'm going to bed."

"I'm not sure I'd know what to do — if there was a problem," he said.

"Oh, you'd figure it out," said Callandra. "The goal is just to keep them both comfortable and breathing. It's pretty straightforward at this point."

She walked over to the woodstove and served herself a bowl of stew, which was still warm and, to her hungry mouth, delicious. Ethan went to see his new son while Callandra picked up the flickering candle and found her way to the bedroom where the fire in the fireplace was smoldering. The bed was empty. Sam was asleep on the rug on the floor, his back to her, with only his coat draped over him for warmth. Quietly, she went into the next room and found the girls asleep in Una's tiny bed.

She came back into the room, but Sam didn't stir. She felt suddenly self-conscious, unsure of what to do. It seemed too bold to wake him and invite him into bed with her. Or was it? He was not properly covered, and it was cold in the room; he would catch a serious chill lying like that all night. She could throw more wood on the fire, but that would wake him, and she wanted to figure out a plan before he awoke.

She studied him lying there — his tousled hair, his sturdy shoulders, his strong arms lying outside the coat. She remembered when she'd first encountered him years ago, how he'd held Lottie so protectively in those arms. Callandra felt a longing for him to hold her, too. And not just as a brother. If there'd been confusion in her mind back then, there was none now.

Suddenly he stirred, then turned over toward her, catching her off guard.

"You shouldn't be sleeping on the floor," she said.

"I'm all right," he responded, raising himself onto an elbow.

"No, no," said Callandra. "You'll catch your death of cold."

He didn't move. There was a pause, then he asked if the baby had come.

"Yes — a boy," she said, as if talking about something that happened months ago.

Still, Sam made no move to get up.

"Please, come in the bed," she said. "I won't sleep knowing you're cold on the floor."

At that, he got up and came over. They were standing on either side of the bed, fully clothed, facing each other. She pulled back the covers on her side and got in. He did the same, leaving a respectful distance between them. For a while they said nothing, and he made no move toward her.

"I thought you liked me, Sam," she said, immediately regretting her choice of words, knowing she did not want to talk him into something.

"Of course, I like you."

"Before — back in Scotland — we didn't like each other ..."

"Sometimes I liked you back then," he volunteered.

"But I thought all that bad feeling between us had changed," she said, unsure where she was going with this; the words just came out.

They were now facing each other.

"Yes, it's changed. I do like you now. I like you — a lot," he added. She could see his face in the flickering candlelight. So handsome; so inscrutable.

"But, I mean ... the way we liked each other that night in the cabin."

There, she said it!

He didn't respond, but kept looking at her.

"Don't you remember?"

He rolled over on his back, eyes staring upward. "Of course I remember."

There was a long silence. He remained on his back, not looking at her. "Do you think this is easy for me?" he said.

She felt encouraged.

Then he rolled back on his side, facing her. "Look, we can't do this, Callandra. It's wrong …"

"Wrong?"

"Yes, wrong."

"I don't believe that."

"You must. It would be wrong."

"I don't understand."

"You've got to trust me on this," he said.

"But —"

"It wouldn't be good for you …"

"Let me be the judge of what's good for me!"

He was silent for a few moments.

"I can't stay," he said firmly.

"You can stay *tonight*. That's all I'm asking." She could hardly believe she said this.

He looked over at her quizzically, giving her a chance to withdraw the remark.

"You don't understand —" he said.

"I understand what I need to understand, that I want you …"

She didn't wait for his response. She knew what she wanted, and needed to know if he wanted it, too. She was finally being honest. Maybe it was her sheer exhaustion or the feeling of having just participated for hours in something so basic, raw, and human that there was no place here for games of feminine modesty. She was happy to toss centuries of all that to the wind. She was in search of a simple truth, no longer imprisoned by the need to play coy about her desire, about her love for him.

She moved toward him, trembling with excitement, her heart racing wildly. She moistened the tip of her finger and gently pressed it to his lips, just as he'd done to her that night in the cabin. Then she moved right next to him, placing her lips delicately against his, astonished and animated by her own boldness.

He seemed astonished, too. He watched her, transfixed, motionless. Then he reached over and touched her face and gently pulled her toward him.

"Callandra," he whispered softly. "Callie."

She hadn't been called that since she was a child, but it sounded so right and so intimate coming from him now in this wondrous moment.

He kissed her, tentatively at first, his lips shyly exploring the contours of her face.

"Callie," he repeated, then opened her mouth and kissed her hungrily.

The candle flickered. There was a sound of a baby crying, a world away.

"Callie … Callie … Callie …"

Chapter Seventeen

For Rosalee, the favoured circumstances disappeared as quickly as they had appeared. Instead of continuing to prepare supper — a supper she had briefly envisioned sharing with Sam and Emma in Callandra's absence — she was now washing their clothes. She had come to dislike Callandra for her imperious ways, her pretense of caring about others, her silly ideas about men and women. Realizing she needed to make more soap, Rosalee began rolling the barrel into the kitchen and searching for the tallow. Her one consolation was that while Callandra may be in the wagon with Sam, it was clear that he preferred Rosalee — in the way that mattered.

Rosalee decided to leave early and was just preparing to go when there was a knock at the door. It was Allan Grayson. Their last encounter — furtively reading Callandra's diary in the grove beside the house — had ended abruptly when she'd become fearful of Callandra returning early from her outing.

"I hear they've left town, so I thought maybe we could take another look at the diary," he said.

Rosalee liked Grayson, whom she'd met at a social gathering. She had responded with her natural sociability and fondness for gossip, and they'd become friendly. She had shared Callandra's diary with him — which was clearly wrong. But they didn't get caught, and the experience left Rosalee trusting him enough to invite him into the house now.

Besides, Rosalee wanted to know if Bert and Callandra were intimately involved and she felt sure the answer lay in the diary, but she couldn't read.

She went into Callandra's room to get it, and was surprised to discover it gone. It was usually in her bottom drawer, along with the silly book about women that she was always reading. The book was still there, but not the diary.

They started searching the house, assuming Callandra had hidden it somewhere, perhaps because she suspected Rosalee's snooping. This unnerved Rosalee, but also made her more convinced it contained the information she wanted.

"Have you seen any guns around?" asked Grayson, after they'd fruitlessly searched the house.

"Guns?"

"Well, yes, muskets. You know, for fighting."

"Oh no."

"Remember you mentioned there was a meeting here? Tell me about it again."

"Oh, I don' know," said Rosalee. "I'm not sure it was a meetin'. Just some people came over. I guess it could have been a meetin'. Just some planning about the church."

"But you said Colonel Van Egmond was there …"

"So? … Why are you so curious about all this?"

"Well, some people think that meeting might have been about planning for a rebellion."

Rosalee looked at him quizzically. She had heard about the American Revolution, which wasn't well regarded by her family, to the extent that such things were ever discussed. Certainly, a rebellion didn't sound like a good thing. Like something against the king. Or now the queen.

"I don' think so," she said. "Who thinks that?"

"Just some people in town," he replied. "But have you heard about Bert being involved in something like that?"

Rosalee now felt distinctly uncomfortable. She had no interest in getting Bert into trouble. On the contrary.

"I don' wanna get involved," she said. "Maybe you should go."

"You already are involved," he responded. "You showed me the diary."

"That was different." She backed up a few steps, suddenly afraid he might grab her.

"Don't worry. I'm not going to hurt you. You've done nothing wrong," he said, striking a softer tone. "It's just that you could be very helpful."

He went over to a satchel he'd left on the kitchen floor and pulled out a burlap bag full of barley — enough to make many pots of soup.

"It's a gift," he said, passing it to her.

"Why? What d'you want?" she asked, suspicious he wanted some sort of sexual favour.

He sensed her fear. "All I want is for you to deliver something for me," he said, pulling a letter from an envelope in the satchel. "I want you to take this to Colonel Van Egmond."

"Why don' you just take it yourself? You know where he lives."

"Because it has to come from you. I want you to tell him you found it in the house here, when you were cleaning, and you thought he should see it."

"What does it say?" she asked, looking it over.

"It's a letter from Bert, applying to be a minister in the Anglican Church."

"Why would he do that?"

"I guess he'd like a nice soft life as an Anglican minister," he said. "Your employer may not be the hero he seems to be."

"But that don' mean he's involved in a rebellion," said Rosalee.

"Quite right," replied Grayson. "And he probably won't be involved in any rebellion — once this is known about him. The rebels won't trust him anymore. And that's a good thing ... unless you favour a rebellion."

"No, I don'."

"So, then you shouldn't have any problem delivering this letter to the colonel. You're only letting him know the truth ... and maybe helping stop a rebellion. That would keep Bert out of trouble."

Grayson returned to his satchel, pulling out a tiny paper packet and handing it to her.

She opened it to find three little chocolates. She'd had chocolate once before, when she was a child, and remembered the seering delight of the taste.

"Now how bad is that?" he said smiling.

Entering his private chambers to change for dinner earlier than usual, Thomas Mercer Jones inadvertently surprised his wife. She was getting dressed in the large adjoining dressing room, but was still in her undergarments, with her maid tightening the stays. Jones sensed Mary's embarrassment, as she instinctively put her hands up over her semi-clad body, covering spots where she bulged at the edges of her corset.

The extra weight she'd put on from her pregnancy had made her even more modest than she'd been in the early days of their marriage. Jones wasn't sure what he found less attractive — the slight bulging or her excessive modesty about it. Either way, he couldn't avoid thinking of how poorly she compared to the smooth-skinned girl whom he'd been quick to dismiss as a potential dinner guest, but who regularly occupied his innermost thoughts. For an awkward moment, Jones considered simply exiting the chambers he shared with his wife and returning when her dressing was complete.

But that would only highlight the discomfort they both apparently felt. Better to pretend all was easy and natural between them. So he merely nodded in her direction, greeting her with "my dear," and proceeded to his own, smaller dressing area on the far side of the room. The presence of her maid made it necessary for him to close the door to his dressing space, sparing him further views of his half-naked wife.

As he dressed, he felt confident about his decision not to invite Van Egmond to the dinner party planned for later that week. Jones had considered inviting the colonel and using the occasion to inform him about Norbert Scott's attempted defection to the Anglican side. Van Egmond would undoubtedly regard such behaviour as opportunistic and unprincipled, making him suspicious of the clergyman's loyalty to the rebel cause. But Jones also realized that Van Egmond likely wouldn't trust the information if it came from the Company. Grayson's idea of having the servant girl deliver Norbert's letter had struck him as clever; Grayson continued to impress.

There was a knock on the door of the bedchamber and Jones, now fully dressed, opened it to find his butler.

"A mail delivery just came in, sir." It had been only a few days since the last one. Could it be that, with talk of rebellion in the air, the Executive Council was starting to appreciate the importance of communicating with the outlying regions?

Jones spotted a letter from the archdeacon's office and opened it first.

My dear Mr. Jones,

I write this to follow up on my last letter to you regarding your inquiry about the Reverend Norbert Scott.

As mentioned in said letter, Reverend Scott did apply to become a minister in our Church, and we did decline his services.

I have looked further into this matter on your behalf and learned that Reverend Scott was not even granted an audience with the archdeacon. His application was dispensed with at a preliminary level by members of the adjunct committee who considered him unsuitable for preaching due to his pronounced stutter.

I trust that this information will be helpful, and that you and your family are well.

With my very best sentiments,
Most revered Arthur Potter,
Secretary to the Archdeacon

Rosalee returned the following morning, determined to find the diary. This was a good time for a more thorough search, since Callandra and Sam wouldn't likely be back before the next day, providing an opportunity for her to get together with Grayson again and finish reading the diary.

She'd accepted his barley and his chocolates, and been tempted by his hint of more to come. She hadn't yet delivered the letter to the colonel, but the more she considered the matter, the more she realized there was no reason not to deliver it. If it kept Bert out of a rebellion, that would be a good thing. The fact that he had tried to defect to the Anglican Church didn't bother Rosalee; it certainly didn't diminish her attraction to him. If anything, it did the opposite. Why shouldn't a man try to better himself in the world? If one Church offered more opportunity than another, surely it made sense to switch.

After taking clothes and bedding out of the closet in search of the diary, she'd gone to the kitchen to make tea and, looking out the window, noticed a wagon coming down the road. It was hard to believe they would be home so soon, but as the wagon drew closer, she could see Bert and Callandra, with Emma between them. She rushed to put the closet back in order, but there wasn't time to do so properly. As they pulled up in front of the house, Rosalee rushed back to the kitchen, trying to think of how to explain what she'd been doing in Callandra's closet.

Looking out the kitchen window, she noticed Callandra's hair was loose and flowing freely around her face, and that she looked happy. Bert got down and tended to the horse, while Callandra helped Emma, who came running into the house.

"You're back so soon. Did everything go all right?"

"Yes. It's a baby boy ... I helped," declared Emma proudly.

Through the window, Rosalee could see Callandra reaching for bags from the back of the wagon, and Bert reaching over from behind her. He was standing close to Callandra, almost brushing against her.

"What are you staring at?" asked Emma.

"Nothing. I'm not staring," said Rosalee. She went quickly into the bedroom, scooped up items on the floor, and put them back in the closet.

It wasn't long before Callandra came in the front door, followed by Sam carrying the bags. They both greeted Rosalee. He then went back outside.

"I hear it's a boy," said Rosalee.

"Yes, a healthy boy," said Callandra.

"You must be tired."

"It was a long night."

In fact, Callandra didn't look tired. She went into her room and closed the door. Rosalee fidgeted nervously.

After a while, Callandra came back out holding a dress from her closet. She asked Rosalee to take it to the seamstress, and to wait at the woman's house while she fixed the buttons and redid the stitching along the front panels. Callandra suggested Rosalee take Emma with her.

There was no mention of the closet's disarray.

——— * ———

Callandra watched Sam chopping wood behind the house. He had taken off his coat despite the chill in the air. What a fine physical specimen he was; so strong and powerful, yet not domineering, like so many other men. She had come to love watching him, no matter what he was doing, observing his strength and sense of purpose — qualities that blended perfectly with his rebellious streak, his easy confidence, his wry smile. And into this mix of wonderfully desirable traits, she now added another: his longing for her. This final one was crucial, the one that gave all the others meaning. Until last night, it had fit uncertainly into her narrative about him. But that had changed. She had initiated things, to be sure, but he had taken charge, overwhelming her by the intensity of his desire.

Now it was possible to believe he had always wanted her, but had held back out of a sense of honour. She felt elation, rooted in the centre of her being, radiating to every nook and crevice of her body. All the way home in the carriage, she'd felt alive as never before, blissfully inhaling the dank, musky smell of the forest, marvelling at the splendour of this cold, remote place. If only they could remain lost here forever, now that they had so completely found each other.

He came in with an armful of wood and began building up the fire. He was facing the blaze, his back to her. She wanted to go over and put her arms around him. Their bodies had felt so naturally entwined last night, but here, in the place where they'd lived together yet so far apart, she had a sudden sensation of their separateness.

"I'm sorry if I got carried away last night," she said playfully, anxious to engage with him about their new intimacy.

"I forgive you," he said, returning her playfulness as he moved toward her, taking her hand.

"I promise to be more respectful in the future," she said.

"That's good to know. Otherwise, how would I be able to sleep, knowing you might just start kissing me?"

"Oh, so you'll trust me enough to come into my bed?"

"I assume you would demand it," he said, pulling her against him.

"Do I strike you as demanding?"

"A bit, but I like that about you," he said, smiling softly and twisting a strand of her hair. "You know what you want."

She was more interested in hearing what *he* wanted — specifically, that he wanted her.

"Well, maybe I learned from experience," she said, more seriously. "I ended up in an unhappy marriage because I didn't assert what I wanted."

"You didn't want to marry Norbert?"

"Oh, good heavens, no!"

"Even with all the advantages he offered?" She realized he was referring to their conversation long ago about the advantages for Lottie in marrying Reverend Blair.

"Oh, no, no," she insisted. "It broke my heart to marry Norbert. I only did it to help my family. Otherwise they would have been forced off the farm, after my father died ... it all happened so fast ... Didn't Lottie tell you all this?"

"No," he said.

"Didn't she tell you that I was different than Norbert and his family, that I disliked all their meanness and haughtiness?"

"Well, she told me about you confronting some guests at a dinner party — which I found impressive. But she said you were mostly concerned about the plight of women."

"Oh ..." said Callandra. "I know you don't think women are oppressed —"

"Actually, I'd never thought about it before I met you," he said.

"And now that you've thought about it?" she asked, hopefully.

"Uh, maybe in some ways they are. I'm not really sure," he said. "But I like that you think about it."

"You do?"

"Aye."

"Really?"

"It shows that you question things, that you don't just accept the world as it is ... that you're strong and rebellious in your heart."

She basked in the praise, feeling for the first time that he truly respected her.

There had been a shift in his tone from teasing to serious, underlined by the way he put his hand beneath her chin and gently lifted up her face, so that their eyes locked.

"But," he continued, his hand still under her chin, "You should know — I also want you as my toy ... my rattle."

"Oh," she replied, not knowing quite how to respond. He kissed her on the forehead, then let his lips explore her face.

Being his toy — surely that was wrong; she had to register some objection. And yet, the way he said it, it felt so right, so sweet, so strangely lovely.

She was giddy, thrilled by his touch, by the confident stroll of his lips over her face and neck. Her head was spinning with delight and confusion. He had just said that he admired her strength and rebelliousness, and yet she felt weak in his arms, dizzy and woozy with desire for him, ready to submit her whole body and self to him.

He pulled her closer, planting his mouth fully on hers, kissing her deeply and urgently. Then he picked her up and carried her into her room, closing the door behind them.

---- * ----

A knock on the door woke her up. She was momentarily disoriented as she recovered from the deep sleep she'd fallen into. The afternoon sun was streaming in through the window and she was lying naked next to him under the covers. How strange and exquisite that felt. Sam had awoken, too, and pulled her over against him.

Then a thought hit her: Norbert.

Surely not.

The knock came again, this time more insistent. She grabbed Sam's arm.

"Callandra, are you in there?" Rosalee asked from the other side of the door.

"What is it?" Callandra responded.

"There's a pastor here to see Bert. But I can't find him," said Rosalee.

She looked at Sam in panic. "What if it's Norbert?"

"It can't be," Sam whispered, trying to calm her. "Probably just a travelling Methodist."

It wasn't unusual for Methodist preachers to seek lodging with local ministers.

Callandra pulled the sheet up against her naked body.

"He's come all the way from Toronto," Rosalee shouted through the door. "His name is Reverend Blair. Do you know where Bert is?"

Callandra and Sam looked at each other. Relief that it wasn't Norbert gave way to a new uneasiness.

"What's *he* doing here?" Callandra gasped to Sam.

They stared at each other. The impenetrable forest had been breached.

Callandra scrambled out of bed, clutching a blanket to cover herself, just as Rosalee opened the door. The girl was startled by what she saw — the look of panic on Callandra's face, the clothes strewn all over the floor, Sam in the bed.

Rosalee quickly retreated and shut the door.

"I can't remember whether Blair ever met Norbert," Callandra whispered to Sam.

They stared at each other; if the two men had met, there was no possible explanation for what was going on now.

Callandra's hands were trembling as she fastened the clasps on her dress. She had them almost done up, and then realized she'd put them through the wrong holes, leaving the dress improperly aligned. She started over, unattaching and then reattaching them properly. She realized how dishevelled she looked, how little she resembled a minister's wife. And Sam, of course, didn't at all resemble Norbert.

"They may have met back in Glasgow," Callandra whispered frantically. "I just can't remember."

Sam was now fully dressed and came over to where she sat, trying clumsily to organize her hair into a bun — a task she could normally perform effortlessly.

He put his hand on her shoulder to calm her.

"It's possible they never met," he said. "We should play it as if I'm Norbert."

"Yes, of course," she said. "I'm sorry ... this is all my fault."

"No, I could have left at any point. I chose not to," he replied.

She didn't argue, although she knew she had subtly pressured him to stay.

Pulling her into his arms, he insisted, "Whatever happens, we're in this together ..."

Their lips touched tenderly, lingering momentarily longer than they knew they should.

——— * ———

She opened the door, and felt a chill as soon as she saw Blair in the sitting area just off the kitchen. Unlike Sam, he was wearing a clerical collar. And he looked pious and dutiful, whereas Sam was big and easy in his ways. Suddenly the absurdity of Sam as a man of the cloth — an absurdity that had somehow gone unnoticed in Goderich — seemed unmistakable.

Blair rose to greet them, the look on his face revealing instantly that Sam was not the man he was expecting.

Callandra reached out her hand to him. "It's so good to see you, Reverend Blair," she said, hoping against all odds that she was misreading his expression. He was surveying Sam, almost gawking at him.

"It's good to see you, Mrs. Scott," Blair began, taking her hand.

"Oh, just call me Callandra." She worried that Blair's formality didn't bode well.

"I don't believe you've met my husband," she continued, her voice quivering. She was aware of Rosalee watching from the kitchen.

Blair held back for a moment, still looking over Sam with curious eyes and an arched brow. Callandra felt sure he was suspicious.

"It's a pleasure to meet you," said Blair, eventually taking Sam's outstretched hand, but still scrutinizing his face closely. "I believe we were both at a meeting of the Glasgow Colonial Society, but we weren't formally introduced."

"Yes, that's correct," said Sam. "I recall seeing you at the meeting."

"Hmm," said Blair, struggling to revive his memory of the event. "I had just returned from Upper Canada, and I guess there were many faces in the room I didn't recognize."

"Aye, you were a busy man that day. A lot of people wanted to talk to you, I recall," Sam ventured, impressing Callandra with his confident assertion.

Blair nodded modestly. "Well, yes, they were keen to learn about the colony. I tried to provide a full picture in my remarks to the gathering. But there were still many questions."

"I remember you spoke very well," Sam added.

Blair looked pleased, the doubt draining from his face.

"And then I missed you in Toronto," Blair continued. "I must say, you're very different than I expected."

"Well, it's good to finally meet you, Reverend," said Sam. "And *you're* very different than I expected. I thought you'd be much older. You seem young to have a position of such responsibility."

"Well, thank you," said Blair, looking flattered that the heavy load on his shoulders was recognized.

They sat down together while Rosalee served tea.

Blair continued, "I'm honoured to have been given the task of ensuring members of our flock have access to a minister of our faith, although it does at times seem like a large burden for one man … And, indeed, I haven't had a chance to thank you for helping out with that. I deeply appreciate your sacrifice in coming all the way to this distant place. In case no one has formally thanked you on behalf of the Church, let that thanks finally come from me. And know that it is heartfelt."

"You're most welcome," said Sam warmly. "Of course, we're delighted by your visit — although surprised to see you so soon. We hadn't expected to see anyone from Toronto until next summer, or spring at the earliest. Is everything all right?"

"Oh, yes."

"And Lottie?" interjected Callandra. "Have you seen her?"

"Yes, I have visited her a number of times, as you asked me to. She is doing very well, and making an excellent recovery."

Callandra pressed for more news about Lottie. Blair obliged, filling out the picture with details about her slow but steady mending.

"Yes, things are well in Toronto," he repeated, producing several letters from his satchel and handing them to Sam. "I'm glad to personally deliver these. This one appears to be from your mother."

Sam thanked him, looked at the letters appreciatively, and then put them aside for later.

"You're quite right," said Blair. "I hadn't planned to come until next summer. But I heard there was a special steamer bringing up some soldiers and equipment, and I was able to arrange passage at the last minute."

Callandra asked him how his voyage had been. He responded with a somewhat lengthy description, comparing travel by coach and by steamboat. Rosalee served honey biscuits. Callandra followed her into the kitchen and suggested that she take Emma down to the harbour to see the steamboat, then ushered them out the door. By the time Callandra returned to the sitting room, Blair was again praising Norbert, this time for his role in building the church, which he'd heard about from people at Feltie's, where he was staying.

"Well, I'm just helping with it," said Sam modestly. "The Presbyterians of Goderich are determined to have their own church. I'm happy to assist in any way I can."

A surprisingly congenial tone had been established in only a short while. It was clear that Blair had great respect for Norbert Scott, without ever having met him.

"Well, there is a reason for my visit," said Blair, looking poised to deliver some very good news. "I am delighted to advise you that there will be an opening for a minister at St. Andrew's Church in Toronto. I've come all the way here, quite frankly, to urge you to apply for it." Then, lowering his voice as if imparting an important confidence, he added, "The congregation must approve all appointments, of course, but I have reason to believe you would have an excellent chance of securing the position."

When Sam didn't immediately respond, Blair simply continued, "It is the leading Presbyterian Church in Upper Canada, and its minister sets the tone for all of our work in the colony. I think your willingness to forsake comfort in Glasgow and go wherever God commanded you reveals a selflessness that is exactly in the spirit of what we are trying to instill in our parishioners — and our ministers, for that matter. I believe you are just the sort of man we need at the helm of St. Andrew's."

"I'm honoured by your confidence in me, Reverend Blair —"

"Oh, please, do call me Jonathan. I assume I would not be taking too many liberties in calling you Norbert?"

"No, not at all," said Sam. "And, as I mentioned, I'm honoured by your suggestion, and will certainly give it serious thought."

"More than serious thought, I hope! There is not much time," said Blair, leaning forward. "There are influential individuals in the congregation who are set on having a new minister in place by Christmas, and there really aren't any suitable candidates in Toronto at this time. I happen to know, however, that three new ministers will be arriving on the ship from Ayr early in the new year. If you were to present yourself to the congregation sooner, I am confident that you would be very favourably regarded."

"Well, that is not much time," said Sam.

"Exactly. Time is of the essence," Blair said. "I'm sure your mother would be proud for you to have such an important position in the Church."

"No doubt."

"And of course, I know how delighted you would be, Callandra, to be reunited with Lottie in Toronto."

"Yes, I would ... but Lottie could always come here," offered Callandra.

"I suppose, yes, if she were healthy enough," said Blair.

"I thought you said she was doing very well? The plan was that she'd recuperate over the winter and come here next spring or summer. It sounds like she's well on the way to recovery, isn't that right?"

"Yes. Yes, she is," said Blair hesitantly. "But spring is a long time to wait for a reunion."

"Well, as I say, I will give it some thought," said Sam. "But I should point out that I feel committed to completing the church here. The people of Goderich would be very disappointed if I were to abandon the project."

"Of course, I understand the sense of duty that keeps you here, but ..." said Blair.

"Not just duty," Sam interrupted. "I'm not really the selfless creature you take me for, Jonathan," he continued, exuding an ease noticeably at odds with Blair's formality. "Yes, I came here to this faraway place. But now that I'm here, I've come to like it. I'm very happy here — happier than I've ever been."

With this, Sam took Callandra's hand and held it gently, an intimate gesture, almost a provocative one. But then, why shouldn't he take his wife's hand, as he described his contentment with their life together in Goderich? As their eyes met, she felt confident that at least this part of what he was saying was true and that the happiness he referred to was connected to her. It was even more thrilling to have him say it in front of Blair like that — a secret that they were dangerously, deliciously sharing.

"Oh, I see," said Blair, obviously disappointed.

"So, as I say, I will give it some thought," said Sam. "I owe you that much for making the trip all the way here. When would you need an answer?"

Blair looked up sheepishly. "Well, I had been hoping you'd come back with me on Thursday on the boat. Your family could follow later. The window of opportunity at St. Andrew's is very small."

"Thursday! You mean two days from now?"

"Aye."

"Oh, I don't think that would be possible," said Sam. "I've got to finish the church roof before snowfall."

"But surely the parishioners can complete the church without you. You said you were only offering assistance."

"Yes, but I want to see the project through ... I don't see how I could possibly do that and accommodate your request ... I regret that you came such a long way only to be disappointed."

"Well, I am disappointed," said Blair, clearly dejected. "But I remain grateful to you for your service to the Church."

"Is there anything else we could do for you?" Callandra asked.

"Uh, well," said Blair. "Yes, I do have one other question: How is Sam?"

"Sam? Oh, he's well," said Callandra.

"I was hoping to see him," said Blair.

"To see Sam?" she responded.

"Aye."

"He's not here right now."

"When will he be back? I can wait."

"Uh ... he's gone ... for a while," said Callandra, evasively. "He ... he's helping build a road. I'm not sure when he'll be back."

Blair clearly felt thwarted, now for the second time. "Oh no. I really do want to see him."

"I didn't know that you knew him," said Callandra, puzzled.

"I don't. But I want to be able to report to Lottie that I've seen him, and confirm that he is well. I know she's upset that she hasn't heard from him."

"Oh, well, she shouldn't worry," said Callandra. "I can assure you he is very well. You can tell Lottie that he is in excellent health and in great spirits — and looking forward to her joining us here."

"With all due respect, I'd like to see him myself, to be able to report back first-hand."

"Well, I'm sure Lottie will take my word for it, Reverend Blair. We are the closest of friends, as you know," Callandra said, a touch of indignation creeping into her voice. Even as she said this, it occurred to her that Lottie apparently hadn't been upset about not hearing from *her*.

"I mean no disrespect, ma'am," said Blair, the formality returning to his voice. "But I do very much want to see Sam myself."

"But he's not here, Jonathan," Sam interjected, trying to diffuse the tension that had suddenly overtaken the visit. "You can be sure that he is well."

"Where's he gone?"

"He's out somewhere in the bush ... on a road-building crew, with Colonel Van Egmond," Callandra scrambled to add some detail to make the story more credible.

"Van Egmond?" Blair asked with surprise.

"He lives just outside town. He has a contract with the Company," explained Sam.

"Yes, I've heard of him. But doesn't he side with the radicals?" Blair shot back.

"Oh, I don't know about that," said Callandra. "In any event, they're just building roads, I'm sure."

"And what would it matter, if Van Egmond sides with the radicals?" asked Sam, softly but pointedly. "Our Church is no fan of the Family Compact."

"Aye, that's true," replied Blair. "But this hothead Mackenzie would cause real problems for our Church. He doesn't support our claim to an equal share of the Clergy Reserves. He wants to abolish the reserves altogether, and hand the money over for public education."

"But surely that's a good idea!" exclaimed Sam. "The problem is privilege — whether it's for the Anglicans or for us. All those vast lands properly belong to the people, and the people should benefit from them. Public education is exactly what's needed."

"Well, but the people need churches, too, and not just Anglican ones!" Blair was flustered and upset to find himself arguing with someone he held in such high esteem. "Surely you agree with that, Norbert?"

Callandra looked pleadingly at Sam.

"Yes, of course," said Sam, backing off.

With that, the tension in the room dissipated. Callandra poured everyone more tea.

"It is important however that I see Sam," said Blair. "Yes, I really must see him. You see, I plan to seek Miss Lottie's hand in marriage again, and I want his approval."

Callandra and Sam were both momentarily silent.

Blair continued: "I've seen a great deal of her lately, and have reason to believe she's developed feelings toward me. I think there's something special between us."

"Why don't you just ask her to marry you," said Callandra finally. "Surely you don't need Sam's permission."

"Well, he is her older brother and has charge of her. And frankly, I think I made a mistake with my last proposal. I didn't seek his approval, and I believe that may be why I was turned down."

Again an awkward silence followed. "Perhaps she just didn't feel inclined to marry …" ventured Sam.

"Well, it's certainly possible she didn't consider me an adequate suitor. I have many shortcomings. But I don't see that hesitation in her any more."

"I wasn't suggesting there was anything lacking in you," said Sam, "I just meant that — who knows what a woman wants? But I'm not sure you can conclude her brother meddled in the decision ..."

"Well, she told me herself that he didn't approve. And I know he has great sway with her. She worships him."

This should have felt like vindication to Callandra, but it didn't. Her disputes with Sam over Lottie seemed distant and irrelevant now. For the first time, Callandra was struck by the thought that Sam was now more important to her than Lottie. She looked over at him, hoping to somehow signal with her eyes that none of this mattered anymore.

"Well, we can certainly plead your case with Sam when he gets back," she said to Blair. "It might even be more persuasive coming from us, rather than directly from you."

Blair shook his head, revealing a stubbornness that Callandra hadn't noticed in their earlier encounters. "I'm not the most articulate man, I know. But I feel I could convince him of my devotion to his sister, if only I could talk to him ... this is of great importance to me. I've come all this way ..."

This then had been Blair's real purpose, Callandra thought. For all his talk about the need for an inspiring minister for St. Andrew's, what he really cared about was getting Lottie to marry him. Even the plan to bring Norbert back to Toronto was really about ensuring that Lottie didn't end up far away in Goderich.

"We simply don't know when he'll be back," said Sam.

"Well, could you take me to him, then?" asked Blair.

"That would be difficult. They're far away. Somewhere north of Point Clark, I believe. I don't actually know where. It would be difficult to find them," said Sam.

"We could try ... you're a sturdy fellow, Norbert. I'm sure you could make it through the bush. I'd be happy to undergo a little hardship."

Sam paused before shaking his head. "I really must focus on building the church ... I appreciate the importance of matters of the heart, Jonathan, but I'm sure you can see what must be done here."

With the issue framed this way — as duty versus personal desire — it was harder for Blair to keep pressing his case. He had no immediate answer and looked flummoxed.

"I'm going to talk to Sam about your marriage proposal when he returns," said Callandra, trying to soften the blow. "Your dedication to Lottie will surely impress him. It's been so good of you to watch over her in Toronto — as I asked you to."

Blair seemed pleased to be reminded that he had acted out of duty.

"Yes, I will tell Sam emphatically about your devotion," Callandra continued.

"I doubt if your intervention will help," replied Blair. "Again, with all due respect, ma'am, Lottie says that her brother doesn't trust you."

"Oh," said Callandra. "I think that may have changed ... I get along with him much better now. In any event, I'm going to write a note for you to take home to Lottie, assuring her that Sam is doing just fine. I know *she* trusts me. So that should be a comfort to her."

Blair asked whether he might be able to find the road crew on his own. As Sam tried to discourage the idea, Callandra disappeared into her bedroom to compose the note. At her writing table, she fumbled trying to get the ink into the pen. She could hear the front door open and Emma and Rosalee moving about in the kitchen, while in the adjacent sitting room the two men continued to talk.

She hurriedly wrote the note, concerned that it was far too short, after months of unexplained silence. But she was anxious to get back to the sitting room to ensure that the conversation didn't return to the subject of Sam, now that Rosalee was back and no doubt eavesdropping. That girl was far too curious.

All Callandra managed to write was:

My dearest Lottie:

I am writing this to assure you that Sam is healthy and well.
    I will send you a proper letter by mail shortly, giving full details of our life here in Goderich.
    I am so glad you have recovered. I miss you terribly.

With sincerest love,
Callandra

She folded up the note and rushed into the kitchen, trying to keep Rosalee occupied. "How was the steamboat?" Callandra asked.

Emma expressed delight at seeing the boat, and Rosalee mentioned that there were soldiers down by the harbour. Callandra thanked Rosalee for taking Emma to the harbour and then told her to take the rest of the day off, guiding her toward the door.

"You won't be needing me?" she asked.

"No," said Callandra, handing Rosalee her coat.

But Rosalee didn't seem interested in leaving. "I know where the road-building crew is if the pastor wants to find it," she said to Callandra. "My cousin is working on it. I could take him there. It's not far."

"That won't be necessary," said Callandra tersely.

The men apparently hadn't overheard Rosalee's offer, but it nonetheless sent a jolt through Callandra. She escorted Rosalee out the door, directing her toward the shed at the back, out of sight of the men. "Uh, have you seen the barrel of apples? I was looking for it but I can't seem to find it. Would it be in here?" said Callandra, desperate to get Rosalee away from the house.

"No. It's in the pantry, where it always is," said Rosalee in a huffy tone.

Callandra realized she was only stoking Rosalee's curiosity with her odd behaviour. Still, it was imperative to keep her out of the house just now.

Summoning authority into her voice, she insisted that the girl go home, then returned to find Blair standing inside the front door, putting on his coat. If he left right away, he might easily catch up with Rosalee, with one of them likely to question the other. Together they knew too much.

"Oh, you're not leaving, Reverend?" asked Callandra. "There is so much more to talk about. Let me serve you more tea. Perhaps you'd stay for supper?"

"No, that's kind of you, but I should be going." It almost seemed like he was trying to catch up with Rosalee.

"Oh, please, don't rush off," said Callandra, directing him back into the sitting room. "Here's the note I wrote for Lottie. Have a look at it. I could add to it, if you could wait a few minutes more."

Through the kitchen window, Callandra could see Rosalee down the way, but not out of sight.

Blair sat down and read the note, thanked Callandra for it, but said he had to go.

"Oh, please. I want to hear more about Lottie — and your plans for marriage. I do think it's a splendid idea."

That picked up Blair's interest. "Really?"

"Yes, I can see that you truly love her. Your devotion is clear. She deserves that kind of love," said Callandra. All of this was true. Still, Callandra wanted to signal something to Sam, in case he took offence at her encouragement of the marriage proposal. Surely he would understand the need to stall Blair, to keep Blair and Rosalee apart.

"True enough," said Blair, getting up. "But I must go."

"I don't know if you remember our daughter Emma," Callandra continued, summoning the child. "You met her back in Scotland, I believe. Emma, you remember Reverend Blair?"

"Yes," said Emma shyly, taking the cue from her mother.

"Hello, young lady," Blair said stiffly.

"Please sit down, Jonathan, so Emma can show you the picture she's been drawing."

Emma went to the alcove to retrieve her drawing, while Blair sat down, clearly frustrated that he was unable to make his exit without appearing rude.

Emma returned with her drawing of a horse. Blair complimented her on it, and then followed up with a few polite questions. Callandra slipped over to Sam across the room and whispered that they had to keep Blair there until Rosalee was well gone.

"Yes, his name was Prince," Emma was saying. "But he drowned in the river."

"How did he get into the river?" asked Blair.

"He fell in, along with the carriage. We were all in the river."

At this point, Callandra gently grabbed Sam's arm.

"What?" Blair asked Emma.

"On the way to Goderich. Our carriage went into the river."

"And the horse drowned?"

"Yes — and the hired man. They both drowned."

"The hired man? He drowned?"

"Yes."

"You mean the hired man who came from Scotland with you? Sam?" asked Blair, scrutinizing Emma closely.

"Yes."

"You're sure? This isn't a story? You're not making this up?"

"Oh no. It's true. I promise."

Chapter Eighteen

The mid-afternoon sun was already low in the sky; its rays brightened the kitchen, providing a false sense that there was plenty of daylight left. Callandra gathered up the salted meats and wrapped them in cloth. There was enough to last him five or maybe six days. Emma, following her mother's example, began wrapping apples and carrots. She had stopped crying, but her face was puffy, her eyes dark balls of sadness and fear.

Sam emerged from his bedroom, wearing his warmest clothes. They wouldn't be enough against the late November weather, with snow expected any day. It was unlikely any of the roadhouses would still be open. Callandra shuddered at the thought of him camped out in the woods. She had gathered six blankets from around the cottage, but he had only packed two into his saddlebag, insisting that was all he needed. While she felt devastated at the prospect of him leaving, he seemed calm, almost sanguine, about this sudden, strange twist of fate.

His calmness had been crucial in the wake of Emma's revelation. An eerie silence had followed, before the girl had run to her mother, a look of confusion and anguish on her face. It wasn't her fault. It had been Callandra who had called her over, in a desperate attempt to delay Reverend Blair's departure. And Emma had done just that; she had kept him busy, answering his questions. And her answers were no different than ones she'd given before, without any problem.

Callandra had immediately denied Emma's story, noting the girl was only five years old and often got things wrong. But Callandra's faltering voice undermined her denial. And by then Emma had started sobbing. Callandra had picked up her daughter, trying to comfort her. But she only cried harder, struggling in her mother's arms.

"It's all right," Sam had said soothingly to Emma, taking her from Callandra and rocking her gently in his arms, looking every bit her father.

In the commotion, Blair had said nothing.

"I've changed my mind," Sam said to Blair. "It's obviously important for you to be able to assure Lottie that her brother is all right. So, we should go together to find the road-building crew."

"Good," said Blair.

"If we set out at daybreak tomorrow, there should be time to make it back before nightfall," said Sam, still rocking Emma, whose sobs grew less intense.

"I will be back here at first light," Blair replied, putting on his coat. Before leaving, he added: "I appreciate this very much, Norbert."

They watched him disappear down the path before Sam reached out and put his arm around Callandra, huddling them all together.

"I'm going to have to leave," he said quietly.

Callandra looked up into his eyes. The thought of losing him was too much to contemplate. "Oh no," she said softly.

"I'll have to be gone before he comes back tomorrow morning. Otherwise he's going to expect me to take him to the road-building crew."

"What if you went looking for it but couldn't find it?"

"There are too many people in town who know where they're working. That would only increase his suspicion."

"What does it matter if he's suspicious? He's got no proof of anything," Callandra insisted.

"Yeah, but what if he starts asking questions? Lots of people in Goderich know the story about the hired man drowning."

Emma had grown quiet, burying her face against Sam's chest. Callandra could feel the warmth and strength of Sam's arm around her.

"Maybe we should just tell him the truth," she suggested, revitalized by the thought.

"What? That Norbert Scott died and we never told anyone?"

"We could tell him the truth about the accident. Then he could return to Lottie and tell her honestly that he met her brother, and that you're safe and well."

"You're forgetting that Blair is a minister, and one of his fellow ministers is dead. He's not going to accept that Norbert drowned and we covered it up, and that I posed as Norbert — and slept with his wife."

Callandra wanted desperately to argue that Blair could be trusted with the truth, but she wasn't sure she believed that herself.

"It's better just for me to go."

"Where will you go?" she asked, tears welling up in her eyes.

"I don't know ... maybe somewhere to hide and wait for the rebellion."

There was silence again.

"Maybe to America," he said.

"Then take us with you!" Callandra pleaded.

At this, Emma joined in. "Yes, yes, let's all go!" she cried.

But Sam shook his head, as he wrapped his arms more tightly around them both. "It's a long way. Don't you remember how long?

And now it's cold, and we don't even know if there are places to stay at night. It's much too risky for Emma — and for you. You've only just recovered."

"We'd be all right if we were with you!" Callandra insisted.

"Think of what will happen if Blair arrives tomorrow and we're all gone. They'd know we were running away. We'd be fugitives."

"Yes, but if we made it to America, they'd never find us."

"We'd never make it that far. They'd easily catch up with us."

"But what happens when Blair gets here tomorrow and discovers you're gone. What am I to tell him?"

"You can tell him I had to leave suddenly."

"But why?"

Sam was silent for a minute, filling Callandra with hope that he'd agree their lie was as good as discovered and they should all leave together, while they could. They would make it through the woods somehow. The thought of all being together, even stranded in the winter forest, was strangely exhilarating. She could feel her heart pounding furiously. Going to America, to start a new life together as a family!

"That letter — the one from Mrs. Scott," said Sam, putting Emma down and going over to the table in the sitting room. "Yes," he said, looking over the letter without opening it. "You can say that Norbert's mother is very ill and that she begged him to come home quickly so she can see him before she dies. So there was no choice; I had to leave immediately."

"But then why wouldn't you go back on the boat with Blair?" said Callandra, desperate to find flaws in his story.

"There was no time for that. The boat isn't leaving for two days, and it's much slower than horseback."

Callandra sensed it didn't matter what she said; Sam was going to leave. Emma began to cry again.

"Just make sure you burn the letter," said Sam.

Maybe it was then that her doubt began to return. He was warm and loving, but able to think it all through so rationally. He didn't seem blindsided or disoriented, as she was.

Callandra finished wrapping his food, by now caught up in the logistics herself. She'd packed all the salted meat, but it didn't seem enough. Insisting it was more than he needed, Sam put some back on the table. He said he would find places to stay along the way, possibly spend the first night at the Van Egmond homestead, and then set out before dawn the next morning.

He went outside to chop more firewood for them. While he was out there, Callandra returned the salted meat on the table to his bag. She also fetched Norbert's velvet sack, with its two remaining gold coins, and placed it inside the folded-up map he had packed. She knew he wouldn't accept the coins if she handed them to him, but if he discovered them during the journey, he would surely use them.

"That's enough wood," she called to him. "There's not much daylight left."

She watched him, mesmerized, as he sent the wood flying under the force of his blows. Surely, being with him was the safest place to be.

The final minutes with him, after he saddled up the horse, were slow and painful. Emma offered him her pillow, and a little stuffed doll she'd made out of cloth and straw. He thanked her, saying he didn't have room for the pillow, but that he'd take the doll because it reminded him of her. Then he picked her up in his arms, drawing Callandra in as well.

"Please take us with you," pleaded Callandra, unable to hold back tears.

"It's too dangerous," he said. "We'd never get away. But if you're still here and you offer a believable account of why I left, that will dispel their suspicions, or at least buy us time. If I get to Toronto before Blair, I can get Lottie to convince him to keep quiet about the whole thing."

"Oh," said Callandra. She hadn't thought of that. Of course, Blair wouldn't do anything that would upset Lottie. Still, this was all too much to absorb. And now there seemed to be a change of plans. He was going to Toronto — not to America? Maybe just stopping in Toronto on his way to America? Maybe he and Lottie would go together to America?

She felt dizzy, all of these questions crowding her mind. But there was little time left; should she ask the questions or just keep pleading with him to take her and Emma along? Or had he already moved on, with a plan to go to America with Lottie and put this whole Goderich episode behind him?

He put Emma down on the ground, and pulled Callandra close to him.

"I love you, Callie," he said, then kissed her fully and deeply. It was impossible not to be thrilled by his words, feeling so close to him, enfolded in his arms.

"I'll come back for you," he said, then looking down into Emma's upturned face, "for both of you ... I promise."

Callandra found herself believing him.

He gave her one last, lingering kiss. Then he gently released her and moved back a few feet, just looking at her, as if to imprint her image in his mind.

Emma clung tightly to her mother's dress. The air was crisp, with a touch of frost, as he got on the horse and rode off.

Callandra was up and dressed before dawn, feeling weak, exhausted, scared and cold, wondering if she'd slept at all that night. She put a couple of logs on the embers in the woodstove, prepared tea, and then sat down at the kitchen table, waiting for Blair. What if he had reported his suspicions to authorities, and Thomas Mercer Jones had figured out Sam was an imposter? Would Blair arrive now with Jones — and soldiers? If so, it was good that Sam was gone, even if she never got to see him again. Of course, she had to be convincing in providing the reason for his sudden departure. She went over the story about his mother's illness again in her mind, checking for flaws.

She realized she'd forgotten to burn the letter. She quickly found it in the drawer. There was no time to read it now, so she tossed it unopened into the woodstove.

The darkness was starting to lift when she spotted Blair coming down the road, alone.

"Hello Reverend Blair," she said, opening the door before he had a chance to knock. "Do come in." Now she was the one being formal, but she found it difficult to sound familiar when trying to lie convincingly.

"My husband is gone," she said as soon as he'd closed the door behind him. "His mother is very ill, so he had to leave right away."

"What?" Blair's eyes showed disbelief — or was it just surprise, concern?

"That letter you brought yesterday contained the bad news. She begged him to come home immediately."

Blair stood there, not knowing what to make of this sudden turn of events.

"I've got some tea ready. Do have a seat."

Blair took off his coat and sat down. "Do they know what's the matter with her?"

"A heart problem. It runs in the family. The doctor doesn't think she'll last long."

"How did he go?"

"On horseback."

"He should have come back on the boat with me. That would have been easy to arrange. It's much safer this time of year."

"I urged him to do that. But he felt he couldn't wait. He said he could make better time on horseback. He's so devoted to his mother, you know."

"I find it odd," said Blair slowly. "I received a letter from Mrs. Scott about the same time that letter arrived for your husband, and she made no reference to her poor health."

"She must have written you before she took ill. She said her condition came on suddenly. That's the way it often is with heart problems, of course."

Callandra was now embellishing the story beyond what she'd planned. She hadn't anticipated that Mrs. Scott would be corresponding with Blair.

She served the tea.

"What was the date on her letter?" he asked.

"I don't recall."

"Well, can we look at it?" he asked.

"It's not here." She had considered the possibility he might ask to see the letter, and then concluded he wouldn't be so obviously mistrusting. But this was different. He wasn't asking out of mistrust. He was suggesting they both look at it — to check the date, a reasonable request.

There was silence; he was clearly waiting for an answer.

"Norbert took it with him," she said.

This was plausible; she only wished she'd thought of it sooner, rather than letting that uncomfortably long silence hang in the air. "He left so quickly. He barely had time to read it. So he took it with him."

"I see," Blair said at last. His disappointment was evident, and Callandra sensed he was suspicious. Everyone and everything he wanted to see kept disappearing.

"I'm sorry to hear of Mrs. Scott's illness," said Blair, returning to polite formality as he put on his coat. "I pray your husband makes it to see her in time,"

"I regret this visit has been so disappointing for you, Reverend Blair," said Callandra. "Please give Lottie my letter and assure her that her brother is safe and well. I wouldn't lie to her about that."

She said this in earnest, only later realizing she had unintentionally suggested there was a distinction between what she wouldn't lie about and what she would.

Thomas Mercer Jones had been puzzled and intrigued by the report he'd received a few days earlier that Reverend Scott had a stutter. But he was now surprised by a different bit of news — that the new minister had abruptly left town to visit his dying mother. The commissioner's initial disappointment by this sudden departure was replaced by a relief that the popular clergyman would at least be gone for a few months. That would give Jones time to ensure that the local Presbyterians knew about their pastor's willingness to desert them for a richer Church, thereby guaranteeing that Reverend Scott would return to a hostile reception.

But when Longworth told him that Rosalee had made it out to the Van Egmond homestead to find the colonel gone, and his wife claiming she didn't know where he was or when he'd be back, Jones felt angry and thwarted.

"What? Now Van Egmond and Norbert Scott are both gone?" gasped Jones, staring at Longworth from across his desk. "Is it possible we've been duped, that they've headed off together for a rebellion?"

The colonial authorities in Toronto had not given much credence to rumours that a rebellion was imminent. Sir Francis Bond

Head, the lieutenant-governor, had only been in Upper Canada for a year and didn't seem to grasp the depth of resentment against the Family Compact. He had unintentionally stoked that resentment himself with his arrogance and contempt for the popular will, including his widely reported comment deriding "the low grovelling principles of democracy."

It occurred to Jones that he now had information that might help Sir Francis see the extent of the danger he faced. The fact that Van Egmond had mysteriously left home could indicate he was on his way to Toronto, where men were reportedly gathering north of the city. The possibility that Norbert Scott was with Van Egmond certainly increased Jones's suspicions — and would presumably increase those of colonial authorities as well, if they were made aware of Norbert's role as a local agitator against the Company.

Jones realized he should immediately convey all this information to Sir Francis, and also to Colonel James Fitzgibbon, head of the Toronto militia, who was known to be more worried than Sir Francis about a possible uprising. As Jones set about to write the letters, he ordered Longworth to bring Rosalee to his office at once, so they could be sure they learned as much as possible from her.

Outside his window, Jones could see six soldiers patrolling. He was struck by the thought that he had more security around his home here in Goderich than Sir Francis had around his official residence in Toronto, where an insurrection was far more likely to occur. Of course, this was due to the lieutenant-governor's curious nonchalance about his own security, as well as the fact that the archdeacon's daughter was here in Goderich. Still, if Van Egmond and Norbert Scott had ridden off to join a rebellion brewing in Toronto, it did seem unfortunate that, of the small contingent of soldiers left to guard Upper Canada, twenty-four had been relocated to Goderich.

By the time Longworth returned with Rosalee and Grayson half an hour later, Jones was pacing impatiently around the room.

"Finally," he said as the girl was directed to a seat in front of his desk. She appeared shocked by the opulence of the house, which was undoubtedly grander than anything she'd ever seen.

Jones peppered her with questions about her visit to the Van Egmond farm, and she related what the colonel's wife had told her.

"Were there other men there?"

"I didn't see none."

"What about Norbert Scott? Did you see him?"

"No, sir, I didn'."

"This is very important," he said in a quiet but intimidating voice. "There may be plans for an uprising — and there's reason to believe Colonel Van Egmond is involved."

"I don't know nothin' about that," said Rosalee.

"And Reverend Scott — we suspect he's involved, too."

"Oh, I don' think so," she said.

Jones scrutinized her carefully. "Your father owes the Company a lot of payments."

"Aye, sir."

"You wouldn't want your family to have to leave the farm, would you?"

"No, sir."

"There's reason to believe Reverend Scott is not who he says he is," Jones continued. "If you helped us uncover this, your family wouldn't need to worry. And you personally would be well taken care of."

"Aye, sir."

"The real Reverend Scott has a stutter. This man obviously doesn't."

Rosalee tried to sit more upright, pushing loose strands of hair off her face.

"Oh, yes, he does," she said, summoning a tone of confidence. "I've heard him stutter. He mostly doesn', but at times, yes, when he's flustered, he stutters."

The December snow blanketed the main road through town, lacing the trees with sparkly bits that glistened in the sun as it sunk low in the sky. Callandra was chilled by the coldness underfoot as she walked in the sleigh tracks, unable to keep the hem of her skirt from becoming heavy with snow. If she and Sam and Emma had set out for America, this snowfall would have stopped the wagon in its tracks, stranding them in the bush. Or maybe they would have made it to America by now. It was impossible to know, or to stop churning the possibilities over in her mind.

There were some children playing in the snow, but fewer people walking about than usual, which was fine with Callandra. She realized, with Sam gone, how much she had related to the town through him and how uncomfortable she felt here without him. Lonely, to be sure, and missing him terribly — but also less certain of herself, and how the townspeople regarded her.

Struggling to keep her balance on an icy patch, she noticed Glenna MacLeod, a young Presbyterian woman, approaching with her three children.

Glenna asked Callandra if she'd had any news from her husband. "Not yet."

There was nothing menacing in Glenna's question, yet Callandra felt scrutinized.

"You heard about Josh Mandridge?" asked Glenna.

It took Callandra a moment to recall that he was the boy who had aggressively approached Mrs. Jones's carriage; Callandra had heard the story.

"No. What's happened to him?"

"He's disappeared, too — along with Colonel Van Egmond ... You heard about the colonel leaving?"

"Yes."

"Well, they say he's gone to Toronto to lead a battle against the authorities. And now with Josh gone, too, people think he may have followed the colonel. That boy always was a hothead."

Glenna and her children moved on, leaving Callandra freshly worried. It was getting harder and harder for her to believe that Sam hadn't gone with the colonel. Was it possible he had known of the colonel's imminent departure and hadn't told her, that he would have left that night anyway, even without Blair's arrival and Emma's blunder? She found that difficult to believe; he had seemed so happy and relaxed on their way home from Ethan's farm earlier that day, and so loving and passionate with her that afternoon.

The sky had darkened and she trundled on against the snow, wrapping her cape tightly against the sharpening gusts of wind and the fears rising inside her. In a snow-cleared area in the square, a small group of men with muskets were lined up, taking drill instructions from a soldier. She recognized a couple of them, and realized they must be part of a local militia training to fight rebels, right here in Goderich. For some reason, she had assumed that the townspeople were supportive of the rebel cause, perhaps because of their strong feelings against the Company. But it was one thing to hate the Company, and quite another to support an armed rebellion against the British monarch; that would be treason. Only those truly committed and incredibly brave — or hotheads — would take the risks involved. Glenna's denigration of Josh suggested she sided with the authorities.

Callandra made her way quickly past the men with the muskets, afraid to look at them for fear of giving away her treasonous thoughts. She walked quickly into the hotel section of Feltie's and headed straight to the front desk to inquire about the mail, only to be told there'd been no mail that day.

She headed back toward the door, bracing for the cold and lonely walk home, when she spotted a newspaper on a table. She recognized the banner of *The Constitution*, Mackenzie's broadsheet, and walked over to get a better look. "We the people of the State of Upper Canada" was the headline, in large, bold letters. She noticed the date — November 24 — more than three weeks earlier. Picking it up, she began reading in earnest. It called for free secret ballots to elect all officials — including the governor himself — and a ban on religious and legal discrimination. All this was to be ratified by a Reform convention to be held in Toronto. At the bottom of the page, in heavy type, it urged every man to arm himself with a musket because "the crisis of liberty is approaching."

"Is that your newspaper?" asked a male voice. She gasped unintentionally as she looked up into the face of Seamus O'Reilly, the tall, thickset Company agent whom she'd seen but never actually met.

"No. I just saw it lying here," she said.

"You interested in the rebellion?" he asked.

"Not really."

"You seemed pretty interested in reading about it. Concerned about your husband, maybe?"

"My husband has returned to Scotland to see his ailing mother," said Callandra.

"Well, then I guess he wasn't in the fighting at Montgomery's Tavern."

Callandra tried not to react.

"That newspaper is out of date," he continued. "The rebels staged their little uprising about ten days ago, but they were quickly routed. Lots of them were killed or taken prisoner."

Callandra felt something collapse inside her.

"But then, I guess you wouldn't care much about that," he said, "since you're not interested in the rebellion ... and your husband is in Scotland anyway."

She moved past him without comment. His lips curled up in a taunting gesture as she bundled her cape around her and headed out to where the men were still practising with their muskets in the swirling snow.

The next morning, Callandra answered a knock on her door and found O'Reilly standing there, hands in his jacket pockets, an imperious expression on his face. She was glad that Rosalee was there, making her feel less alone.

"We need to review your file, Mrs. Scott," he said, stomping the snow off his boots as he walked into her sitting room and seated himself without an invitation.

"Rosalee, could you prepare some tea for us, please," said Callandra. Emma was with Rosalee in the kitchen.

"My file?" Callandra tried to sound unafraid.

"Yes, as you know, the payments on this property are in arrears."

"No, I didn't know that," said Callandra truthfully, as she sat down. "I believe it's leased by the Presbyterian Church."

"That's correct. But they missed the last payment."

"Oh. I didn't know that. Who usually makes the payment?"

"Your local treasurer, William Cosgrove."

Callandra recalled the man whom she believed to be Mr. Cosgrove.

"Perhaps it was just an oversight. Did you ask him what happened?"

"No. That's not my concern. You'll have to work it out with him."

"All right, well, I'll speak to him."

"Today," O'Reilly said, clearly as a command.

This was ostensibly the end of their business, and Callandra rose from her chair.

"I'm waiting for some tea," he said, smiling. He remained seated. "Although I'd prefer whisky if you have it."

"I don't." Callandra noted Emma's fearful expression. "I'm sure we can straighten this out about the payment, Mr. O'Reilly."

"I certainly hope so, for your sake." A broad smile spread across his face, pushing up his heavy, dark sideburns.

"There's no need for us to have tea. You prefer whisky, and I have none to offer you."

"You can offer me other things," he said. "Sit down."

"No, I have nothing to offer you," she said.

"I worry about what's going to happen to you if you can't come up with that money."

"I'm sure it's just an oversight." She didn't dare ask how much money was involved. For all she knew, he was making the whole thing up.

"I'm not so sure," he said. "I assume that if, for some reason, Cosgrove doesn't come up with the money, you'll be able to cover it."

"Yes," she said.

"Because otherwise you'd have to leave."

"There's no need to worry about that," she said, as Emma came running to her.

In the kitchen, Rosalee was arranging a tray for the tea.

"The tea won't be necessary, Rosalee. Mr. O'Reilly is leaving now."

This time she stood up with resolve, pushing Emma gently toward the kitchen. O'Reilly stood up, too, smirking.

"It must get lonely for you here without a man," he said, edging closer to her.

"No. Not at all. And my man will be back soon." She backed farther away from him until she felt the wall behind her.

He put his hand against the wall just over her shoulder, without touching her. If she moved again, it would look as if she were running from him, acknowledging that she'd lost control of the situation.

"I wouldn't count on that," he said.

It was impossible to know if O'Reilly had some information that she didn't have, and she didn't dare ask.

"What if he doesn't come back?" he said, this time gathering a lock of her hair in his hand and dragging it gently across her face.

"Stop this, at once," she said, feeling enraged as well as scared. "Get out of here."

"Oh, now don't go getting all upset," he said, leaning forward to kiss her on the lips.

She pushed him away. "If you don't get out of here right now, I'm going to report this to the commissioner."

"Oh really?" His nonchalance seemed real. He leaned in to kiss her again.

She went to slap him, but he grabbed her hand and pushed her back against the wall. She screamed and called to Rosalee to run for help.

"Where should I go?" asked Rosalee, frozen in her spot.

"Get someone, anyone!" cried Callandra.

"Don't bother," O'Reilly said to Rosalee as she started out the door with Emma. "We don't need any help here."

With this, he clutched Callandra's wrists and held them behind her back. She struggled to get free, and ended up falling to the ground. He pinned his arms around her from behind, so that she couldn't get at him. She was screaming now, but he put his hand over her mouth and half-carried, half-dragged her into her bedroom, throwing her down on the bed and climbing on top of her.

"You'll regret this."

"No, I won't," he said.

He grabbed at her breasts and ripped her dress. He lowered his mouth toward the exposed skin below her neck, but she managed to get hold of him by the hair and pull his head momentarily back, allowing her to manoeuvre out from under him.

Then he hit her across the face with considerable force, stunning her and breaking the skin on her cheek.

"Just lie still and you won't get hurt." He ripped her dress open at the top and severed a seam on one side connecting the skirt to the bodice.

She tried to spit up at him, screaming, "My husband will kill you for this!"

"I don't think so," he said, smiling through gritted teeth and reaching up under her dress. "I'm just keeping you warm for him."

As he reached down and opened the front of his trousers, she managed to slide off the bed. But he jumped on top of her, pressing her down flat and grinding the back of her head against the wooden floor. She was trapped by his heavy body, one of her hands wrenched behind her back, helpless against his violence. With each struggling movement, she only inflicted more pain on herself.

There were voices in the front part of the house. Evidently Rosalee *had* gone for help.

Callandra's head was pressed against the floor, pointed away from the door, with blood congealing on her cheek. She flipped her head around as about a dozen children tramped into the room in their boots and coats, watching with confused faces.

"What are you doing here?" O'Reilly called out.

There was no response. Indeed, the room had gone quiet. But she could feel his grip on her losing its intensity.

After a few more moments, O'Reilly got up, turned away, straightened his clothes and walked out the door, the curious, blank faces following his departure in silence.

Callandra recognized some of the children now, even spotted Emma among them.

Gradually sitting up, she pulled her torn dress together and dabbed at the blood from her cheek.

---- ❊ ----

It was later in the day, after feeding the children pudding and milk, that she learned Rosalee had run away, and that Emma had rounded up the children playing in the snow after a couple of men had ignored the child's plea for help.

---- ❊ ----

With a shawl covering one side of her face, the bruising around the eye was less visible. She knew she had nothing to be ashamed of. It was O'Reilly who should be ashamed — indeed, in jail. Still, she felt it best to keep her face down as she and Emma walked toward the little market just off the main square. To be visibly bruised would only draw attention to herself, raising questions about her activities and the absence of her husband.

She hadn't expected to see Mrs. Jones and her niece pull up nearby in their grand carriage. The two ladies, wearing coats with elaborate fur trim, were helped down onto the road only a short distance away. With the driver a few feet behind them, they ambled, arm in arm, in Callandra's direction. Her face down, Callandra eased Emma to the side, ensuring lots of room for the ladies to pass. She caught a sideways glimpse of Mrs. Jones and noticed her kindly demeanour.

Suddenly emboldened, Callandra, with Emma in tow, caught up to the women.

"I am sorry to trouble you, Mrs. Jones, but I want to alert you to something," she said.

"Move away," the driver said to Callandra, inserting himself between her and the ladies.

"That's all right, Henry," Mrs. Jones intervened. "Let the lady speak."

"Thank you, Mrs. Jones," Callandra said. "I just thought you might want to know that some of the Company agents are being rough with the townspeople."

As she said this, she pulled back her shawl, showing the bruising around her eye and the cut and scratch marks on her cheek.

Both Mrs. Jones and her niece gasped.

"A Company agent did that to you?" asked Mrs. Jones. "Who was it?"

"I'd rather not say his name. I don't want any more trouble. I just thought you should know about it. Thank you for listening," Callandra said, tipping her head in gratitude, wondering how Mrs. Jones would react if she heard the whole story.

"I'll tell my husband about this. If you have any more trouble, you come to see me," said Mrs. Jones, as Callandra moved to walk away.

"Oh, thank you, ma'am," said Callandra, a little overwhelmed. She had never encountered such kindness in a member of the upper class.

Crossing the street, she heard the driver say something to Mrs. Jones about "the new pastor's wife." Glancing back, Callandra could see the young niece staring at her with a look of acute interest, as she placed a finely gloved hand over her mouth.

Standing at the counter in the little shop on Richmond Street in Toronto, Reverend Blair felt an acute sense of anticipation.

The jeweller returned from the back and placed the gold poesy ring on a velvet mat on the counter. It was as fine as Blair remembered. He picked it up and checked the inside rim. He'd been torn about what to have inscribed. My Beloved described how he felt, but he had never said those words to her, so it seemed too much to say them first on the inside of a ring.

Now that he saw the inscription, he felt pleased by his choice of words: Axletree of Love. The mention of love was subtle, rather than possessive. And it referred to something that had been shared between them — an appreciation of that exquisite phrase (even though it had originated with McAndrew). The phrase had helped Blair confirm that his feelings for Lottie were about more than her physical loveliness. There was something deep in their souls — a shared sense of beauty, perhaps — that united them.

He decided to walk all the way to her flat, even though the slushy streets and heavily clouded sky gave the city a bleak feeling. It was more than just the weather; the city was still in shock due to the uprising the week before. By all accounts, it had been easily and speedily crushed, but there was still unease over the nighttime raid that had brought the rebels within a mile of the city. The newspapers carried reports that few soldiers had been in Toronto at the time, suggesting that the rebellion might have succeeded had it not been for the last-minute rallying of the militia, and the arrival of reinforcements from Hamilton. The large contingent of British soldiers that had been moved to Lower Canada didn't make it back to Toronto until two days after the rebellion had been crushed.

He was relieved that the revolt had been suppressed; Blair was no fan of the extremism of William Lyon Mackenzie. However, Mackenzie's rout had the effect of reinforcing the power of Sir Francis and the Family Compact, and this would mean even more favouritism toward the Anglican Church. Thus, the sight of so many British soldiers in the streets — such as the troop parading down Yonge Street as Blair approached — was an annoying reminder that the possibility the income from the Clergy Reserves would be shared with the Presbyterians was now more remote than ever.

Blair waited for the soldiers to march by, as a gaggle of well-wishers waved British flags and cheered them on from the sidewalk, evidently comforted by their presence, however late their arrival. He moved on once they'd passed, feeling optimistic about his prospects with Lottie, despite some setbacks. To his great disappointment, he'd come home without a letter from Sam, without even locating her dearly loved brother, raising questions about Sam's whereabouts — questions that had only become more puzzling due to the strange comments of the little girl, Emma.

Luckily, Blair at least had the brief note Callandra had written, confirming that Sam was fine. Surely there was no need to mention the comments of a five-year-old, who had almost certainly been confused. At least, no need to mention them today, spoiling the celebration that would accompany his proposal.

The separation had confirmed for him that they should be man and wife. There were few moments in the past month when he hadn't been thinking about her.

Indeed, the splendid aspects of marriage had become especially clear to him that day in Goderich as he had sat waiting in Reverend Scott's cottage. The reverend and his wife had apparently been in bed together in the middle of the day. So this is what married couples did, in their love for each other! Perhaps this explained Norbert's willingness to accept a life of hardship in the backwoods. Nothing was too difficult, no sacrifice too great, if one had this sort of all-encompassing love in one's life. With Lottie at his side, Blair felt he too could reach a higher level of service to the Lord.

That moment of insight had been abruptly interrupted by the opening of the bedroom door, with Callandra and Norbert emerging. In his endless musings on the life of Norbert Scott, Blair had never envisioned him looking as he did — so tall and strapping and … well … handsome. The piety that usually lurked in the face of a pastor was notably absent in his. But then that fit the easy, almost casual manner Norbert had about him, reinforcing Blair's hunch that the passionate and the spiritual were at peace together somewhere deep in this man's soul.

A cart was stuck in the snow as Blair turned the corner onto King Street. He went over to help dislodge it but was relieved when several stronger young men came along and took over, sending him on his way. His heart quickened a little, realizing he would soon be at Lottie's door.

Chapter Nineteen

Lottie was sitting on the love seat in Mrs. Tinsdale's parlour, wearing a shawl over a moss-green woollen dress, which Blair had seen before and especially liked.

"It is such a pleasure to see you again," he said, bowing and kissing her hand.

There was an awkward moment as he struggled to decide whether he dare sit next to her. He hesitated too long, missing a chance to look spontaneous, so he sat down opposite her, on the stiff-backed chair he'd occupied on previous visits.

Mrs. Tinsdale served tea and cookies then disappeared into the kitchen.

Lottie was surprised and excited to learn Blair had visited Goderich on his travels, and he assured her that all was well there.

He went on to describe the town — a simple outpost with a delightful perch over the lake, where the Company commissioner had built a fine home. Blair noted that Reverend Scott's cottage was small and humble, but not uncomfortable, and that there was a local girl helping with the housekeeping.

"And my brother? How is he?"

"He's well," Blair began, having spent a great deal of time figuring out how to handle this question.

"Oh, I'm so glad to hear that." Lottie flashed her soft half smile, which highlighted the dimple on her chin.

After a pause, she continued, "Really? He seemed well?"

"Yes, very well."

"Did you tell him you've seen me?"

"Uh, well, I didn't actually see him," Blair conceded. "He was off on a road-building crew, and I was only in Goderich briefly. I had other parishes to visit."

"You didn't see him?" The pretty smile disappeared, taking the dimple with it.

"No, but both Reverend Scott and Callandra assured me he is very well." Blair reached into the inner pocket of his jacket and pulled out Callandra's letter and handed it to her.

"That's all she wrote? After all these months?" exclaimed Lottie after reading it.

"She told me to assure you she'd write more soon. She probably already has, but the mail is very slow."

Blair felt deflated by Lottie's obvious disappointment.

"Did Callandra seem well?" Lottie finally asked, breaking the awkward silence that had developed.

"Oh, yes — better than I've ever seen her," said Blair, thinking of how happy Callandra had appeared that first day in Goderich. "It seems she and Reverend Scott have adjusted very well to life in the backwoods."

"Oh. That's good," said Lottie, distractedly.

"Yes, although in truth I had hoped to convince Reverend Scott to consider trying out for the position at St. Andrew's."

"You mean here in Toronto?"

"Yes, I believe he would be perfect — such a leadership figure for our Church. And, of course, it would mean the whole family would return to Toronto. Sam, too."

Lottie looked more hopeful.

"But, sadly," he continued, "Reverend Scott wasn't interested in St. Andrew's. He seems very committed to the people of Goderich."

"Really?" said Lottie, surprised.

"I guess that's just the way he is — committed to serving the Lord, wherever he can be most useful. It really is a wonderful aspect of his character. I aspire to be more like him myself," said Blair, casting his eyes down with a look of humility.

Lottie was silent for a few moments. Blair looked up and, in a fleeting glance, caught sight of where her shawl had slipped off one shoulder, revealing the tight cross-lacing on her bodice, and how nicely it tapered down to her slender waist.

"Perhaps Sam will come home on his own," Lottie ventured. "If Callandra and Reverend Scott are happy in Goderich, and Sam is off working on a road crew, maybe they don't need him there after all. What happened to the church he was building?"

"It's coming along well. It looked impressive. The roof isn't on yet, though."

"Well, why is Sam off building roads if the church isn't finished?"

"I suspect he was badly needed to help with the roads."

"I'm surprised Reverend Scott is willing to share him like that, when the church is unfinished."

"I believe Reverend Scott has taken over much of the building of the church himself," said Blair.

Lottie let out a little laugh. She appeared on the verge of saying something disparaging about Norbert, but didn't.

"Well then, maybe Sam really can come back," she said, filling Blair's teacup and dropping in two cubes of sugar. "If he's not needed for the church."

"Well, he might be needed for something else now," said Blair, sipping his tea and savouring the thought that Lottie remembered how he liked it. "You see, Reverend Scott had to return home to see his ailing mother in Scotland. So Sam will be needed to take care of Callandra and the little girl while Reverend Scott is away."

"Reverend Scott has gone back to Scotland? I thought you saw him?"

"Yes, I did. But I took him a letter that had news of his mother, so he had to leave suddenly."

"So he came home with you?"

"No, he was in a terrible hurry. His mother is gravely ill. So he left on his own, on horseback."

Now Lottie looked at him incredulously. "On horseback? I'm sure he doesn't know how to ride a horse, and he would never make it through the woods alone. He's such a timid little man."

Blair smiled. "You're obviously joking."

"No, not at all."

Blair looked bemused. "He's tall and strong and broad across the shoulders. He looks like he could lift an ox, and grapple with a wolf bare-handed."

"Oh, my goodness," Lottie said, putting her hand to her forehead. "You've mixed them up. That's Sam, my brother, you're describing."

"No, no," insisted Blair. "I'm sure the man I met was Reverend Scott."

"No, you're wrong. That tall, strong man you just described — that's my brother."

"That's not possible," said Blair, shaking his head firmly. "Reverend Scott was in bed with Mrs. Scott when I arrived. They are clearly married."

"What? ... The tall man was in bed with Callandra?"

"Yes, exactly."

"No, I'm sure you're wrong," said Lottie.

"Well, they came out of the same bedroom together, in the middle of the day."

"Perhaps he was fixing something in her room."

"With the door closed? I don't think so," Blair continued. "They were clearly intimate with each other. They held hands and presented themselves as husband and wife."

Lottie said nothing, and Blair was suddenly horrified by the thought that the man in bed with Callandra may have been someone other than her husband.

"If that man was your brother, where is Reverend Scott?" asked Blair.

"I thought you said he went to see his mother."

"The man who went to see his mother was the same tall man who presented himself as Reverend Scott. I met him and Callandra the day I arrived in Goderich. Then I went back the next morning, because he said he would take me to the road-building site, to see your brother. But when I arrived the next morning, he was gone. The tall man was gone."

Lottie looked deeply puzzled.

"If that's your brother, where is Reverend Scott?" Blair repeated, emphatically.

Lottie remained silent, withdrawn into her own thoughts as she tried to piece it together.

"And if that's your brother," Blair continued, "he should have made it to Toronto by now — unless something happened to him. I better contact the authorities."

"Oh no, don't do that," said Lottie. "There's no need to do that."

"Well, something is amiss."

"Yes, but we don't know what."

"Well, we have to find your brother. The authorities should be notified."

"No … no. That could cause trouble," she said.

"Well, I at least have to report that Reverend Scott appears to be missing."

"No, no. You can't do that," said Lottie, suddenly insistent and forceful. "That could get my brother in trouble. We mustn't do anything until we know what has happened."

Blair swallowed hard. "I have to report Reverend Scott's disappearance," he said.

"Shhhh," she said, putting her finger to her lips and motioning with her head toward the back of the house. "You mustn't speak of this to anyone."

"We can't just ignore it," said Blair. "A minister is missing …"

"*Appears* to be missing," Lottie corrected him, whispering. "We don't know what's going on."

"But that's why we need help. We need to know what's happened to Reverend Scott, if something has happened to him."

"What could have happened to him?"

"I don't know. Perhaps he's come to some harm."

"Are you suggesting that my brother might have harmed him?"

"No —"

"I can assure you my that brother would never do such a thing."

"No, of course not. I'm not suggesting that at all. But it is my duty to report that a minister is missing — a minister I recruited and supervised! He may be in danger somewhere."

Lottie abruptly rose from the love seat and dropped to her knees in front of Blair, looking up beseechingly at him.

"I implore you," she said. "I couldn't bear if anything happened to my brother. He's everything to me."

The look on her face was intense.

"Lottie, my dearest, nothing will happen to your brother. I'm sure he is blameless." Her body was pressed against his legs. Her hands gripped his knees. He had just called her "my dearest"; the phrase had come out spontaneously.

"If we do what's right, the Lord will take care of us," he said, finding strength in their sudden physical closeness.

"No, he won't! He never does!" She was trembling.

"We must be strong. We must believe in the Lord and do his duty."

"No! We must protect my brother!" she said, looking at him with an intensity that made him flinch. Her shawl had fallen to the ground, and he could feel her breasts pressing against his legs. "I'll do anything you want. I'll do anything to save my brother."

"Will you marry me?" Even as he blurted out the words, he realized how utterly inappropriate — even ridiculous — they were. He felt deeply foolish, ashamed.

She looked at him with incredulity, pulling herself back, as if shaken that he had misinterpreted her desperate gestures so completely. She picked up her shawl and covered herself. The distance between them suddenly felt immense.

And then, in a soft, barely audible voice, she murmured: "Yes — if you promise not to do anything that could hurt my brother."

There was so much to think through on the long, cold walk home that he was almost back at his flat when he realized he'd completely forgotten to present her with the ring.

Chapter Twenty

It was late April 1838 when news of Samuel Lount's hanging reached Goderich. The story was on the front page of *The Christian Guardian*, which was posted in the foyer of the hotel. A couple of men, whom Callandra vaguely recognized, were reading it. She joined them, determined to learn the full extent of the dreadful news right away, regardless of who might be watching.

For months since the failed uprising, the newspapers had been full of reports about the fate of the rebels. Only a few had been killed. Mackenzie had somehow escaped to the U.S., but dozens of others had been captured in the rout at Montgomery's Tavern — including Colonel Van Egmond, who died of pneumonia in a Toronto jail after almost a month of captivity. Josh Mandridge, only fifteen years old, still languished in that prison.

There had been no reports of any kind about Sam. About Reverend Scott.

Trials of the other captured rebels were underway, but Lount and Captain Peter Matthews were the first to be convicted and executed. It was Lount's execution that dominated the story in the *Guardian*. An elected Member of the Assembly, he had been widely respected among the rebels. After his arrest, his wife had collected five thousand signatures across the province on a petition pleading with the authorities to spare her husband's life. To no avail. Callandra gasped when she read at the bottom of the article that, in addition to their widows, Lount left behind seven children; Matthews eight.

She realized she was pregnant again, making Sam's return all the more vital.

The executions showed how vindictive the authorities planned to be. It was rumoured that Archdeacon Strachan had been advising the new lieutenant-governor, Sir George Arthur, to deal severely with the captured insurgents in order to smother any fires still smoldering in the hearts of rebels or their sympathizers. There was to be no mercy.

Callandra moved on to the front desk where, to her surprise, there was a letter for her — or at least a letter for Norbert, from his mother. She put it in her purse and left.

Making her way home through the muddy roadways, she thought of how much more tense things had become in the four months since the rebellion, even here in Goderich, where there'd been no uprising. The Company agents, including the loathsome O'Reilly, walked around with considerably more swagger, generating a whole new level of fear among the townsfolk. All eighteen Goderich residents who had signed the petition to spare Samuel Lount were visited by Company agents who grilled them about their activities and their loyalty to the monarchy.

Thousands of acres of Huron Tract land, rightfully belonging to the Van Egmond family, were seized by the Company. And the Mandridge family, already in despair over their son's imprisonment, had been evicted from their modest farm and were living with relatives. Meanwhile, men who had signed up for the militia were served first at the Company store, and even given free bags of seed.

The menacing words of a little verse, published in the *Cobourg Star*, which Callandra had seen at the hotel some weeks ago, kept churning in her mind:

> Now the rebellion's o'er,
> Let each true Briton sing,
> Long live the Queen in health and peace,
> And make each rebel swing.

Callandra noticed that nobody stopped to talk to her on the street; one Presbyterian couple crossed to the other side, apparently to avoid her. Although "Norbert" was officially home visiting his mother — and no one had questioned this to Callandra's face — his radical ideas and defiance of the Company were widely known. What had once endeared him to the folks in Goderich now evidently made him, and her, people to be shunned. Without him working his magic on the town, she found herself treated like any single woman — with suspicion.

She headed into the woods not far from her cottage, anxious to read Mrs. Scott's letter without Rosalee seeing it. The ground was wet and marshy beneath her feet, and the tree branches overhead thick with buds.

> My dearest Norbert,
>
> I am very disturbed that I haven't heard from you in such a long time. The last letter I received was from Toronto, dated August 18, 1837, many months ago.
> I am grateful to Reverend Blair who has written to me and reported that he saw you in Goderich in November and that you are doing well. I was surprised, however, that he expressed great concern about my health, which has been fine.

Callandra scanned quickly through the rest of the letter — about activities in Glasgow and Scott relatives. She was extremely relieved that Reverend Blair apparently hadn't figured out that the Norbert he met was not the real Norbert. Nor did Mrs. Scott sound particularly suspicious, despite Blair's unexplained expressions of concern about her health. The letter ended with a plea for Norbert to respond right away.

She put it back in the envelope and contemplated what to do with it. Clearly, it had to be destroyed, since it indicated that Mrs. Scott wasn't ill and hadn't requested her son return home, exposing Callandra's explanation of his departure as a lie.

As she began ripping it up, she noticed with alarm that the seal on the back of the envelope appeared broken. If the envelope had been steamed open and resealed, there was enough information inside for someone to begin putting together a case against Sam for assuming a dead man's identity, or worse — killing him in the first place.

---- * ----

Unlike the headquarters of the Anglican Church, Presbyterian House was austere. Blair had sat many times in the cushion-less antechamber waiting to see Reverend Nesbitt, his supervisor, but this was the first time he recalled feeling distinctly nervous. He was eventually ushered into Reverend Nesbitt's large, unadorned office.

"I received a letter from our dear friend Mrs. Scott that makes little sense to me," Reverend Nesbitt began, after minimal salutations. "I'm hoping you'll be able to shed some light on its meaning."

"I will certainly try, sir," said Blair, abandoning hope that this summons was unrelated to the disappearance of Norbert Scott.

"The lady says she received a letter from you last January, indicating great concern about her illness — even though she has not been ill."

"Uh, well, perhaps there was a misunderstanding," said Blair. "When I journeyed to the Huron Tract last November, I took Reverend Scott a letter that his mother had sent him, care of our office." Blair was aware that his lines sounded rehearsed, and strained to make the words flow more easily. "Of course, I didn't see the contents of the letter, but Norbert later expressed concern about his mother's health. So when I returned to Toronto, I wrote to Mrs. Scott and wished her a speedy recovery. You know how these things sometimes get misconstrued."

"Hmmm," said Reverend Nesbitt. "That was last December. Her letter here is dated February 2. And she says that she still hasn't heard from her son. Have you communicated with him?"

"No, I haven't, sir."

"You thought his mother was very sick, yet you let the matter drop? Did you not feel the need to follow up with him?"

"I should have," Blair stated, eyes downward.

"Yes, indeed, you should have." Reverend Nesbitt was often abrupt but rarely accusatory, as now. "As a minister, you have a responsibility to pay attention to the well-being of members of our Church. And Reverend Scott is not just a member of our Church, but a minister, under our care and supervision …"

"Yes, sir."

"And his mother is a very good friend of our mission in Upper Canada."

"Yes, sir."

"She says that he has always been a devoted son. Yet she's written him several letters and had no response. She finds his silence very disturbing."

"Yes," said Blair, aware that he'd exhausted what he could say without outright lying.

"Well, you should write to him immediately. Tell him we need to know that all is well, and that he must write his mother at once."

"Yes, sir, I will," said Blair, rising on this perfect cue to go write the letter and get it posted before the mail left that morning. But Reverend Nesbitt directed him to sit back down.

"I don't know if that's enough. Perhaps we should contact the colonial office," said the older man. "Do you think it's possible something has happened to him?"

Blair was conscious of beads of sweat forming below his collar. What could he possibly say to this very pointed question? Fortunately, he was saved by a knock on the door. It was the clerk, notifying Reverend Nesbitt that the bookkeeper needed to speak with him.

Blair offered to leave and return later.

"No, no. Just stay here," said Reverend Nesbitt, stepping out of the office himself.

This little reprieve, while welcome, couldn't possibly last long enough to allow Blair to figure out what to do; he'd been grappling with this question for months. Of course, he *knew* what to do. Tell the truth; he had a duty to tell his spiritual superior that one of the Church's pastors was inexplicably missing, and possibly dead.

Lottie, too, surely understood what had to be done. She knew right from wrong, good from evil. It was just that she was deeply concerned about her brother. Her lack of trust in society — even in the Church — was troubling.

Lately, she seemed to have withdrawn from Blair as well, creating an awkwardness between them. He had eventually given her the poesy ring, and she had smiled at the inscription — although not the lovely dimpled smile he craved to see again. But she never wore the ring, explaining she was too upset to think about happy things like marriage now, and that she was keeping it safe in her top drawer. Blair would have preferred it on her finger, and until it appeared there he understood that, whatever the status of their engagement, it was not yet time for a public announcement.

The uncertainty of their situation made Blair's struggle with his conscience all the more challenging. For months, he had acquiesced to her wishes and had not reported his suspicion that something serious had happened to Norbert Scott. Now the letter from Mrs. Scott crushed Blair's faint hope that Norbert was somehow alive and well back in Scotland. Lottie was asking so much of Blair — demanding his silence — yet she provided him with no warmth or support as he wallowed in moral anguish.

"Do you think it's possible something has happened to him?" Reverend Nesbitt's question hung in the air as Blair awaited his return.

It required a direct answer. Silence was one thing, but it would be unconscionable for him to directly misrepresent the truth — to lie — to his superior about a matter of life and death involving a minister of the Church.

Help me, Lord! I know I must follow in Your righteous path. Give me the strength to tell the Truth so that I can serve You, so that I can be worthy of You ...

But if he did so, Lottie would never forgive him. She'd left no doubt about that. His dream of marital joy would come to an end.

Reverend Nesbitt returned and sat back down behind his desk.

Blair felt like he might faint, but realized that too would be wrong: cowardice did not serve the Lord. He mustn't dodge the question; he had to face it.

"Now where was I?" asked Reverend Nesbitt.

"Umm, I believe, umm, you were talking about ... you had, I think, some concerns ..." Blair scanned his brain for vague words. Was it possible to switch topics? No, it wasn't. "... some concerns about Reverend Scott."

"Exactly. What do you think?" Reverend Nesbitt asked.

"What do I think?"

"Aye, do you think something could have happened to Reverend Scott?"

"It does seem strange that he hasn't written his mother in such a long time."

"When you saw him last November, did anything seem odd to you about his behaviour? Was there anything that gave you concern?"

"You mean at the time?"

"Then — or now. Do you think there are any grounds for concern about Reverend Scott's well-being?"

Blair felt like the world was closing in on him. Reverend Nesbitt was scrutinizing him with eyes that seemed capable of penetrating to the depths of his soul.

"No ... I don't think so."

Lord forgive me ...

"Are you all right, Reverend Blair? You seem very pale."

"I'm fine, sir," he replied, even though he was sure that, after a lifetime of struggle at the entranceway, he had just passed through the gates of Hell.

———— * ————

Startled by a knock on the door, Callandra immediately feared O'Reilly. She and Emma were alone in the house, making her feel especially vulnerable.

Looking out the window, she was relieved to see the fine carriage that transported Thomas Mercer Jones and his family about town. It looked strikingly out of place here, on this muddy little roadway of cottages, stopped right in front of hers.

Callandra rushed to the door, overwhelmed at the thought that Mrs. Jones was kind enough to pay her a visit, to ensure that she and Emma were safe. But she opened the door to find an impeccably dressed gentleman whom she knew to be Thomas Mercer Jones. Was *he* following up? She decided that she would identify O'Reilly if he asked.

"I'm honoured to have you come to my home, Mr. Jones. Please come in."

"No, that won't be necessary," he said in a voice that suggested a comfort with giving orders. "You are the wife of the Presbyterian pastor, Reverend Norbert Scott — is that correct?"

"Yes, sir," said Callandra, with Emma wrapped in the folds of her skirt, which no longer hid her pregnancy.

"I'd like to speak with your husband."

"He's not here, sir."

"Well, where is he?"

"He's gone back to Scotland. His mother is very ill. He had to make an urgent trip home."

"Really? You're sure his mother is ill?"

"Yes, sir. She wrote herself to plead with him to come home."

At that point, the carriage door was pushed open from the inside. The driver rushed to assist a well-dressed middle-aged woman emerging.

Emma was the first to react. Upon seeing her grandmother, she let out a high-pitched shriek. Callandra gasped and swept Emma up in her arms.

"I am perfectly well," Mrs. Scott said with clenched teeth, as she advanced up the path toward the house. "I never wrote my son asking him to come home."

Mrs. Scott looked every bit the tormenter Callandra remembered — the stern features, fierce countenance, and stabbing grey eyes. She could feel herself shaking as Mrs. Scott confronted her. "Where is my son?"

"I don't know. He left at the end of November."

Mrs. Scott pushed past Callandra into the house.

Callandra was now aware of Rosalee getting out of the carriage and approaching the house, avoiding Callandra's glance. Soon they were all inside.

"Where did my son sleep?" Mrs. Scott demanded of Rosalee.

Rosalee headed toward the tiny bedroom. "Here, ma'am."

Mrs. Scott and Mr. Jones followed her into the room, with Callandra and Emma stopped in the doorway.

"What a horrid little room!" Mrs. Scott exclaimed. "My son living in such a place!" She looked about the room in disgust, then addressed Rosalee once more. "Show me his clothes."

Rosalee began going through drawers, and quickly produced a pair of folded-up trousers.

"My son never had trousers like these." Then she held them up, allowing the pant legs to fall down to their full length. "These do not belong to my son."

Callandra felt an impulse to grab Emma and run. But where? Suddenly dizzy, she backed up against the wall, and then slumped down onto the floor. Emma was pressed up against her, her little arms clinging around her mother's neck like a drowning child.

"Take the child from her," Mrs. Scott ordered Rosalee. As Rosalee tried to do as instructed, Callandra kicked her. Abruptly, Callandra felt strong male hands pulling her back by the arms, and she looked around to see the carriage driver. Then Emma was gone from her arms, scooped up and carried out of the room by Rosalee.

"Stand up, at once," ordered Mrs. Scott.

Callandra struggled to her feet, straining to see where Rosalee had taken Emma.

"Have you killed my son?"

"Oh, my God, no!"

"Something has clearly happened to him. You made up that story about me summoning him back to Scotland. Why are you lying? What are you hiding?"

"You know you could be charged with murder," interjected Jones.

"No, no. That's not what happened."

"Then what did happen?"

"There was an accident on the trip to Goderich. The carriage went into the river," Callandra said, and then paused. There was no good way to say it. "Norbert drowned."

As she spoke the words, she felt a tinge of sympathy. Mean and vicious as her mother-in-law was, Callandra knew that she loved her son deeply.

"I'm sorry to have to tell you such bad news," Callandra continued. "I feel terrible about what happened."

Mrs. Scott's face looked cast in stone.

"You feel terrible, do you?" she said, her tone confirming there would be no forgiveness. "But you didn't bother to let me know. You pretended he was still alive. Who was the imposter?"

"It was all a misunderstanding …"

"Who was he? Who posed as my son?"

"Sam."

"My husband's carpenter?"

"Yes."

"Why would you pretend he was your husband?"

"It was a misunderstanding. When we arrived in the town — after a long trek through the woods — the people who greeted us thought Sam was the new minister."

"And you didn't feel the need to tell them the truth?"

"I should have. Of course, I should have. I was sick. I don't remember much."

"So you just lived here together, posing as husband and wife?"

Callandra could hear Emma calling for her from the next room, but she didn't dare respond right now.

Mrs. Scott and Jones were conferring quietly, beyond Callandra's earshot.

Then Jones spoke to Callandra: "So the carpenter left at the end of November — just in time to join the rebellion?"

"I don't think he joined the rebellion."

"Well, where did he go?"

"I honestly don't know."

"Honestly?" Mrs. Scott said contemptuously. "You expect us to believe anything you say?"

"He didn't tell me where he was going."

"Did you and he plan this together?" Mrs. Scott asked. Her grey eyes felt like knives stabbing into her flesh.

"What do you mean? Plan what?"

"The carriage going into the river."

"Oh Lord, no! It was an accident. We all nearly drowned. It was terrifying."

"But somehow only my son drowned," said Mrs. Scott, moving closer to survey Callandra's face. "It all worked out pretty well for you, didn't it? You preferred him to my son. He's from your social class … and … perhaps you found him handsome?"

"No."

"You don't find him handsome?"

"It wasn't like that."

From the next room, Rosalee interjected, "Yes, he is handsome. Tall and handsome."

"I guess you didn't notice," Mrs. Scott said sharply. "You were too busy mourning the death of your husband."

"I was sad about his death."

"Don't lie to me, you strumpet," said Mrs. Scott, slapping Callandra across the face. "You seem perfectly happy to have a new husband."

"It wasn't like what you're saying. We slept in separate rooms," said Callandra.

"Really? Is that true, Rosalee?" asked Mrs. Scott.

"Yes. Callandra's room is there," she said pointing to it.

"And they slept separately?"

"Yes ... well, I think so."

"You think so?" Mrs. Scott asked.

Callandra looked at Rosalee, trying to meet her gaze, but Rosalee evaded it.

"Well, they did sleep separately ... at least most of the time." Then Rosalee finally looked straight at Callandra, with eyes that were stone cold. "One time I found them in Callandra's room together — with the door closed. Just before he left." Rosalee continued, "And she's pregnant, as you can see."

What followed was mostly a blur. She heard the words "murderer" and "harlot," and felt the hands of the carriage driver on her again, this time more roughly. The last thing she remembered, as she was dragged out the door, was Emma's terrified face across the room, her little body trapped in the firm, loveless grip of her grandmother.

In retrospect, it had been obvious all along that concealing Norbert's death would have severe repercussions. It was hard to reconstruct what she'd been thinking during those early weeks in Goderich when she'd mostly pushed that thought from her mind — even when Sam kept raising it. She was stunned now by her recklessness. Feelings of guilt, remorse, and shame preoccupied her during the long, seemingly endless days in her cell. The only deeper regret was that she hadn't been able to convince Sam to take her and Emma with him.

Her cell was tiny, with only one small window, from which she could see that she was on the second floor of a building, overlooking a storage yard. The air in the cell was musty, and there was barely enough room for its minimal contents: a narrow wooden bench, a straw mattress on the floor, a bucket for her bodily functions.

There were bars across one side of the cell, separating her from an empty adjacent room, where a paunchy guard appeared from time to time, bringing her water or a stale piece of bread. At night, it was pitch-black and eerie, making her crave sleep as an escape. But the sleep just wouldn't come, leaving her even more tormented by her thoughts and fears.

"My daughter? Do you know where she is?" Callandra asked her jailor, finally getting the courage to speak on the second day of her confinement.

The man regarded her with a scowl, although when she peered into his eyes, he looked more dim-witted than mean.

"Don't know" was all he said, as he passed her an apple and carrots, along with her bread and water.

Later that day, the jailor told Callandra that she was being held in the Company office, which was the only jail in town.

"We had to release a couple of thieves to make room for you," he said, "since your crime is so much worse."

The fact that her jailor seemed scandalized by her "crime" suggested that there'd be little sympathy for her in the town. But, above all, she worried about Emma.

After a couple of days, two well-dressed men appeared, and she was taken to a room where she sat on one side of a table opposite them. Her initial hopes that they were there to help her in some way soon faded, when they explained they were lawyers and that they worked for the Company.

"Do you know where my daughter is?" she asked them, imploringly. "Please, please. I just want to know that she's safe."

"She's in good care. You needn't worry," said one of the men, who was heavy-set and balding. "But we're here to talk about you and your case."

She didn't believe them or trust them, but felt she had no choice but to co-operate.

They turned out to be less accusatory than Thomas Mercer Jones and Mrs. Scott had been, and they listened closely to the details of her story, making notes from time to time. The heavy-set man in particular asked her a number of questions relating to the mix-up that happened the first night in Goderich, and even appeared somewhat sympathetic when she described her miscarriage.

The other lawyer, younger and more judgmental, kept asking about her relationship with Norbert, suggesting that they'd had a very unhappy marriage.

"No, we weren't unhappy," Callandra said. "We were looking forward to a new life in Goderich."

This last sentence was at least partly true; they had both been hopeful their lives might improve in Goderich, despite being together. Surely, if she stayed near the truth, she would have more chance of sounding convincing.

But as the interview wore on, it became clear that the young lawyer didn't believe anything she said. When she insisted that she'd been upset by her husband's death, he simply smiled.

After a while, some food was brought in on trays. Even though she knew the meeting was going badly, she was pleased to have something substantial to eat. She readily devoured the boiled eggs and potatoes on her plate, while the lawyers ate beef with Yorkshire pudding.

The session continued for a long time. At the end, the young lawyer told her that she had been charged with murder and would stand trial in Goderich.

She was so devastated that she had trouble walking the short distance back to her cell.

Later that day, a dowdy, silver-haired woman named Mrs. Murphy appeared in the anteroom and announced she was replacing the male guard. Any hopes that Mrs. Murphy would be kinder were soon dashed; she told Callandra that her arrest had scandalized the town and been reported in newspapers as far away as Toronto and Kingston. Mrs. Murphy clearly regarded her prisoner as a deeply sinful woman, an adulteress and likely a murderer — of a clergyman, no less.

The next day, Mrs. Murphy let slip that Emma was living in the servants' quarters of the Jones household. This was good news; strangers would almost certainly be more caring than Mrs. Scott. It was also clear Mrs. Murphy knew this first-hand; she was from the Jones household staff, having been reassigned here on orders from Mrs. Jones herself.

This openness was a momentary lapse, however. As the days wore on, Mrs. Murphy declined to provide further information about anything happening beyond her cell. Callandra lost track of time. She struggled to prevent her thoughts from straying onto memories of her childhood on the farm, let alone anything to do with Emma or Sam or Lottie. She was trying to drain herself of feeling, hoping to dull the pain.

Some days later, she awoke one morning to hear workmen outside. They were putting bars on her little window, even though she had made no attempt to escape. Later that day, her hands were cuffed in front of her and she was put in the back of a carriage, along with Mrs. Murphy. Could this be her last chance to escape? Before she could decide whether to try, Mrs. Murphy said they were going to Callandra's house, where her detention would continue.

She slumped back in her seat, feeling some relief. The carriage pulled around the side of the Company building. People had gathered in the square, making it hard to see, but she caught a glimpse of a wagon parked in front of the building. She watched as several soldiers roughly pulled a man, his hands and legs shackled, out of the wagon and half-dragged him into the building.

Mrs. Murphy said the man was Samuel Hunter. Staring at Callandra with derision, she added that he'd been arrested in Toronto and brought back to Goderich to stand trial with her for murder.

Chapter Twenty-One

It was a warm day in late May when the trial began.
There were surely more people in the town square than the entire population of Goderich.

Callandra had never seen it so full, nor the people so unruly. Skirmishes broke out here and there between factions of young men. From the window of her carriage, she spotted some of Sam's loyal followers, including Joe and Randall. Mostly, however, the crowd was calling for punishment, holding up signs saying SINNERS GO TO HELL and DOWN WITH THE REBELLION. The most common message was simply a hand-drawn noose.

The carriage slowed as the crowd grew thicker in front of the Company building. Faces pressed up against the window, screaming, "Here she is!" and "It's the preacher's tramp, hahahaha!" After days of isolation, the world was closing in on her.

The room that served as a courtroom was large by Goderich standards, with windows overlooking the square. As she was led in, wearing the stiff black dress that had been issued to her, people turned in their seats to stare and whisper. It was only as she was seated, at a table near the front of the room, that she caught sight of

Sam sitting at a table parallel to hers. In between were men in robes who were largely blocking her view.

Still, in her furtive glance in his direction, Callandra could see that Sam was unshaven, his hands were cuffed, and his cotton shirt was ripped across one shoulder. He was staring straight ahead of himself, so she could only see him in profile. But his presence in the room changed everything, and she could feel her heart pounding furiously. She wanted to lock eyes with him, to somehow communicate all the love, fear, terror, passion, and everything else she felt being near him again. But she didn't dare. She was supposed to be indifferent to him, focused on the tragic drowning of her husband.

The heavy-set lawyer was seated on the far side of her. There was also a group of men seated separately at the front, presumably the jury. She recognized a few of them, without knowing any by name. They looked like upright citizens, no doubt scandalized by the behaviour of the fraudulent clergyman and his harlot.

But it wasn't until Mrs. Scott took the stand as the first witness that Callandra felt a cold rush of despair. The fact that her mother-in-law had stayed on in Goderich to testify against her hinted at Mrs. Scott's determination to see stiff punishment meted out.

Instead of coming across as the mean woman Callandra knew, Norbert's mother sounded kindly and gentle, almost submissive. Dressed head to toe in mourning black, she spoke lovingly about her son — how close they'd always been, how proud she was when he took up the calling, how much she'd missed him when he moved to the New World. Her quiet conviction captured the attention of the silenced room. The young lawyer was questioning her, and his powerful voice highlighted her apparent meekness. There was a touching moment when she revealed that Norbert had had a stutter, making her feel especially protective toward him.

When the lawyer asked Mrs. Scott about her daughter-in-law, she continued in the same soft voice, fighting back tears, "I had always hoped Norbert would marry a loving girl — someone who appreciated him for his kindness, and was willing to overlook his stutter."

"Take your time, Mrs. Scott," said the judge, who was mostly bald and wore spectacles.

After giving Mrs. Scott a few moments to compose herself, the young lawyer resumed his questioning. "And did your daughter-in-law turn out as you'd hoped, Mrs. Scott?"

"Sadly, no."

"Could you elaborate for the court, please, ma'am. I know this is difficult."

"Well, I don't think she ever loved my son."

"Please explain."

"Well," Mrs. Scott continued slowly, as if reluctant to criticize her daughter-in-law. "She was just a simple farm girl. Norbert gave the eulogy at her father's funeral ... I think she spotted an opportunity to escape a life of poverty."

Callandra gasped, putting her hand over her mouth. She leaned over to the heavy-set lawyer and whispered that that was a lie.

"You didn't meet at your father's funeral?" he whispered back.

"Yes, that's true. But not the part about me seeing him as an opportunity to escape poverty."

Of course, that was true, too, but not in the way Mrs. Scott described it.

The lawyer put his finger to his mouth, signalling silence.

"Her father had just died," Mrs. Scott continued, "but at the wake, she was flirting with my son. She was clearly determined to marry him. It all happened very quickly."

Callandra felt angry listening to Mrs. Scott's fabricated account. Or, was it possible that Norbert had presented the story this way to his mother? For that matter, this distorted version wasn't much different than what Sam had once believed.

"It was obvious when she came into our home that the marriage had been a terrible mistake," said Mrs. Scott, her face seemingly contorted in pain beneath a heavy black bonnet. "We are a very loving, close family, but she never wanted anything to do with us."

Callandra leaned over to her lawyer again, whispering, "That's not true! They were so mean to me."

"But I think she did like living in a grand home," Mrs. Scott said, her voice remaining steady and almost sweet.

"I hated every minute of my life there!" Callandra whispered to her lawyer.

"And what about Callandra's relationship with your son?" the young lawyer asked.

"It was clear that she never loved him. My son was a very trusting soul, and I believe he was fooled by her. After they were married, and she'd gotten what she wanted, she paid no attention to him. She seemed embarrassed by his stutter."

Callandra let out a grunt of disbelief, and her lawyer looked at her admonishingly.

"She was always closer to the servants. Lottie in particular."

"Could you please tell the court who Lottie is," the young lawyer requested.

"Lottie is Samuel Hunter's sister. That's him there," she said, pointing at him.

The lawyer urged her to continue.

"Sam worked for my husband as a carpenter. And he asked my husband to hire his sister to work in our household. She was only fourteen and we didn't need her, but we hired her anyway, out of consideration. She wasn't a good servant. Later, when Callandra arrived, she and Lottie became very close. I believe that's how Callandra and Sam became involved …"

"Really?" said the young lawyer, folding his arms across his chest, allowing the voluminous sleeves of his robe to billow. "Could you explain, please?"

"I heard from my housekeeper that Lottie and Callandra made a great fuss whenever Sam came over. At first, I didn't make anything of it. But then, when my son decided to come to Canada — to continue his calling here — I noticed how determined Callandra was that Sam come, too. It seemed odd to me. The original plan had been just to take Lottie, but Callandra insisted they take Sam, as well."

"Perhaps she thought he would be useful to have along?" the young lawyer asked.

"Well, you could tell by the way Callandra looked at him that there was more to it than that," Mrs. Scott said. "She certainly never looked at my son that way. Of course, I knew she didn't care for Norbert, and that she was the kind of woman who didn't take her marriage vows seriously ... I happen to know she's a devoted reader of Mary Wollstonecraft, who takes lovers with the same freedom as men."

Amid clucks of disapproval in the room, the young lawyer paused, allowing the notion of women's sexual freedom to be digested by the men of the jury.

"So you suspected that your daughter-in-law and Sam were involved — in that way — even before they came to Canada?"

"Yes, I was pretty certain."

"This is outrageous!" Callandra said in an increasingly exasperated whisper. "Everything she's saying is a lie!"

"Was your son a strong man, Mrs. Scott?"

"Not physically. He was small and not very muscular. He was concerned about matters of the soul, not the body."

"So Sam could have overpowered him?"

"Easily," she replied.

The lawyer asked Sam to stand up, and he did so, allowing everyone to observe that he was unusually tall and powerful-looking.

"How tall was your son, compared to the accused?"

"Norbert would have come up roughly to his shoulder."

There were sounds from the crowd; the lawyer told Sam to sit down.

"And did your son carry a weapon?"

"No."

"So he would have been vulnerable, if another man — particularly a big, strong man — had attacked him?"

"He would have been helpless. I suspect it was my daughter-in-law's plan, that she saw an opportunity —"

"This is outrageous. Can't we protest in some way?"

"Not now. Shhhh."

"— to take my son's money, and then to live with a man she preferred. And now she's going to bear that man's child …" Mrs. Scott shuddered, still speaking softly while managing a look of moral revulsion. "I didn't know such depravity existed."

Sam looked over at Callandra, clearly affected by the news she was pregnant. Her head was spinning as the young lawyer indicated he had no further questions.

The judge called on Callandra's lawyer, who rose to his feet. "No questions, your honour," he said.

Mrs. Scott's distortions were just the beginning. Next came Seamus O'Reilly. The very sight of him made Callandra recoil, yet she had to sit still throughout his testimony. O'Reilly decried how he had been peacefully collecting rent from one of the farmers when Sam intervened and punched him.

"There were no problems in Goderich until *he* arrived," O'Reilly testified. "He's a radical, and he got people here thinking about rebellion. He was supposedly building a church, but he was really organizing a political revolt."

There was grumbling from the spectators. It was unclear, however, whether the grumbling was sympathetic to O'Reilly. Or did it reflect anger against the Company and the Family Compact — anger perhaps shared by some of the jurors?

Rosalee's testimony sparked further hope. Without directly contradicting O'Reilly, she softened Sam's image, implying he had only been trying to help her family in their problems with the Company. She also testified that Sam and Callandra had slept in separate bedrooms, and that she had never noticed much romantic feeling between them. The one time Rosalee had found them in Callandra's bedroom together, Callandra had looked confused and panicked. There were no follow-up questions, leaving it unclear what had transpired. Rosalee also suggested, to the further annoyance of the young lawyer, that Sam wasn't a radical, just a popular figure in the town who naturally attracted supporters. Perhaps Rosalee's infatuation with Sam might save him, Callandra thought.

Things were looking a little more hopeful when the young lawyer called to the stand Stewart Kilgour, a name that meant nothing to Callandra, nor apparently to those in the courtroom. There was silence as the stranger came forward from the back of the room.

Callandra soon realized she had seen him briefly once before. He was the innkeeper of the roadhouse in Clinton, although he looked cleaner and better dressed now. The young lawyer quickly established that Kilgour was the last person, besides Callandra, Sam, and Emma, to see Norbert alive. Under questioning, Kilgour described the tension between Sam and Norbert in front of the roadhouse that afternoon.

"The pastor did not want to stay, but the hired man did," he explained.

"And why didn't the pastor want to stay?"

"I think he felt it was too rough a place for his wife and daughter."

"And was he correct about that?"

"Aye. There was a road crew staying at the inn, and they weren't too used to being around ladies," said Kilgour.

"So Reverend Scott was acting to protect his family?"

"I believe he was."

"And did it strike you as unusual that a hired man would question the judgment of his employer, who also had moral authority as a man of the cloth?"

"Yes, it did strike me as odd."

"And out of line?"

"Aye. But, of course," Kilgour continued, "the hired man was very big and strong. And he seemed used to getting his way. The way he spoke to the minister was not respectful."

The lines appeared rehearsed.

"Really? Can you tell us more about their conversation?" the lawyer prompted.

"Well, it became quite heated. There was obviously bad feeling between them. I remember the pastor accused the hired man of trying to steal his gold — and his woman. Yes, I remember those words very clearly."

There was a gasp in the courtroom.

Instinctively, Callandra turned toward the other side of the room, glancing past a blur of faces that included Thomas Mercer Jones, his wife, and niece. Her eyes found Sam, who was already looking over at her. In that moment, she felt sure of two things: that all hope for a favourable verdict was gone and that nothing had changed between them.

When Sam finally took the stand, placing his hand on the Bible, the young lawyer asked him if he appreciated the importance of telling the truth.

"I have little knowledge of the Bible," Sam responded. "But I have great regard for the truth."

Undeterred by the menacing tone of the lawyer's questions, Sam went on to explain events described by Mrs. Scott in ways that made them sound considerably less sinister.

"It's true that Callandra pushed for me to come to Canada, but not because we were intimate with each other. We were not. She wanted me to come only because she knew that if I came, Lottie would want to come, too. Lottie was always the focus of her attention."

Callandra nodded, pleased to hear the truth spoken so clearly.

"And you — why did you want to come to Canada?" asked the lawyer.

"I didn't," Sam said. "I liked my job in Glasgow. I saw a future there. But Reverend Scott was determined to come to Canada, and wanted me to build a church for him here. I figured I could build the church, and then Lottie and I could leave for the United States. I'd heard there were opportunities down there for skilled carpenters."

"So it was always your intention to leave for the United States? You felt no loyalty to Reverend Scott?"

"I had agreed to build his church, and I was committed to doing so."

"But didn't you, in fact, feel hostility toward Reverend Scott?"

"No. Not hostility …"

"But you disliked him?"

"I didn't particularly like him."

"You disliked him because he was born into privilege — isn't that right?" asked the lawyer. "You disapprove of privilege, don't you, Mr. Hunter?"

"I do disapprove of privilege," Sam said. "But my feelings about Reverend Scott had little to do with that. I disliked the way he treated his wife and child. He was cruel to them."

"You're neither a husband nor a father, and yet you presume to judge one who had the duties and responsibilities of both those positions, including discipline?"

"I don't believe it's a man's job to discipline his wife — or to be cruel to his child."

"So you and Callandra shared a dislike of Norbert?"

"I didn't talk to her about him."

"According to Mrs. Scott's testimony, Callandra never liked Norbert."

"From what I could see, it was more a case of him not liking her."

"And what about you? Did you like Callandra?" the young lawyer stopped directly in front of Sam as he asked this.

"Yes," Sam answered. "She was kind to me."

"Did you like her ... in the way a man likes a woman?"

"She was married, and her husband was my employer," Sam responded.

"I didn't ask you if it was appropriate for you to desire her. I asked you if you *did* desire her?"

Sam hesitated. "Well, as any man would. She's a beautiful woman."

Callandra's heart soared, even though she knew Sam's comment contributed to the dangerous narrative the young lawyer was constructing.

"As you say, she's a beautiful woman, and there you were in the forest with her all those days, with only her husband in the way. And you both hated her husband."

"Hate is too strong to describe my feelings. And I can't speak for her."

"Well, she would have had grounds to dislike him, if he treated her badly. So let's just say that you both disliked him, and that he stood in the way of the two of you being together, with access to his money. And there was no one around to witness any misfortune that might befall him — like the carriage going into the river."

"The carriage went into the river because the bridge collapsed. If anyone bears responsibility for the death of Reverend Norbert Scott, it's the Company — for allowing that bridge to deteriorate."

The courtroom erupted at the audacity of the accusation. Nobody dared talk about the Company that way in Goderich — certainly not since the rebellion. Callandra glanced over and saw Mr. Jones's face stiffen. Mrs. Jones and her niece fanned themselves nervously.

"Why don't you put your questions to the Company commissioner?" Sam continued. "He's sitting right there in the front row. I believe you know him; he's your employer."

Sam's impertinence was stunning. Thomas Mercer Jones was the most powerful man in the Huron Tract, and here was Sam openly taunting him. *Why was he being so reckless, so brazenly insulting to those with power?* Callandra wondered. Perhaps he was hoping that at least some of the jurors would side with him, as many townspeople had in the past, precisely because he'd dared to stand up to the Company.

The courtroom was buzzing, prompting the judge to call for order.

"Let me remind you that it's you who is on trial here," the lawyer snapped. "And how was it that you managed to save Callandra and the child from the river, but not Reverend Scott?"

"I was focused on saving mother and child."

"And when you got them to safety, you just ignored Reverend Scott?"

"No. Callandra pleaded with me to go back and look for her husband."

"And did you?"

"Yes. She was insistent."

This was a pleasing embellishment of the truth, Callandra thought, making her sound like a more devoted wife than she'd been.

"And what happened? I suppose you tried to save him?" said the lawyer, undercutting any heroics Sam might try to claim.

"Actually no," said Sam. "I went back across the river. The carriage was partially submerged in the water, and he wasn't inside. I swam around looking for him, but couldn't find him. It was dark and the current was strong …"

"And this?" asked the lawyer, picking up a small velvet sack from the table. "Can you tell us what this is?"

"That, I believe, is the coin purse that was taken from me when I was arrested."

"And where did you get it? Was it yours?"

"I got it from the coat of Reverend Scott — which was inside the carriage."

The crowd was hushed.

"So you took this sack of gold coins from Reverend Scott's coat, and then did no more to find him."

"I didn't believe there was anything more I could do. I assumed his body had been swept away by the current."

"Of course, there were no witnesses. So we have no way of knowing if what you say is true." The lawyer's tone turned nastier. "I put it to you that you found Reverend Scott alive and killed him — so you could take his money. And his identity."

"That's not true."

"So you say," said the lawyer more softly, leaving the murder allegation dangling. "You then continued on to Goderich, with the dead man's wife and child, and presented yourself as the new pastor."

"No, I didn't. That was a misunderstanding. The first family we encountered in Goderich mistook me for him."

"And you didn't bother to correct them?"

"I should have," said Sam slowly, sounding sincerely regretful.

"You should have, but you didn't?"

"That's correct."

"And I suppose you also expect us to believe that you were never intimate with Reverend Scott's wife?"

"No, I don't expect you to believe that."

"I thought you said that?"

"I indicated that I was not intimate with her earlier, back in Glasgow."

"So, you admit that you became intimate with her later?"

"Yes, in Goderich."

"So, after you had taken Norbert's identity, you also felt entitled to his wife?"

"No, I didn't feel entitled."

"But you wanted her?"

Sam said nothing, as the crowd awaited his response. But, eventually, he responded, "Yes."

The room buzzed with reaction. Some of the jurors looked disapproving, or did Callandra imagine that?

"And I guess it worked out well, since she wanted you, too."

"No, she didn't. She was upset about her husband's death. He'd been cruel to her, but she felt some loyalty to him. She told me to stay away from her."

"And did you?"

"Initially. We spent the night in a cabin …"

"This was in Goderich?"

"No, before we made it to Goderich. Right after the accident. We were on the road between Clinton and Goderich. Just off the road, there was a cabin … I believe it's owned by the Company. We spent the night there."

There was a pause before a lawyer, sitting next to Thomas Mercer Jones, rose to his feet and objected, insisting the Company owned no such cabin.

"Somebody owned it," Sam continued. "There were supplies there. Even liquor."

The young lawyer walked over and briefly conferred with the lawyer next to Mr. Jones.

"Just to clarify, your honour, the Company built that cabin before the town was settled, but it no longer uses it," the young lawyer said.

"Well, someone left liquor there," added Sam.

"Probably poachers or surveyors," the young lawyer suggested. "But, in any event —"

"No, this wasn't cheap liquor," Sam interjected. "It was brandy — in a silver flask, covered in fine leather."

There were chortles in the crowd, prompting the judge to pound his gavel.

"I fail to see the relevance of this," said the judge.

Sam was clearly annoying the young lawyer. And, looking around, Callandra caught sight of Jones, whose face was flushed and contorted, as if struggling to contain anger.

It suddenly occurred to her that maybe the brandy they'd been drinking that night in the cabin had belonged to Jones. The silver flask was too fine to have been Longworth's.

Indeed, maybe it had been Jones who'd been involved with the servant girl, Daisy Howard. Perhaps he still was. Of course, having affairs with young girls is what powerful men did, married or not. But then Jones was no ordinary powerful man; he was the son-in-law of the all-powerful archdeacon, who would have little patience for such depravity, particularly when it threatened the well-being of his daughter and his family's good name. As Callandra scrutinized the near-desperate look on Jones's face right now, he certainly seemed like a man who'd been caught.

The young lawyer turned back to Sam: "So you and Mrs. Scott spent the night in the cabin. Did you make love to her?"

"She wanted nothing to do with me. She pushed me away when I touched her. But she quickly learned I wasn't going to take no for an answer ... There was no one there but the child to hear her screams."

Callandra felt faint. It was one thing for him to falsely paint her as a loyal wife, but another to falsely paint himself as a rapist. She realized he was trying to take all the blame, to portray her as an innocent victim. But that was wrong. If anything, what had happened had been her fault. At the very least, they should share the blame.

But then what about Emma? Of course, that's what he was thinking.

"So, you forced her to behave like your wife?" the lawyer's voice boomed.

"Well, not exactly my wife," Sam responded slowly. "It was never my intention to stay long in Goderich."

"But you had a sexual relationship with her?"

"Yes; she had no choice," Sam replied, looking straight at Callandra. "She became my toy ... my rattle."

The courtroom exploded in hoots of disapproval. But at the mention of those words, against all reason, Callandra felt a sudden, unstoppable thrill. She looked straight at Sam and, for an exhilarating moment, it felt as if it were just them alone in the courtroom.

The lawyer continued, "What happened to Reverend Scott's gold?"

"We spent some of it. What was left I took with me when I left Goderich last November."

Now he was portraying himself as greedy and treacherous. "No, that's not true —" Callandra called out. But the judge ordered her silent.

"So you're a thief, as well?" the lawyer asked Sam. "A killer, an imposter, an adulterer, a thief! Oh, yes, and one more thing — a rebel! A hanging offence all on its own!"

"No," said Sam.

"You left for Toronto late last November, just before the rebellion started?"

"Yes."

"Your rebel sympathies are well known. Yet you expect us to believe that you didn't join the rebellion?"

"I did not."

"I suppose we can add 'liar' to his list of transgressions!" said the lawyer, building to a crescendo, speaking directly to the jury.

"Actually no," said Sam with a clear, strong voice. "I have always been sympathetic to the rebel cause, but I did not take part in the rebellion."

"Oh really?" the lawyer sneered, turning back to Sam. "Where exactly did you go when you left Goderich?"

"To Toronto, to see Lottie."

"You were going to see your sister?" smirked the lawyer, a twinkle in his eye. "You expect us to believe that?"

"I said I was going to see Lottie."

"And that's your sister, right?"

Sam paused, his eyes connecting with Callandra's for a moment. Then he turned back to the lawyer. "No ... I don't have a sister."

"So now you want us to believe you do not have a sister?"

"I am simply telling the truth. I do not have a sister."

"So, you don't know this person Lottie?"

"Yes, I do ... I know her well ... but she's not my sister."

Why was he saying this? Callandra couldn't figure out what he was trying to suggest, but she called out impulsively, "That's not true —"

The judge looked at her sternly. "If you speak out one more time, I'll have you removed."

"It is true," Sam said, over the loud banging of the gavel and talking in the courtroom. Then speaking just to Callandra, with the din in the room a background blur: "I'm deeply sorry ... I should have told you."

Deeply sorry? He should have told me? What on earth did he mean?

"So, she's not your sister?" said the lawyer, surprised to be thrown off his line of questioning.

"No."

"I fail to see the relevance of this, counsel," said the judge. "What does it matter if Lottie is his sister or not?"

"Well," the lawyer responded, regaining his composure. "It shows one more lie. He lied about Lottie being his sister to his employer — the man who trusted him and promoted him. He appears to have lied about Lottie to Callandra as well. The accused is clearly a chronic liar. No wonder he was so comfortable lying to the people of Goderich. That's what he does. He lies. He's a con man — and a killer."

In the background, Callandra could see the judge, the jurors, the lawyers. Everything was closing in, the walls advancing toward her.

If she's not his sister ... then what was their relationship? What is their relationship?

The room started swirling around; her head felt light and woozy. Sam was talking again, to the room, not to her. Voices were speaking, but she didn't follow what they were saying. Then, in the moment before she fainted, she could see Lottie — smiling, lovely, radiant — just as she'd looked in Sam's arms back in the shed in Glasgow.

Callandra regained consciousness outside of the courtroom as her hands were being shackled. She was surrounded, scores of people in the hallway pressing for a closer look at her. Two constables led her to a small, windowless, unfurnished room. They closed the door, leaving her slumped on the floor, strangely disconnected from what was happening. It was hard to know what devastated her more at this moment: her likely conviction for murder or feeling betrayed by two people she'd trusted completely.

She found herself consumed by the betrayal. So, Lottie had never been truthful to her. This was the secret that Lottie had refused to divulge. Despite all the closeness and trust that had seemed to exist between them, Lottie had resolutely hidden this fact — undoubtedly the most important fact in her life. Callandra was flooded with memories of life in Glasgow, realizing now that there was so much about Sam and Lottie that she hadn't understood at the time — that she'd been prevented from understanding. They weren't siblings; they were lovers!

Lottie was only fourteen when she came to work in the Scott household; Sam nineteen. Were they fully involved then, or just in the throes of delirious romantic love and anticipation? It had always seemed believable to Callandra that they were siblings, but in fact they looked very different. That they were both so physically alluring didn't point to common parentage, but to a raw attraction between them. How had Callandra missed that?

Of course, she missed it because she was trusting. Why should she not believe what her dearest friend told her? Why had Lottie been so dishonest? It made sense that Lottie had lied to the Scotts; otherwise Mrs. Scott would never have hired her. But why lie to Callandra? Surely Lottie trusted her not to tell her in-laws? Of course, back then, Sam didn't trust Callandra, and he had probably insisted that Lottie keep their secret from her. And whatever he said, Lottie followed.

Sam's betrayal stung much more. Callandra had opened herself to him more than to anyone in the world. Now it was clear that he hadn't reciprocated, hadn't even been truthful about the basic facts of his life. Indeed, he had knowingly deceived her, leading her to believe that there was another obstacle to their involvement, that it had something to do with his need to join the rebellion. If he'd simply told her the truth, she would have backed off, determined not to do anything that would have hurt Lottie. Why had *he* been willing to betray Lottie, whose loyalty to him was so strong and clear?

Beyond pain, there was anger and jealousy. She now realized he'd gone to Toronto to see Lottie. She thought of their reunion, of their desire for each other after those many months apart. Images that had always made her feel inadequate now came back to haunt her in a new way — Lottie's hypnotic beauty, her generous lips, her bewitching green eyes, her flaxen hair, soft skin, and fulsome breasts. Then there was her sweetly feminine manner, with its touch of mystery. Of course, Sam would have loved her and wanted her — no doubt from first sight.

Callandra, on the other hand, had to chase after him, to practically plead with him to make love to her, and on such easy terms. *You can stay tonight; that's all I'm asking.* Her own words came back to taunt her. How thrilled she'd felt by her own boldness, how happy she'd been when he finally gave in. She cringed at the memory of it all.

She wondered if he'd confessed his infidelity to Lottie. She would surely have forgiven him, making their reconnection all the more intense, infused with pain, jealousy, and remorse. Perhaps this wasn't the first time he'd wandered. Perhaps there'd been other occasions when temptation had been dangled in front of him, offered up casually and without strings attached. Callandra thought of Rosalee, the girl at the roadhouse, Jones's niece — and the way they had all reacted to Sam. Lottie must have seen other girls flirting with him, but she would have known he'd never stray for long, and that he would always come back to her.

It was uncomfortable on the bare wooden floor, and Callandra was thirsty, hungry, and depleted. How long had she been here in this grim little room, slipping in and out of consciousness, battered by memories? There were so many images — from Glasgow, the ocean crossing, Mrs. Tinsdale's, Ethan's farmhouse. All had to be reassessed, filtered through a new lens. Almost everything that had seemed good in her life these past five years was connected to Lottie or Sam — although never both together. Was any of it true?

How should she even think about Sam now? He had deceived her with his silence, his refusal to disclose something crucial. And yet, in court, he had clearly been trying to save her, saying things that incriminated himself to make her look blameless. But then, it wasn't as if he had come back to save her. He'd been captured in Toronto — where he'd no doubt been staying with Lottie. Once he'd been brought back to Goderich, he would have known there was no hope for himself; he had posed as Norbert, and Jones had always hated him. He faced conviction for sure. There was no reason for him not to try to save Callandra — if only for Emma's sake.

Exhausted, she fell asleep. It was morning when a sour-looking constable opened the door and informed her that all charges against her had been dropped and she was free to go.

Emma came bounding down the path toward where her mother was standing, arms outstretched, just behind the little wooden gate. Pushing it open, Callandra scooped her daughter up into her arms, joyful to see her for the first time in more than a month. The girl's cheeks were flushed and almost as pink as the ribbons in her long, dark tresses. Her big brown eyes glistened with excitement. Callandra held her tightly, assuring her that they would always be together now. A smile lit up the child's face, and she nestled her head against her mother, her little body pulsing with emotion.

"You don't have to go back to jail?" asked Emma, as Mrs. Murphy came out of the house and caught up with them.

"No. I'm going to be with you," said Callandra. The reality of her freedom hit Callandra with fresh impact when she saw what it meant to her daughter.

The sun was bright and it was already very warm. No matter what else, she had Emma. Standing there outside the imposing Jones home, Callandra felt suddenly grateful. She had an impulse to thank Mrs. Murphy — for what? For supervising her imprisonment? For delivering Emma from the servants' quarters just now? Or simply for softening her look of disapproval, now that Callandra had been cleared?

"Thank you, Mrs. Murphy," she said.

"It's good that you're free," the woman replied, her face less dour than usual. "This girl needs a mother."

"Thank you," Callandra repeated, holding Emma tightly.

"Well, it's Mrs. Jones you should be thanking."

"Mrs. Jones?"

"Yes. Her testimony really helped you."

"I didn't know she testified," said Callandra, standing up.

"Yes, after you fainted," Mrs. Murphy continued. "I think it was because of her that they dropped the charges against you. Mrs. Scott clearly thought you should be punished, and she's very powerful. But Mrs. Jones is more powerful."

Callandra was taken aback by Mrs. Jones's intervention, not quite sure what she'd done to win the great lady's support.

This also explained Mrs. Murphy's softening. If Mrs. Jones was sympathetic to Callandra, it wasn't surprising that Mrs. Murphy would rethink her own disapproval. Perhaps there might be some forgiveness in the town, as well.

Still, Callandra wanted to get home now without encountering any townspeople. She had managed to slip unnoticed out the back door of the Company building after her unexpected release that morning. It had been early and there hadn't been many people in the square. But Sam's trial was continuing today, and by now there would be a crowd as big as yesterday's.

Emma asked if they could go down to the harbour and watch the ducks. It seemed like an odd thing to do in the midst of such turmoil, but it would take them away from the courthouse and all the curious onlookers. Besides, it was what Emma wanted.

They headed toward the harbour. Emma's moist little hand held on to hers tightly, jubilantly. They followed the narrow path to where the land sloped down to the water's edge. Across the lake, the water gleamed near-turquoise in the sun. Like the day, it was improbably beautiful — a glorious sight that highlighted the starkness between life and death, freedom and captivity.

She was exhausted after her anguished, mostly sleepless night. Sitting on the warm, dry ground, Callandra gently probed Emma for details of her life since they'd been apart. It became clear the child had not been mistreated. She talked of missing her mother and crying every day, but there was no mention of punishment. She had not seen Grandmother at all. She had made friends with the children of the serving staff, and Mrs. Jones and her niece had been kind to her.

Emma wandered down by the shore, where the ducks waded in the shallow water on the sandy side of the harbour. They let her come up close to them before suddenly fleeing en masse. In the warmth of the sun, Emma seemed so happy. This wasn't the time to intrude into her childhood bliss to tell her that Sam was on trial, and that it was almost impossible to imagine a good outcome.

It wasn't until they were heading back home, on a route that avoided the centre of town, that the question of Sam became unavoidable. Randall appeared in the distance, walking toward them, apparently on his way home. Callandra felt her heart speed up. She hadn't talked to him in months, but had noticed him in the courtroom yesterday. So why wasn't he there now? Was the trial over?

As he approached, she held Emma's hand more firmly. What terrible news was the little girl going to hear about the man who had been like a father to her?

Randall quickened his pace when he noticed them.

"I'm so glad you're free," he began.

"Aye, me, too," said Callandra.

"You seem to have recovered. Are you all right?" he asked, and she realized that the last time he saw her she was being carried out of the courtroom.

"Yes, I'm fine."

"Sam's trial is over," Randall said.

Callandra's heart was thudding. Emma looked up curiously. "Where is he?"

"He's here in Goderich," Callandra answered.

Emma, her face brightening, asked, "When can we see him again?"

"I'm not sure," said Callandra, trying to make her voice sound calm. She looked pleadingly at Randall, as if to say: *If it's not good news, don't tell us now.*

"The jury is deliberating," he said.

"How does it look?" she said, ignoring her own caution.

"It's hard to tell. The prosecutor made a long speech about how Sam had always hated Norbert, even back in Scotland."

"That's not true. I doubt he ever thought about Norbert back in Scotland," said Callandra.

"Well, the prosecutor said that Sam had planned the whole thing — the murder, posing as Norbert and then" — Randall paused, searching for a polite phrase — "taking advantage of you."

"He never took advantage of me," said Callandra. "I understand Mrs. Scott's anger over Norbert's death, but she had no evidence against Sam."

"Maybe not. But Mrs. Jones did."

"What?"

"She testified about how you had come to her with cuts and bruises all over your face."

"But that had nothing to do with Sam! I told her that one of the Company men did that to me. Sam wasn't even in Goderich at the time. Didn't she make that clear?"

"No. She made it sound as if that were proof Sam was violent and was forcing you to —" Randall interrupted himself again.

"That's absurd," cried Callandra. "Besides, what does that have to do with Norbert's death? Nothing!"

"Well, the prosecutor went on and on about it. He said it showed Sam to be a violent man, capable of murder."

"That's so wrong —"

"But it fit with what Sam had said himself, about the way he treated you."

"But he was lying about that …"

That's what he does. He lies.

Still, after a night of jealousy, rage, disbelief, she knew she didn't want him to die.

A cluster of people appeared down the road, so Callandra said goodbye and, taking Emma by the hand, proceeded down another passageway. But even this way, she could see people approaching.

She abruptly switched directions, heading out into the forest that surrounded the town. It was a longer route home, but it would spare them from encountering the crowd from the trial. She knew she would have to face the town's disapproval eventually, but not now.

She and Emma walked in silence through the woods, following a footpath Callandra had taken once before. It was more overgrown than she remembered, making it harder to walk, but giving her space to think.

That's what he does. He lies.

Chapter Twenty-Two

Mrs. Scott had returned to her bedchamber in the Jones mansion to rest and await the verdict.

After delivering her testimony the previous day, she felt relieved but exhausted. These past few months had been the most miserable and tumultuous of her life. The discovery that her dear son was dead had been horrifying, made worse by the treachery and deception that surrounded his death. Since then, she had been consumed with grief and rage, focused on seeing that punishment was meted out, and without mercy.

Sitting by the fireplace in her bedroom, still fully dressed in black, she felt confident that there would be a conviction. But she was also distracted by the news she'd received from one of the lawyers as she left the courtroom that morning: the charges against Callandra had been dropped.

Mrs. Scott had sensed how much the commissioner wanted to see Sam punished, as much for his rebel sympathies and his troublemaking as for his role as an imposter and possibly a murderer. Punishing Callandra had always seemed a secondary concern to Jones. For Mrs. Scott, the priorities were reversed.

She felt sure that it was Callandra who had initiated the relationship with Sam, thereby creating the circumstances that led to Norbert's murder, or at least to his abandonment in the river by aspiring lovers wanting to be rid of him. It was Callandra's deep disloyalty to her husband that had been the root of the wickedness.

Mrs. Scott thought back on how much she had always disliked and distrusted Callandra. From the outset, she had found the girl selfish and overly assertive; memories of her self-centred behaviour in Glasgow came flooding back now. Mrs. Scott vividly recalled the afternoon when Callandra had appeared in the parlour with that beret perched jauntily on her head, prompting Norbert to make the perfectly reasonable request that she remove the silly garment before meeting his cousins. Yet Callandra had responded with an ostentatious display of tears, drawing Mr. Scott's attention to herself and making Norbert the object of his father's mockery.

Callandra had shown that same desire for attention at the dinner party where she had needlessly inserted herself into the conversation the men were having, insulting those very gentlemen for no reason other than that they were high-born. While Norbert's impeccable behaviour that evening had gone unnoticed by his father, Callandra's smug intervention had amused Mr. Scott, who seemed all too ready to be charmed by the girl's flagrant coquettishness.

Mrs. Scott also angrily recalled how Callandra had tried to indoctrinate Isobel with the ideas of Mary Wollstonecraft, and how Isobel had seemed interested in reading that scandalous book, prompting Mrs. Scott to take it away from her. The fact that Callandra had had the audacity to praise the work of such an adulteress should have alerted Mrs. Scott to the kind of woman Callandra truly was, and the danger she posed to her son.

Indeed, Callandra's licentiousness reminded Mrs. Scott of the adulterous ways of her own husband. Such behaviour was even more deplorable in a woman, and it enraged Mrs. Scott that she'd been unable to protect her poor, vulnerable son from the sort of pain she herself had so long been forced to endure. While she couldn't make Mr. Scott suffer for his cruel infidelity, Callandra was not beyond her reach.

Mrs. Scott decided she must act. Writing a quick note, she summoned a butler to take it down to Mr. Jones.

She soon received a reply, inviting her to come to see him in his study.

Although she'd been a guest in his home for four weeks, this was the first time she had actually been in his study, and she was impressed by the fineness of the room's decor. Jones came out from behind his desk and bowed his head respectfully as he directed her to an upholstered settee by the window. He came over and sat in a leather wingback chair nearby. Tea was ordered.

"It shouldn't be long now, Mrs. Scott," Jones began. "The lawyers are confident of a guilty verdict."

"I am grateful for all you have done in the interests of justice, Commissioner," she replied. "And, of course, for your generous hospitality."

"Not at all — we are pleased to assist in any way we can," said Jones, projecting the tone and manner of a longtime member of the Family Compact, despite his recent arrival in those ranks. "We know what a difficult time this has been for you."

Mrs. Scott studied the commissioner, concluding that his wide sideburns were adequately groomed, even if she personally disliked such a display of facial hair. She was aware of the commissioner's modest roots, and this knowledge boosted her confidence, which was already strong and deeply ingrained. Undoubtedly, Jones would have been informed about her wealth and the prominence of her family in Glasgow by his father-in-law, the archdeacon, whom she had made a point of visiting in Toronto before proceeding to the Huron Tract. In fact, it had been the archdeacon who had been good enough to arrange for her and the maid travelling with her to stay with his daughter and son-in-law while she was in Goderich.

They briefly discussed the splendid view of the lake. "There is a matter I must urgently bring to your attention," she declared, ending the pleasantries. "I am deeply concerned that Callandra has been set free."

"I see," said Jones, knitting his dark eyebrows together in an arc that made his face appear even more densely haired.

"I do believe she bears considerable guilt, and I should like to see her punished," Mrs. Scott continued.

"I understand," he replied, pulling at the edges of his perfectly starched shirt cuffs in a show of fastidiousness, if not nervousness.

The arrival and serving of tea put a temporary damper on the conversation.

When the servants had gone, Jones continued, "Of course, our focus has been on ensuring the conviction of Sam, who most likely did the killing and who posed as your son."

"His guilt is evident," she said crisply. "But Callandra was clearly his accomplice."

"Well, was there not some doubt about that, ma'am?" Jones ventured in a careful, respectful manner.

"There was none," stated Mrs. Scott firmly, with a voice that underlined her sense of her own authority.

"Well, there was the testimony of my wife about bruises on Callandra's face." His voice sounded uncertain, as he pulled again on his cuffs.

"I'm sure Mrs. Jones was mistaken," Mrs. Scott said. "At the very least, the matter needs more investigation. Certainly, Callandra and

Sam were living together in sin. Is that the sort of behaviour that you, as commissioner, condone? Do you think that the archdeacon would find that acceptable?"

"No, no, he wouldn't," said Jones, stiffening visibly at the mention of his father-in-law.

"Well, I think Callandra should be charged again — as an accomplice to murder."

They sipped their tea in silence for a short while.

"Of course, there's the question of the child to be considered, Mrs. Scott."

"What does that have to do with Callandra's guilt? Should she be allowed to get away with murder, just because she has a child?" Mrs. Scott's face was shaking slightly, her eyes becoming more focused and pincer-like.

"No, of course not, ma'am ... I'm just thinking through the consequences, and how we would deal with them."

"That should hardly be your concern, Commissioner," she said.

"Well, I would have to concern myself with it. We don't have facilities for orphans in the Huron Tract. Perhaps the child could be returned to her mother's family back in Scotland. I understand they have a farm."

"Not any more, but that's of no consequence," Mrs. Scott said, reflecting on how glad she was that she had held on to the deed to the property.

"Well, then maybe the child could return to the servants' quarters here. I'd have to check with my wife, but I suspect she would be willing to allow that. She's fond of the girl."

"That wouldn't be necessary," Mrs. Scott said.

"No?"

"No. You needn't concern yourself with the child," she said, resolve etched unmistakably on her face. "I would take her."

"Oh," said Jones, visibly surprised.

"I am her grandmother."

"Yes, of course."

Mrs. Scott had given the matter considerable thought and had decided that, in the event something should happen to Callandra, she would be willing to take Emma back to Glasgow with her. With rigorous discipline — and a new Christian name connected to the family — the girl could be made to forget these years under the influence of her wayward mother, and be raised to become a proper, God-fearing woman.

There was a knock on the door of the study. The butler entered and handed an envelope to Jones, who opened it immediately, arching his eyebrows.

"Guilty!" Jones declared, a look of vindication spreading across his face. "Samuel Hunter is to be hanged — at noon on Saturday!"

Mrs. Scott felt a deep sense of relief, murmuring only: "The Lord be thanked for his justice."

Now, if only she could secure Callandra's lifetime imprisonment or execution, she would feel she had done what she could to set things right by Norbert.

——— * ———

When Callandra and Emma made it back to their cottage, Randall and Joe were there waiting for them, and the look on their faces conveyed the terrible news. Callandra immediately put her hands over Emma's ears, although she knew there was no sparing the girl from what lay ahead.

Randall and Joe stayed for a while and they all talked with dread and sadness about what was happening, without being specific, for Emma's sake. With the windows open, they could hear hoots and hollers coming from the town square as news of the verdict spread.

Callandra asked them if they would stay awhile with Emma, but the girl, crying and confused, not understanding what was going on, refused to let her mother out of her sight. So Callandra simply put on her bonnet, took Emma by the hand, and headed out the door.

They took a back road that was mostly empty. A few young men rushed by, then turned to stare at them. A woman leaned out a window as they passed and called Callandra a strumpet, adding that her unborn child would be a bastard. Without asking, Emma seemed to know what the words meant.

As they headed down West Street toward the Jones mansion, Callandra could feel Emma's grip tighten.

Unlike the wooden gate at the servants' entrance, the wrought-iron gate at the front of the house was heavy and intimidating. Callandra opened it, walked with her daughter up to the porch, and knocked on the imposing front door.

When a male servant answered, Callandra asked to speak to Mrs. Jones.

"And your name, ma'am?" he said.

"Callandra ... She knows me."

The servant indicated that he would return and then closed the door, leaving them outside. Waiting, holding Emma's hand, Callandra sensed her resolve slipping away. She felt she must speak to Mrs. Jones, although it was hard to imagine that even Mrs. Jones could stop Sam's execution. The longer she waited, the more doubts she had.

They stood there for what seemed like a long time. Perhaps the servant had forgotten, or had never intended to seek Mrs. Jones.

It wasn't too late to leave. Yes, they should leave.

But the door finally opened, and Mrs. Jones's niece appeared, by herself. She immediately reached out and embraced Emma, who responded warmly.

"We haven't formally met, but I know you're the pastor's wife," Annabelle said to Callandra. She was immaculately dressed, her light brown hair formed into distinctly shaped curls, and she spoke in a sweet, small voice.

"Aye," said Callandra, heartened to observe Annabelle's kindliness toward Emma.

"I was hoping to speak to your aunt."

"She's unavailable right now. Is there something I can help you with?"

"I have something important to tell her."

"You can tell me. I could convey the message."

This wasn't as good, but perhaps her only chance. "Please tell her that Samuel Hunter never hurt me. Those bruises on my face were caused by one of the Company agents."

"Oh ... yes, I remember you saying that."

Callandra now recalled that Annabelle had been with Mrs. Jones that day.

"Sam is not a violent man. He would never hurt a woman," Callandra continued, encouraged by Annabelle's willingness to listen, with eyes full of sympathy. Despite her polished appearance, the girl seemed to have some of Mrs. Jones's decency.

"Please tell your aunt —"

But Callandra was interrupted when Mr. Jones appeared behind his niece in the front hallway.

"What's going on?" he asked tersely.

"This lady has something to tell Aunt Mary," said Annabelle.

"Really?" said Jones. He picked up Annabelle's hand gently, directing her away from the door. "Thank you, dear. I'll handle this."

Annabelle moved back but stayed in the hallway.

"What is it you wish to tell my wife?" he said to Callandra. "You can tell me."

"Well," said Callandra cautiously. "I thought she should know that Sam never hit me. Those bruises were from Seamus O'Reilly."

Jones hesitated before answering, finally responding: "How are we supposed to keep track of all the men in your life?"

"Whatever you think of me — Sam is not a violent man. He certainly didn't kill Norbert. That was an accident. Sam doesn't deserve to die."

"He was convicted by a jury of his peers."

"They didn't have all the information."

"It would not have made a difference," he said, dismissively. "Besides, it's too late now."

"No, it isn't," said Callandra. "You could pardon him. Yes, you could … I plead with you to pardon him …"

"And why would I do that?" he said disdainfully.

Then Annabelle stepped forward. "Please, Uncle. I believe she is telling the truth about the pastor."

"He's no pastor. He's a fraud!"

"But he's not a violent man …" Annabelle persevered.

"My dear, you don't understand," Mr. Jones spoke to his niece softly but firmly. "That man is a fraud and —"

"He rescued me and Auntie from the mob that day, down by the creek."

"My dear, you're mistaken," said Jones. "Look, this matter is out of my hands. The jury has decided. I can't intervene —"

"But Grandfather could!" said Annabelle, with an animation that seemed at odds with her prettily twirled strands of hair. "He's the most powerful man in the colony. Everybody says so. *He* could intervene!"

"Good gracious, child!" said Jones, shocked by his niece's audacity. Then with clenched teeth, he added, "The highest authorities in Toronto have already made clear they want the scoundrel punished — either for this or for treason. He will not walk free, that I can tell you."

Callandra felt a knife through her heart. It now seemed truly hopeless.

"But," he said, turning to Callandra. "You just said something of interest. You admitted that Sam wasn't violent toward you, that you weren't coerced …"

His eyes seemed to brighten as he continued: "So you were his mistress, his willing harlot."

She pulled Emma in closer to her, backing away.

"You conspired with him, to kill your husband — just like Mrs. Scott said."

"No —"

"The proper place for you is jail!"

Jones rang a small bell attached to the wall, and the butler quickly appeared.

"Summon Captain Henderson to come to the house at once," he ordered.

"Yes, sir."

"Oh, please no!" cried Callandra. "What will happen to my child?"

"She'll go with her grandmother back to Glasgow," said Jones through clenched teeth. "Mrs. Scott has already said she'd take the girl."

"What! Oh, my God, no!" cried Callandra, but her words were drowned out by a piercing scream coming from Emma, who held her mother, visibly shaking.

"You should have thought about the consequences before killing your husband …" Jones continued.

"I did no such thing! Please, please let me talk to your wife …" Callandra begged.

"My wife?" he scoffed. "My wife is a virtuous woman, the

daughter of the archdeacon. I can assure you she would have no sympathy for an adulteress."

Emma was now sobbing uncontrollably.

"Really?" said Callandra, emboldened by her daughter's despair. "Your wife dislikes adultery? Then, pray, what does she think about the servant girl?"

"What are you talking about?" said the commissioner, his words clipped.

"The servant girl," Callandra repeated. "Daisy Howard ... I believe you know her."

Jones looked at her with fury, then stepped out to join her on the front porch, pulling the door shut behind him.

"I don't know what you're talking about," he said menacingly, grabbing her roughly by the arm. But did she also detect fear?

"I believe you're the father of her child," Callandra boldly continued.

From inside the house, Mrs. Jones's voice was audible: "Who is it, dear?"

Jones let go of Callandra's arm. "Get out of here," he whispered to Callandra.

But before she could grab Emma and leave, the door opened. Mrs. Jones and her niece stood at the entrance, engulfed in a cloud of perfume.

"Callandra, why are you here?" the lady asked.

"I ... I wanted to tell you that Sam didn't hurt — "

"What about the servant girl?" Annabelle interjected.

Jones looked with astonishment at his niece as she continued, "I heard Callandra say something about a servant girl, before you closed the door."

There was silence.

"A servant girl?" asked Mrs. Jones, in her soft voice. "Who is that?"

"Nobody," insisted Jones. "Annabelle is confused."

"Didn't you say something about a servant girl?" Annabelle asked Callandra.

"Uh ... uh ..." stammered Callandra.

"I'm sure I heard you say something about her," Annabelle persisted.

Callandra stared hard into the eyes of the commissioner, then composed herself.

"I only said that the servants here were nice to Emma, and I appreciate that," she said.

Emma had stopped crying, and now ran over to Mrs. Jones and asked, "Is Momma going to jail?"

"No, no, the trial is over, little one," said Mrs. Jones, patting Emma's head.

"We should be going now," said Callandra to Emma, pulling the girl toward her.

But she froze at the sight of four soldiers coming up the street toward the house.

"You summoned us, sir?" said Captain Henderson's gravelly voice from just beyond the gate.

"Yes," said Jones hesitantly. "Uh ... I heard there was disorder in the square ... I trust you've secured the Company offices."

"Yes, indeed, sir. They're well-secured, with guards stationed there overnight," the captain continued. "Was there anything else, sir?"

Jones said something inaudible.

"Sir?" the captain asked again. "Can we be of further service?"

"Uh, yes," Jones answered stiffly, searching for words. "This, this lady here ... and her daughter," he motioned to Callandra and Emma huddled together. "Take them home ... See that they get home safely."

The captain saluted. "Yes, sir."

At that, Jones ushered his wife and niece back into the house, closing the door behind them.

Callandra took Emma by the hand and walked past the soldiers, who watched her curiously and cautiously.

When she hesitated about proceeding, Captain Henderson went out in front of her.

"Follow me ... ma'am," he said, then motioned to the other three soldiers to come forward beside him. Together, with muskets over their shoulders and one carrying a torch, they proceeded to lead Callandra and Emma down West Street toward the town square.

It was just getting dark, but there were still men hanging about in the square; most were young and drunk and disorderly. A particularly raucous group of youths came toward her, yelling insults. Callandra distinctly heard one of them call her "the tramp ... the preacher's tramp."

But he backed off abruptly when one of the soldiers pointed a bayonet at his chest. The young man stumbled, as he scrambled to move away from the blade. The others who'd been cavorting with him went silent and backed away, too.

After that, the other men in the square stood and watched, but didn't interfere as the soldiers escorted Callandra and Emma through the centre of town and then the rest of the way home.

The first hanging in the Huron Tract was expected to draw a considerable crowd. Callandra was resolute she would not attend, but Randall and Joe insisted she must: her absence could be construed as sympathy for Sam, undermining the story that she'd been his victim.

Rosalee complicated things. If anyone understood that Callandra wasn't a victim, it was Rosalee, who had competed with her for Sam's attention. So Callandra was wary when Rosalee appeared at her door a couple of days after the verdict. Much as she distrusted her, it was dangerous to risk antagonizing her. She invited her in for tea.

They began mutually lamenting the verdict. But then, seemingly out of nowhere, Rosalee switched topics, saying that Sam had kissed her at the barn dance.

So that was the purpose of the visit? To torment her? Callandra didn't believe that Sam had kissed Rosalee. Still, she hated Rosalee for reviving her insecurity, for poking around in her jealousy. She wanted Rosalee to leave, but the girl just sat there, sipping her tea and talking about the many new people she'd met at the trial.

Callandra was ready to demand she depart when Rosalee announced that she was going. She was almost out the door, fiddling with the latch, when she mentioned she'd tried to discourage Sam from kissing her at the barn dance, feeling it was wrong, but that he had insisted. "He was always looking at me that way," she said, before walking away. In the flurry of Callandra's tortured thoughts, it was hard to know what to do with this one.

On Saturday morning, Randall and Joe showed up at the cottage, as Callandra had requested. She had accepted that she must appear at the hanging, but was determined that Emma be spared that horror. The girl cried and cried, insisting she never wanted to be separated from her mother again. Callandra explained that this would help ensure they never would be, and somehow Emma stopped crying long enough for Callandra to slip out the door.

The large square was packed with people, including many from out of town. Men wearing military insignia and bearing muskets surrounded the substantial wooden platform built for the occasion.

The Company evidently wanted to show it didn't scrimp on things that mattered. Fixing a bridge could take months or years, but when it came to hanging an offender of public morals, who had stirred up people against the Crown, action was swift. This was to be a celebration — the triumph of good, the punishment of evil, the final crushing of the rebellion.

Callandra was conscious of curious onlookers whispering about her. She had dressed modestly, covering up her dark navy dress with a cloak, despite the hot sun overhead. A group of Presbyterian women, Glenna MacLeod among them, surveyed her from a distance. She sensed the skepticism in their gaze.

The sound of bagpipes could be heard, causing the crowd to strain forward for a better view. Callandra let people press in front of her.

Then abruptly, above the bagpipes, she heard a child's cry and turned to see Emma running toward her. She scooped her daughter up in her arms, even as Randall arrived, apologizing that he hadn't been able to stop her. She put Emma down on the ground, blocking the girl's vision of the gallows by burying her little face in the folds of her skirt. She tried to calm the frightened child, even as her own heart pounded wildly.

The crowd went silent as Sam was paraded out, hands tied behind his back. He looked magnificent, so strong and unbowed.

She ached as she watched, even as she struggled to keep Emma from looking up.

Callandra tried to conjure up fresh thoughts about how he'd betrayed her, how treacherous he'd been in concealing his relationship with Lottie — even while making love to her. But she just couldn't summon any anger. That well had gone dry.

In fact, Sam had warned her that it was wrong for them to be together. But she'd refused to listen, unwilling to hear anything that might prevent her from being with him.

One thing was clear to her, as the sound of bagpipes filled her soul: no matter what, she would always love him.

A parade of images raged through her head: the ride home from Ethan's farm, when every joy seemed possible, to now, when joy seemed unimaginable.

Men with muskets marched, stomping in unison. To the side of the platform was a row of chairs for the dignitaries. Thomas Mercer Jones sat in the middle, next to Norbert's mother, who was no longer in black, but rather wearing a light, maroon-coloured dress that, by her standards, seemed almost festive. Mrs. Jones and her niece were noticeably absent.

With armed men around him, Sam mounted the steps. He stood tall, seemingly unafraid, even as Callandra felt despair spreading through her body.

A minister she didn't recognize opened a Bible in front of Sam. Yes, this would be regarded as the restoration of rightful religion as well, after the religious fraud that had been perpetrated on the town. The minister mumbled as he read from the Bible.

Sam was told to step forward.

The crowd surged closer for a better view. Emma pulled at Callandra's skirt, tears streaming down her face.

"I don't want him to die," the girl sobbed.

Then, Sam's faraway voice could be heard in the square.

"I apologize to those I've hurt through my deception," he declared loudly, holding the rapt attention of the crowd. "But I have no regrets about supporting the working men and women of Upper Canada in their battle against corruption and special privilege!"

He sounded almost triumphant, as if he were going to his death for the cause. The crowd responded with silence, uncertain how to react to this recasting of the narrative.

Another man's voice could be heard from the back of the throng: "Long live the rebel cause!" There was silence again, and then more cheers from others nearby. Slowly, the cheers spread, coming from different parts of the gathering until they were loud enough for Jones to look disturbed and angry. He motioned to officials to speed up the proceedings.

At the front of the crowd, some waved Union Jacks and yelled "Traitor!" to drown out those applauding the radical cause, which only seemed to make the rebel cheering grow louder and more vigorous. There was pushing at the front, and it looked like fights might break out.

The men surrounding the scaffold removed the muskets from their shoulders and looked out at the increasingly disorderly scene in the square. On the platform, the hangman moved quickly, reaching up and putting a sack over Sam's head and pulling the noose tightly around his neck.

Unable to bear the sight, Callandra gasped and looked away. The crowd surged forward. Then suddenly a howl rose up — wild cheers mixed with wails of impotent rage. The taunts from the crowd told her that Sam was hanging by the neck.

She collapsed to her knees, pressing Emma's tear-stained face against her own and wrapping the child tightly in her arms. The world went dark all around her.

Epilogue

1862

It is just like Luke to aspire to something dangerous — but also bold and principled.

I am horrified; the thought of him joining the Union army fills me with unbearable images of him dying on a faraway battlefield, although I'm proud of him for risking so much to fight slavery.

Momma would have also been proud. I remember her reading to us about slavery, and saying how wrong it was to celebrate the United States as the land of freedom when it tolerated such a blatant assault on freedom. The stories she read us — about the floggings and slave markets and wealthy plantation owners — affected me deeply, much more than tales of wrongdoing by the Family Compact. They had a huge impact on Luke, too, feeding his desire to follow in his father's footsteps in standing up against injustice.

I had been so happy when Luke got on the train. As we hugged in the aisle, I was struck by what a strapping young man he'd become. But he had barely settled into the seat beside me when he told me of his plan to join the Union army. I was distraught, particularly because I fear there will be no talking him out of it.

But try, I must. After all, I promised Momma I'd take care of him. He meant so much to her. After the hanging, I'm sure it was a great solace to her to have Sam's child, allowing Sam to live on in her life. She would have been devastated at the thought that this beloved child would meet a violent end, just like his father.

The train is crowded with people and their belongings, and it's lucky I managed to save the seat beside me. Now that I may actually lose Luke, his closeness is all the more treasured. I can feel my nose tingling and tears forming in my eyes, but I want to hold them back, at least for now. I look out the window as the train gains speed, my head turned away from him, so I don't have to confront the sadness he suddenly represents.

But he isn't sad, and he playfully urges me not to mourn his passing yet since he is very much alive. My urge to cry subsides as he peppers me with questions about my quiet little life in Brantford.

I've done well, people say, for someone who spent a good part of her childhood as an orphan. I was lucky to marry a good man who owns a small dry goods store, and we have two young children. With so much to be grateful for, I sometimes feel guilty for not being happier. It's just that I never seem able to escape the pain and sadness of my childhood. And I'll never stop missing my mother.

Some of my fondest memories involve her reading to us. It didn't matter what it was — a book, a newspaper, or a magazine — she read us things that she thought we should know, about politics or history or the rights of women. She taught us not to trust everything people wrote or said, especially if they were in positions of power. I remember a newspaper article that said the rebels should be executed because they had betrayed the queen. Momma explained who the queen was, and how the rebels had sided with the ordinary people against her. After that, when I heard people in Goderich say that rebels should be hung, I knew they were wrong, although I kept that to myself.

Momma particularly liked reading *Tait's* magazine, which we received occasionally, all the way from Scotland. It had some women writers, and I know Momma wanted to write for *Tait's* herself. She sent them an article, and I remember her waiting and waiting for a reply that never came. She concluded she wasn't good enough to write for such a fine publication. But she kept writing anyway, in her diary, and sometimes she'd share what she wrote with me. I really loved her writing, and told her so. She'd just smile and say, "That's because you're my daughter."

I sit back and let the train's motion rock me. My thoughts turn to what awaits us in Toronto and how I'll deal with the death of someone I barely remember, but who was once so important to Momma and me.

———✲———

I'm often unsure of how much I actually remember from my childhood, and how much is based on what my mother told me and I later embellished. I suspect my memory of Sam as he rode away from Goderich is an image I've embellished. Momma described the little stuffed doll I gave him. I remember that doll, but I don't really remember giving it to him or him riding away.

There are other memories, however, that I'm sure are actual recollections. One is my first sight of Momma after our long separation, as she stood on the other side of the little wooden gate. Every time I think of her standing there, her arms reaching toward me, I feel like crying. Another memory that I'm sure is real is very unhappy: Momma's face, right after I blurted out to Reverend Blair about the hired man drowning. If there is anything I could do to put those words back in my mouth ... but, of course, I just have to live with that mistake forever.

So it was jarring to see Reverend Blair again, for the first time since that sorrowful day twenty-five years ago. I wouldn't have recognized him after all these years, except that he approached us as we got off the train and introduced himself. He is a little heavy, has thinning hair and wears spectacles. If that day long ago made him think negatively of me, he doesn't show it. He's been so nice to us since we arrived. It was his idea that we come and stay with him so that we could attend the funeral.

I didn't really understand the invitation at first, but now I do. There were only a few dozen people for the ceremony in the church, and at the graveside there are fewer still. I don't mean that we were invited to swell the ranks of mourners, just that even people on the fringes of her life, like us, seem important, given the isolation of her later years.

After only a day in Toronto, I've already picked up enough to conclude that Lottie's marriage to Reverend Blair was part of the tragedy of her life. I believe what his housekeeper said about him being very devoted to Lottie. Momma always said that he idolized her. And when I look over at him now, standing by her grave, I see a man who is not only saddened by her death, but was also saddened by her life, or his lack of space in it. The deep recesses around his eyes reveal a man who's been unhappy for a long time.

It is drizzling rain as the graveside ceremony ends. Reverend Blair talks quietly to a few people who are leaving; most are coming back to his home nearby. As we walk toward the house under umbrellas, I can see from the look on my brother's face that this situation is affecting him much less than me, which is not surprising. He never met Lottie or Reverend Blair. He wasn't even born when Momma knew them. And although I don't recall much about either of them, I have a rich roster of embellished memories of Lottie.

I know that she was very beautiful, and that her warmth and affection made Momma's life bearable back in Glasgow. I also know that Momma was deeply hurt by Lottie's coldness in later years, by her refusal to see us again. Of course, it must have been hard for

Lottie to deal with what happened — finding out about Momma's relationship with Sam, when she herself had been in love with him for years. The hanging took him away from both of them.

About a dozen people make it back to Reverend Blair's two-storey home on Bond Street. Mrs. Garrett, the housekeeper, has set out china cups next to the large teapot on the dining room table, along with biscuits and small custard tarts. I talk to several ladies, explaining that my mother had been Lottie's dearest friend many years ago.

"It's hard to imagine her having a really dear friend; she kept so much to herself," says one, dressed in a black, high-collared dress.

"We never saw much of her," says another, whose stiff black skirt and jacket are livened up ever so slightly by a grey blouse.

The portrait they paint doesn't fit with the embellished memory I have of Lottie as tender and caring. Of course, it's not hard to imagine Lottie's lack of interest in socializing with these dull clergy wives. Still, their description of her fits with Mrs. Garrett's, confirming my sense of how lonely her life must have become. Perhaps Lottie took Sam's execution even harder than Momma. I'd always thought that Lottie's marriage to Reverend Blair indicated she'd been able to rebuild her life but, in some ways, hers seemed even more damaged than Momma's.

In the parlour, the woman in the grey blouse sits down beside me. Speaking in a semi-whisper, she suggests that Lottie was not a good wife to Reverend Blair, nor much of a wife at all. Perhaps realizing the inappropriateness of such talk only an hour after Lottie's burial, she changes topic and asks me about my children. Forced into official politeness, I retreat into private memories of Momma and the tragic events that engulfed our lives.

When all the guests have gone, Mrs. Garrett serves us a light supper. Reverend Blair is tired, but is putting forth effort to make us feel welcome in his home. After he learns of Luke's plans to fight in the American war, he gently discourages the idea, much to my delight. The conversation moves to more mundane topics, allowing my mind to drift back to childhood memories. I realize there is so much I'd like to ask Reverend Blair, but can't possibly, because the subject would be too painful for him. He is probably the only person who could answer questions now freshly crowding into my mind: Where did Sam go after he left Goderich? Did he see Lottie? Were they living together in Toronto when he was arrested and taken back to Goderich to stand trial for murder?

These questions must have plagued Momma, although she never discussed them with me. For that matter, she didn't talk much about Lottie, except to recall what a dear friend she'd once been. She said even less about Sam; I think it was just too upsetting for her to talk about him. She certainly never spoke ill of him. I remember her once describing him as a champion of the common people.

I now see what a hole he left in her heart. The happiest I ever saw her was riding in the wagon with him, me on the bench between them. I remember looking up at her — and this I do remember unembellished — and she was smiling and laughing, her hair flying in the wind. She never seemed more alive than that. I can still see joy all over her face.

Of course, our life in Goderich was very difficult after his execution. Some of the townspeople took pity on us. We were allowed to stay on in the cottage, and Momma was given work cleaning and doing laundry for the church. We didn't have much to live on, though, especially since Momma sent money back to Fenwick whenever she could, after the family lost the farm.

It was hard to know whom to trust in Goderich. We avoided Rosalee and people who blamed Sam for stirring up dissent in the town. But there were others who considered Sam a hero; Momma said that was evident at the hanging. Then the next day, the commissioner posted a notice condemning Sam as a traitor and threatening to arrest anyone who had helped him incite rebellion.

Given that heavy-handedness, it was surprising that there weren't severe repercussions against Momma. But Jones never took action against her; indeed, after that night when the soldiers escorted us home through the town, no one ever tried to hurt us again. None of the Company agents bothered us, either.

I recall a lady at the church telling Momma that this showed what a decent man Thomas Mercer Jones was, how he wouldn't tolerate mistreatment of women. Momma and I knew better.

Mr. Jones left us alone because of what Momma knew about the servant girl. Momma kept her part of their deal — if that's what it was — and never mentioned to anyone about his relationship with Daisy Howard. Everyone in town assumed Daisy's child was Longworth's son, and that Longworth had abandoned the boy, just like the other children he'd left behind in Ireland. We didn't see much of that boy in town, nor his mother; they kept to themselves. He was always regarded with curiosity, though, since everyone knew he was the son of a high official in the Company. They just didn't know how high.

But I knew, and it always amazed me to observe him and realize how different he was from Mr. Jones's other two sons. Those boys were educated in the Jones mansion and never played in the square. We'd occasionally see them driving by in their carriage with their well-pressed shirts and high-and-mighty looks, even as youngsters. They would have been mortified if they'd known that they had another brother who grew up in the servants' quarters of a nearby home.

After supper, Luke coaxes me to come with him to visit a friend who moved to Toronto a few months ago. I'd like to go, just to be with him, but decline, feeling too preoccupied with thoughts of the past to be able to socialize.

Reverend Blair and I sit in the parlour, making pleasant but superficial conversation after Luke leaves. I'm more and more convinced that it would be wrong for me to pose my questions, that any reference to Sam — the love of Lottie's life — would be cruel. And so nothing of substance is said, and I take my leave to retire upstairs for the night.

That's when he tells me that he has something for me and goes into his study, returning with a finely embroidered folder. He hands it to me, and I open it to find an envelope addressed to Lottie — in Momma's distinctive handwriting. This is the closest I've come to feeling Momma's presence since she died. I turn it over and discover, even more to my surprise, that the envelope is still sealed. I look up at Reverend Blair searchingly.

"I found it a few days ago, when I was sorting through Lottie's things," he explains, his eyes looking soft but remote. "You can see from the postmark that it arrived seventeen years ago. Your mother must have written it shortly before she died. I don't know why Lottie never opened it."

So, this was the extent of Lottie's anger or withdrawal from the world, that she would not even open a letter from my mother many years after Sam's execution?

I feel too fragile to open the envelope in front of Reverend Blair, so I thank him and head up to my room. I'm sitting by the window, looking out at the street in the advancing dusk, when Mrs. Garrett knocks and enters with a cup of hot milk.

"Oh, thank you. That is so kind," I say. "You shouldn't have gone to such trouble."

"It's no trouble," she replies. "Lottie always liked hot milk before she went to bed. I think it was her favourite part of the day."

The notion of Lottie and Reverend Blair drinking hot milk before bedtime conjures up a homier image than I've encountered so far. As she leaves, Mrs. Garrett notes that Lottie always drank her milk here alone by the window, and I now realize what should have been obvious last night when I slept in this room; this was Lottie's room, with Reverend Blair's room down the hall. One more reminder of the lovelessness of this marriage.

I sit quietly sipping the milk, my fingers tracing the embroidery on the cloth folder, until I feel calm enough to confront what lies inside the envelope.

> Goderich
> April 17, 1845
>
> My dearest Lottie:
>
> I am ill with pneumonia, and the doctor doesn't expect me to recover. Before I pass on, I feel compelled to clarify some important matters.
>
> There is no way I can possibly express the depth of my regret over what happened. But I want you to know that I have spent the past seven years living with a profound sense of guilt for what I did.
>
> Sam's execution never would have occurred had he followed his heart and gone back to Toronto right after the carriage accident. He clearly wanted to return to you, but felt obligated to help Emma and I get settled in Goderich. As you know, the townspeople mistook him for Norbert, and we foolishly didn't correct this. But he always wanted to leave. In retrospect, I see that I put a great deal of pressure on him to stay. That was very selfish of me. I wanted his support, and increasingly I wanted him.
>
> You should know, however, that my interest in him was not reciprocated. We slept in separate

rooms and he made no advances toward me. Without realizing the special relationship he had with you, I tried to reach out to him. He resisted my overtures repeatedly — out of loyalty to you, I now see. But one night he was obliged to accompany me when I was called upon to midwife a birth on a remote farm. I am deeply ashamed to confess that, when he and I ended up assigned to the same bed at the farmhouse, I virtually pleaded with him to make love to me. I'm sure he later regretted that he did. He left the next day for Toronto.

It is clear to me now that he always loved you, and that it was utterly wrong for me to attempt to win his heart. For what it is worth, I failed in that attempt, and I apologize unreservedly for trying.

Although it will offer you little comfort, you should know that I have suffered a great deal for my wrongdoing. I have not told this to anyone before, but I want to tell you now.

Soon after Sam left for Toronto, I was raped by a vile and vicious man who works for the Canada Company. It is he — not Sam — who is the father of my son Luke. I have tried my best to create a distance in my heart between Luke and that dreadful memory. I have raised Luke to believe Sam was his father, because I thought it would be better for both of us. It hasn't been easy; I've never felt close to Luke the way I've always felt so close to Emma. Still, I've struggled to make him feel included, and to love him as much as I love and cherish Emma.

> My darling Lottie, you were such a wonderful friend to me back in Glasgow. I will never forget your sweetness and warmth, which makes it all the more painful to me that I have caused you such great sorrow.
> With sincerest love and deepest regret,
>
> Yours,
> Callandra

Luke's friend, I have now discovered, is a young lady. I was distracted the night of Lottie's funeral, and that possibility hadn't occurred to me — even though Luke did seem unusually happy when he got home later that evening. I was still sitting by the window, in a sleepless daze, when he came sauntering toward the house. I went down to greet him, and we talked in the parlour for a while. His elevated mood allowed me to easily do what I had already resolved to do — avoid any mention of Momma's letter.

So my departure is less painful than it otherwise would be. Luke and Reverend Blair have brought me to the train station and, after four days in Toronto, I'll be glad to get home. I'm encouraged that Reverend Blair has invited Luke to stay on with him in Toronto so he can look for work here. And, although Luke continues to talk about joining the Union army, he hasn't yet said no to Reverend Blair's offer. Perhaps a position and a budding romance will be enough to keep him here, far from death on the battlefield. Surveying him now, with his wavy dark hair and intense charcoal eyes, I realize I love him as much as I always have, even though knowing his true pedigree has somehow turned my world upside down. Better mine than his.

Reverend Blair has certainly been kind to us; he said he regards us as family. And now, waiting for the train, he surprises me with a beautiful gold necklace that had been Lottie's. I am deeply moved by the gift, and freshly saddened by the tragedy of his life. Lottie clearly crushed his dreams, leaving them both trapped in lives of isolation and loneliness. But he isn't bitter. Rather he seems to treasure the memory of her. His openness to me and Luke tempts me to seize this opportunity to do what I couldn't bring myself to do the day of Lottie's funeral — ask him the questions I have now formulated clearly in my mind: Did Sam come back to Lottie? Did she forgive him? If he hadn't been arrested, would they have left for America together?

The conductor rings a bell and announces the train is ready for boarding. My stomach is churning, and I am suddenly wracked by the thought that I could be deluding myself, that these might well be my last moments ever with Luke. Should I tell him I love him dearly and always will, or would that just start me crying? Is there anything wrong with crying now? And should I say something to Reverend Blair that could prompt him to open up? He might even welcome a chance to unburden himself of long-kept secrets, to talk about his suffering and sadness, with people he considers family.

And yet, with final hugs, I am boarding the train, having imparted nothing meaningful to my beloved brother, and having walked away from perhaps my only chance to uncover the central mystery of my mother's life — a mystery that has dominated much of mine as well. As the train pulls out of the station, I wave goodbye and treasure final glimpses of the tall young man who I now know to be the result of a horrible assault. For all these years, I thought I had saved Momma from that appalling fate, but it turns out that I only arrived with the entourage of children after the assault had happened. I vow that I will never tell Luke, even though he has a right to know who his father is. He will certainly never know that his mother never really felt close to him. Instinctively, I pull out the embroidered folder from my bag and reread the passage, although I know the words by heart, *"I've always felt so close to Emma ... as much as I love and cherish Emma."*

I am savouring those words in the anonymity of the train, with forest and field fleeting by outside. Since Luke will never know it was a struggle for his mother to love him, I can, without guilt, feel joy at her expression of love for me — the same joy I felt the day I saw her behind the wooden gate when I was five and I knew our separation was over at last.

The folder slips off my lap and, retrieving it from the floor of the train, my fingers detect a hidden sleeve in the inner lining. The elaborate embroidery has somehow camouflaged the existence of two more slim envelopes up the sleeve. I pull them out with shaking hands, not knowing which to open first. One is addressed to Mrs. Jonathan Blair, and has previously been opened. The other is addressed to Momma; the Goderich address has been crossed out and replaced with the address of the Presbyterian office in Toronto. This one is still sealed. I tear it open.

> Editorial Department
> *Tait's Edinburgh Magazine*
> 221 Victoria Street
> Edinburgh, Scotland
> March 17, 1839
>
> Dear Callandra Scott,
>
> Thank you for your submission. Enclosed is a copy of your article "Morals and Misdeeds in the Upper

Canada Rebellion" as it appeared in our journal earlier this month. It has received much favourable feedback from our readers.

Your writing is strong and clear, and I am personally delighted by your astute observations about the position of women in Upper Canada, and how you interweave these observations with the thoughts of Mary Wollstonecraft. There is a growing interest in the Woman Question, as you know, and also in much else about that part of your continent which has been neglected in our rush to know ever more about America. The rebellion you describe, and its nasty aftermath, has left our readers keen to learn more about what is going on in your part of the realm.

I particularly like the diary format you used, mixing politics and personal thoughts. In fact, it is with great pleasure that I invite you to write a regular monthly post in this style. We could call it "Letter from Upper Canada." We could pay you one pound, fifty per post.

I look forward to hearing from you at your earliest convenience.

Enclosed is a money order for your first article.

With warm regards,
Harriet Martineau

Police Headquarters
48 Wellington Street
Toronto
December 3, 1838

Dear Mrs. Blair,

I apologize for the delay in responding to your request for information about the arrest of Samuel Hunter.

I am obliged to correct some misinformation in your letter. The arrest did not take place in Toronto, but about twenty miles outside Hamilton. A report by the Hamilton Police Board has confirmed that it was carried out by two constables on May 6, 1838. The constables took Samuel Hunter into custody after a farmer rode into town to report he'd seen a tall traveller fitting the description of the man wanted in connection with the murder of a clergyman near Goderich.

I regret that I cannot confirm the exact location of the arrest, but the report indicated that Hunter was on foot and appeared to be walking west in the direction of the Huron Tract.

I trust this will satisfy your inquiry.

Yours truly,
Nathaniel Hartford
Superintendent, Toronto Police

Acknowledgements

The manuscript for this novel has long been in my bottom drawer — a labour of love that I worked on from time to time and dreamed I would finish someday.

So I am very grateful to those who gave me early support: Ellen Vanstone, Barbara Nichol, Bill Reno, and Ken Alexander were all extremely helpful, as well as being important friends. Anne Collins and Deirdre Molina devoted considerable time and expertise to developing the manuscript.

I was fortunate to have the editing insights of Adrienne Kerr, who provided excellent suggestions as well as encouragement.

And I am particularly grateful to my editor, the talented Shannon Whibbs, who came up with thoughtful questions and ideas that forced me to really work at improving the manuscript. She was also a delight to work with. She has described the relationship between author and editor as a "dance" in which two people move to the music as one in their creative partnership. That's what it felt like working with Shannon.

The historical setting of the novel provided many challenges, and I am grateful for the help of two academics with expertise in the 1830s in Upper Canada — Eben Prevec, who is completing a Ph.D. in Canadian history at Queen's University, and the late William Westfall, longtime history professor and coordinator of the Canadian Studies program at York University.

I want to also thank my hardworking agent, Lloyd Kelly, as well as a number of friends and family members who offered valuable feedback, help, and support — Gordon Laxer, Cynthia Farquharson, Daniel Wright, Susan Wheeler, John McQuaig, Janet Allen, Wendy McQuaig, Fred Fallis, and Anna McQuaig.

Finally, I'm very much indebted to the terrific crew at Dundurn — including publisher Meghan Macdonald, who kindly accommodated my request to move up the publication date, as well as Erin Pinksen, Laura Boyle, Megan Beadle, Karen Alexiou (for the wonderful cover), Elena Radic, Kwame Scott Fraser, Kathryn Lane, and Meg Bowen.

About the Author

Photo by Brenton Alexander

Linda McQuaig is well known as a journalist and author of non-fiction books, including eight national bestsellers about how the wealthy and powerful dominate our politics. As a dogged young reporter, she won a National Newspaper Award for investigative reporting that led to a public inquiry and the imprisonment of a political lobbyist. She has been called controversial, and she insists her proudest moment was when an enraged Conrad Black, in a national radio interview, called for her to be "horsewhipped." McQuaig's work takes a new turn in *The Road to Goderich*. The product of many years of dreaming about and piecing together the intricate story, this is her first work of fiction.